# Treading Softly

## A Novel

## Victoria MacLeod

Published in 2012 by FeedARead.com Publishing – Arts Council funded

First Edition

He Wishes for the Cloths of Heaven (from The Wind Among the Reeds 1899) by W.B Yeats (1865 - 1939) reproduced with kind permission of A.P Watt Ltd on behalf of Gráinne Yeats.

A CIP catalogue record for this title is available from the British Library.

*to those who inspired and encouraged me*

*thank you*

*you know who you are*

# HE WISHES FOR THE CLOTHS OF HEAVEN

Had I the heavens' embroidered cloths,

Enwrought with golden and silver light,

The blue and the dim and the dark cloths

Of night and light and the half-light,

I would spread the cloths under your feet:

But I, being poor, have only my dreams;

I have spread my dreams under your feet;

Tread softly because you tread on my dreams.


W.B Yeats (1865-1939)

# LEN

I hear my name, but I am frozen to the floor. I cannot look at him. I cannot move.

"Professor Thomas, do you understand what I've just said?"

His voice is kind, but persuasive. He wants me to look at him so that he can draw this conversation to a close and get the hell out. The silence hanging between us is excruciating. I can't look at him, can't let him see that I understand. Maybe we could just stand here forever; the words spoken, but not acknowledged. I haven't accepted what he's giving me. And I can't. I don't want it. I don't want this conversation, this room, this happening. He places his two hands very deliberately on my arms and stares me in the face.

"Professor Thomas, your wife is dead."

The statement. He's caught me out. He's bypassing the question. Now he doesn't need an answer. It's slipping out of my control. He's made it real, without my agreement. He's made it happen. Still I can't move, but strangely I start to view the whole scene as a bystander. I see my stricken expression, my feet planted, no *glued* to the carpet; the doctor, nervous about this unscripted part of the conversation. As if you could call it a conversation! I haven't spoken a word yet. The man of words lost for words.

"Is there someone I could call for you…family… a friend?"

Suddenly, the whole situation seems so bizarre. He's telling me my wife is dead. We're standing in a hospital in the middle of Edinburgh, the blinding winter sun streaming down my face, the noise outside of cars, vans, buses pulling in and out of the drop-off space beneath the office window. Beyond the door I can hear trolleys bumping past and voices, lots of voices. Where is she, I wonder? As if recognizing the change in my demeanour, he visibly relaxes and I hate myself. I've let him see that I understand. I've taken his information. I've believed it. I am responsible now.

The door closes gently, a barrier between us and I realize he's taken his leave. I imagine he's glad to be free of me. How uncomfortable when people don't take on their expected roles. I can feel my body, heavier than before. I doubt whether I'll ever be able to lift my foot off this floor. Staring down, I wonder if my body has actually stopped working. Maybe the extremities give out first, then the vital organs one by one. I know my brain has spiralled out of my head altogether. I cannot move, cannot speak. Perhaps I just stand here and slowly everything stops. Are they waiting outside for me to die too?

A muffled cough and I realize I'm not alone. I still can't move, can't turn round to see who is there. Soft words, though; the most gentle voice I think I've ever heard. Words flow liquid over my head, across my face and drip down past my fingertips; soothing, familiar even. Is it my mother? No my mother and father are busy outliving us all in their frantic, New York-paced style. But it's a mother's concern and that voice - it's tearing at my gut. I feel with every delicate word uttered another handful of my soul scraped agonisingly out. If this doesn't stop soon, I know my body's going to rip apart and spill my heart out all over the place. I feel my fear rising. I know I'm on the verge of exploding. I can't contain this pain. It sears inside my chest. I need her to stop. I open my mouth to shout at her to stop and feel the words jumble themselves up almost choking me. I gasp for air and groan as another sob escapes my shaking body. Now they come, tumbling out one upon another and all control is gone. My life. My everything.

I guess there isn't a good moment. Would I like to spend some time with her? Some time? Yes I'd like to spend the rest of my life with her actually. That was the plan. That was always the plan. Then again, I understand that this is the next step. First the bad news must be broken. Funny turn of phrase, that isn't it? Break the bad news. We don't hand over bad news or offer it. We break it. We smash it into people's faces and grind the splinters into their eyes. And the more gentle, the more caring the deliverer of the news, the more painful the experience for the recipient. First that. Well I've got through that bit, now I should see her. Spend some time with her. Spend the last time I ever will with her. Shouldn't this be special? Like a first date. How much thought goes into that and here we are at the end, totally unprepared.

I am shown into another room and left alone. But I'm not alone am I? Here's Claudine. Lying sleeping, eyes closed. I tiptoe over to her bed. I don't like to disturb her, she looks so peaceful. And so pale. I think, "This is what a dead person looks like. This is what my wife looks like when she is dead." I stroke her beautiful hair back from her forehead and come face to face with her killer. An angry hole gapes wide across her skull; an opening out of which her precious life flowed. My poor Claudine. I touch her wound and she doesn't flinch. My fingers marked with her blood, her life-force spilled out everywhere. Where are you Claudine? I look around the room expecting to see her. She's not within her darling body. She must be somewhere. The stillness of the room is agony. Where do I look for her, my beautiful girl? I can't believe it; this morning so alive, taking a shower, preparing for the day ahead. A few hours later, your life ebbed away at the side of a road. I touch your face. You feel like glass. No wonder you broke so easily. I fumble under the starched sheet for your hand. Your icy fingers hang limp. There is no life left here. There is no Claudine, who laughed and cried and at the end screamed. No Claudine. No us. No me.

Coming home from the hospital without Claudine was the strangest experience of my life. I still can't quite get my head round the fact that I left her there. I came home without her to carry on the rest of my life without her. How can this be? I wonder now if she ever thought about death. When the time came, did she know? Did she see her life flash before her, any bright light? Did she think, "I am dying here by the side of the road, on my own. I am dying and Len has no idea, Len who is busy being an important person doing an important job at an important university, Len who was in too much of a rush to say a proper goodbye this morning." This thought turns me suddenly cold. I was in a hurry this morning, didn't say goodbye. Where does that leave me now? My wife died this morning and I didn't say goodbye. Was it only this morning? Suddenly I am almost suffocated with exhaustion. Each breath is such a huge effort. I feel my lungs fill and empty and wonder if I have sufficient energy to repeat the process. My chest continues to rise and fall. I breathe. I breathe.

On waking I have the distinct impression of having been wakened. I listen for a sound, the sound which a few seconds ago stirred me from sleep, but hear nothing. In fact, the stillness is quite chilling. I strain my ears to hear a noise, but the quietness rings louder and louder in my ears and I am unable to hear anything else. Gradually my heart thumps less ferociously, making room for other sounds inside my head. Still I hear only silence, a familiar silence.

Then all at once I am transported back to my childhood and memories of waking to discover the first snowfall of winter come fondly back to me; the almost disturbing stillness, the instinctive sense of snow falling softly, silently. I reach for a corner of the drapes and tug gently to reveal the shrouded landscape. Large, heavy snowflakes drop endlessly, hypnotically past my window. Sitting up, I see that already a thick blanket covers what was yesterday our backyard, now transformed into an unblemished carpet of white. Snow falls upon snow falls upon snow. Mesmerised, I try to track the route of a particular flake as it drops silently past and on until it is lost among the vastness of the multitude already dusting my window-ledge. And then I feel it. Right bang in the middle of my being, a kick so hard I lean against the window to steady myself. The pain scorches through my core, deep, deep inside and I reel from the shock. The beauty beyond is lost to me now. I am turned in on myself, consumed with pain. She's gone.

I have to get out of this house. Its walls stifle and I crave fresh air. Dressing hastily, lacing my boots and shrugging on a jacket, I am out in the garden before I think to lift gloves and scarf. It doesn't matter. I want to feel the cold anyway. I just want to feel something. Trudging heavily, my feet drag me to the end of Rowan Avenue and out onto the main street. Here the snow is piled up in dunes by the side of the road and cars slush cautiously in either direction. Sprayed by icy water, my clothes cling frozen to my aching body. My legs move me onwards, directionless - the momentum thankfully occupying my mind so I don't have to think.

After a while I realize the snow has stopped falling. In the distance the sky unfolds revealing a rich red sun. Dawn. I am in awe of the beauty before me. Pink and red and orange painted painstakingly across the horizon in bold, beautiful strokes. As I approach the town centre I pause to appreciate the sight. I know there is a public garden nearby, not sufficiently grand to be called a park, more a sort of stopping off place for walkers to rest. Spotting the opening in the hedge, I venture in and settle on a bench. No matter that my seat is soon soaking as the snow seeps through my jeans. I have a good vantage point from which to watch the sun rise. All around me is still. The city hasn't yet woken up. Moments like these are savoured by the few who are on the move early: nurses hurrying to catch the first bus that will take them to their early shift, dog-walkers and fitness fanatics exercising before the business of the day impinges on them. Old people who can't sleep, having gone to bed at teatime exhausted on account of rising so early the day before; a self-perpetuating insomnia. And me. I sit and watch the sun grow and grow and the sky unfolding little by little to accommodate its vastness. Wooded silhouettes become trees, their branches glittering with new-fallen bounty. The sun edges forward, fuller and brighter each moment, the sky radiant in gratitude. After a time, I am conscious of people around me, bustling by on their way to work. Buses crammed with sleepy schoolchildren speed through the slippery streets. The day has awoken, the moment gone. Shakily I stand and realize I have been sitting for a while. My legs, cold and stiff are reluctant to move again. I am colder than I ever remember. My hands, purple and numb, feel as if they are no longer part of my body. I allow my feet to guide me and unthinking head for warmth.

The outer door resists my touch, so I peer through the glass and watch as Sebastian prepares for the day ahead. A tray of crockery is despatched upon the tiled counter and methodically redistributed around the surrounding tables. Gingham tablecloths are smoothed and adjusted at the perfectionists' fingertips. Glancing around the room, satisfied, he turns toward the door and catches sight of me gazing inwards. Hurriedly he stumbles over locks and the familiar jingle beckons me inside. Nothing is said. Sebastian ushers me to a booth and sits opposite me. I am vaguely aware of voices echoing around the kitchen and utensils clattering distantly. After a time I notice a mug of coffee on the table in front of me. I hug it to my chest feeling the warmth through my wet clothes. When I drink, it scorches my throat and I cough uncontrollably. Sebastian, my oldest friend, is the one who can look me in the eye. He doesn't say a word. He knows, as I do, there is nothing to say. We have been friends for so long.

The first time I met Sebastian I was a stranger in his homeland and grateful for his friendship. I had come to Paris on completing my degree, to do a PhD at the Sorbonne. I had long treasured the idea of being an American in Paris. I suppose I wanted to walk the path of my idols. Living in poverty in a pension close to the Seine, drawing inspiration for my writing from the flavours of France, I imagined myself as Ernest Hemingway or F Scott Fitzgerald. An illustrious author self-exiled from America, living in shabby surroundings, soaking up the mystery and romance of the city and consequently producing a work of incomparable worth. This was always my dream for as long as I can remember. Of course, strictly speaking I was not an American in Paris. Having lived much of my life in Montreal, I was more of a French Canadian in Paris. This gave me the advantage of pretty good French, but I did always harbour some doubts over my authenticity. In the end it was this to which I attributed my lack of creativity during my years in Montparnasse. I didn't write my book, but I did meet Sebastian and his girlfriend Helen. And I did meet Claudine.

My most lasting impression of my stay in Paris is that of time. At no other point in my life have I been so conscious of having time: time to stop and chat, time to do things, time to think. I used to escape the university confines at every possible opportunity. Each day at lunchtime I strolled to a park to spend an hour in relaxed contemplation. I used to decide at the last moment where I would go and I always went unaccompanied. This was *my* time. Sometimes I headed for Jardin des Plantes and rooted out a comfortable spot close to a fountain, basking in the therapeutic chatter of the flowing water. Other times I might saunter into Jardin de la Republique and enjoy the fragrance of the freshly mown grass, and watch with amusement the butterflies dotting around from flower to flower. This was personal space at its best and always fuelled me for the rest of the day. My favourite place became Place des Vosges, but that was because of Claudine. It was a bit farther than my other haunts, so to begin with I didn't often reach it. After I spotted Claudine, though, I learned to quicken my step and found myself sitting in a little oasis in the heart of Paris most days. She wasn't always there. On those days I contented myself watching old ladies feeding the birds and children pottering about in the sand, my eyes glancing frequently towards the gate to catch a glimpse of her. Did I stop to think what I was doing? I don't think I did. This wasn't real. She was unreachable and I had no plans to bridge the chasm between us. I wasn't too good socially in those days. I had friends and girlfriends too, but they always accidented upon me. I didn't really know how to win people over and it wasn't an issue because I enjoyed the life I had. Things changed once I noticed Claudine. I became more aware of my inadequacies, less sure of myself, more conscious of failure.

The first time I caught sight of her I shocked myself at how captivated I was. I tried not to look at her the whole time, but without fail my eyes strayed in her direction. I was enchanted. She formulated my impression of the ideal woman, but she was like a character in a

13

book to me. I thought, 'This is beauty,' and even 'This is what I want,' but never in a tangible way. She was a painting that I couldn't drag my eyes from. Of course she didn't notice me, but that was okay. I couldn't watch her if she knew I was looking could I? Anyway she was always absorbed with her notebook. She seemed to be sketching, one of many who frequented this walled garden and utilised its seclusion for creativity. We continued like this for weeks and I felt secure in the predictability of our situation. I looked forward to seeing her each day and then one day I didn't. She wasn't there. The next day was the same and the day after that. I was in turmoil. My cosy routine had been disrupted but it was more than that. I missed her. I knew this was ridiculous, I didn't even know her name and I realised the probability was that I'd never see her again. Then one morning she literally walked back into my life.

I was taking a class for my supervisor; American Feminist Poetry. It wasn't really my thing and I wasn't enthused at the prospect, but I had studied Emily Dickinson in depth back home and knew it would be routine enough. Imagine my surprise, no shock, when minutes into the lecture I turned to the heavy wooden door heaving open and in she walked. I stopped short then caught myself and scanning my notes for my place hesitatingly continued. There was no apology. She strode up the steps of the tiered theatre and ignoring the empty seats at the end of the row, squeezed past several disgruntled students until she was seated bang in the centre of the room, directly in my field of vision. The sideways glances I had been sneaking over the past few weeks suddenly seemed pathetic in the face of her confidence. I stumbled through the rest of the lecture, hardly aware what I was saying, losing my French, trembling. The podium became my crutch as I desperately tried to keep it all together. I reached the end of my notes and dismissed the class, taking no questions. Thirty or so muttering students dragged themselves from the room, but she remained. I gulped my tumbler of water, shuffled my papers, waited; for what, a word, a smile, eternity? I was beginning to panic. Speechless, I shoved my notes haphazardly into my case wondering what to do. This was not me. I was out of my depth, lost in unfamiliar territory.

"Vous avez un accent interessant." Her voice touched my soul. "Est ce que vous etes Americain?"

I realized she was waiting for my reply. "I'm more comfortable with English," I whispered. She was listening. I went on, "I speak French, but I'm more comfortable with English. I'm Canadian." For a moment I wondered if she understood.

Then when she spoke her words were so soft she was almost inaudible, "You have a beautiful voice. You are beautiful." Reaching into a duffel bag, she pulled out a notebook and flipped through a few pages. "You see?" I stepped down from the stage and reached across two rows of seats to receive the offered object; a sketchpad. Glancing down I saw my own face locked in concentration. I looked back at her, confused. "There are more. Regardez!" she gestured to the book. I turned the page and saw myself hunched against the cold, reading. In another I looked weary unwrapping my lunch, another depicted me sitting cross-legged helping a little boy untie a tangled kite-string, page after page.

"You were drawing me all the time?"

"Oui."

"You knew I was ……." I fumbled for the right word in English, French, in any blessed language, "….admiring you?" I faltered.

"Bien sur…and I you, as you see."

I took a deep breath. Suddenly the ludicrousness of the situation enveloped me. I smiled and she smiled back. Instinctively I reached my hand out and helped her to her feet. That was the beginning.


That was the beginning and this is the end, I think, as I watch Sebastian clearing a nearby table. Would our life together have been different if we had seen the whole package at the outset? I suspect it would. If I had known in that moment, when she took my hand and we started a new life together, that we would have sixteen years or thereabouts and then I would be on my own again. I feel robbed. Death has cheated me of the rest of my life.

The numbness of the past few days begins to dissipate and with the thaw I feel so much. Welling upwards from deep inside I sense an explosion. Gritting my teeth hard together I try to keep a lid on it. Breathing deeply, I force the anger deep down inside. Push it down. Push it down. I struggle with the fire of this emotion. It is hot, so hot. Unbuttoning my jacket, I shake it from my shoulders and try to free myself from the intensity of this heat. I've never felt so angry. I am consumed with pain, filled to overflowing with rage. In a moment I am on my feet. A vicious sweep of my arm and the gleaming white crockery scatters smashed across the floor. I stagger to the door and step out into the freezing morning air. Blinking back stinging tears I stumble blindly across the road, vaguely aware of screeching brakes and sounding horns. Onwards. What else is there to do? Keep pushing. Keep pushing on.

Slithering through the slippery pavements I am heading instinctively for home. My eyes hurt so much I can barely see and each heaving breath rattles painfully around my chest. Passing the entrance to the Walkers' Rest, where I watched the sunrise a few hours ago, I hesitate, lose my footing and lurch to the ground. I kneel to try and regain my balance and a pain shoots up through my leg. Moaning I fall back despairingly into the snow.

"Let me help you, mon ami."

At this moment in time I cannot bear to see Sebastian. He is too inextricably linked to Claudine. He is part of the pain. I understand that he followed me out of concern, but I can't let him into my grief. Shaking off his arm, I pull myself to my feet. Things are bad enough. I honestly sense that Sebastian being around will make things worse. Limping gingerly, I follow the pavement round and into Rowan Avenue. In the distance I can make out our house, *my* house, distinct from the rest on account of the whitewash with which my wife painstakingly coated the outer walls last summer. I feel terrible. I am reminded of a lame dog I once saw dragging its battered body home to die. It occurs to me that perhaps this homing instinct I have is indicative of a similar fate. If only. The fear I once had of death has been replaced by a far greater fear of living without Claudine. The very thought of her name sends an ache of devastation through me. On I go. My feet continue to carry me and I am thankful for that. Reaching my front door relief is quickly replaced by rage filling every pulsating beat of my heart. Peering through the misted glass I see her, staring straight at me, smiling; beautiful on our wedding day and beside her, a younger version of myself, deliriously happy. Fury fills me. My fists smash through the window sending a multi-coloured shower of glittering glass cascading inside and out over the snow. Bloodied hands cover my face as tears stream uncontrollably. I am embraced in the warmth of friendship and have no energy left to resist. Leaning against Sebastian's strength I am guided indoors. I feel myself falling and hope that I never get up.

Repeated knocking on the front door stirs me from the depths of sleep. I hear voices and strain to hear who has arrived now. I have never really been one to share my private space with anyone other than Claudine and yet my house seems now to be permanently full. The first sign of tragedy and people you barely know are clucking all around. I know I'm being unfair. Friends, neighbours, colleagues are all trying to help. It occurs to me that this is the kind of thing I might say at Claudine's funeral: "Thank you to all my friends, neighbours, colleagues who have been such a help...." No! Will this never end? I hadn't given the funeral any thought at all. How will I ever bear it? The knocking continues and I wonder why one of the voices doesn't open the bloody door. The door! Of course, someone is repairing the broken door. How pathetic I must seem lying up here while Sebastian or whoever is now downstairs takes care of things. It's just so hard. It occurs to me that maybe someone else will organise the funeral. Life appears to be going on around me. Other people still seem to be capable of everyday functions of which I am not. Let them do it. The bedroom door nudges gently open and Sebastian's large frame fills the doorway.

"How are you Len?"

"You still here?" I bark.

"Len, I know this is really hard. Things are needing to be done… the undertaker, he called twice…he...he needs to speak with you….arrangements, you know?"

I can't do this, I think. I'm not doing it.

"Someone is needing to sort things for the… the …funeral." He breaks off and I realise I'm not the only one hurting. Sebastian has known Claudine as long as I have. He has lost a friend, a dear friend.

During our Paris days the four of us spent all our time together. Sebastian who welcomed me when I arrived, Helen his girlfriend, Claudine and I. Sebastian shared an apartment with me and also many good times. I had never had a friend like him before. He was an artist in his own right, a chef experimenting with new and wonderful creations each day. I ate very well while I lived with him and marvel sometimes that I never picked up any culinary tips whatsoever from him during that time. He would cook for the four of us. We almost never ate out, but instead enjoyed a social life of togetherness at home. We would sit around our kitchen table late into the night, our conversation awash with cheap table wine. As the evenings lengthened and the candles dripped the last of their wax over the rim of the chianti bottle placed with precision by our host, we relaxed in our companionship. We were the centre of the universe then. Untouchable.

Watching Sebastian now I see his grief, but I can't feel it. I am immune to everything outside of myself. My own pain is so total. He reaches out to me and I turn away. Even as I do I am conscious of how callous it is, but I cannot comfort him. Wiping his face with his sleeve, he stands, hesitates, leaves.

This is bad, so bad. I close my eyes and try to shut it all out again.

# SEBASTIAN

What do the British do when there's nothing to be done? They make tea. Fumbling with cupboard doors in this unfamiliar kitchen, I search for the trappings of the make-it-all-better brew. No tea, no milk, no teapot.  Exasperated, I wrestle open a pottery canister and inhale the familiar smell of coffee. A French kitchen, of course! Grinding the beans, the repetition of this second nature activity soothes and I start to calm down. I could have hit Len upstairs just now. He has the monopoly of mourning being the grieving husband. Who am I? Just a friend. For so long I've been just a friend.

Looking around this house the sense of Claudine is so strong. I'm not a religious man, but I'm having difficulty accepting that something so vibrant has simply disappeared. I hear the soft tread of her step on the wooden floor, her laughter ringing round the walls. Her touch is everywhere. Her artwork decorates each room; paintings, photographs and her precious pots all lovingly crafted with her beautiful bare hands. How I longed for that touch. The coffee pot splutters and spits, enveloping me with its scent. Filling a mug, I wander through to their sitting room and am surprised to find Len hunched over the dining table, scribbling frantically.

"Tu veux un café?" I ask. Nothing. I grit my teeth, trying to keep my annoyance under control. It would help no-one to start fighting now. "Len!" He glances up. "Coffee?"

"No…..thanks." He smiles awkwardly.

"What're you doing?" I ask, peering over his shoulder. No reply. He is intent on his work, but doesn't stop me from looking. He has written:

LIST OF THINGS TO DO
1. FUNERAL
2. SORT OUT HER STUFF
3. PHONE CALLS
4. SORT MY CRAZY HEAD
5. GET RID OF SEBASTIAN

This latter is because I'm reading it, I know. Maybe I should go though. I could do with clearing my head and Len seems pretty focussed here. "Okay I'll go. Call if you need me." Nodding, he continues with his mission. That's as much as I'll get I know. Pulling on my coat, I slip out the back door, snapping it closed behind me. I'm surprised by the darkness as I step outside. It's a beautiful evening. The sky is clear, almost cloudless. Light from the low winter moon dances over this afternoon's snowfall, giving the impression of daylight, while endless stars dot across the night's expanse. I shudder as a buried memory creeps unexpectedly from my psyche. I haven't been troubled by memories for a long time, but Claudine's death seems to have awakened images which I had put to sleep. The last few days I've revisited my past so often that it all feels fresh and new again. I don't know if it's therapeutic to start going over things again or just stupid. Is this an excuse to indulge in thoughts of what was, what might have been? I haven't allowed myself to go down this road for such a long time. Can't do any good to rake it all out, but I feel helpless to stop the memories. Tonight I want her back.

Reaching the restaurant I'm pleased to find it locked up, in darkness. The cheerful jingle grates on my nerves as I enter, flicking the light switches as I go. The girls have done a good job. The place is immaculate. No evidence of this morning's *dommage*. Automatically I turn on the espresso machine and reach for a cup. I won't be sleeping tonight I already know. Placing a bottle of scotch beside the coffee, I heave my aching body into a chair. I feel like a stranger to myself. Why am I here? Why am I even now not sitting on that bus heading for home? Helen will be waiting, expecting. I don't know what I'm doing, but I know I need space. I need to think. I don't want my thoughts interrupted. No small-talk, no conversation, nothing where anything is expected of me. I want to think, to remember. I haven't allowed myself to do this for so many years. Any ripple of a resurfacing memory in all that time and I defiantly quashed it, pushed it away. It was finished after all. I told her it was finished. Who was I kidding? It was never finished. She's remained part of my life since I met her. I've carried her with me, treasured her. I wonder did she realise. In the early days I was convinced they would all read it in my face, but they didn't seem to. Then gradually I began to live the lie I had created and I suppose somewhere along the line accepted it.

We grew up together. She was literally the girl-next-door. I can remember playing in her sandpit, squabbling over toys, falling out and back in again. We knew each other inside out all our lives. Our parents were friends and used to spend many social occasions with each other. All our childhood achievements were celebrated together. Her mother loved me like her own son and Claudine was a second daughter to my parents. I was as comfortable in her home as I was in my own and vice versa. We didn't have secrets from each other. I knew all her embarrassments, all her fears. We went through school together and I was so proud to be associated with her. Everyone loved Claudine. She was smart, cool, beautiful. She had it all and she knew, but not in any precocious way. She simply knew as a matter of fact and accepted it as her good fortune. We were used to each other for so long that I can't even pinpoint when I started loving her. Maybe I always did. The moment I remember is when I realised that she loved me. Only then did I acknowledge my feelings for her to myself. Perhaps fate was preparing me for the future when I would need all my powers of denial to endure the pain ahead.

We were in our final year of school and had joked for years that if we couldn't get a partner for the end of year dance we would go together. I must admit I didn't try hard. I wasn't bothered too much about a school dance, but Claudine was. Of course she was. The school's princess had to be there, glittering in all her glory. She had done great in her bacalaureate and had secured a place at a prestigious art college. I forget now which one, because she never went, but no matter. This was her moment and I knew she'd be there. I was curious to know whose offer she would accept. When she asked me who I was going with I replied that I wasn't. She assured me I was, because she wasn't going without me. As she took my hand in hers, I lifted my head and met her steady level gaze and I knew. In that instant I knew we were meant for each other. That she loved me now as I had long loved her. That each completed the other. We became the golden couple, spending every minute together, enjoying each other, getting to know each other all over again. We laughed so much. And talked; talked about everything. I had met my perfect match. I felt safe. Her touch electrified me. Her conversation thrilled me. Who could ask for more? Was there more than this? If there was, I never found it. I knew she had planned a year out before college and when she announced she was going to New York I wasn't too surprised. I didn't really have any fears about her trip. I felt strong in our love. I thought we were unshakable. Inseparable.

The first few months of her stay I missed her desperately. I didn't expect it to *feel* so far away. I threw myself into my course. I was training to be a chef, working long hours, studying in between. Time passed quickly. When I met Helen it felt so unremarkable that I thought little of it. We spent more and more time together, because it was nice to have the company. She was very sweet, holidaying with girlfriends from Scotland and pleased to meet someone who would admit to understanding her awkward French. I guess if I'd had time to have any other interests, right then, I would never have got involved, but hindsight as they say…   The truth is she was so unlike Claudine, so completely incomparable that I didn't even consider her in the same way. What I didn't see and should have is that she was becoming more deeply attached. I didn't recognise the signs. I let it happen. I was so unemotionally involved that I couldn't see it was different for her. Stupid, stupid. What a stupid mistake.

To cut short a long story, Claudine came home and we picked up where we left off. It was so good to have her back. We fitted back together and put the previous year behind us. It didn't matter to either of us that we had seen other people. We were together again. Complete. What I didn't reckon on was Helen. Helen by this time thought she loved me. It hit me suddenly that she had assumed Claudine and I were finished. She had no idea what our love was. Helen a lovely girl, but rather superficial, based everything on her own experience. I realized I was going to have to spell it out. I didn't relish this prospect, but for Claudine and me to move on I had to. I know it sounds naive, but my feelings for Claudine were so intense I thought everyone knew. I truly thought Helen knew she was nothing to me. I know that sounds really harsh now, but back then, the way I felt, it seemed reasonable. Anyway, a month or so after Claudine returned we were deeply imbedded within each other again. Stronger. I thought forever. I asked her to stay with me, to marry me. She said, "Yes!" but she didn't want an extravagant engagement. She thought it a meaningless state and wanted us simply to marry. I bought a simple gold band and arranged to meet her. Everything would be perfect. The only thing was, first I had to sort the Helen situation. I didn't expect it to be so hard. I was young.

We went out for dinner and I kept trying to bring the subject round, but she wouldn't take me on. I tried a different tack, talking about Claudine all the time. Still no. I was nervous. I had a few drinks; two, maybe three glasses of wine. I wasn't drunk, but nevertheless it was my fault. The police said a lapse in concentration was just that if the driver was stone cold sober, but after a few drinks it was drunk driving. Drunk driving! I maintain it wasn't the alcohol, but the pressure I was under that night, but no one listens to a drunk driver do they? Maybe I took the bend too fast. I don't know. I've been over it so many times I hardly know what happened at all now. In my mind the many variations of what might have happened have all become real and now I just don't know.

The car was messed up but what's a car? Helen was another matter. It was so odd. She didn't have a mark on her, not a scratch. I had broken ribs and a dislocated shoulder, but bones heal and shoulders relocate. Helen was not so lucky. The doctor thought at first her sight would return after a few days, that it was just her body's response to the shock of the accident. But it never did. Blind. Because of me. The idea was unbearable. The guilt weighed heavily and I began to realise I wouldn't be able to leave her. The final decision was made when she said in her statement to the police that it was she who had been driving. She kept me out of jail, preserved my future. I owed her.

Claudine came to visit and it was the most painful thing I had ever endured. We walked out into the night and I broke the agonising news to her. She accepted it as it was. I was responsible. I had ruined Helen's life. I owed her.

"What about us?" she asked simply. I didn't reply. She knew the answer. There would be no more us. No more us.

# LEN

Staring at my list for the hundredth time I know there is nothing written here that I will ever do anything about.

1. The funeral. No. I'm not doing that. Surely no one expects me to let that go ahead. Let them bury my wife? Put my darling, beautiful wife in a box in the ground? Are they out of their minds? I finally spoke to the undertaker; told him not to bother me, that there would be no funeral. He said he would speak to me in the morning and hung up. Guess he's heard it all before.

2. Sort out her stuff. Her stuff's fine! I love her stuff. Glancing around the room, I see her touch in everything. Her creativity dazzled. She transformed the most mundane item into an objet d'art. It was her way.

3. Phone calls. Oh I never could cope with those foreign phone calls. I can't really understand properly unless I can see the person speaking. They talk so fast and their accents are so much more pronounced on the phone. Anyway, what is there to say? What would I actually say? No phone calls.

4. Sort my head out. Now there's one. I am so completely screwed up I doubt I could spell my own name tonight. Will I ever think straight again? My head hurts with the effort of thinking. Every thought is painful and takes all my strength to push it out of the way to

make room for another one. It feels like all these thoughts are just sitting in my mind, jumbling up amongst each other, going nowhere.

5. Get rid of Sebastian. I only put that there because I knew he was watching and I wanted to stop him talking to me. Anyway, he sorted that one for me. It occurs to me that maybe Sebastian could sort some of the others too. He could deal with the funeral. He could more than deal with the foreign phone calls. Don't know about her stuff. Don't suppose he could do anything about my head. Still, I resolve to speak to him and pass the list on, see what he makes of it.

Disturbed by the quietness of this house, I move into the kitchen to try and generate some noise. Clattering pots and pans out of cupboards, spilling assorted grocery items from the counter, the sounds all echo hollow around the empty walls. I'm no cook. I don't even know what half these things are for. I discard several packets before deciding to make some toast. The toaster hums gently as it browns the bread, but it's not enough. I pull the cord for the fan heater and a soft murmuring accompanies the toaster. Pleased with this small success, I move along to dishwasher, washing machine, tumble dryer and nudge the switches to ON. Suddenly the kitchen bursts into a melody that satisfies me. Rummaging in a low cupboard I pull out a small transistor radio and the room fills with a sports commentary. I have an idea then and wander round the house switching on every appliance I can find. Televisions, stereo systems even the vacuum cleaner buzz within the rooms. Not only does this have the desired effect of drowning out the silence, it also makes it difficult to think. What a bonus!

Back in the sitting room I'm congratulating myself on this stroke of mastery when I catch sight of her watching me. I remember the day this photo was taken. I remember the moment. We were camping in the Camargue four, maybe five years ago. We'd built a fire and sat around it in the half-light savouring the last of the day. Her face is partly in shadow and her hair curls softly over her cheek, giving more an impression rather than a distinct image. How beautiful she is.

*Was*. In a second my emotions flip. Tenderness replaced with anger. I can't look at her. I can't bear the agony of her smile. Turning the picture face down, I systematically work my way back around the house turning over every photo I find. There. The house is singing, every light in the place burning. From outside it must look like a beacon. And still it feels so empty. Collapsing on the couch, I suddenly feel very frightened. Heathcliff said it before me: "How can I live without my life? How can I live without my soul?" It occurs to me that getting through this night, arduous as that seems at this moment, is only the start. I have to live the rest of my life without the love of my life, without the meaning of my life. Groaning, I feel the all too familiar ache welling inside. This is suffering indeed.

I'm woken early as daylight peeps through my half-open drapes and am surprised to find that I must have slept after all. Not for long I admit, glancing at my watch, four hours maybe? Still it's better than I'd hoped for last night when sleep seemed out of reach altogether. The house is quiet again. I guess most of the appliances ran through their cycle then ground to a halt. A faint murmuring from the kitchen tells me the radio is still going though. The most resilient item in the whole place I decide.

Drawing back the drapes I can't remember if I didn't close them properly last night or didn't open them properly yesterday morning. The sun today is big and bright, reluctantly rising from the duvet of clouds hanging heavy still with snow. There has been a snowfall during the night, but the morning is clear and sharp. In another hour I could walk slowly down to the corner shop and meet Bobby opening up. I have a powerful urge for a cigarette. Strange, as I haven't smoked in ten years, but the feeling this morning as potent as if I quit only yesterday. I know. I could wash up now and change my clothes and that would pass some time. Reaching the bathroom I am struck by pangs of hurt emanating from the memory of the last time I saw her. Right here, in this very space, we both stood, both breathed, both lived. Slamming the shower screen hard against the wall, it shatters into the bath. Turning I catch sight of myself in the mirror. I barely recognise the face staring back at me. Pale and stubbled, red-ringed and shadowed, hair in my eyes, I look the way I feel. I look like shit. Defiantly I lift the mirror from its hook, raise it high and smash it across the tiles. My boots crunch through the debris as I exit the bathroom, heading downstairs and out.

How many days has it been I ask myself? I decide three, but am not totally convinced. Time has blurred past and I have very few points of reference. Everything has changed so fast. This emptiness is all-pervading. It seeps throughout my body, my mind. How do I get a grip back? I wander the streets aimless. It's a beautiful morning. Blue skies provide an impressive backdrop to the silver skywriting which snails its path behind a shimmering distant aeroplane. Here and there a slab of snow shunts its way slowly down a roof and shatters onto the pavement below. She would have loved a walk on a morning like this. Reaching Bobby's shop I fumble in my jeans for money. Gratefully I buy my cigarettes from a woman I don't know. Someone who won't ask me how I'm doing, who won't care how I'm doing. Drawing deeply on my first smoke in years, I open myself to its therapy, relieved that something can still touch me.

Maybe I should go into work. Obviously I'm not going to be able to do any work, but maybe I should go in and sort some things out. Work! How little anything matters now. I feel so fragile, so inadequate. Reaching the bus stop I pause to light another cigarette. I'd like to spend some time in my office, I decide. The familiarity might be quite reassuring. It might help to be there. Wondering how long till a bus shows up, it dawns on me that it doesn't remotely matter how long it takes. Time has no meaning to me now. There is nothing, no one waiting for me. I have no schedule, no commitments. This lack of parameters unsettles me. I feel untied, loose.

I notice a couple of students on the bus. They know. I can tell that they know. They don't know what to say though. It's easier to pretend not to see me than to confront the awkwardness of the moment; suits me better this way too. The last thing I want is people's pity. Arriving on campus I am disturbed to see so many people about this early. I hope to pass my colleagues' offices without being seen and to reach the sanctuary of mine uninterrupted. I wonder absently if I might have become slightly agoraphobic in the last few days. Can grief do that to you? Closing my office door finally behind me I realise I am sweating. This was harder than I expected. The room is as I left it moments after receiving the phone call; the call, which burst uninvited into my life and turned it upside down. The phone sits innocently now on my desk, beside it a bundle of papers. What had I been doing? Lifting a sheaf I remember Carly Adams failing her exam. That morning she had seemed so important. Today I struggle to put a face to her name. Still, I pull out my crumpled List of Things to Do and add 6) Carly.

The room is peaceful, restful and I feel now that I could sleep here. My answering machine flashes, indicating messages, which I don't want to hear. Instinctively I press play and to my horror find myself listening to Claudine's voice. "Len?" she asks. That's all. I replay; again, again. Claudine! When did she phone, before the accident, after? Was she phoning for help? Did she know she wasn't going to make it? Was this, "I love you"? Was this, "goodbye"? Trembling I listen to her voice again, one word in her distinctive accent; soft, tender, final. Pressing delete, I turn to leave as my wife's voice is erased forever.

# SEBASTIAN

I wake from my alcohol-induced sleep aching all over. I must have passed out eventually sitting at this table. The specifics of last night are hazy. The empty bottle lies accusingly at my feet, although my throbbing headache is evidence enough that I overdid it. It's light outside, but still quiet. It feels early. Rising from the table; stumbling against the chair, an excruciating pain cracks through my knee; the final insult. Helen will wonder where I've been. I'm not in the habit of staying out all night without calling. I wonder if she has rung looking for me, but there are no missed calls on my phone. Perhaps she has assumed I've got caught up with Len. Maybe I stayed with him last night so he wasn't alone.

I clear the table as a matter of course. I like things to be tidy. This place looks good. We've done well here. How ironic that I've messed up the rest of my life so effectively. A psychologist might say that's the very reason I'm so meticulous. That I'm still trying to sort out the debris of the past. There could be something in that. My head is killing me and I wonder if I could get away without baking this morning. Could I get away with not opening at all? I realise that I no longer care if the place shut up for good. We worked so hard for this. I invested years of my life into establishing Café Helene as a reputable restaurant, not to mention all our money. In the space of a few days it has all become meaningless. What would people think, though, if I caved in now, in the wake of Claudine's death? Having disguised my feelings so effectively while she lived wouldn't it be crazy to let everyone in on it now that she's gone? I begin the morning preparations. Lights on, ovens on; the ritual is easy on my mind. I can stop thinking for a bit. A couple of hours on and things are ticking over as always. A rap on the outer door drags me from my preoccupation. Morning staff! Is it really that time already? I am confused by their cautious entrance, sideways glances darting between them. Then it dawns on me how I must look. "Bit of a rough night…" I mutter. "Will you guys be okay for a while if I go home, straighten myself out?" They are enthusiastic at this suggestion and I understand that I look terrible. Still it gets me away from the place for a couple of hours. Heading out I watch them assume their respective roles and am grateful to have such reliable people.

The sun is burning bright this morning, stinging my eyes as they adjust to daylight. I don't want to go home. I don't feel ready to resume the act. I haven't finished mourning yet and I know I'm going to have difficulty tempering my feelings to a more appropriate level. A guy doesn't crack up completely over the death of his friend. After all she was Helen's friend too and she's keeping it together isn't she? I am envious of Len able to let go, able to grieve openly. I have long been envious of Len, though.

After Claudine and I broke up she disappeared. I mean literally disappeared. Her mother called me to ask if I knew where she was. Of course I didn't and I had to endure the blame for that too until a postcard arrived at her home, absolving me of responsibility. She went to stay with friends in London apparently. Improving English was the agenda. Several months later I heard by chance that she had teamed up with some travelling French students and drifted up to Scotland. She stayed away for about a year; long enough presumably to get herself together. She would never have broken down amongst people she knew. Long enough also to miss matriculation for Art School and long enough for me to have promised Helen I wouldn't ever leave her. I always thought I would know instinctively that she was back in town. I thought about her often, dreamed about her all the time. Strange dreams in which I had either no voice or else we didn't speak the same language and couldn't understand each other, couldn't communicate. Maybe it's just as well she left. Surely I would have turned back otherwise. Oh, if only… I know I broke her heart, but I also smashed my own to pieces. I was never the same person after Claudine.

So when I bumped into her one afternoon at le Marche aux Puces de Saint-Ouen, the flea market nearby, I was stunned. I wandered through here from time to time usually in search of clothes or something a bit different. I had just bought a jacket and was entering another dimly lit cavern that purported to be a shop. The midday sunshine burned down on the streets and pavements outside and only very few had skipped siesta. I paused to allow her to pass through the narrow entrance, her face completely obscured by shadows as she approached. She on the other hand would have seen me clearly. Perhaps she even spotted me before she exited. Either way she was ready. Poised; perfect. I was a wreck the moment I recognised her. My whole being yearned to gather her in my arms, to put right all the wrong I had caused. I had imagined this moment many times. I had rehearsed hundreds of different combinations of conversation. In each version there was one common factor, I said the right thing. When the moment chanced upon us it wasn't like that. I barely said anything and what I did was so stilted, so distant. She stood before me yet out of reach. It was over too quickly. Minutes, seconds and she was gone again. Her perfume lingered a while and her image added itself to the dozens already in my memory. The words: "I've missed you" hanging unsaid in the air between us.

The next time I saw her, she was being introduced to me as Len's girlfriend.

I met Len at the College Club, a pretentious place which provided leisure facilities for teachers and lecturers. I was working there at that time. I guess I was one of the few students to access that hallowed, strictly invitation-only area. I hadn't completed my course, but I was gaining experience with some of the exclusive restaurateurs in the city and had managed to secure an apprenticeship with the college chef. The only snag being that I didn't get paid for the privilege of providing the finest food to the city's finest academics. I did have opportunity though to experiment and to develop a unique style at my employer's expense so it cut both ways. I was living in really poor conditions back then. The apartment was in a desperate state. I was the only remaining resident in a block of six, everyone else having either moved out or taken the cheaper option of living on the street. Because I rented I was the exception. My landlord was in no hurry to let the lease lapse and anyway I had nowhere else to go. Trouble was I couldn't pay the bills and people weren't exactly tripping over themselves to move in with me.

The day I met Len things were rock bottom for me. I had finished for the day, but always as I vacated the kitchens there were a few stragglers left drinking on into the night. Usually I merely nodded and made for the door. I was really tired by this time. On this night though, Emile Duflot was nursing a brandy in the company of a guy I never saw before. I knew Emile a bit. He worked in the English Literature Department and as I crossed the floor, he signalled to me to join them. Well I wasn't in a hurry to go home to face my problems, so a drink seemed a good alternative. Emile introduced Len as a brand new associate lecturer to his department. I knew this meant that he would be studying for a PhD as well as teaching. He seemed very young, about ages with me and I surmised he must be a bit of a high-flyer. Emile headed up a rather salubrious staff and this guy obviously had the right credentials. I liked Len immediately. I'm usually cautious with new people but Len was so matter-of-fact, so down to earth that we seemed to connect very quickly. I liked his sense of humour, his self-deprecating wit. I enjoyed his intelligent conversation and stories of his native Canada. It transpired through this conversation that Len was hot off the plane and staying in a hotel until he found accommodation. I joked that I had a spare room and listened with incredulity as he queried the logistics of living in the Latin Quarter. I decided to burst his bubble before expectations were any further raised, but he merely asked in that quiet-spoken, even, intense voice of his if he could come look around. I laughed, knowing how unsuitable the apartment was likely to be, but he was insistent so it was arranged. The following afternoon, sure enough he came by. I thought

33

if the graffitied entrance with its peeling paintwork and urine-stenched stairway doesn't put him off, the interior sure will.

A few minutes wandering through and he smiled broadly, "It's perfect. When can I move in?"

I was stunned. Surely this guy could do better. It was much later when I knew him well that I understood his desire to live like his literary idols in a kind of Americans in Paris sort of thing. Anyway it was to my benefit, because, of course I had someone with whom to share the unbelievable rent. Unknown to me at that time, though, this guy was to become a hugely important person in my life.

We shared the apartment for around two years before he ever brought anyone home. That was understandable, of course. It wasn't a place you'd be dying to show off to all your friends. We were like brothers, doing our own thing a lot of the time but always had time for the other. We spent many evenings at local pubs or cafes just talking. Sometimes there was a crowd of us, his friends or mine, but always there was room for each other. He was very relaxing company to be in. My initial impressions proved to be correct. High-flyer had been an understatement though. He was etching a memorable impression at the Sorbonne. You could tell his colleagues admired his work, enjoyed his company. He was the kind of person who said things the way you wished you had said them. He could express your thoughts better than you could yourself. He was also very funny and as a result very popular. Sometimes I had the impression, though, that popularity was something he would have happily avoided if it hadn't chanced upon him. He didn't appear to have to make much effort with people. I guess you could say he was a natural people person. I later discovered this was far from the way he felt, but this is the impression he gave. He was also very attractive to women although seemed happy to be just friends with many who I know harboured hopes for more. He only went out on the odd date during the first two years of his stay and it wasn't through lack of interest. I knew, therefore, when he told me he'd met someone, that this was someone special. Just how special I realized the night he brought her home. Claudine.

# LEN

I decide I can't be on my own anymore. I couldn't bear to stay in that office after hearing Claudine's haunting voice. I can't look at her picture, can't listen to her message. Even thinking about her hurts beyond belief. Where will I go? Suddenly I feel very alone. Where are all my friends? I lead a very busy, social life and yet at this moment I can't think of anywhere to go, anyone to call. The only place where I know I'll find someone who understands is the Café and I don't want to be with him. I can't keep running back to Sebastian. After seeing how shaken up he was the other day I realised that he is also grieving and it isn't fair to put more pressure on him. On the other hand I want to be with someone who cares and I desperately need companionship right now. Helen! What about Helen? I wouldn't need to explain anything, she would understand and her company might just distract me from this hideous feeling for a while. Resolutely I hail a taxi, something I never do, but I can't face meeting anyone on the bus. Maybe I should call first. I fumble in my pockets for my phone, but the battery's gone. That probably explains the lack of calls today, though, which was welcome relief. The cab drops me outside their block and I hurry up to the main door still worried about the possibility of meeting people. I don't even know anyone else in this neighbourhood, but I feel as if everyone has heard and is talking about me. Number 8. CHARPENTIER. I buzz and wait for her to answer.

"Who is it?" The voice answers more quickly than I expected. It also isn't the voice that I expected. Surprised, I stand in silence. "Hello?" the voice urges.

35

"Em… it's me… Len."

"Come on up."

A sharp sounding click follows as the door is unlocked. I am obliged to go in. As I approach the bend at the top of the stairs I see Sebastian waiting at the open door. He welcomes me as always with a warm handshake and ushers me inside. The flat is immaculate. Nothing is ever out of place here. People think it's so that Helen can always find her way around, but Sebastian has always been like this. When we lived together he kept that grotty apartment really nice too. He cooked and cleaned, sorted out the bills, shopped. I don't think I contributed much as a flatmate, but then I didn't have to because Sebastian had everything under control. It occurs to me that he moved on from looking after me to looking after Helen. It must be difficult at times, to have someone so completely dependent on you. Who looks out for Sebastian I wonder, when it all gets too much?

I suddenly feel like a pretty rubbish friend. I haven't ever really given Sebastian's situation all that much thought. Helen was the only girlfriend I knew him to have, although I believe he had a substantial romantic history. I was stunned when he announced that he and Helen were to marry. She's lovely sure, but she never really struck me as Sebastian's type. Still, what would I know? I don't suppose we can understand someone else's love-life can we?

"What are you doing home at this time of day?" I ask as he follows me into the kitchen.

"So it's not me you're looking for then?" he asks, smiling.

"Well no, actually I came to see Helen. Thought she would be someone to talk to."

"Afraid she's not here. Hospital appointment I think. You should have phoned first. You want a drink?" I take the beer he offers and remark that he isn't having anything. "No, still recovering from last night. Head's killing me." The whole time I have known Sebastian I have never known him to miss a day's work. He has that self-employed martyred work ethos. I must admit he does look pretty rough this morning. I wonder at him going out partying at a time like this. I thought he was really cut up yesterday. He doesn't feel like the right person to be speaking to about Claudine and I wish desperately that I hadn't come. "You doing okay?" he asks.

"Yes… no… well, you know…."

He nods.

Unusually I am lost for something to say. I'm starting to feel really stupid when I remember my list. "Wondered if you could help me with something," I say holding out the piece of paper. He scans it quickly, looks up puzzled. "I made a list of things that need to be done." His gaze is levelled, waiting for me to go on. "I can't deal with this stuff just now. I know I'm pathetic, but I can't do it."

He nods again, reassuringly. "Okay, let's see..." I sit down and soak up the beer while Sebastian reads over my list again. "Right, well, d'you want a hand with funeral arrangements?"

"Definitely. I want you to handle it."

"Well, I don't know if it's really my place..."

"Please Sebastian if anyone else can do this it's you. You cared for her almost as much as me."

He says nothing. Glancing back to the paper, he murmurs thoughtfully, "Well I can certainly do the phone calls. I'll do them today if you like. Who is it? Claudine's folks? Anyone else?"

"No that'll do. They can pass on any information themselves."

"Right. Her stuff?"

"No that's okay I can deal with that later." A look resembling relief flashes over his face.

"Not sure I can do anything with your head. Never understood what went on in there!" He smiles and again I feel the warmth of his friendship. It's strange how I've wavered between wanting Sebastian and not being able to have him near me these past few days. He is a good friend, has always been there for me. It's just with Claudine, I don't know, I guess I always wondered if he perhaps admired her from afar. I wouldn't blame him mind you. He wouldn't be the only one. Many men were attracted to her. I never worried, but with Sebastian I think I just had a niggling doubt. They got on so well, their friendship was very natural and easy. Maybe I'm being paranoid. I seem to be extremely sensitive just now. The slightest ripple disturbs my equilibrium. He reads on down the list, "Sure I can stay away if you want me to." He looks hurt.

"Forget that one," I reply.

"Carly?" he asks.

"A student. Forget her too."

"Okay, so I phone the Rousseaus and help you with the funeral. Is that it?" I nod. "No problem, mon ami and anything else you think of."

"I should get going." I rise to leave.

"Stay, Len. I'll make you something to eat. Helen won't be back for ages. I'm not doing anything." Always Sebastian was hospitable and welcoming. I feel bad now about thinking he might have been interested in Claudine.  I am so tired I can barely think. Leaning back in the chair I decide to let him look after me. Closing my eyes, the restful atmosphere of his home washes over me and I let myself sink, deeper and deeper into oblivion. The familiar sounds of Sebastian setting to work in the kitchen become more and more distant. His trademark coffee disperses its aroma throughout the apartment and I am taken back to happier times. Paris. Claudine.

# SEBASTIAN

The evening Len brought Claudine home I was busy in the kitchen. We had had friends over for dinner, Helen had gone home with them and I was sorting stuff out. I'd had a bit to drink and was looking forward to finishing the last bottle off in the comfort and quiet of the apartment. I finished up in the kitchen and, lifting the wine and a glass, made for the living room. I was busy flicking through some music, deciding what to play when I heard voices outside. Laughter and chatter rising steadily up the stairs. The key scraped in the lock and they fell into the room still laughing. They looked good together; that was my first thought. Len with his black shirt and jacket, black eyes and hair, a glint of silver from his earings. He had the look. He had the personality and now he had the girl. He was animated, drinking her in. I knew in an instant he was besotted. Claudine, beautiful Claudine. She wasn't surprised to see me. As always she was controlled, measured and appropriate. I didn't know what to say. Len started to introduce her when she interrupted with, "Sebastian!" Len was as surprised as I. "I already know Sebastian. We grew up next door to each other. I've known him all my life. How are you Sebastian?" So that was what we were reduced to; childhood friends. It was so hurtful. I watched as he made her comfortable, made her a drink, made her laugh some more. My Claudine here in my home with someone else and no acknowledgement that I had ever been anything; it was agony. I couldn't speak. I just sat burning up inside, wanting to scream, wanting to cry. I waited for a sign. When Len left the room I was sure there would be a smile, a look. Nothing, not a flicker. We sat

39

in silence till he returned. She showed no glimmer of remembering what we had been. She was in perfect control. This set the scene for the way we were to conduct our future relationship. Not once did she crack. Even on my wedding day I watched for a sign, anything from her and who knows what I'd have done, but she was impeccable. I wondered and still wonder why she didn't tell Len about us. As far as I know he never had any idea that we had a past beyond *childhood friends.* Why did she keep that from him? I like to think it was because I still meant something to her. That she wanted to protect what we had shared. Some of me wonders, though, if she had simply closed the door and shut off all feeling. Maybe for her it was truly finished and not worthy of mention. I don't know. I do know that it hurt and goes on hurting. I did the wrong thing, made the wrong decision. All for the right reasons, but it was wrong. We should have been together. Instead I've spent the rest of my life regretting letting her go.

## LEN

When I wake I have the sense of having slept for a long time. I feel stiff and uncomfortable and I haven't a clue where I am. Standing to stretch my back I glance around the room; wooden floors, blank walls, minimalist verging on empty; Sebastian's place. We always referred to it as Sebastian's, never Helen and Sebastian's, probably because it was so much an expression of his tastes. It looks to me like a bachelor pad, very like an upmarket version of our apartment in Paris, in fact. That flat also had Sebastian's mark stamped across it and little evidence of me. He is such a strong character, the type whose presence turns heads when he enters a room. At times I used to think he played it a bit. You know the kind of thing, pretending he didn't notice someone showing an interest. He was charming and flirtatious and girls loved him. He was a really good mate too. It was down to him that I settled so quickly in France. I mean the work was great and I developed skills in research which set me up for life. I also established important contacts which have proved beneficial to me over the years. Yes my time at the Sorbonne definitely helped boost me up the career ladder. Sebastian, though, taught me the value of friendship. He was the first friend who I felt I could trust implicitly. He was solid, dependable and also very considerate. I remember when I didn't know anyone else outside of work he would always include me in his plans. He introduced me to his friends and his family and before I knew it I was relaxed in their company too. I wasn't ever very comfortable about making friends or instigating relationships, but Sebastian kind of did it all for me. One thing he wasn't good at was sharing his feelings

41

and I think that's still true. In some ways he is quite a private person, doesn't talk a lot about himself. He's the sort of person you feel you'll never totally know. For example, I don't think he has ever told me anything that is troubling him. You can tell of course; sometimes he seems quite distant and sad, but if mentioned he laughs it off. There are definitely hidden places where access is denied. Like with Helen. You're not telling me that's a match made in heaven. Helen is a nice girl and pretty, but Sebastian and she have nothing in common, and I mean nothing. When she's hot, he's cold, when she's tired, he's full of life. Sebastian likes to socialise and talk, is charismatic, entertaining, Helen is very quiet, doesn't go out a great deal, sometimes she doesn't even seem to enjoy his company much. More than this though, they don't have any spark between them. When I think of Claudine and myself and the excitement, the chemistry between us, I am surprised that Sebastian has settled for this. I did wonder if he felt sorry for her after the accident and if that was why. But then as Claudine used to remind me, we don't know people, not really and what is between Sebastian and Helen we'll never know, because that part of their life is just for them. I was shocked all the same when he told me they were getting married. I actually remember when he told me, I didn't automatically congratulate him, I asked him why, and he replied simply, "Why not?" Nothing has ever surprised me more. Not until the last few days that is. The shock of this week outstrips everything.

I can hear his voice now through in the kitchen. French. He's talking on the phone. I can't understand much, the Parisian accent is so unlike the way people speak back home. My home that is, in Montreal. I struggled with that a bit too when I first arrived in Paris. It's almost like another language from the French I grew up with; a very distinctive accent and also very fast. I'm sure I survived the first few months by picking up key words in conversation and then trying to do much of the talking myself so as not to have to listen to the unrelenting, incomprehensible prattle. At this moment I can't even pick up any key words. I'm so tuned out to all things French now. Claudine and I didn't speak French to each other. Not ever. It seems to be almost universally accepted that English-speaking people continue to speak in English when in foreign company and that was true with us. I was the foreigner and I spoke French all day at work, but when I came home, Sebastian would speak his almost perfect English to me; later Claudine too. I suppose when we became established as a foursome, there was Helen who hardly spoke any French at all, to consider. Strangely, Sebastian and Claudine who had grown up together didn't speak to each other in French either. I can't make out what he's saying, but I know he's talking to my in-laws on the phone. I am so grateful to him for this. I would have found this particular call really hard in any language. It's quiet for a few seconds and then I see him peering round the door, "Oh you're awake. I've got Cecile on the phone." Strange how I never felt comfortable calling my mother-in-law by her Christian name. Sebastian is more at ease with my wife's family than I ever was. I always guessed that she would have rather had Sebastian as a son-in-law than this upstart Canadian who she couldn't even understand. I shake my head vigorously and nodding knowingly he returns to the kitchen.

I wander over to the window and am shocked to see dusk falling. Across the rooftops, the sun is settling down in a final blaze of burnt orange glory. I've never liked sunsets and in this recognised a kinship with Saint-Exupery's Little Prince. Even I, though, have to marvel at the magnificence of this one. I often wish I could paint. Claudine could capture the essence of this sunset on canvas, but I wouldn't be able to do it justice. She used to say that the only reason a person was unable to paint beautifully was if they didn't see the beauty before them, if they didn't know how to look. Maybe that's me after all. Maybe I just can't see what's in front of me.

I hear Sebastian's tone change and realise he's onto goodbyes. I breathe a sigh of relief.

"She wanted to speak with you," he says returning to the room.

"I know."

"They're coming over."

"I thought they would. Who's all coming?"

"Cecile, Antoine, Christophe. Maybe Dominic and Luc…they don't know, they'll try." Claudine's parents and brothers, that's good, no extended family.

"When are they coming?"

"I said I'd ring them tomorrow when we… when you have things arranged." Another awful phone call! I wonder what on earth they were talking about all that time, if that's all he has to say. I know they can be a bit long-winded, but even so. Of course, he would be giving them the detail. They would want to know precisely what happened, when, how etc. Sebastian runs his hands through his hair, "This is so…" breaking off he turns, leaving the room. I feel relief. I'm thankful that things are starting to happen without my involvement. I wish everything else could just happen. I don't want to be asked to do anything, don't want my opinion sought. I just want it to happen and be over.

Following Sebastian through to the kitchen I find he has cooked. Tossing a bundle of cutlery onto the table he asks when I last ate. I actually can't remember. Even now all I feel like is a cigarette.

"I hope you haven't made much, I'm not hungry."

"I've made enough for two and Helen isn't coming so you'll have to have some," he replies. Chicken, rice, salad, bread all prepared with precision. He reaches into the fridge for a half-empty bottle of wine and with a gesture invites me to sit. I have never really grown used to this custom of storing opened wine bottles in the fridge and then drinking red wine cold. Tonight, though, the wine is welcome; quenching my dry throat, dulling my senses.

"Where's Helen?" I ask and immediately feel awkward.

He hesitates. "Staying with her sister… she rang earlier. She sometimes does. Stay with her sister, I mean… quite often in fact."

"Are things okay?" I ask and hope he isn't going to choose tonight of all nights to open his soul to me. I really couldn't take it. I don't want to know, cannot offer an opinion or give advice. I'm having difficulty thinking. Keeping track of the conversation is hard. I have a sudden longing to get completely drunk and not be able to think at all.

"Things are fine," he says finally.

I feel terrible. Clearly things are not fine. He is as uncomfortable with this as I am. I should have realised that Sebastian doesn't open up. I needn't have feared any outpouring of feelings. Sebastian keeps it together. Finishing the meal, I realise I must have been hungry after all. The obligatory cup of coffee appears together with an ashtray and Sebastian lights up. I reach over to help myself from his cigarette packet. He says nothing. I like that about Sebastian, he doesn't pass comment unnecessarily. Inhaling deeply I start to relax. I am using every crutch available to me at the moment and things don't feel any easier. Normally this would worry me, but I don't have the energy to worry about anything anymore. I am existing completely in the moment. I have no past, no future. At times, I feel I'm barely existing at all. I'm here and that's about it. I'm here and she's not.

Our meal finished, I have an overwhelming urge to be on my own. This pendulum of emotions, swinging from desperation for company to a desire for space is exhausting. I step out from the warmth of Sebastian's home into another freezing night. Most of the snow seems to have melted away during the course of the day. The roads are clear, but sparkling with frost and smeared with a dirt trail left in the wake of the plough. Only the pavements and gardens remain white with ice-packed snow. It is solid underfoot but my boots churn the snow up into a spray of flakes as I walk. The full moon hangs low and heavy in the sky, lighting my path and all around me. The keen night air crawls through my clothes, leaving me shivering. My head is clearing, though, for the first time in days. My mind feels sharp and focussed. A semblance of control attempts to nudge its way back into my head on the breath of a fresh breeze. It is a beautiful night. Raising my eyes, I see a multitude of stars blink in the darkness overhead.

Arriving home, the house looks dark and unwelcoming, the only one in the street with no lights. A dusting of wood shavings decorates the front step where the joiner left off yesterday. Was it yesterday or the day before? Time has stopped for me. The thud of the door echoes around the empty house. Switching on the lights, its emptiness grows in front of my eyes. It is freezing, the walls seep coldness through them. I scrabble about in the linen cupboard for the dial which beckons heat into the building and hear the comforting sound of the boiler firing.

The house feels enormous, the emptiness all-pervading. I would like to scream just to hear what it sounds like in the silence. I know I will never sleep tonight. I have slept all day, lulled by comfort and companionship. Tonight my mind is clear and alert. A sense of calm descends over me. I feel more in control now than I have for a while. Maybe the combination of rest, food and exercise has done me good. The trouble is I'm bound to think now. In actual fact maybe I want to think. An image of Claudine creeps into my open mind and I smile back at her. She is walking with me through a field of flowers, a beautiful part of Provence where we holidayed last year. Claudine's brother is at college in Marseille and we visited during our summer vacation. She looks so relaxed, so carefree. We are choosing a spot to have a picnic and finding the perfect one, stop to spread out a travelling rug and lay out our banquet. Claudine unpacks the basket and fills our plates with cheeses, meats and bread. A bottle of beer each and we clink glasses, "Santé!" Suddenly I am overcome by a desperate need to preserve this image. I want to remember every detail. I want to protect all my memories of Claudine. Aware of how little I remember of my childhood, a panic rises within me that one day I might not be able to bring Claudine back to mind in all her colour and warmth. Fumbling through a drawer in my desk I grab a pen and some paper. Settling inside my study, a familiar place in which to concentrate my efforts, I write:

LIST OF THINGS TO REMEMBER
1) The way her eyes dance when she smiles
2) The softness of her skin
3) The tilt of her head while she decides what to say
4) Her gentle handshake
5) The melodic lilt of her accent

6) The fragility of her thin shoulders

7) The way she rubs her eyes when she is tired

8) The way she plays with her hair when she is distracted

9) The way she sleeps curled up like a baby

10) The way she whispers "I love you"

I could go on and on. Resolutely I decide to note down anything which comes to mind, anything that I want to remember and fear forgetting. Reading back over my list I am again assaulted by a barrage of pain pummelling to be let back in. I want to feel it. I want to think about her and for it to hurt so much I almost can't bear it. I want to make her real in my mind and I know that will hurt, but where else can she be if not there? Music, I think. Put on her music, that will bring her close. Sifting through our collection I pause at some of Claudine's favourites and pull out The King. As the mellow tones of Elvis filter through the house, my imagination is once again captivated by the sight of my beautiful wife. Lifting my pen once more I continue…

11) The way she blows a kiss

12) Her expression of concentration while she works

13) Her hair wet from the shower

I cannot write in the past tense. She is here with me, each image stronger, more real than the last. I am enjoying her company, enthralled by her conversation, engaged by her beauty.

14) The way it feels to be loved by her

Tears fall fast. I let them flow. The pain is worth it if it brings Claudine back. I can endure all of it if it allows me to be with her.

15) Her subtle wit

16) Her quiet confidence

17) Her melodramatic exaggeration

My writing is almost illegible now, smudged by tears and sweat. I am writing furiously, faster and faster. The pen skids across the page tearing through my words. I scribble over and over what I've written, big black lines digging deep into the page. I feel the pain rising higher and higher wrestling to take over. Snap! The pen breaks between my gripped fingers and I fling the fragments to the floor. Deep breath. Another. It's okay. It's going to be okay.

Restless now I rise from my desk and wander from room to room. Breathe, I tell myself, breathe. Pausing for a moment on the stairs the familiar blink of messages stored on the answering machine catches my eye. The repetitive on- off on-off is therapeutic, calming. I watch the little green light flickering out and in, like a candle in a draught. Finally I press the button and my reverie is broken. "You have 2 messages. Message 1 recorded today at 1445." Beep. 'This is a message for Mr Len Thomas. Mr Thomas it is Donald Mackenzie, the undertaker. It is absolutely imperative that I speak to you soon. Please call me back at your earliest convenience.' Beep. "Message 2 recorded today at 1456." 'Hello, Mr Thomas? This is Staff Nurse Riordan phoning from the Royal Infirmary. I wonder if it would be possible for you to call in tomorrow. We have the death certificate ready for you to collect and also some personal items belonging to your wife.' For the second time today I press erase and wish everything else was as easy.

## SEBASTIAN

Standing in the darkness beside the window, I watch as Len emerges from the entrance below, turns down the street and disappears from view. He looks cold, his hands stuffed into pockets, his body hunched against the evening air. The streetlights send shadows into my room, across the floor, up the wall. A neon light on the building opposite shines luminous as the night unwraps itself. I'm glad he came round this morning. I feel we've been quite disconnected this past couple of days. He looks lonely, a solitary figure wandering the streets. I wonder how he's going to be. He worshipped Claudine. I know he counted himself lucky to have her, never took her for granted, just loved her. In that I am pleased. I couldn't have taken it if she had married someone who didn't treat her well, someone who didn't appreciate what he had in her. At least I always knew she was alright, that she was happy. It's a very strange way to live your life, watching from the side-lines. I guess because we all became such good friends it has been natural to remain a part of her life. I knew this would be difficult and at times it has felt almost unbearable to stand back as her life with Len unfolded. And yet I'd far rather that than nothing at all.

When Helen and I got married it was a lavish affair. We flew over here to Edinburgh where Helen's family all live and tied the knot in a big marquee amidst hundreds of guests. It wasn't my kind of thing at all, but Helen wanted the works and her dad ensured she had what she wanted. The day passed in a blur. I drank too much and have little memory of the event itself, other than one distinct image. I can still see her clearly as if it were yesterday; Claudine seated beside Len, beautiful, elegant; perfect. I noticed them as they entered, everyone did. They were a stunning couple after all. I watched her scanning the room, eyes darting all around the place, looking for someone. I met her gaze and for a moment we froze. Just a moment, what was it seconds, less? In that instant she was mine and I was hers. It was all still there, I know it was. And then it was gone. She didn't smile, didn't wave and didn't call out to me, didn't rush over and beg me not to go through with it. She simply turned away. My heart wrenched inside my body. I wanted so badly for it to be me she was with, for it to be us who were pledging our lives to each other. The rest of the ceremony seemed to take place without any involvement from me. Very little was expected. I had to say, 'Yes' a couple of times and that was about it. I couldn't tell you what was said, what promises were made that day, but I do know that each word took me farther away from Claudine. I understand I disgraced my wife that afternoon, a result of drinking too much, and wasn't fit to be in company. Nevertheless, I doubt if I would have gotten through it any other way. We didn't go on honeymoon, instead we headed straight back to France to pack up all our stuff and prepare for a new life in Scotland. We were home for about six weeks in total. When we returned Claudine and Len had married. They didn't have a fuss of a wedding, just the two of them and a couple of strangers picked off the street to witness their vows taken in a small registry office in the city. I was completely shocked. I know it sounds like double standards. Somehow though, this seemed so wrong. I mean it seemed wrong for me and Helen to be together, but that was because I had to. I felt I had to. This felt like betrayal. I didn't imagine for a moment that Claudine would put her life on hold, wait for me to be free one day, maybe never. All the same, the reality of her declaring her lifelong love for someone else dug holes in my heart that have never healed. I never got over her marrying Len. I never got over her not marrying me.

At first I found it hard to be around her. It was difficult not to see her, because they had settled in a neighbouring part of town. I did try to avoid her in the beginning, but it didn't really help how I felt. You see I missed her. I was incomplete without her. After a while I realised it was better, though more painful, to have her in my life as a friend, than not at all. And so the foursome we had become in younger days in Paris was reunited again in Scotland. This way I still got to spend time with her. I loved her company, the way she spoke, the things she said. She was funny and intelligent and very thoughtful. I loved the way she walked, the way she moved. I loved all the things she created; her artwork was beautiful, like an extension of herself. I loved her deeply and never stopped. It didn't get easier, but I did begin to accept our situation. I had to, this was it. I couldn't live without her; that would be like dying, so this arrangement became acceptable to me. She remained in my life and I in hers. It was the best I could hope for at the time.

# LEN

Wandering restlessly from room to room, I wonder how I'm supposed to do this. I'm obviously not the first person to have lost someone they love. Lost! What a funny turn of phrase. I've lost Claudine; as if I've absentmindedly left her somewhere and can't remember where. Do people really think that by euphemising they take the sting out of it? Lost, Gone, Passed On… Whatever you like to say it means the same; dead. She's dead and I don't even know what that means. I don't know what or where dead is. I'm struggling, I know. I've lost my footing, lost my grip on reality and I don't know what I do about it.

Pushing open the door to our room, I am drawn to her bedside and all her little things. These are her trinkets: boxes of assorted sizes containing earrings, bracelets, rings. A watch lies beside them and a book. What was she reading? I am shocked that I didn't know what book my wife was reading. I could tell you what 31 Honours students, who I barely know, have been reading, but I had no idea that Claudine had selected Sylvia Plath. I wish I'd realised. How I would have loved to discuss this poetry with her. I never really shared my academic life, my love of literature with Claudine. Tonight it feels like the most natural thing in the world. A wave of despair swamps me now that the chance is gone. I wonder how many other things I didn't realise about her. Our lives were so busy, so full. If only I had realised we were running out of time, maybe I would have savoured everything that little bit more. And yet just knowing the end was approaching would have, by definition ruined, it all, wouldn't it? She has a notebook beside her book and a pencil. What was that for? Flicking through the pad I see she has left herself various reminders, a shopping list, bank details… There is nothing remotely personal here but I feel like an intruder. I would never have gone through her stuff and can't imagine she would have mine. We didn't have secrets and I'm sure there's nothing I would have minded her finding. It's just the principle, I think. It's about respect.

I suppose at some point I'll need to go through all her stuff and sort it out. What do I do with it? What do you do with a lifetime of personal belongings? Opening her top drawer, my fingers smooth over scarves; velvet, chiffon, silk. Feeling my way through layers of luxuriant fabrics I enter farther into its depths. Her sensual fragrance envelopes me. Gathering an armful of these treasures, smothering my face in them, I breathe in her scent, long for her love. Placing the delicate scarves gently back into the drawer, my cuff catches on a buckle. Reaching in to unhook the sparkling belt from my sleeve I lean too heavily and the drawer spills out, emptying its treasures abundantly around me. Carefully I rescue each item, one by one, gently folding and refolding and returning them to their rightful places. Scarves and belts, stockings and gloves, I place them all back where she had left them. It's so hard to imagine that she will never again wear these lovely things. As I close the drawer, I notice a leather glove lying on the floor. Stooping to retrieve it, my hand brushes a paper hidden beneath. Lifting both items I push them also into the drawer. Almost as an afterthought, I turn the paper over and see Claudine's familiar handwriting, neat, precise, tidy. It is an envelope rather than a piece of paper. Curious, I retrieve it and read the words she has written:

'In the event of my death…'

Stunned I re-read those words. Claudine had considered her own death! She never mentioned it, never made any suggestion that she had made any preparations.

'In the event of my death, please forward the enclosed.'

Disbelieving, I read again. Claudine's words, her thoughts, her wishes. She must have known I would be the one to find this so why is it written so formally? Why didn't she tell me about it? I don't understand. What was she thinking? Then I realise that she's given me something here. She's given me something that I can still do for her. I will send this letter, or whatever it is, because that is what she wanted. She knows she can rely on me, trust me. I'll do this for her. Resolutely I fold it and push it down deep into my back pocket. Tomorrow my love I'll do this for you. I'll do it and I won't ask why.

# SEBASTIAN

Repeated, impatient buzzing rouses me from sleep. The door, someone is at the door. Staggering through the mess of the living room, pressing the door release button, I am only half-aware of my surroundings.

"Good morning Mr Charpentier. I'm Donald Mackenzie, the undertaker… so sorry for your loss."

Shaking my head, trying to clear the cloud of confusion permeating my brain, I stand aside and allow him to enter. Almost immediately I regret directing him into the living room. Now more awake I see the room as he must see it. Clearly I have slept in here, most likely an intoxicated slumber as evidenced by the empty bottles scattered around the place. An ashtray has been knocked onto the floor spilling dusty debris over the rug. All the lamps are on and the curtains closed despite the time of day. I am also a part of the mess, unwashed, unchanged. His sweeping glance takes it all in and I wish I hadn't been caught like this. Clumsily I start to gather the bottles in an effort to minimise the impact of the scene.

"Don't worry Mr Charpentier, I've seen it all before," he says morosely. I would have preferred him to pretend he hadn't noticed.

"I….it's just…..I find it difficult to sleep," I stammer. "Sometimes this helps."

"You don't need to explain," he continues. "There's very little would shock me. Not after all I've seen."

"Who did you say you are?" I ask, bewildered by this conversation.

"The undertaker… I was told I would find you here."

"But why?"

"Professor Thomas phoned me this morning and instructed me that you would be making all the funeral arrangements for his late wife." I stare at him blankly. "Mrs Claudine Thomas or Rousseau?" he prompts.

"Yes I know who you're talking about, I just wasn't expecting this," I am short with him, but he's taken me quite off guard. I see he is becoming exasperated.

"With all due respect Mr Charpentier, someone needs to start taking charge of this situation. Someone must now… *today*… start making some decisions. A good place to start would be to authorise the removal of the deceased from the hospital. It is highly irregular for things to go for so long without any …"

I wave him to stop. "Let me get this straight. Len Thomas has contacted you and said that I will take care of the funeral. Is that what you're telling me?"

He sighs, "That's what I'm telling you."

"And you're here right now so that I can make these…arrangements with you?"

"That is correct." He smiles, satisfied that at last the penny has dropped.

I remember Len running this past me yesterday when he produced that scrawled list of his, but I didn't realise… well, what does it matter? I did say I'd help him.

"Right… yes, I can do this, but first I need a chance to think."

A look of frustration sweeps his face. Nevertheless I am undeterred. There is no way I'm going to churn out any old suggestions for Claudine's funeral. I need to think what to do. I need a bit of time. "Perhaps we could meet later, maybe this afternoon," I suggest hopefully.

He hesitates and I'm sure he had hoped to have it sewn up here and now. Resignedly, he agrees. "Can I ask that you grant permission for the body to be released into my care, at least? Otherwise…"

I assure him that will be fine and he reluctantly takes his leave, settling for the promise of further direction later in the day. Left to myself, I survey the scene of squalor before me. I am really going to have to find some other way of getting to sleep at night. Drinking myself unconscious is not going to be possible with Helen around. What if that had been Helen coming home? She would wonder why I wasn't at work. Where is Helen anyway? Why *am* I not at work? Checking my watch, I groan. Nothing will have been ready for the early staff arriving this morning. I'm losing it. I better phone, apologise, see if everything's alright and let them know I'm on my way. Reaching over the debris for my phone I dial the restaurant.

"Good morning, Café Helene, how can I help you?"

"Helen?" I'm confused. What is Helen doing down there? She doesn't usually come down until the evening. For a panicked moment I wonder what's gone wrong. Did they try to get hold of me and failing then called Helen?

"Yes Sebastian, it's me. You sound surprised!"

"Well, yes. I didn't expect you to be there."

"It's just as well I am, though. This place is going like a fair and you aren't here!"

"Why are you there Helen? Is something wrong?"

"The only thing wrong Sebastian is with you. We're managing fine. I knew you wouldn't make it in this morning and we can't expect the girls to carry everything for a third day can we? Is that all? I really need to get on!"

"I guess if you're there then everything's fine," I reply. Of course I understand that the very fact Helen is there is indication enough that things are far from fine. She obviously thinks I've lost it completely, that she's had to step into my role. Part of me wonders if she might be right. Opening the curtains I allow the day to sweep away the gloom. Pushing open windows I release the cigarette-clad air which has choked this room all night. I bin the bottles, empty the ashtray and start once again to compartmentalize my grief. I need to keep a lid on things. I can't allow myself the luxury of crumbling openly like this. I don't know what's going on with me and Helen just now. The truth is I'm not really bothered either. In comparison to how I'm feeling she seems like a minor irritation. I wish she would give me some space. I would like to know she wasn't going to walk in at any moment, especially now that I'm aware she's noticed my behaviour. I don't really care, but I also am in no state to cope with a confrontation. I need to try and keep things ticking over. I need to try and conceal my feelings from Helen. It shouldn't be too difficult. I've been doing it for the past twenty years after all.

## LEN

The bus steams through the wet streets, reluctantly slowing down it seems, to allow passengers on and off. It feels like the driver is in a hurry. Maybe he can finish his shift once he has completed this route. It must be hugely annoying, therefore, that people actually want to make use of this transport, forcing him to lose time at almost every stop. I like travelling by bus. I mean once I've caught one, that is. I wonder wryly if that's why the term, "catch" is used, because it is so difficult to predict when one will ever come along. I find it relaxing. It's restful to sit and watch the world shooting past, while taking my time to order my own life. I've always found it productive thinking time. After work it is good to have a chance to sort out my thoughts, put the day's hassles to bed, before reaching home. It means I almost never bring my worries home with me. In the morning it's good too. I can get my head round the day before actually arriving at the office. I find it calming. Unfortunately today is different. Isn't every day different now? A pang of hurt reminds me that this is what it is like now. Every day is like this, a day that I don't want to think. It's quite ironic that now I have all the time in the world, I want nothing less than to be so preoccupied that there's no room for thought at all.

It's hot on the bus and I feel inappropriately dressed. After the last few freezing days, I have habitually worn warm clothes and now, in the damp heat, I am sweating uncomfortably. The windows are all steamed up. I can still make out the vague outline of a name finger-written by an earlier passenger. This is all I have to do today. I'll finish up at the hospital and then what? I have no structure to my day, no routine. I miss the safety of my usual parameters. I obviously relied heavily on my normal boundaries to keep me in my rightful place. It occurs to me that the French contingent will be arriving any day now. I wonder if they will stay with me. I don't want them to, but it might seem like the natural thing for them. The family have never all been over to visit at the same time; Claudine's brothers have flitted in and out, usually on their way to another destination and have used us as a stopping off point en route. Her parents have stayed only twice. I'm not sure why. It strikes me as strange that the adored daughter wasn't visited more often, though at the time, I must admit, I was relieved at their reluctance to intrude. We were a private couple. We liked our own company, our own space and it did feel like guests were in the way. At least to me it felt like that. I don't remember ever asking Claudine. It occurs to me that there were many things I never asked Claudine. I suppose we just assumed that we had endless time ahead of us. Doesn't everyone?

Although the family didn't visit a great deal, we were almost always planning a trip back to France. If we weren't just about to go, we were discussing when we would and on our return always decided when the next visit would be. Claudine missed Paris. She didn't complain about living here, in fact I think she quite liked it, but I know her heart was still in France. I wonder now if we made the right decision deciding to settle in Scotland. It was opportunistic really. We came over here for Sebastian and Helen's wedding soon after I finished my doctorate, so I was available for work should the right job present itself. We had also more or less run out of money, and although I wouldn't say the pressure was on, we did realise that a decision needed to be made. There were a few realistic proposals to consider. One was a post in Berlin, which was fairly attractive in a work sense, but as neither of us had German I felt it was always going to be a tall order. There was another back home in Canada, but Claudine wasn't keen and I had been away so long by then it didn't really feel like home. Then when we knew we were coming to Edinburgh for the wedding we thought it would be a good chance to check things out at the university, see what the English Department was like. Well, we arrived a day or two before the wedding and used that time to tour about and get a feel for the place. The day after the wedding I had an interview. I liked the look of it all. For me it would be good, I knew but I wasn't sure what Claudine thought. We both knew there was also a job waiting for me at the Sorbonne and I did expect Claudine to push for that. She loves her country and her people. When I was offered the post in Edinburgh I actually felt quite nervous about telling her. I wasn't prepared for her response but she was delighted. She clapped her hands like an excited child and threw her arms around my neck, telling me how clever I was and how proud she was of me. I told her that of course I wouldn't accept the offer if there was any possibility that she wouldn't stay too. She just smiled and said that now we could settle down and get married, put down some roots, find a place to stay and live happily ever after. You wouldn't believe my delight. I had it all. The girl of my dreams, the one person I could imagine myself with for the rest of my life, mirroring my own emotions. We were in a spin, everything was happening at uncontrollable speed. We decided just to run with it and were married three weeks later. In fact when Sebastian and Helen returned from France, our wedding had already taken place. I don't think either of them really believed us at first. It was great, though, living so close to them, particularly for Claudine because she didn't have a job as such. I'm not in any way demeaning what she did. She was a talented and well recognised artist and her work is much sought after. I feel another stab of pain as I realise that she won't ever make anything else. Her talent just like her beauty, her warmth, her love - all gone.

The bus is slowing down. I wipe my sleeve across the misty pane to clear a field of vision and spot the hospital signpost off to the right. I haul myself to my feet, joining the queue of people pressurising the driver to pull over. I walk slowly up the hill and across the car parks to the main entrance. I can't help myself from searching for a sign for the mortuary and seeing it, feel my stomach heave. I wonder if she is still there. I was asked to allow the undertaker access and permission to collect her, but I just told him to speak to Sebastian, that he was in charge. I feel happy with that. I know there's nothing he'll suggest that I wouldn't be in total agreement with. He knew her so well.

I hate to think of her just now. Remembering back is okay, well it hurts like hell, but I can take it. Thinking of her as she is just now, lying in a fridge somewhere or in a few days being buried, well I just can't go there. I stop to lean against a wall surrounding a little rose garden, feeling increasingly sick. I'd put money on this being a memorial garden. It's a little haven within a busy conurbation. Sweet-scented roses, elegant benches placed occasionally here and there. It looks like somewhere for people to have some quiet time, space to think. I wonder where this misguided idea of grieving people needing to think has come from. The worst thing, the absolute worst thing is to have time to think. Unfortunately at the moment I seem to have an abundance of it.

# SEBASTIAN

Now that I've had a chance to clear up and make myself more presentable I should really head down to the restaurant. I could go take over from Helen, let her see that I'm still in control, that nothing's changed. I know I can do it, but I seem to be losing the will. This is a worry. Nothing good can come out of letting the charade drop now. Maybe while Claudine was alive if I had, then who knows? I often wonder about the life not lived. Once, while over at Len and Claudine's place I remember absent-mindedly lifting a book from Len's mammoth bookcases. It was a book of poetry. I've never really been a poetry man, I leave that kind of thing to Len, but skimming through it I settled on a particular poem: 'The Road Not Taken' by Robert Frost. I was captivated by the words. For a moment I guess I understood the attraction of the study of literature. There in that poem, someone was describing my feelings and emotions more precisely than I could ever have articulated them myself. I can't remember the words exactly, but I recognised myself as I had been, standing at the point of a decision which would change my life. The poet selects one of two routes and following his chosen path forever wonders where the other would have led him. Where would we have been Claudine, had I decided differently? Would we have been together? I've always been convinced we would, but who knows? Maybe Len would have won your heart anyway. At least in those circumstances, though, I would have felt it was a fair contest. The way it turned out I more or less handed everything over.

It's a strange way to live your life, to be living out a role constructed from a single lie. I do not love Helen. I care for her and feel responsible for her. I am reasonably happy with her and the life we have made. Day by day we move in and out of each other's space, allowing time to propel us forward at increasing break-neck speed. We must appear to have a fairly good life. We have each other, a beautiful apartment, thriving business, our life together must seem very full. We have filled it with nothingness though. It overflows with emptiness. I feel like a shadow of myself. Sometimes I feel so colourless I hardly notice myself at all. The writer in the poem ultimately decides that taking the less walked road is always the right decision. Me? I chose the moral high ground and I wish I could turn back.

# LEN

"Professor Thomas? Dr Jamieson will see you now." Instinctively I glance at my watch and immediately wish I hadn't. I'm not exactly in a hurry. Embarrassed, I overdo my thanks to the nurse and again wish I was acting more appropriately. I decide I will just keep my mouth shut in the doctor's office and try to avoid offending anyone. I didn't actually expect to see a doctor today. I thought there would be a bag waiting for me to collect at reception, but when I arrived I was directed from the main entrance upstairs to a secretary's office and then re-directed to this row of plastic chairs, lined against the corridor wall. The nurse indicates a particular half-open door and I enter. I feel awkward. I feel as if I have taken on another role; this time it's poor, ignorant relative. I am expecting him to speak loudly and slowly in an effort to communicate basic information to me. He gestures to me to sit and introduces himself. He says we met before. I look back at his face. In response to my presumably puzzled expression, he replies, "I was here the day your wife came in, the day of the accident."

Of course - the doctor who had the misfortune to have to break the news of Claudine's death! I feel bad for him and wish for more than one reason that this was over.

"Mr Thomas, thank you for coming in this morning. I know this isn't easy. I have a copy of your wife's death certificate..." His words begin to merge into each other. I'm finding it increasingly difficult to concentrate. I feel almost overcome with exhaustion. I struggle to focus, my mind wandering all over the place. With a huge

65

effort, I fix my eyes on his and channel all my reserves of attention into the words he is speaking.

"….so now that we have the post mortem results I am finally able to authorise the death certificate. I apologise again for the delay. I know this must be extremely distressing for you."

The words, 'post mortem' catch my attention. They've been busy cutting my wife up these past few days and I didn't even realise. As if reading my thoughts (I remember he was pretty good at that the last time) he explains that a post mortem was necessary to establish the exact cause of death, that I had agreed to this.

"Which was?" I ask.

He looks surprised and I remember too that I hardly spoke at our last meeting, so he was probably expecting a similar monologue today.

"The cause of death was trauma–induced cerebral haemorrhage," he replies and offers me a piece of paper. I see the words printed on a certificate of death. For some reason this makes me smile. I am thinking that even the most stupid person will in death attain a certificate of some merit. Trauma-induced cerebral haemorrhage.

"I guess that means a bleed in her brain caused by two-tonne of lorry smashing it open." I look at him and dare him to hold my gaze.

"In a manner of speaking…" he says simply. But he does indeed keep eye contact and I think perhaps I misjudged him.

"Well thank you for your time." I rise to leave, but he signals me to stay.

"Just a moment, Mr Thomas… I know how uncomfortable this must be for you and naturally you're keen to get going. There's something else I need to tell you." I sit again and lift my head to face him.

"There's no easy way to say this. Were you aware Mr Thomas that your wife was pregnant? I wondered if you knew. You have the right to know."

I stare at him. Pregnant. Claudine.

He continues, "Your wife was thirteen weeks pregnant. She had an ultrasound scan here two weeks ago. I have a picture… perhaps that's something you would want to have."

He hands me a small piece of paper. The image is grey and very fuzzy, but I can make out a profile; head, nose, mouth. A baby… My baby! The room spins; my collar and back are drenched with sweat. I think I'm going to be sick. I rest my head in my clammy hands and try to breathe deeply. After a time I am aware that I am following instructions. A gentle voice is urging me to do just that. It is the same voice whose words brought me to my knees on my last visit to this place. Glancing up I see the young nurse who must have accompanied me into the room. This is why she's here, I realise. A glass of water is produced. Sipping it, my throat is quenched by icy-cold liquid and I am startled back to the present.

"My wife was pregnant." I state the words rhetorically. I don't need any reply. She was pregnant. I just wanted to hear what it sounded like to say those words.

Funny to think about it now, but Claudine and I never discussed having children. Not ever. Is that strange in a marriage I wonder or is it in fact indicative of a good marriage? I was aware, of course, of other couples around us having babies. Babies, more babies and in some cases even more babies. It just didn't seem to be something which was for us. Claudine more than satisfied me. She was everything to me. My life was complete. I can't imagine us sharing what we had with anyone else. I guess I felt that a third member in our relationship might dilute our love in some way. Now of course I'm wondering if Claudine was happy with that situation. You hear of women having a maternal instinct. Is it possible that secretly she did yearn for a baby and never told me? Why wouldn't she though? My head is thumping. I feel really ill. The effort of concentrating throughout this conversation and lack of caffeine in my system is making me light-headed. I also feel like someone is hammering on my skull from the inside, clamouring to get out. I wonder if my head can contain this pain or if it will burst out in an explosion of emotion.

The doctor stands, leans forward to shake my hand. This particular conversation is drawing to a close. The trouble is I'm no longer very good at responding to social cues. I know I should stand also, let him know it's okay to leave, put on a brave face. I find it impossible. I remain seated, staring, thinking. All this bloody thinking is doing my head in. If only I could close my brain down temporarily; give it a good rest. Maybe then I'd feel more able to cope. He lifts his bundle of papers from the desk between us, tucks the folder under one arm.

"If I can be of any help to you, if you want to discuss things further at a later date, you know you can arrange to come back," he says sympathetically.

I reason he must be happily married, maybe with a couple of kids, to feel for me in this way. Either that or he is particularly good at relating to people, not a trait commonly found in doctors in my experience. He has to squeeze his way past me and unable to move, I don't stand to allow him an easier passage. Stumbling, he reaches out to steady himself and his file drops to the floor. My fault, I think and I feel bad for him. He's actually been very considerate. I am surprised for I assumed that this stark, clinical environment would have dissipated any empathetic feelings which a young doctor might once have held. Guilt prompts me to move and I kneel down to assist with gathering the various documents strewn across the floor. Words, lots of words: all something to do with my wife. I pick up another little picture, an ultrasound he had said, of our unborn baby, our never-to-be-born baby. This one is less clear, cloudier. I can't make out any of the features. Presumably that's why he gave me the better one.

"When was this one taken?" I ask. He doesn't straightaway answer. "Is it an earlier one? It's much fuzzier. I can't really tell what's what in it."

Taking the picture from me, turning it over he says, "No this is from the last time. It's older, different quality. The scanners these days produce a much higher definition."

I must look really stupid, just staring at him. I've done a lot of that this morning.

"What last time?"

"The last pregnancy…." he tails off. Clearly I have no idea what he's talking about and for the second time today, I feel like a bomb's just gone off inside my head.

## SEBASTIAN

I'm getting nowhere pacing around this flat. The place looks respectable now. I could safely leave without facing any repercussions when Helen comes home. It's funny how someone who is blind can be so aware of her surroundings. In actual fact, I rarely think of Helen as being blind now. In the beginning, yes it was terrible. It was a disability. She had a very difficult time coming to terms with what had happened. Surprisingly, she never seemed to blame me. I wondered at times at her wanting me around. Her family took it all very badly and wished me out of her life completely. I was cold-shouldered for months and had it not been for Helen's desperation and I suppose my own sense of responsibility, I would have gladly walked away. Those first few months after the accident were so hard. I felt like a criminal who had evaded punishment. I guess in a way I was. I sometimes wonder if that's the reason I sought to punish myself more appropriately. Anyway, Helen's family gave it a good go too. Claudine's family also awarded me the dubious honour of, "most hated." A home where I had been welcome all my life closed its doors to me. People crossed the street when they saw me approach, ignored my attempts at pleasantries, ridiculed my apologies. Claudine simply disappeared out of my life. It was as if she never knew me. There was no contact, either arranged or contrived; nothing. What did I expect? I caused a horrific accident, ruined a young girl's life. I walked away from it unscathed, chose to abandon my girlfriend and turned my back on those I had grown up with. I can see how it looked, of course I can.

Why did I do it? Simple; I thought it was the right thing at the time. I thought it was the right thing to do.

The rain has petered to a drizzle. Soft, feather-light raindrops brush my face and hair as I set off for the bus. Tugging my collar up round my neck I prevent them from crawling on down my back. The clouds are low and visibility is vastly reduced. Crossing the Meadows I can hear the sounds of the funfair packing up long before I catch a glimpse of it. As I near, I begin to make out grey shadows moving busily around the attractions. Voices shout to be heard above the noise of engines revving with their loads secured. They seem to be preparing to leave in convoy, lining up, waiting for the last few. I step onto some plastic tarpaulin and crackle my path across, suddenly conscious of my own steps. Litter is strewn over the site, cans, bottles, sodden cardboard boxes. Debris left behind from the fun of the fair. It occurs to me that there must be few more depressing sites than a deserted funfair on a miserable February morning. I walk on into the gloom and leave the mist enveloping the scene behind me. Downhill I head and turn right into The Royal Mile. My usual route is left past the castle and on down The Mound to pick up my bus in front of the art gallery. Today I am feeling contrary. I am going right just because I don't usually. The cobbled streets are slippery underfoot and I have to tread carefully. Passing the High Court I pause to allow two police officers and their handcuffed charge to lunge out of a hazard-lit van and cross the pavement in front of me. Iron gates clang closed as they approach the temple of justice. I wonder what he's done and hope earnestly that his punishment befits his crime. I sometimes wish I had been tried in court for my stupid *malfeasance*. Tried and punished. At least then I could have served my time and been granted release from blame. My own self-served punishment has been very harsh; a life-sentence so to speak.

Ducking in and out of alleys, down stairways, through courtyards I trace the shortcuts which years of familiarity have nurtured. Approaching the end of The Royal Mile, I see the Palace of Holyrood rise majestically in front of me. Admirable as it is, this however is not what interests me. On my right, I spot the small gallery shop which hoards Claudine's work. The art itself was crafted in a little outhouse-turned-studio in their back garden, but this was Claudine's outlet for selling her creations. From the outside, nothing much to look at, but this place is well-known for hosting exhibitions of aspiring, gifted artists. Claudine was loved here. The owner displayed her work at every opportunity and bought everything she offered. This was probably where she got her big break. The publicity attracted by her debut exhibition of paintings heralded success and Claudine embraced and surpassed expectations. Year on year she displayed artistically superior work and acclaimed critics gathered here to catch a glimpse of her latest triumph. I was so proud of her! Looking through the window at all her things, I have an urge to buy something, to own a piece of her. Rows and rows of pottery dishes, vases, plates, decorate the shelves. The walls are adorned with her distinctive style of painting. Amazingly I only have a single item of Claudine's artwork in my home. That seems suddenly very strange, given how close we all were. On my thirtieth birthday, Len and Claudine gifted me a beautiful painting which she had apparently made specially. I still remember when she presented it to me. It was the highlight for me. Trembling fingers unwrapped brown paper and knotted string to reveal a huge disappointment. Oh yeah, the painting was fabulous, her trademark style of Mediterranean colours, yellows, reds, orange but depicting an unfamiliar, nondescript scene; a part of southern France which meant nothing to me, to us. I praised and thanked and said all the right things, but I was hurt that she hadn't taken this opportunity to make it more personal. Here, I thought was the perfect chance to paint something which meant something to us and only us, something special, a sign. She didn't take it. Instead her painting hangs thoughtlessly in my hallway, its emptiness accusing me daily of my own missed opportunities.

Entering the gallery, I feel uncomfortable; I am intruding into a world in which I have no part. Gazing lovingly around at all her work, I realise this is as close to Claudine as anyone can now get. I am in her presence here. Her personality shines vibrantly through the character of her creativity. Her art, brought alive by her hand, mirrors her beauty and depth. I soak up all that is here. I love each item. What can I have that will go unnoticed by Helen? Being blind, surprisingly, is not a hindrance to seeing, where Helen is concerned. She is so finely attuned to her surroundings that almost nothing is lost to her. I lift a tiny pottery pig from a glass shelf and cradle it fondly between my fingers. I know she made these out of the bits of clay left over from the largest, most impressive pots. I watched her make them several times. Yes, this will be fine and I hand it over to the assistant to wrap. Scraps for Sebastian! How apt.

# LEN

After a time I am aware of the caring young nurse guiding me from the bad-news-room and into a kind of waiting room. It's not a typical waiting-room. Armchairs and a sofa replace hard-backed chairs; a coffee table dominates the central floor space, magazines stacked neatly in the middle. It is comfortable in a simple, restrained fashion. I decide it's a relatives' room, established for just this kind of occasion, perhaps not often used. Anyway, it's good, because it means they have somewhere to put me. What am I actually waiting for? Glancing at the nurse who has seated herself opposite me I realise she is busy doing something with a mobile phone.

"There's no one home, Mr Thomas. Shall I scroll down and see who else you have in your phonebook?"

I nod without comprehension. I'm not sure what's going on now. I barely understand the words she is saying.

"Arthur! Is that a friend, Mr Thomas? Will I try him and see if he's available to come for you?"

A second nod; I watch her press in the digits of a phone number then pause, listening. I see her speaking to someone; even hear her soft, indistinct accent. Is she Irish I wonder? I can't follow the conversation. It feels as if I'm watching this scene from the other side of a window. I'm not a part of it.

"That's fine, Mr Thomas, Arthur is on his way over to collect you. He was very nice, said it's no trouble at all. He's pleased to be able to help."

She asks if I would like tea while I wait. I shake my head. I've settled on random nods and shakes in response to all the unheard questions and it seems to be working quite effectively. Time passes. How long I have no idea. We sit in uncomfortable silence. I count the tiles which depict a floral pattern along the side of the wash-hand basin. Then I count the rings from which the ugly drapes hang around the window. Counting like this is calming me. It is less disturbing than thought. 1,2,3,4,5,6,7,8. Then again, 1,2,3,4,5,6,7,8. Numbers don't do it for me in the same way as words though. I search the room for inspiration. Mentally I start a new list.

LIST

(Of things in this room) (Things which mean nothing to me) (Things which I don't need to remember) (Things which distract me from thinking of anything else)

1. Dated country-cottage wallpaper.
2. Thin, threadbare drapes.
3. Magazines – women's, out of date.
4. A glass ashtray (I thought hospitals were non-smoking places now).

One way to find out I think, reaching into my jacket pocket and fishing out the packet and lighter. Lifting my eyes to her face she is shaking her head apologetically. Right. Still, there is something mildly comforting about feeling the cigarette between my lips even without lighting it. We resume our waiting. I notice a carrier bag placed beside the nurse on the sofa and recognise it as having been in the last room.

"What's that?" I ask without really caring.

"Oh, this is for you. It's your wife's belongings…the things she had with her the day she was brought in here."

"What's in it?" She offers me the bag and I stretch across the table for it.

"Her personal things…the clothes she was wearing…some jewellery…her bag."

I nod again and clutch the bag tightly. I am suddenly struck by the enormity of death. Its all-powerful, total consumption of life is awesome. Evidently it has no need for material objects or the things we view as essential everyday items. No need for clothing or possessions or even for a body. Death creeps in when we least expect it and steals our essential force. My head is starting to hurt again and I realise I've inadvertently resumed thinking. Must keep a tighter hold on my thoughts:

5. The nurse in front of me – Sandie Riordan the name badge states.
6. A shelf of books – none that I recognise.
7. A tray set with two cups, saucers, plates.

The phone rings interrupting my flow, not my mobile which the nurse, Sandie Riordan still holds, but a phone clamped to the wall behind her. She speaks a few words, then replaces it and gestures me to rise.

"He's here. Arthur: down at the main entrance. I'll show you the way."

I follow her into a lift and retrace my morning's steps along corridors, through doors, more corridors until we happen upon the broad expanse of the foyer and reception. Arthur greets me with a hug, his favoured mode of welcome, although not mine and I wince at his touch.

"Why didn't you tell me you were coming? I'd have brought you over and waited as well. You shouldn't have been on your own for this. I told you just to call…"

On it goes: the unrelenting barrage of meaningless chatter. My phone is pressed firmly into my hand. I look back at her, intending to thank her, but no sound comes out of my mouth. I nod instead and she smiles understandingly. Turning to Arthur I mutter, "Let's get out of here." Striking the lighter in readiness, I lead the way through the revolving doors back out into the real world.

# SEBASTIAN

My entrance to the restaurant is heralded by the usual jingle and it feels as if all eyes immediately turn to me. I have always disliked that bell. It's not at all in keeping with the ambience I've sought to create in here, but today I actually despise it. I yearn to burst open the box above the door where it hides and destroy it. The bell however, is essential for Helen. It's how she knows people are entering or leaving and it must remain. Helen's needs are always paramount because she is blind. It's simple really. Whatever I might want or need, will always be secondary to Helen's wants or needs because she's blind. This is the formula on which our lives are based. Anytime I might start to feel unhappy about something or choose to go against Helen's wishes, I am quickly reminded that she's blind and life is more difficult for her. As if I could ever forget.

Wandering through to the kitchen, removing my jacket as I go, I sense an awkward atmosphere. My staff seem embarrassed and focus more than is necessary on their tasks. The kitchen empties within seconds of my arrival, leaving me and Helen alone. "It's me," I say, fully aware that she knows. No response. I continue, "Something wrong?" She laughs, a forced, sarcastic laugh, which I hate. Taking a deep breath I start again, "Helen?"

"I wondered when you'd show up," she says. "Is there something wrong? I don't know. Is there Sebastian?"

I'm not in the mood for this. I know she deserves an explanation, but I don't have the energy to fabricate one and I can't

77

possibly tell her the truth. This is getting too hard. I'm not sure I can do it anymore. Pulling my jacket back on, I turn to leave.

"Sebastian, don't you think we need to talk, sort things out?" she says more softly, desperately. Facing her I stare, momentarily wondering where to begin. I don't honestly know where I'd start and more worryingly, I'm not at all sure where this particular discussion would end. I need more time; time and space to think. Can't she understand that? "Sebastian?" she pressures, "Sebastian!"

I never speak French to Helen, never.

"Nous ne parlons pas la même langue!" She stares uncomprehending. "We don't speak the same language, Helen. We never have."

What do I do now? I can't hole up at home like a recluse. I couldn't stand its confines; that's really why I came out. I can't go into work, because Helen's there and we're just not communicating at all right now. Where will I go? I wander aimlessly for a while and then decide to call on Len. It's hard being with Len too, but at least he's a connection with Claudine. Also there's no pretence that life is just carrying on the same regardless of her death. Len is devastated. That's how it should be. We should all be devastated. I'm a bit surprised at Helen taking it so much in her stride. So what if we had to close the restaurant for a couple of days? Would that be such a bad thing? Claudine's dead! Doesn't that count for anything? Reaching into my pocket I search in vain for my phone. Damn! Must have left it behind! Well I'm not going back there now. I'll just leave it and go round to Len's in person. It'll give Helen and the girls a chance to screen my call log. I smile bitterly. She won't find anything untoward. I never called you Claudine, nor you me.

Two more different people you couldn't find. I guess that's why my family were so surprised at me leaving Claudine for Helen. They understood, of course. I think they maybe even thought it was the right decision. After the accident, things were so bad. It wasn't just the self-inflicted sense of responsibility that I had to live with. Helen's family descended en masse and I had a steady stream of visitors dishing out advice, ensuring that I was kept informed of every detail of her condition. There was to be no running away from this - that was clear. I was to blame and I was being well and truly blamed. I suppose deciding to marry Helen gave my family some relief from the terrible association I had brought upon the household. I don't know what it was like for them. I know *I* was shunned by people I had trusted and respected. It seemed to be difficult for friends even to be seen in my company. Only Claudine remained the same and I ruined that myself.

It occurs to me that her family will be arriving soon. The days are blurring together in a meaningless fashion. Of course, things are fine between me and Cecile now. I think once Len came along and her darling daughter was happy again, forgiveness was easier. Len kind of relied on me a bit to help him with the language then and bridges were built. It amazed me that someone so fluent in French could have so much difficulty with the accent. After all Len was bilingual! He insisted, though, that it was very different, almost like a different language. I'm not convinced. I think there was a convenience associated with not quite understanding or being understood: an in-law thing which has allowed him to keep his distance from them over the years. He could understand Claudine well enough couldn't he?

# LEN

"Right sir, homeward!" Arthur: always so upbeat, even when he doesn't quite know what to say. Especially when he doesn't know what to say! I'm not actually sure that poor Arthur has ever known what to say to me. We didn't get off to a great start professionally, that's certain. He didn't like me even before I arrived at Edinburgh University. I think I was too young in his eyes. Either I wasn't going to have the experience warranted of this post or I would have it but I'd be a smug young upstart, I'm sure that's what he thought. I smile when I remember my first departmental meeting, the one where I was being introduced to the rest of the team. I had met a few of them at interview, but to most of them I was a new face. Poor Arthur, I don't know who he thought I was, but in blissful ignorance opened the meeting with a tirade against me. He obviously thought I was late and hadn't pitched in yet, so took the opportunity to warn his colleagues off me. There was no way, in his mind, that I could have done all I claimed in my CV. He doubted if I would last the year. I was scruffy, looked more like one of the students and probably wouldn't know how to relate to them professionally. It continued for a few minutes, the others in the room shuffling uneasily around him. I caught a glimpse of some whispering at the far end of the table, someone thinking about putting Arthur in the picture, no doubt. I decided to make things easy for them. Standing, I crossed the room to where Arthur was seated, held out my hand and assured him I would fit in quite well. His face turned from puzzled, through disbelief to horror in a matter of seconds. I didn't push it, just shook his hand and returned to my seat whereupon our boss entered, oblivious to the circus around him and took charge of the meeting. Despite this, Arthur and I have now a good working relationship. We don't really mix socially, our common ground being literature, but at work I think he accepted me once he saw I could deliver. I glance over towards him concentrating on the traffic and smile as I remember it. He senses me looking and turns momentarily.

"What is it?"

"Nothing," I reply shaking my head, still smiling.

"I'm very sorry, Len…I don't know what to say…she…Claudine was lovely…"

I interrupt because I know this is hard for him. It's hard for me. "That's all there is to say, Arthur. She was lovely wasn't she?" I turn to look out of the window so that he knows the conversation is finished, and watch the world spin past. We continue in silence for a few minutes, but it's not an easy silence. It's funny, I can sit with Sebastian all night without talking and feel totally relaxed and at ease, but this is really uncomfortable and I know he'll start talking again just to break it. Sure enough,

"Thanks for doing that reference for me, by the way. I got a letter this morning. I didn't get the job but that's the way it goes… probably for the best... not sure I'm ready for a move anyway."

He continues on and on. I'm sure he's worried that if he pauses I might say something and he's not really wanting to deal with me, with my problems. Things like this don't happen to Arthur. Things like this don't happen to me, I think. I tune him out and resume watching the fields of sheep rushing by. Letter! Suddenly I remember the letter! Delving into my back pocket, I retrieve the now crumpled envelope and smooth it out on my knee. Claudine's meticulous handwriting stares back at me. The clouds start to close in again. Oh Claudine, what is going on? I don't like the feeling I have about this. Last night I was sure you had sent me a message, let me see something I could really do for you. After this morning's meeting I don't know what to think. I am weary. I feel emotionally stripped.

From the feel of the envelope I can tell it contains another envelope inside. In order to forward it I need to open the first, there being no address on the outside. I know, therefore, I can safely open this envelope, which I hold in my hand, without breaking Claudine's trust. Carefully I slip my finger beneath the seal and gently edge it open. I prise open the envelope which my wife's lips have closed, pull out the paper which Claudine's fingers folded. When did she do this I wonder? Was I in the house, downstairs, in my study? Was it opportunistic or something she planned? So many questions but what I need to decide now is do I want to know the answers? Again I read Claudine's beautiful script, this time a name and address:

Mr James Harris
177 Rowmore Street
Leith.

This means nothing to me. In itself, not a remarkable fact; there were many people who Claudine knew that I had never met, perhaps never heard of and likewise people in my life that Claudine would not have known. The difference here is that this person, whoever he might be, was someone whom Claudine wanted contacted if anything should happen to her. Not only that, but he was important enough that she was prepared to put me in this situation, knowing how difficult it would be. This is a man that Claudine wanted contacted at all costs. What could matter so much to her that she would omit to tell me about it? Oh, Claudine I don't like it. I don't like this mysterious side to you. I am aware that the fact of it being a male name on the envelope is grating on me. I suddenly feel an overwhelming desire to know, to get some answers. I need to put this feeling of jealousy to rest. I'm sure there's an explanation, but right now I'm having difficulty coming up with an acceptable one. Turning to Arthur, I realise he's still talking. How can he be still talking when he's been getting no reaction from me for the past ten minutes! He must think I'm in shock. Am I? No I'm far too focussed for that. He seems to be prattling about work, the reference I wrote for him or something like that.

"Arthur!" I interrupt.

Surprised he turns to look at me and the car swerves across the road. Horns beep from both sides. Correcting his steering wheel and righting the car on the carriageway he apologises, then staring ahead, keeping his eyes safely on the road, asks cautiously, "Yes?"

"Do you know where Rowmore Street is?" I ask.

"Rowmore Street? Yes I think I do. Not much there though, a few pubs, a bookies, mostly flats. Why?"

"Do you think you could take me there?"

"What, now?"

"Yeah."

"Well, I suppose…don't you think you'd be better at home…get some sleep or something…"

"I'm not really sleeping these days, Arthur. I could do with getting over there today. 177 Rowmore Street. There's something I need to do."

"Alright," he answers and signals to turn off at the traffic lights.

We're driving back upon ourselves somewhat and I can't but think that is somehow significant. I'm going back to uncover something Claudine dealt with sometime ago. Gazing at the letter again, I can't believe that I didn't know anything about this. Is that the bit that hurts the most, the idea of her having a secret from me? And yet today I've discovered Claudine did indeed have secrets from me; the kind of secrets that a wife shouldn't have from her husband. Claudine was pregnant! Twice! She must have miscarried the first time and never told me. There's another mystery. Why wouldn't she tell me? Did she think it would hurt me? Was it too painful for her to speak of? Was she worried I would think I wasn't enough for her, that I'd fail to understand her desire for a baby? My head is spinning. I know I need to rest. I can hardly bear this but I'm so unsettled now that I have to do something. I really feel that. Even if it turns out to be the wrong thing, I need to physically take some steps to explain this to myself. I wonder was she planning to tell me about this baby. Surely, after all she would have been showing in a few weeks. The doctor said she was thirteen weeks at the scan. Maybe she was already showing and I didn't notice. Oh God forbid that I didn't notice! We were going to have a baby! An unbelievable sadness swamps me as the reality sinks in.

"I think that's it there." Arthur's voice shatters my reverie and I am dragged back to the present. Glancing out of my window I see a banal-looking, non-descript building. The kind of place you could live next door to all your life and never wonder what purpose it served. There is a sign outside, its message obscured by obscene graffiti. "Do you want me to come in with you or will I just wait out here?" Arthur's offer is clearly weighted toward the latter.

"Don't bother to wait. I could be some time." He doesn't look about to budge. The last thing I need is Arthur receiving me when I come out. I don't know what Pandora's Box I'm about to open and I don't want any witnesses to my reaction. I see he needs a push. "I'm meeting someone," I lie.

"Oh right...well in that case..." He seems relieved. He can go now without guilt.

"Thanks, Arthur. I appreciate your coming. You've been a big help."

"Oh it's nothing," he says, but I know he's pleased. He can go back to work now, update everyone and give himself a portion of credit as personally featuring in the story. I don't mean to be unkind. That's just Arthur. I can read him like a book. And I've read many books in my time.

# SEBASTIAN

As I approach Len and Claudine's house the clouds start closing in. The drizzle has ceased and with the darkening day's end, the temperature has once again plummeted. Night falls early this time of year. This is the moment of half-light that briefly washes away the grey skies of day, before darkness descends. It's a strange time of day, kind of like standing in a dimly-lit room. It's difficult to see things properly. Shadows are mistaken for moving objects. People step out of the gloom and into focus. Impossible to grasp long enough to examine, dusk sweeps soundlessly across the sky, down the mountains, into the city streets like a majestic bird. Night follows close on its heels, mopping up any remnants of daylight that remain. Underfoot, gems of frost already glitter, scattered haphazardly over the pavements and roads. My breath puffs out into the air before me, clouding my vision further. The street is quiet, empty in fact and I feel suddenly very small as the vast night unfolds in front of me and all around. My boots hammer on the ground disturbing the silence, each step in synch with a beat of my heart. On and on and on and on and on… They halt at the end of the driveway and the quietness that falls is strangely unnerving. I feel like an intruder, out of place, unwanted. A movement in the doorway catches my eye, but the light is too poor, I can't make it out. Blinking a couple of times, straining my eyes I can see a shape, no more than that. There are no lights on inside the house and I know already Len isn't home. Who is hanging around the house I wonder. Whoever is there knows I am standing here, that's for sure. My footsteps echoed all the way down the street to this point.

Contemplating what to do next, I light a cigarette, the orange glow signalling my presence like a beacon. Digging my hands deep into my pockets, a vain attempt at warding off the chill, I head up the drive toward the doorstep.

"Can I help you?"

She turns at my words. Even in this dim light I see her blush. A young face, pretty, embarrassed. She smiles awkwardly, stutters an apology, makes as if to leave. Something about her unsettles me. She seems nervous, stressed even.

"Who are you?" I ask, aware as I do that this is none of my business. She seems to feel the need to explain, but is having difficulty with the words. For a fleeting moment I wonder if she understands me. All of a sudden it dawns on me. Claudine's family must have arrived. I don't know this girl, but she must be one of them. A cousin perhaps; a niece? I'm not good at gauging ages, but I've met all Claudine's immediate family, so it must be someone from out of town.

"Vous me comprenez mieux quand je parle du français? Etes-vous arrivé aujourd'hui avec Cecile?"

No response.

"Comprenez-vous que je dis?"

Nothing.

"You haven't a clue what I'm saying have you?"

A smile… "No".

Did she speak? Her lips moved but the sound…no more than a whisper. I still can't be sure what language was uttered.

Clearing my throat, I start again. "Hi," I say simply.

"Hi." Another shy smile.

"Can I help you?"

"No…Yes…I don't think so…I'm sorry I shouldn't have come." In a flash she springs from the doorstep like a startled rabbit and sets off down the path.

"Wait," I call, my voice ringing loud through the empty street. She half-turns, pauses; long enough for me to catch her up, "Why did you come here? Who are you looking for?"

She starts walking. I let her go, feeling suddenly that I've overstepped the mark. There's just something about her. Vulnerable I think. Frightened? I walk behind her, slowly, hanging back so she doesn't think I'm following her. Retracing my steps I start to wonder where Len might be. I wish I had my phone. I feel lost without it. It is properly dark now. Somewhere in the midst of our conversation, night has caught up with dusk, banishing it from the ever darkening skies. Mist floats through the frigid air dampening my hair and face. Visibility is really bad; I can barely see the girl now, moving in and out of the fog maybe a hundred yards ahead. It occurs to me that it's probably not a great idea for her to be out on her own on a night like this and for the second time tonight I am conscious of pushing the boundaries of appropriate interest. It's nothing to do with me.

Rounding a bend, she disappears from view and my thoughts drift back to Len. I could really do with getting hold of him. I need to tell him about the arrangements I made with the undertaker this afternoon. Not all that many as it turns out, but all the same… I can't remember the man's name, but he introduced himself with a fancy-sounding title which meant he was the undertaker's sidekick. I guess the main man finally got fed up with our lack of enthusiasm for his field of expertise. It crosses my mind that undertakers must surely have no social life out with their own professional circle. Who wants to make small-talk with a man who is measuring you up in more than one sense? Anyway, he seemed to have his own ideas about what would be necessary and that was fine with me. He asked for personal touches. Personal touches? The concept is alien to me. Funerals are not something you think about are they? We all live out our lives in the certainty of death and yet we never give any thought to the final event itself. How strange we human beings are. So advanced physically and intellectually but still without the capacity to control our own destiny. I decide I've spent too much time thinking over the last few days. Morbid thoughts such as these are not my norm. Usually I shy from thinking about death in any shape or form, but I suppose Claudine's 'passing' as the undertaker-person liked to call it, has brought it uncomfortably close. Anyway, I let him guide the plan for the funeral.

It sounds pretty predictable. For personal touches the only thing I could think of was flowers. These guys arrange everything so I only had to say what I wanted. Lilies…white lilies… lots of them. There is an association, of course and I wrestled with the idea, wondering if it was completely out of order to request something so personal to me. Would that in itself be a betrayal of Len? And then I thought, well wait a minute, didn't he instruct me to make the arrangements as I chose? And anyway, didn't he get everything else? Is it so much to ask for a simple recognition of my memories of Claudine? No one else will even realise. So I asked for lilies and have been wracked with guilt ever since.

I gave Claudine lilies once. I gave her flowers often; she loved them so much, but lilies just once. It was the night of our school leaving dance. The night that we let people know we were a couple. I guess you could say it was our first date. I picked them out for her because they looked so elegant; tall, statuesque stems, magnificent in their simplicity. When I called round for her I knew she would look beautiful. Her mum opened the door and from the expression on her face I could tell she was the proudest mother in Paris. We got on great and I knew she was pleased that Claudine and I had "teamed up" as she put it. She knew me well, knew I would look after her daughter, would treat her right. She knew I was for real. I can only imagine the shock when Claudine told them we were finished; that I was leaving her for someone else, a girl I hardly knew. I push this thought out of my mind and concentrate again on conjuring up the previous image, that of Claudine descending the stairs to meet me, her friend, her partner, her love. She was dressed in red; long and sleek, perfectly accentuating her beautiful body. Her fair curls framed her face then fell softly down her back. Simple jewels sparkled from a bracelet on her left wrist. She was breathtakingly lovely and she was mine. The dance was all that she had hoped. She stole the show of course; no one there could rival her presence and Claudine revelled in playing centre-stage. She mingled expertly. She had an amazing way of making everything she said sound really incredible. People were in awe of her, mesmerised by her, keen to be associated with her. Of course what greater honour than to be there as her boyfriend? She held tight to my hand throughout the evening, while she laughed and danced and talked. This was just Claudine's kind of thing; the princess in all her splendour. I didn't want the evening to end. I was besotted by her engaging smile, her eyes full of promise. She came back home with me that night and we talked into the late hours. Time ceased to have any meaning for us. We watched dawn break in a kaleidoscope of colours, exploding across the retreating night sky and wished the moment would never end. I gave my soul to her that night. Right then, I knew I would never love another girl like this. This was it. She was the one.

# LEN

A steep flight of stairs beckons upwards, so summoning a huge effort, I start to climb. Behind me I hear the irritating hum of Arthur's car engine signalling his continued interest. Fixing my gaze straight ahead I consciously don't look round. With each step I expect him to get the message and drive off. The drone is grating on my nerves now, but still he waits. Surely he isn't going to sit there until I come out. I told him I was meeting someone. Didn't he believe me? I'm beginning to wonder if he has been humouring me, afraid to upset me in my fragile state and I'm beginning to credit him with a degree of sensitivity I hadn't before noticed, when I hear the car lock into gear and edge slowly away. Reaching the top of the stairs, I momentarily question the benefit of piecing together this puzzle. I don't need to do this. I could easily turn back right now. I could turn back and leave the unknown where it belongs. I could go home and mourn the loss of my darling wife and never uncover her secrets. And yet… I've come this far just because I now know that there is more. I can't un-know and so I have to create some kind of understanding or else it will drive me crazy. Resolutely I lean into the swing door and push it open. Frustratingly a second staircase looms ahead, nothing else, just an empty lobby with stairs leading to the next floor. These people don't really welcome visitors, I think. Anyone who wants to reach them obviously has to be prepared to endure this initiation; no passing interest expected here. On I go each step a mammoth effort of will. I consider I must appear a sorry figure. I am so unlike the person I was a mere week ago. It's as if everything has slowed down. My physical movements command already desperately low reserves of energy. My mind plods sluggishly through unfamiliar ground. It's as if I'm running on empty. I have little interest in life at all. Halfway up I round a turn in the stairway and catch sight of my reflection in a window. I am barely recognisable to myself. I look tired. So tired.

Another set of swing doors lead me into a kind of foyer or a waiting area of some sort. Two men are doing just that at the end of a row of seats. Beyond them, behind a window, people are bustling to and fro. Phones ring and different voices answer them. Several girls sit working at computers, people wander in and out of the office lifting pieces of paper from wire trays. As I approach the counter an overly made-up face appears behind the dividing window, a false smile twisting her expression in a contorted fashion. "Good afternoon, sir. How may I help you?" I understand that she isn't the slightest bit interested in helping me as she utters her mantra.

"Good afternoon," I reply undeterred. "I'm looking for someone." I wait for her to say something, to give me some indication that she is listening, a cue that I should continue. She is looking at me, waiting. That's enough. I go on, "…a Mr Harris, James Harris?" She just keeps looking straight at me. I'm beginning to wonder if the happenings of the last few days have completely altered my perceptions of social norms. I seem to have difficulty now with all forms of communication. I feel misunderstood on all levels. Taking a deep breath I plough on. "Is there anyone here of that name?" I ask impatiently.

She is shaking her head. "Sir, do you have a birth, death or marriage that you wish to register? Otherwise I'm not sure that I can help you."

I feel foolish. I should just go before I embarrass myself. Turning to leave, my gaze sweeps the reception area and I realize that there is nothing here to suggest what this place is. There are no signs, notices, no indication of any kind. I'm surprised they do any business at all. I guess registering births, deaths and marriages are the kind of things you make a special trip to do. Just then I remember the death certificate given to me this morning. Was it only this morning?

Turning back to face her, my fingers fumbling through a polythene bag marked Patients Clothing, I find what I am searching for.

"A death," I say. My voice sounds nothing like it should. I wonder why I am whispering.

"Excuse me?" she says.

Don't make me say it again. My eyes plead with her. She is looking at me once more. What is it with this girl? Why doesn't she understand me? Digging deep I dredge up the will to repeat myself and push the piece of paper, the certificate awarded to my wife in death, under the window. She seems pleased with this. At last, the evidence that I do have the right to be here.

"If you'll just take a seat, sir, I'll be with you in one moment." She disappears from view taking the paper with her. I stand for a few minutes waiting. After what seems like an age she returns, requests my signature and disappears again. I wait another few minutes before wondering if maybe that's it. Maybe she doesn't come back. Maybe I'm just meant to leave now. This is one of the difficulties with my detached state. I seem unable to sense what is expected of me. I don't know how to act or interact. I feel like I'm from a different world to everyone around me. My contemplation is interrupted and I'm startled to see she has returned. "That's fine, Mr Thomas. Everything is in order." Everything in order! How completely different our perspectives are. I have never experienced anything like the disorder of my life right now. Everything is absolutely out of order. A thought jolts me as I remember why I came here.

"Are you sure there is no one here by this name?" I say and hold the envelope up to the glass. Maybe reading the words will help. Maybe she just can't understand me. I feel that she doesn't understand me.

"No sir there's no-one here by that name, but this isn't 177 Rowmore Street, Mr Thomas."

"It isn't?" I check the envelope to confirm the address.

"No sir, this is 175. Number 177 is next door."

# CARLY

I think I always knew I was adopted. I've heard of people who say they didn't know, had no idea until someone broke the news, but to be honest I've never really believed them. I always knew as far back as I can remember. My parents didn't make a secret of it; that's the way they decided to handle it, so everyone knew and I guess I just grew up with it. I don't suppose I really even considered it until I was about nine. Nine was a significant age for me. My ninth birthday an occasion I'll never forget. Up until then I was just an ordinary little girl; an ordinary child with a label which meant very little to me. I know to our friends and neighbours I was the little adopted girl down the street, but it didn't bother me. I was no different, a child typical of everyone else I knew. We lived in a lovely house, a Georgian style villa with loads of rooms we didn't use. I had the prettiest bedroom of any of my friends. Mum was an interior designer so the whole house was regularly re-styled to reflect current fashions. I had a room all to myself with an adjoining sitting room where I could take my friends without disturbing Mum and Dad. Everything in my room matched. Pink and white candy-striped wallpaper, crisp cotton bedspread, sumptuous carpet; it all matched but with Mum's very singular style. I had everything. All the latest gadgets and techno equipment; I had it all. My parents were very generous with their money and I never wanted for anything more than a few days. My friends were so envious. While they saved up for a CD player or waited for Christmas hoping for a DVD player I had them before I even knew what they were. I had a telly in my room before any of the other girls were allowed one and I got to watch anything I wanted even late at night as long as I didn't make too much noise about it. I did appreciate what I had, though. I wasn't one of those spoilt brats who has everything and still wants more. If anything I found it a bit embarrassing. I can actually remember getting new clothes and not wearing them for ages because I knew my pals would make fun of me having more new stuff.

Mum and Dad were very good to me and despite what happened I know if it wasn't for them I wouldn't have had the opportunities which my life has offered me. I didn't blame them at the time. I don't suppose I really understood what it was all about then. It's now I have the issues with them. I suppose that's a good thing in a way. When I was a kid I needed to get on with everyone, I needed them to provide for me and look after me. Now I can manage and being on my own is fine. In fact it's the way I want it.

So what happened to change everything? What turned my life upside down and left me without the love I craved? Strangely it was a beautiful thing that happened. Mum had a baby. On my ninth birthday a little sister was born into our family and I could hardly contain myself. At school that day I was full of it. She was an adorable little thing, Ava Louisa Jayne, named after both my grandmothers and Mum's favourite designer at the time. I was so excited and couldn't wait for Dad to come home and tell me all about her. He was absolutely besotted right from the beginning, producing a wallet full of photos for anyone who showed any interest. And there was great interest. I could not have imagined how sensational this news was to be. Mum and Dad were portrayed as the poor, desperate couple who had yearned for a child all these years and now had been blessed with a miracle baby. And it was wonderful. It could have been so perfect. If only they had still wanted me.

## SEBASTIAN


Rounding a bend in the road, I catch a glimpse of the bus stop through the gloom and wonder whether to chance on a bus turning up or to plough on into the mist. It's becoming really difficult to see. Nothing is clear anymore. The streets are quiet for this time of evening. I suppose those with any sense are safely hoarded up at home. Standing within the questionable shelter of the bus stop I can scarcely make out the blurred image of someone else lacking that sense. As I approach, the figure begins to take shape and my focus sharpening, I see it is the girl from before. I hope she isn't afraid. I'm aware it probably looks like I've followed her and this really isn't a night for young girls to be out alone. On the other hand I'm glad in a way to discover that she has found her way this far and will take a bus home out of the mire. I was concerned for her when she took off so suddenly. I stand self-consciously not knowing where to look. I don't want her to think I'm sizing her up, but it's hard to find anything else to look at. It's so dark and the fog weaving its way around and between us conceals everything I might possibly find to look at. I'm wary. She seemed very frightened when I stumbled across her back at Len and Claudine's place. I felt she would rather have not been spotted there and so I suppose I feel I've intruded on her privacy. I try to glance around at anything that might catch my eye, but nothing does; it's too dark now. Fumbling through my pockets I find only keys, which taking out I examine closely for a few long minutes. Eventually I allow my eyes to turn in her direction and see her looking back at me. How long has she been watching my discomfort I wonder? I don't know what to do so I smile vaguely at her. Politely she returns a half-smile and shyly drops her gaze. I too look away until I feel her eyes upon me again and looking up feel the need to speak, just to break the awkwardness of the moment. "Hi," I say. She nods a reply. I consider explaining that I haven't followed her, that I'm not a lunatic or rapist, but am simply heading home and happen to have landed at the same bus stop at the same time, but I know how clumsy it will sound so I refrain and hope that she works it out.

"You gave me a fright back there." Her lilting east- coast accent is strangely soothing, but her unexpected statement surprises me somewhat.

"I'm sorry. I didn't mean to." She smiles again, still nervous but friendly enough, so I continue, "You took *me* a bit by surprise too."

"I'm sorry." She grins, "I didn't mean to."

I'm starting to relax a bit. She seems happy enough to chat and it beats the uncomfortable silence of before. "It's turning into a terrible night isn't it?"

She looks at me blankly.

"The weather… fog… its miserable."

"Oh I quite like it actually" She's smiling again "I find it very atmospheric, kind of Dickensian if you know what I mean?"

Glancing cautiously in her direction to ascertain whether or not she is joking I am struck by the strangeness of this whole situation. I don't even know who this girl is. "I'm Sebastian by the way," holding my hand out in greeting. Clasping it, her own hand feels tiny in mine and I wonder how old she is, nineteen maybe twenty? I'm not good with ages, though so I could be way off. "Your hand is freezing." I tell her.

"Oh my hands are always cold. Poor circulation I think. I'm Carly by the way." An unusual name! Suits her, I think. A sudden illumination breaks into the pervading mist, casting a beam of light across the road and a bus tracks its lonely route through the night. "Where are you headed?" she asks.

"Em, home I think… Morningside." Up until this point I hadn't given any thought to my direction, but right now I can't come up with anything better to do. "What about you?"

"Home too. Haymarket. Student flat. Dump."

"Aren't student flats meant to be just that? Mine was the worst you could ever imagine. I was the only remaining occupant it was so bad. Everyone else in the block moved out."

She laughs and asks "Where was that?"

"Montparnasse… Paris."

Laughing again she exclaims, "Well I bet a student flat in Paris had a lot more going for it than one in Edinburgh!"

Seated on the bus she seems to want to continue our conversation. I'm happier with it now. I feel she's had opportunity to move on, but she's chosen to sit in front of me and turning round to face me smiles again. I wonder if she's lonely or perhaps a bit naive. I can't help but feel a bit worried for her. I'm not sure she realizes that not all men are as safe as me. I feel she should be a bit more cautious about striking up conversations with strangers. Maybe it's my age. I guess she probably thinks nothing can touch her. At her age I certainly felt that way. I was wrong as it turned out. "So you're a student! Literature is it?"

She looks momentarily puzzled. "How did you know?"

"Oh you've just got that look about you. You know, intelligent, industrious."

"Really?" she asks incredulously.

"No, not really. Well, yes I mean you do look intelligent, but that's not how I know. It doesn't take a genius to work it out though."

"Tell me, how do you know I study literature?" she insists.

"Maybe something to do with the fact I found you not half an hour ago hanging around Len Thomas' house. Len Thomas who, correct me if I'm wrong, is Professor of American Literature at the University down the road."

"Len Thomas!" she seems genuinely surprised. "Prof Thomas!"

"I take it he's your tutor or something?"

"Yes! Yes he is, but I didn't know he lived there!"

"So who were you looking for then?"

"I was looking for Claudine Rousseau. I was told she lived there. I'm sure that's the right address. I checked."

The mention of her name sends a jolt of pain through my core. Our relaxed, carefree conversation abruptly interrupted, my feelings start tumbling in upon themselves. Pain burns; everything else is blocked out. For a moment I forget the girl in front of me, allowing grief to seep back in. My Claudine, my poor Claudine! Only she wasn't mine was she?

"Are you sure that's Prof Thomas' house?" The question hangs limply in the air as she grasps at remote possibilities.

"Yes definitely. I know him well, Claudine too."

"What do you mean, Claudine too?"

"I mean Claudine Rousseau, Len's wife. She lived there too." The choice of tense is unbearable.

"So, Claudine Rousseau, my art teacher, is married to Professor Thomas, my English teacher! No way! This is immense!" she gasps.

"Did you come to visit Claudine tonight?" I probe trying to ascertain what she knows.

"Yes, it's the first time I've called, that's why I wasn't exactly sure if I had the right place. I was a bit worried she might be annoyed and then it turned out there was no one home anyway. Typical!"

My heart sinks as I realize she doesn't know. "You haven't heard about Claudine, have you?" I ask gently.

"Heard what?" she questions.

"Claudine, she…well, she…she passed away… earlier this week."

"Passed where?" the unthinking response.

"She died, Carly. She was in an accident, a road accident, just a few days ago." Her stricken expression startles me as I see her unmasked for the first time. "I'm so sorry you had to hear like this." I could continue with endless platitudes. I've heard them all myself this past week, but I sense there's no need. She doesn't want me to try to make it better. She's taking it in, allowing the news to touch her. I admire her resoluteness, her apparent ability to face things head on.

"Oh," she says simply.

We continue in silence, the monotony of the engine's drone strangely therapeutic. She has turned in upon herself and I sense I won't be able to reach her again so I leave it. Minutes pass and I hate myself for upsetting her in this way. She's so young and probably hasn't had to deal with anything like this before. I can't say I've ever had to deal with this kind of thing myself. Nothing like this pain has ever affected me before. There have been several times in my life when I felt hurt so unbearable that I wondered if I truly could endure it; when Len and Claudine first got together for instance, when I said goodbye to her and closed the door on our chance of happiness, when Len and Claudine married and I realized there would never be a future for us. On each of these and other occasions I honestly felt it was more than I could bear. I thought at times I would crack completely under the strain, the endless ache of lost love. This pain, though, transcends any previous experience. This is something new altogether. This is the worst.

"When is the funeral?" her words spoken so softly, almost inaudible. She seems to have this tendency at times, to speak so quietly that her words barely leave her lips. She did this earlier on back at the house.

"Funeral? It's…em…it's the day after tomorrow… Saturday… three o'clock… Would you like to come?" A brief nod is her reply. "You'd be more than welcome. There's a chapel service first followed by the burial."

"I'll skip the chapel bit if you don't mind. Not my kind of thing."

I resist the urge to tell her it's not my kind of thing either. Claudine's funeral, whatever shape or form it took could never be described as my kind of thing. It's something to be got through, that's all. In actual fact I find it difficult to imagine surviving it at all. But the girl, she's very young. She doesn't understand. She didn't know Claudine like I did, didn't love her like I did.

"Well if you want you could meet us at St Peter's. Do you know where I mean? You don't have to come. It's just if you want to. Please don't feel obliged…" I tail off as she speaks over me, assertive, defiant even,

"No it's okay. I want to. I'll be there." Then, as an afterthought: "Thanks."

The bus lurches to a halt and without warning she gathers her bags and disappears out onto the pavement. No goodbye; again the resemblance to a frightened animal suddenly taking off. I hope she's alright. It wasn't an ideal way to tell her about Claudine, especially since I didn't realise she would just disappear without me knowing how she is about it. I feel for her. She seems so vulnerable, a child needing someone to look after her. I hope earnestly that she has someone.

## LEN

My heart thunders inside my chest as I run through the darkened Leith streets. My breath is heavy and hot around my face, anger welling up inside, spilling out all around me. Who the bloody hell does he think he is? My feet hit the pavement hard as I try to push through the pain. I don't know how to deal with this anymore. I give up. I give up now. Let it all stop. Slowing to a halt, gasping for breath I lean against a parked car. Gradually breathing becomes more regular, less laboured, though my pulse continues to race. I feel it throbbing in my neck and around my temples. I can't stand this pain anymore. Throwing my arms up I shout out loud, "Stop! Please let it stop!" The streets are deserted. No wonder. It's dark and cold and thick fog has infiltrated the city, while I've been cooped up inside those stifling buildings waiting for that guy to stop taking the piss. A shadow sweeps over my mind as I realise none of this will ever stop. There's nothing I can do to end it. Claudine is gone. I am in agony. I can shout till I collapse that I've had enough, that I give up, but nothing will change. This has been dished out and it can't be taken back. I have a disturbing thought that the rest of my life is now something to be endured. There's no way out. This is it. This is my life and I'm not sure I can live it. Not like this. Not without Claudine.

I realise that I'm shivering and wonder whether I am in fact about to pass out under this strain. I am so out of touch with my feelings that I doubt if I would recognise any signals my body is giving me. I don't feel right, that's for sure but I haven't felt anywhere near normal since this all happened. When was it anyway? It seems such a long time since I last saw her, last heard her voice. Persuading my legs to move again I resume my course, this time walking. I decide I'd be better getting home. At least at home I don't need to worry about being found lying in the street should my body give up on me. A glorious thought! I wonder is it possible my own life might decide it's just not worth carrying on. It's all such a struggle. Maybe I could just lie down and die.

That guy back there, James Harris or whatever his name was. How stupid does he think I am? Did he actually believe I would hand that letter over and just walk away? Here you are sir. I don't know who you are or why you were so important to my wife, but here's a letter she wanted you to have should she die! Forget it. Either he explains things to me, puts me out of my misery or else I keep the letter. Fair deal I think. Anyway he can keep his ramblings about professionalism and all that shit. I still have the letter so he's the loser. Of course I don't know that that's necessarily true, because I don't actually know what the hell's going on. I guess I didn't really know what to say. I didn't expect that. I don't know what I expected. I suppose, if I'm honest, I thought maybe this man would be able to give me a reasonable explanation for knowing my wife. I hoped for answers that would be acceptable to me, something that would lessen the pain. Instead I'm left with what? The letter sure, but more confusion than when I came. It dawns on me for the first time that maybe I could open this letter. Presumably there are answers sealed within. Unfortunately the only way to find out is to break my wife's trust. Something I've never done my whole life. A voice tells me I've never been in this situation before, but it still feels wrong. It is wrong. I know she didn't want me to read it. She left explicit instructions didn't she? I was to ensure it reached this James Harris. I've already let her down then haven't I? The crumpled paper remaining in my jacket pocket is testament to that.

I can't go on like this. I don't know much at the moment, but I know I can't continue like this. I need answers. I must have answers. This uncertainty, this doubt will surely finish me otherwise. I feel as if I hardly know Claudine anymore. I think that's the worst part of all of this. We were happy. I thought we were happy. We were just an ordinary couple, in love. Things were good. So where does this secrecy fit into it all? I'm discovering a mysterious side to Claudine that I never dreamt existed and I think I'm scared now of the possibilities.

If I could just get back in control maybe I'd be able to work things out. If I could shake off this feeling of despair, this helplessness then maybe I could sort out my thoughts. I need to be able to think more clearly. I need to get a grip on my mind. Trudging on through the mist I wonder momentarily if I'm lost. I don't see anything familiar, no landmarks that I recognise. I keep moving onwards because I don't really know what else to do. Soft beams of light penetrate the fog sufficiently to pour a dim glow across the pavement and I keep moving forward. After several minutes a recognisable sound pushes its way into my thoughts. Machinery. Engines. People. I must be near the station. It crosses my mind that I could just go and get on a train, any train. I could start playing roulette with my life, stop trying to sort things out and just let decisions, choices make themselves. What if I headed into the station right now and got on the first train I saw? I could go wherever, do whatever. Nothing matters anymore. I am accountable to no one. I have no life to leave behind. I could go and start everything over somewhere new, where nobody knows or cares about me. And what difference would it make? None is the simple answer. I can't run from this. I'll never be able to shake off the pain will I? I could travel to the ends of the earth and still I won't ever find Claudine. I'll never have my old life back. What I need to do is find a way of making this new, unwanted one bearable.

## CARLY

Sitting alone in the darkness I'm trying to get my head round all of this. I'm not being melodramatic, I forgot to buy a new power card and I've run out of units for the meter. No electricity that means, unless I go back out and the weather being what it is, I don't much feel like it. I don't feel like anything really. My world has been well and truly shaken this evening by an encounter with a complete stranger. The room is cold and I'm not feeling too good, but that's nothing unusual these days. Maybe I should go to bed. I'm absolutely exhausted, but my brain is doing overtime and I doubt if I'll be able to sleep. Sebastian his name was. He was nice enough, but has muddled things so much I don't know what to think anymore. I'm not even sure who he is. Sounded like a family friend didn't he? Anyway I guess the big thing is that having finally plucked up the courage and the energy to go round there, it turns out there's no point. I can't believe it. It's still sinking in. I saw Claudine only last week at my Saturday morning art lesson. She was explaining about differences in perspective and I remember being a bit distracted thinking how ironic that was. I had had her address for a while, but with so much going on it just didn't seem like the right time and now it seems I've left it too late. How typical of my life is that? I'm not sure where that leaves me now. Did I have an alternative plan? No. This was it. Do I feel sad about her death? Yes I do but I can't say that I feel it in the way I might if it was someone I had known really well. It's more a sadness for myself, if I'm being totally honest. Of course I'm sorry that this happened to her, but most of what I feel is disappointment at what might have been.

This feeling is becoming all too familiar. I should maybe lie down. Suddenly I feel really wiped out. I'll just stretch out on the couch I think and rest for a while, then later I still have going to bed to occupy me. I like it lying here with the curtains half-open. Lights reflecting the business of the street outside stream through the large bay window, providing some welcome company. Car headlamps rush across my white walls. Voices outside on the pavement nudge in and out of my consciousness; people going about their lives, oblivious to mine.

I'm not feeling well at all now and I'm beginning to wish I had told Shane what I had planned to do today. If I had he would more than likely have come round to hear how things went and then I wouldn't be alone right now. I like my space and I like having time on my own but every now and then I need someone and this is one of those times. I feel sorry for Shane. I know he finds all this really difficult. I never hid the fact that I come with a good deal of baggage and he always said that was part of the attraction. I guess he thought I was more interesting than your average college student simply because of my colourful history. I'm quite sure, though, that now he is realising just how difficult it can be. What I'm not sure is if he understands just how hard it could all get, especially now. Anyway I'm not going to phone him. What can he actually do anyway and I know he needs a night out with his friends. I'll probably see him tomorrow and I can fill him in with the details then. I feel terrible anyway and would make awful company tonight. If I lie still perhaps I can quell this disturbing sensation of nausea. If I sleep I might wake feeling better.

## SEBASTIAN

Pushing the key into the lock I have an instinctive sense of something wrong. Turning it slowly my mind is spinning trying to locate a point of reference, an explanation for this feeling. Nudging the door silently open I am greeted with the sound of voices, lots of them. Closing the door softly behind me I am confused. Who is in the apartment? It sounds as if Helen is having a party. There's no way of course, but I don't understand. The place feels busy. I've just walked into my own flat, into the middle of a gathering of some kind and nobody has noticed. And then I hear it. The familiar sounds of home: French. The living room door swings suddenly open and Claudine's youngest brother stands before me.

"Luc!"

His embrace is desperate. He clings to me as his sobs heave against my chest. No words, just this tactile expression of his loss. I am becoming a bit resentful of all these people who are able to display their emotions without worrying about the consequences. Gradually I peel his arms from my neck and hold him at arm's length. "Luc... I'm so sorry," I say trying to keep my own composure. He nods and the tears continue to stream down his face. Behind him I peer through the open door and see a room packed with people. Absolutely packed! Who are they all? What are they doing here? Easing my way past the despondent boy and into the room I am greeted by Cecile, Claudine's mother. She is clearly distraught and cannot speak to me. She hugs me hard to her, nodding continually. Over her shoulder I am faced with a sea of unfamiliar faces. Where is Helen I wonder? Scanning the people

106

around me I fail to spot another recognisable face. This is all I need. Tonight I had hoped to get some sleep, maybe to try and make some sense of the past few days, try to get my head straight. Not a hope now, not with this lot here. Pushing through several huddles of bodies I manage to reach the kitchen and breathe more easily as I find it empty. The table is littered with open bottles and I realise what is going on. They've all been drinking. Great! Not only do I have the dubious pleasure of playing host to Claudine's relatives and whoever else has tagged along, but they're all drunk! Grief and alcohol, what a combination! A more demonstrative bunch you could not find at the best of times, but now... I guess that's why we're practically having a party here. I sit, rub my eyes, try to think. Maybe I could just turn around and go back out. Nobody would notice that's for sure. The thing against that, though, is I have nowhere to go. I'm also really tired. I could do with getting some sleep tonight. Isn't it strange? I've hardly slept a wink these past few nights and tonight I feel like I'm dying of exhaustion and know I won't be getting much rest. That's how it goes. Again I wonder where Helen might be. She doesn't usually stay out late. I suppose she could be at her sister's again. That would be fine with me. I don't have the energy to justify myself to her right now. It's actually easier just not to see her. I'm in the middle of deciding what to do next when the door opens again and Len wanders through.

"Len what are you doing here?"

"Well the rest of the world and his wife are here so I thought maybe it was the place to be."

He's sober. What a relief. The last straw would surely have been the grieving husband drinking himself into oblivion.

"Any chance of a coffee?" he asks.

I start my methodical makings of our staple drink, glad to at last have some kind of purpose amongst the circus which appears to have taken over my home.

"What's all this?" I ask him.

"The family arrived."

"I see that, but there are so many people..."

"Yeah, I know. To be honest I'm not sure. I think maybe the boys have been out drinking since they arrived and I guess they've probably invited a pile of people to come back. Maybe it's a kind of wake sort of thing."

It's beginning to make sense. I don't like it any better, but at least I understand what's been happening. The takeover of my apartment is temporary in that case. Tomorrow things should be back to normal, whatever that means these days. I join Len at the table and push his mug across towards him. "How'd they all get in anyway?"

"Helen. She called me, said the family had arrived, taken a taxi to my house and finding nobody home rerouted over here. She said you had left your phone so she couldn't get hold of you and could I come over and see them."

I'm annoyed with Helen. Why did she bother Len? Doesn't she understand what he's going through? I would have thought she'd have left him alone. Surely she could have managed here until I got back. "Where is she anyway? I haven't seen her since I came in."

"She left as soon as I got here. I think it was a bit uncomfortable for her. She'd only come back to collect a few things and was met by this rabble. Bad timing you might say."

He's smiling sympathetically and I sense there's something more going on. "So where is she then?"

"Where *is* she? Don't you *know*?"

"Well if I did, I probably wouldn't keep asking you would I?" Even Len is beginning to irritate me, I'm so, so tired.

"Sebastian, she's left!"

"What do you mean, *left*?"

"You're kidding me on! Helen's left you and you haven't even noticed!" He looks truly shocked.

I need air. Huge gulps of oxygen, something to kick-start my brain again. I desperately need to clear the clouds out of my head. I wonder if maybe I'm losing my mind. Everything feels so oppressive, even my own apartment. I have no space, nowhere I can think and it's starting to drive me mad. My life is twisting out of control. I feel that I'm a bystander watching it all unfold, powerless to intervene. When did it all start going wrong? Pacing deserted side-streets I wonder how much more I can take. Surely everyone has a limit to their reserves of strength. How much fight do I have left anyway? Everything worth fighting for died last week. Is there even any point carrying on? Everyone must have a reason to live, I'm convinced of that. Without it what is there? Thing is I'm not at all sure I have one now.

Returning to the flat I am met by Len at the door and ushered through to the kitchen, so avoiding the throng which has dispersed throughout the rest of the place. I am shown a seat, handed a glass. I wonder fleetingly what kind of state I am in to warrant this over-attentive concern. The drink is strong, scorching my throat as I swallow, but it feels good. I don't know what it is or where he found it. Maybe something the boys brought in. They all appear to be in full swing now. I can hear loud chatter and singing interspersed with sobbing and the occasional wail. It was thoughtful of Len to keep me away from them tonight. Perhaps he feels bad that they've all set up camp at my house and not his. Whatever, I appreciate it.

"Are you alright?" His voice is distant, intruding on my self-absorbed reflections. Looking up I meet his gaze and see that he is truly worried about me. I must have lost it. Before I left the flat tonight I must have really lost it. I can barely remember reacting to his words about Helen, but I guess I must have and whatever I did or said has given him reason to be concerned for me. For a moment I wonder if I have been inappropriate in any way. I pray I haven't let my guard down. What if I've said something stupid? Then I realise how unlikely it would be that Len would be sitting in front of me offering tea and sympathy if I had just blown my cover, if I had just divulged how much I loved his wife.

"Do you want to talk?"

Shrugging my shoulders I am aware of how desperately I want to talk. I want to talk about Claudine and everything she was. I want to be like everyone else who loved her and be open about my feelings, drawing comfort from reminiscing. Len would be the perfect person to speak with because he would never tire of discussing every detail. And yet, the constant worry that I might overstep the mark and let the guise slip a little too far. I would never have believed it could get so hard trying to bottle up my feelings. I kept things under wraps for all those years and yet it is now that I'm struggling to keep it together. I long to tell someone. Part of me feels it would give some worth to what we had, what we shared all those years ago. I loved her so much and never stopped, will never stop.

"Sebastian?"

Len's insistence urges me to focus back on him, rousing me from my inner self. He continues to stare at me and I know I'm going to crack. I must get away from him and yet I don't move.

"I feel terrible," I blurt out. "I feel so guilty. I never meant any of this to happen. The last thing I wanted was for anyone to get hurt. Now I feel I've let everyone down, especially the person I care most about. I'm so stupid, should have done something about it long ago. Now look at me. Look at the state of me. I can't sleep and yet I'm wandering around in a trance I'm so exhausted. I can't work. The business can go to hell. I seem to have lost my footing, lost my grip on reality and the things that matter. Nothing seems to matter anymore."

"Hey, Sebastian." His voice is soft, comforting. "It's alright. You've been going through a tough time is all. You and Helen, you can sort this out. You've been together too long to just throw it all away. You'll get through this. I bet once she has a chance to think, once you've put a little space between you, she'll be back."

He doesn't get it! He thinks I'm talking about Helen. He thinks I care about Helen leaving me! The truth is I have hardly given Helen a thought all night. The only thing troubling me is that things are changing. The predictability of the parameters of our lives is shifting too quickly. I don't feel safe anymore. Helen has gone. How do I feel about that? I force myself to consider for a moment what it means to have lost Helen. Intense emotions wrangle inside me. Clamouring for domination I feel anger and bitterness in turn. Why, oh why does she leave me now? Why couldn't she have done this any number of years ago? She could have let me off the hook right at the beginning. She must have known I didn't love her and yet she took everything I had, everything I was, leaving me without hope. She traded on my conscience and that is precisely why I had to give up Claudine. At this moment in time I am glad Helen has gone. I don't think I could bear to look at her again. Fury fills my being. Standing I beat my fist hard against the table and welcome the pain stabbing through my knuckles. Gritting my teeth, I try to contain this rage fearing where it might lead. I like the sensation of releasing my anger. It feels very cathartic, but it also feels out of control and that scares me a bit. I've probably already said too much. I look over at Len and see he is watching me, but there's no sign of judgement or criticism. So far so good. He doesn't realise. Quit while you're ahead Sebastian. What is there to be gained now? Len is a good friend, the best you ever had. Don't waste it; don't let this be the end of everything. Claudine is gone remember, nothing will change that. Helen could leave, return or simply disappear into thin air. It makes no difference.

"I'll never forgive her," I mutter. "Never!"

# CARLY

Sunlight streaming through the open window and zigzagging across the floor explodes in a burst of bright yellow over my bedroom wall. I'm in awe of the beauty of the morning after such a horrible night. Peering through the curtains I discover a sky gilded by daybreak, new and wonderful. A morning like this and hope is easily restored. I still don't feel too good, a bit shaky and shivery but at least I've stopped being sick. The happenings of yesterday, so dreamlike during my wakeful state overnight, have taken on a more realistic quality. It does seem unfair, as if the goalposts have shifted again. At the risk of sounding self-pitying I wonder why, just when I think things are going to be okay, something else happens to destroy my plans. Sighing deeply I reason that this is life. At any rate this is what my life is like, has always been; full of disappointments, full to overflowing.

I decide against breakfast. I don't think my stomach could take it. Opening the curtains properly I watch the morning pour itself into the room and marvel at how much it raises my spirits. What a beautiful sight. It's a good day to be alive. I have a nice view from here. My window looks out over the garden where I like to spend time pottering about. I like planting and tending my flowers, even weeding can be very therapeutic I find. Maybe today I'll clear the overgrown area at the front and start preparing the ground for spring.

Mulling over this course of action something catches my eye and turning toward the movement I register someone turning in through our gate, approaching the front door. We don't have a security entry system so I wait and seconds later hear the predictable sound of footsteps on the stairs. Solid feet tread heavily, deliberately on each step. They pause outside on the landing and again I wait expecting to hear them resume their path further up the next flight. Instead they stop by my door and after a brief hesitation a confident rap rouses me to the arrival of a visitor. I'm not used to people appearing unannounced and wonder if they've got the wrong number. Maybe if I wait they'll just go away. I'm not really in the mood for company and anyway I'm not even dressed. A second knock; this one louder, more impatient than the last and it occurs to me that whoever it is may have seen me opening the curtains and therefore knows that I'm home. I better see who it is. Tiptoeing to the front door I peer through the spy-hole, but it's dark in the stairway and I can't see too clearly. The third knock disturbs me and I am persuaded to answer just to tell them to go away. Opening the door a fraction, my eyes take a second or two to adjust to the change in light and my visitor recognises me before I see him properly.

"Carly!"

"Oh! What are you doing here?"

"Well isn't that a lovely welcome!" He smiles reassuringly and I know he's joking. I'm completely taken aback, though. Why has he come to visit me?

"Aren't you going to ask me in?"

Clumsily I hold the door open wide enough for him to pass and mutter something apologetic.

"Is it a bit early for you?" He's referring to my pyjamas I know. I feel slightly embarrassed but then silently chide myself; after all it's not as if I was expecting anyone. Glancing at my watch I see it's still pretty early, breakfast time for the majority of people.

"It's fine. Come in."

He stands awkwardly in the middle of the room waiting to be invited to sit.

"You're probably wondering why I'm here," he starts.

"Well…yes…I didn't realise it was you at first…" I stammer. Why do I sound so nervous? It amazes me how I can still manage to appear so self-conscious when actually inside I'm quite together. This is my house, my territory after all. He's the one who should be embarrassed arriving like this without calling first.

"I was just wondering if you were alright. I spoke to Sebastian. I understand you two met yesterday at my house and he said he was a bit worried about you." So the Frenchman and the Prof do know each other! He continues, "He said he told you about Claudine, that you hadn't heard. I'm so sorry Carly, I didn't realise you knew her or I'd have gotten in touch myself."

"It's okay Prof, I didn't appreciate the connection myself until yesterday when I met your friend. He pieced things together for me."

"I tried calling you last night and again this morning, but didn't get an answer. In the circumstances I thought I'd better check on you. I wasn't sure how well you had known Claudine and didn't know if news like that would upset you."

He was worried about me. The thought feels very comforting. Lifting my phone from the side table where I left it last night I quickly identify the reason for the missed calls. "No charge," I explain.

He's nodding, "It's okay. I didn't mind coming over. I've been meaning to get in touch anyway to see how you are after the exams and everything."

"Sure you were," I reply sarcastically.

"I *was.* Look at this." He holds out a crumpled piece of paper; a list.

LIST OF THINGS TO DO
1.     FUNERAL
2.     SORT OUT HER THINGS
3.     PHONE CALLS
4.     SORT MY CRAZY HEAD
5.     GET RID OF SEBASTIAN
6.     CARLY

Scanning it quickly I see he has listed me as one of his things to do, number six to be precise, scrawled in different coloured ink to the rest of the list, probably added in later.

"There's been a lot going on this week as I'm sure you understand, but I was always planning to meet with you at some point and help you establish a plan."

"It's okay Prof, I know you've got a lot on your plate right now. I can manage things myself."

"I want to help you, Carly. Why don't you let me?"

He looks at me steadily and I know he means it. I've always liked Professor Thomas. Everyone does. He's the most popular tutor of all. Partly I suppose because he's got a great reputation. He also has a brilliant track record of results for his students. It's known that he handpicks his Honours students and if he selects you, then you know you're going to do well. Bet he wishes he hadn't wasted so much time on me in that case! As well as that, though, he's considered to be the cool guy of the Literature Department. He's much younger than all the other tutors and very good-looking. There are loads of girls who fancy him I know, I've heard them discussing him in class. I always liked him, though, just because he's so nice. I mean he's really easy to talk to and you always get him the same way. I find him a very calming person. Considering the chaos of my life right now, there's probably no one I'd rather find on my doorstep offering help. I nod gratefully, "Thanks for thinking of me. I appreciate it."

He smiles at me, "Now why don't you go get dressed and I'll take you out for breakfast. We can talk."

# LEN

She disappears into another room, presumably her bedroom, leaving me to wait in the sitting room. I decide that student flats haven't changed all that much since Sebastian and I shared ours. That feels like a lifetime ago. My life was just beginning and everything good was before me then. That's Carly now I think, on the brink of everything. I guess that's partly why I'm here. Yes I like the girl and I always had great hopes for her academically. It's more than that though. I think in a lot of ways she reminds me of myself at that age. Seriously lacking confidence, but with so much potential. I was very fortunate. I came across the right people and to a certain extent was steered in the right directions. I was assisted with decision-making and seemed to make the right choices, took the right chances. I feel that Carly needs a little good fortune right now and I want to help her.

Glancing around the room I see her character stamped all over it. I wonder who else lives here, because there's no evidence of any other personalities. Several large canvases adorn the walls. I never knew she was a painter. Moving closer to get a better look, I see how intricate her work is, the detail incredible. She has captured expressions perfectly; her use of colour is beautiful. This is a very talented young lady, not only artistic but creative with words too. I know I was right to come. She can't be allowed to waste this. It occurs to me that, for the first time all week, I've discovered something that I actually care about and it feels good.

She seems to be taking a long time getting ready. Feeling restless I wander over to the window. Not much of a view; beyond the garden, a dingy street. It's not the best part of town. I suppose student land has to be the cheapest of areas. I'll never understand why so little is invested in these kids who, let's face it are likely to become the backbone of our country given half a chance. Along the window ledge little trinkets are grouped according to colour: pale, pastel shades at one end leading through earthy reds and browns to vibrant purple at the far end. The effect is amazing. Dazzling like jewels in the sunlight. Tentatively I pick one up, a thimble, hand-painted by the look of it; a lovely little thing. Next to it a tiny painted dish with two small silver earrings laid carefully upon it, then a row of little pigs. I catch my breath as I realise how like Claudine's these are. Lifting one gently and turning it over I almost choke as I read the initials CR grafted into the underside. Carefully I check each of the others, there are six altogether. Each has the same markings. They scream at me. My wife lovingly crafted these objects, but never again will her fingers work the clay, teasing it into the shape of her choosing. She will never lift her tiny paintbrushes, sent over from France especially for this purpose. She took such care with each detail. Even these little pigs - I know this was something she did with leftovers, but she still treated them with love and precision. That was Claudine's trademark. Nothing was too insignificant to deserve her attention and again I feel that, maybe by helping Carly, I can demonstrate that I learned from my wife. That with a little time and attention I too can help to create something beautiful.

Drifting back over to the couch, I notice a sketch pad lying open on a side table. Sitting down I reach over and begin flicking through it. Pages and pages of pencil sketches fill the book. All of them appear to be faces. Some depict groups of people, students at the bar, children playing in the park. I'm reminded of Claudine sketching, while surreptitiously watching me at Place des Vosges, all those years ago. I wonder if every little thing is going to spark a connection from now on or is it just that here there are so many similarities. And then suddenly I'm hit with the force which continues to jolt me back to my pain in all its fullness. I can't seem to escape it, even when I consciously try to distract myself; this ache which feels like its

117

gnawing away at my soul. I'm looking at a drawing of Claudine. It's definitely her, there's no doubt. The girl is good and she has recreated her perfectly. In fact it's better than many of the photos I have at home. Her hair softly curling around her face, I feel I could reach out and stroke it, feel the silk between my fingers. Pale blue eyes dancing with laughter: her beautiful smile, radiant. Without thinking I tear the page from the pad and hold it up to examine it more closely. I feel like a child yearning to get into the picture to join her. A memory from my childhood flashes into my mind. I remember asking my mother how I could get into a nursery rhyme. I so wanted to be a part of it, to actually live it and not just listen to it. It was so vivid, so real and I had trouble understanding that there wasn't an easy route into nursery rhyme land that would allow me to go and play for a while.

"What are you doing with my stuff?" I am roused abruptly from my reverie. She stares steadily at me, waiting for an answer. I'm not sure what to say, where do I begin? She holds my gaze and I see that she is really angry.

"I…it was just…I'm sorry Carly. I don't know what I was thinking."

Striding towards me, holding her hand out she is waiting for me to hand over the torn page. Reluctantly I hold it out to her and am struck by the strength of her emotion. Taking it quickly from me, she glances down at it and gasps.

"Oh Prof, I'm so sorry. I'm so sorry. I didn't realize. It's your wife, that's why isn't it? Of course you can have it. Take it." The scrappy drawing is once again hanging in mid-air waiting to be claimed. I reach out and take it from her, but say nothing. I feel things are on a different footing now. I came here to see Carly, to talk about Carly. Now it's all back to Claudine. Will I ever be able to have a normal life again? Is Claudine always going to cry out from the grave for attention, preventing me from having any part of my life that doesn't include her? My head is spinning once more. My rational self is slipping away.

After a time, I'm not sure how long, seconds, minutes maybe, I glance over to her and am touched by how young she looks. She doesn't know what to do, how to react to me. She sits looking down at her fingers, lacing them together, unlacing them; examining her nails, anything but look directly at me. My heart goes out to her. Poor Carly, this thing is too big for her to understand.

"I'm sorry," I say quietly, more to get her attention than anything else, although I am truly sorry to have made her feel awkward. She looks up, but doesn't speak. Probably doesn't know what to say. "I'm really sorry Carly. I'm not myself just now. You know… Claudine, well… I loved her so much… It all feels very raw… you know what I mean?" She nods, but I doubt she has any idea. How could she? "Come on, I said I'd get you breakfast. This is meant to be about you." I rise to leave, but she remains seated. She looks very pale. Her eyes are dark blue and shadows accentuate their colour. She has twisted her wet hair into two plaits which snake their way down over her shoulders. She looks like a little girl. Reaching down I offer her my hand. Hesitatingly she places her tiny fingers within mine and I pull her to her feet. "Let's go," I suggest and turn to leave. I don't look back, but I hear her soft footsteps following me and I know she's okay. I need to try to remember Carly is only a child and may not be able to handle something as intense as my situation. I came here to help her not vice versa.

Downstairs we head out and into the bright morning air. It's cold, despite the early sunshine and I wonder if she'll be warm enough. She's wearing jeans and a t-shirt with only a thin denim jacket over it. "Are you cold?" I ask. She shakes her head and I notice that she's actually sweating. Soft droplets of perspiration bead her forehead. "Are you feeling okay?" This time a nod. Sometimes these kids are hard work! We wander aimlessly for a while before turning round past the Student Union. "This do you?" I question. She looks up at me, a surprised expression playing around her face. "Maybe you'd rather not be seen in here with me?"

"No, it's not that!" The first she's spoken since we left. "No I would have thought it would be the other way around!"

"What, you think I'd be embarrassed to be seen having breakfast with one of my students?" She blushes - a very endearing attribute. Smiling I tell her I'm up for it if she is and we go inside.

She doesn't want anything. What is it with these girls? Why the need to abstain from eating? We came for breakfast and I decide she's having some whether she wants it or not. Anyway she looks like she could do with some nourishment. Dismissing her refusal for food, I tell her to go find a table while I order tea and toast for two. A quick glance in her direction and I spot her thin frame sitting by the window. I add cereal, fruit juice and pancakes to the order. I wonder when she last ate, she looks so fragile. I don't think we look after our students well enough, I decide. We're too interested in the work they're producing for us and not enough in their lives. How can someone produce their best work when they're starving or worried about bills or relationships or whatever else might be putting a strain on them? They're only children after all. I endeavour to do something about it when I get back to work. Maybe we could start a kind of guidance service and allocate each student someone to watch out for their pastoral needs. It occurs to me then that I will return to work. Not yet, but I will. What else is there for me after all? It's all I know. It's what I do.

## SEBASTIAN

I wake with a start and for a moment I'm not sure where I am. It takes me a few seconds to get my bearings. My dreams are so vivid just now I actually feel that I'm living them. They're disturbing too. When I waken I'm not sure what's real and what isn't. I'm no psychoanalyst, but I'm pretty sure their occurrence must have something to do with the past week's events and the reawakening of long-stifled memories and feelings. In my dreams Claudine is alive. She is alive and full of colour; happy, beautiful. It's always the same story. I walk into a crowded room and I'm searching for her. Countless heads turn to look at me, but I can't see her. I start to panic because I don't know where else to look. Then without warning the floor clears and I find her in the middle of the room, a spotlight on her. The whole place becomes quiet and I watch as, in slow motion, a ring slips through her fingers, bounces silently onto the floor and rolls out of sight. What is this all about? Missed opportunities? Lost love? It means, of course, that I can't escape the pain even in my sleep. Each morning I waken exhausted. Staring at my face in the bathroom mirror I can see that I'm wrecked. I know I need to find a way of channelling my feelings. This wayward see-saw of emotions is really damaging. My whole life is getting screwed and I don't seem to be able to get back on top of things. This is so unlike me. Usually I am a calm, level-headed person. I'm good at compartmentalising things and so staying in control. This is not part of the script. I feel things are slipping. I'm lost.

It was good to be with Len last night. I appreciated his company. It's a very strange situation though, because in any other circumstances I'm quite sure I would open up to him. I'm not really much of a talker, I tend to keep things to myself, but there are times when I know to share with someone would be a good idea. I'm pretty certain that part of the reason I feel I'm cracking up is a result of this desperate need for secrecy at all costs. I'm unable to share my thoughts, my feelings, my heartbreak with my closest friend, the one person in the world that I trust absolutely. Telling Len anything about this would surely kill our friendship. I must have worked that out fairly early on otherwise I would have spoken up way back at the beginning. Would things have been different had we been open about it at the time? I'll never know. I can speculate over various different versions of events, but I'll never know. What I do know is that if I can't find a way of coping I'm going to completely destroy myself. Things can't go on like this, but what to do?

And what about Helen? There are issues there of course. I'm not bothered about her leaving, but we share a home and we work together, share the business. We won't be able to just leave things as they are. This isn't the break-up of two high-school kids. We have roots which will need to be pulled up. I can't walk away from this, I will need to meet her and talk to her. Picking up my phone to check for missed calls I find two. Dialling up voicemail I discover they're both from Helen. She wants me to call her and then she wonders if we should attend the funeral tomorrow in a show of togetherness. Perhaps it would be the decent thing. I replace the phone without calling back. Not now, not about this. As far as I'm concerned she can have everything. She already has it all anyway. I gave her my life didn't I? I sacrificed my own chance of happiness to allow her to have hers. There's nothing more she can take that would make any difference to me. Let her have the flat, the restaurant. I have no heart for any of it now anyway. All I ever wanted is gone and my life now is empty and pointless. The funeral! Now how am I going to manage that one? I certainly won't be there with Helen that's for sure. At this moment in time I'm not sure that I'll actually be able to go through with it. I can't be certain that I'll be able to keep a lid on things. It would be disastrous if I broke down and spilled my secrets. I can't imagine anything worse. What would it do to Len? What would it do to me? No. If there's any risk of that then I just can't go. I wouldn't mind missing it; it's the last place I want to be tomorrow. The only drawback of course in not attending is what message that would send out. That might actually be worse. I am seriously screwed up. I can't even make a decision anymore. This is so bad.

## LEN

She has seated herself at a table by the window. Maybe she's not mortified to be seen with me after all. From here everyone entering the Union by the main entrance can get a pretty clear view of us. It doesn't bother me a bit. People can think what they like. I'm way past caring about petty gossip. I've got enough to be worrying about. Unloading the tray I offer her the various bits and pieces I selected for breakfast. She stares at each one, but takes nothing. Helping myself to tea from the pot and buttering some toast, I watch her as she casually pushes the food away from her place and looks out of the window. "Don't you want it?" I ask.

"No, it's not that…I just…I don't really feel like anything. It looks great though," she says with distaste.

She couldn't make it any plainer that I've picked all the wrong things. She looks absolutely disgusted by it. I'm starting to get a bit irritated. I'm trying my best and she seems so ungrateful. Taking a deep breath I force myself to ask, "Would you like me to get you something else? Is this not the kind of food you eat?"

"No, it's not that …the food's fine. I just don't want any, that's all."

"Carly, look at you! You haven't eaten today have you?" She diverts her gaze from mine. I know I'm getting a bit heavy, but the girl is practically emaciated and I wonder if this is the root of her problems. How can someone give their all to their course if their brain is starved? Reaching into my jeans pocket I pull out a crumpled fiver

124

and place it on the table before her, "Go and choose something you want."

She speaks evenly, decisively, "I don't want anything," pushing the money back towards me.

I'm becoming increasingly annoyed and it's all I can do not to abandon this mission. I leave it and start to eat, the food's there, I can't make her eat it. I do think she's being very rude but leave it anyway.

"Okay, I think we need a plan." She draws her gaze around to me again and I have her attention at last. "I need some paper," I tell her, "and a pen." She scans the room, then rises and heads over to the counter. For a second I think she's decided to have something to eat after all and am musing over her contrariness when she returns with a paper napkin and a borrowed pen.

"There."

"Right, here's what I think. You've messed up the exams okay, but we can still do this. It's all going to rest on your coursework. To equate with the exam you're going to need to produce a dissertation." She looks shocked. "Well, the regular coursework on its own only brings in sixty percent of your final grade. You need to do a dissertation if you're going to come up to First."

"But I could still pass on the marks I've got and a decent course result"

"Well yes…but that's not what we're after…is it?"

Silence.

"Well…is it?"

"I don't know. I guess I'd hoped for better, but it would do. It would be better than nothing."

"Better than nothing?" My voice is raised, but I can't help it. What is she playing at? She knows I expect more from her than better than nothing. Why does she think I'm here? Does she honestly think I've come over today, putting my own problems to one side, to help her work out how to get better than nothing? Her eyes dart around the room. She's obviously worried about attracting too much attention. "No Carly. We're not going for better than nothing. We're going for First. Understand?" She nods uncertainly. Finishing my drink I allow myself a few minutes to think before I speak again. I decide to ignore her protestations. "Right, have you any thoughts about subject?"

"Subject for what?" she says absently.

"For the bloody dissertation, what do you think?"

She's uncomfortable now I know. I shouldn't have got angry, shouldn't have raised my voice. I certainly shouldn't be swearing at her! "I'm sorry," I add. She seems to be back with me so I continue. "Well, what about poetry?"

"Yes, poetry," she replies. Good, at last she is beginning to focus. I wait for her suggestions but none are forthcoming. This would try the patience of a saint!

"Adrienne Rich? You could use feminism as your focus." I scribble on the napkin:

Possible Dissertation Subjects
1. Adrienne Rich

She shakes her head.

"Okay, what about Elizabeth Bishop?" I add her to the list

2. Elizabeth Bishop

"She was also an artist so you could have a personal slant with that one. That's always good, helps you to get inside the poet's head."

"Hmmm…" her vague response.

I can't help feeling that I'm the one doing all the work here. I don't remember Carly being like this. She's not a difficult student. In fact I've always really enjoyed our tutorials. She's a brilliant student, I remind myself. At this moment she doesn't seem like the same girl at all. Again I wonder if there's something wrong. I glance at her untouched food and drink but plough on regardless.

"Rita Dove?" I ask hopefully.

3. Rita Dove

"What would I do with her?" she asks and I fleetingly wonder if I detect a hint of sarcasm in her voice. I'm prepared to ignore it, but I'm also reaching the end of my rope. I will only give so much while getting nothing back. We're approaching last chance, I feel. What a pity. I had such high hopes for her. The funny thing is I really thought Carly wanted it too.

Speaking more quietly I ask her, "Carly, am I wasting my time here?"

A shrug of the shoulders. That does it. She's not interested. I'm out of here. As I rise to leave, she looks up at me with surprise. I snap. "What? You think I'm just going to sit here and take this?"

"Take what?" She looks puzzled.

I shake my head. "You're taking the piss, Carly. I've come over here today specifically to help you. I've gone out of my way; put my personal problems to one side so as to guide you through this. It might interest you to know I'm having a pretty difficult time right now. I have a lot of stuff going on in my own life, but I came here today because I care about you and what happens to you. Pity you don't offer me the courtesy of showing that you appreciate it."

She reacts instantly, "Oh right. I see how it is." She's standing now too. "Because you take the time to come and speak to me I've to be eternally grateful. Because you buy me a breakfast that I don't want I'm meant to be thankful. I told you I didn't want anything, but you don't listen to a word I say. You've decided I should eat, therefore I should eat. Doesn't matter how I feel. You've decided that I should do a dissertation; therefore I've to come up with a subject. What about the fact that I don't think I can do it? What about the fact that I've got so much going on in my life that I can hardly think straight, never mind focus on a dissertation? At this rate I'll be lucky to pass at all. Yes I care, but it's not the most important issue in my life."

I'm absolutely furious now. How dare she speak to me like that? I've never shown her anything other than respect. I respect her a great deal. She has a fantastic talent, unparalleled in this institution in my opinion. I've put so much into helping her and this is what I get back in return; ungrateful, bitter words of reproach.

"How dare you! As if you didn't know I am burying my wife tomorrow! I am going through the most difficult time in my life and you dare to stand there and tell me that life is hard. You've got no idea, absolutely no idea. You are a spoilt little girl who's obviously never had to endure any hardship in her life and you so lack compassion it's almost unbelievable."

Kicking over my chair I turn to leave. I see the staring faces all around, but couldn't care less what any of them think. If I've given them something to talk about this morning, then good. It's nothing to the hurt I'm bottling up inside. Maybe I shouldn't have come. I'm not ready for this. I realise I'm still holding the crumpled napkin and turning back, throw it onto the table amongst the uneaten food.

# CARLY

The room seems to have become very quiet. People are staring, forks paused half-way to their mouths, conversations ceased. My face is burning I am so embarrassed. Slowly it feels, very slowly, people gradually resume their own business. Cups again clatter onto saucers, knives scrape across plates and the level of chatter begins to rise again. I feel so stupid standing here, Prof's chair lying on its side in front of me. He was so angry! I've never seen him like that. I'm not even sure what triggered it. I'm hurt too. He said some horrible things, unfair things. If only he understood. I know this is probably all about misunderstandings. He thinks he knows me, thinks he knows about my life, but he has me all wrong. I know I should have spoken to him weeks ago about my problems. Shane told me I should in case it started to affect my work and now look. It's certainly done that. I don't suppose he'll give me the time of day now. What will he do? I remember once he threw a student out of a lecture because he was busy reading for another subject in Prof's time, as he said. I never saw that guy again. I wonder if he has the authority to pull me from the course. Surely not, probably he'll just assign me to another tutor. I'll never do it if that's the case. My only hope was having Prof help me and without him I know I've had it. On the other hand there's no guarantee I was going to manage anyway. Anger begins to dissipate and is replaced with a strong sense of disappointment. All my dreams seem to be crumbling around me. I don't feel that there's anything I can do. I feel really powerless and vulnerable. And yet, I chastise myself, someone like Prof tries to offer help and you push him away.

He was wrong about a lot of the things he said about me, but he was right in saying that I wouldn't take his help. It's not that I didn't want to; I'm crying out for help, I'm just not good at recognising the genuine article; someone who really cares.

Gathering my things I head out towards the door, righting his chair on the way. I wonder what people think of the spectacle that just took place in here. A couple of girls from my Renaissance class are crowded round a table near the exit,

"Everything alright, Carly?" one of them asks, smirking as I pass.

Ignoring her I push against the heavy door out into the foyer. It's really busy out here, people queuing for tickets for some band, I forget who they are. I need to get some air, this place is stifling me. I think momentarily of all the germs floating around this hot, dank room filled with sweating bodies. Outside will be better. What a difference to breathe in some cool air. It's a gorgeous morning, clear and fresh. We should never have gone in there. Maybe we wouldn't have fought if we'd stayed outside and kept our heads free of all that stuffiness. Moving on down the steps, I am almost upon him before I notice the huddled shape leaning against the wall. Grey hooded sweatshirt and jeans, he looks much like one of his students. Drawing deeply on a cigarette, he is facing the other way and doesn't notice me approach. Hesitatingly I speak, wondering as I do whether it is wise to disturb him,

"I thought maybe Sylvia Plath."

He turns when I speak and I see his eyes wet with tears, glistening in the sunlight. Wiping his face with his sleeve he nods and whispers, "Plath would be good." I didn't know he smoked, have never seen him with a cigarette before. I guess there are lots of things I don't know about him.

"I'm sorry Prof. I shouldn't have said those things."

He gives me a half-smile and nods. "Thanks, but it's me who should be sorry. I was horrible to you back there." The cigarette balanced precariously between his fingers trembles and I realise that he's shaking.

130

"Are you alright Prof?" He doesn't answer. I feel the need to say something and stupidly blurt out, "I didn't know you smoked" Immediately the words are spoken I think how stupid it sounds. What a stupid thing to say. How would I know anything about him anyway?

Taking another draw he says, "I don't…I mean I used to, a long time ago…this is just…I don't know…helping."

"Do you want to walk?" I suggest, becoming aware of a group of Lit students gathering at the entrance looking over frequently in our direction. I feel that I want to protect him from their gossiping tongues. He nods slightly and starts moving off the steps. We walk side by side for a few minutes without speaking. The street is busy with students hanging around. There's nothing like a little sunshine to drag everyone out of the woodwork.

"I'm really sorry, Carly. I really am." He turns to look at me and I know he means it. "I don't know what's going on with me right now. I guess I thought I was ready to come back to work, but clearly I'm not."

I flinch inwardly at the reference to our meeting as work. It's good to be out in the open, my head is clearing and I'm beginning to feel slightly better. Reaching the park we settle on a bench beside the duck-pond, the sun's warmth suggestive of a preamble to spring. "What was she like?" I ask and surprise myself at the intrusive nature of my question. I didn't really mean to say it out loud.

"Who? Sylvia Plath?" He looks confused.

"No, Claudine. What was she like?"

"Oh, Claudine… What was Claudine like? She was… she was …well, she was very beautiful. Her hair was soft as silk, golden curls, long down her back. Her skin the smoothest, softest texture you could imagine. Beautiful."

"No, I mean what was she like as a person?"

"I thought you knew her." He states the obvious.

"No, not really. I knew her as my teacher, but I didn't really know her as a person." He nods, understanding.

"Well, she was very smart, very bright and creative. She was becoming really well established as a painter. Her work was incredible."

"Was she interested in literature?" I'm gaining confidence because he's engaging with me and I sense that he desperately wants to talk about her.

"She was interested yes, but she didn't share my passion for it. You know, she read a lot, but not always fiction. We didn't like, sit and discuss books over dinner or anything like that. Funnily enough she was reading Sylvia Plath before she died. There was a volume of poems beside the bed, but I didn't even know she was interested in her work at all."

He sighs deeply and once again I feel cautious. I don't want him to think I'm being nosy, but I'm so enjoying hearing about her from someone who knew her so well, better than anyone else I should imagine. "When did you guys meet?" I watch for a reaction, a sign that I've overstepped the mark, but he smiles.

"We met in Paris when I was studying there. I went over to do my PhD in the hope of being inspired to write a book. It didn't happen, but I had a fabulous time, met lots of interesting people and that included Claudine." He recounts watching her over a period of several weeks, before she actually confronted him and they got together. It's really romantic and fits very well with my picture of her.

"How did you end up over here then?" The million dollar question! It's out before I have time to consider the implications of the answer.

"Oh it was work really. Well, we came over for a friend's wedding and there was a job that interested me. It all just kind of tied in, the timing and everything."

"And Claudine, it suited her to stay even though her family were back in France?" He thinks for a while before speaking. I hold my breath waiting to hear what he has to say, feeling like I might burst if he actually comes out and tells me. He doesn't and I feel deflated.

"She was quite happy to stay. I guess by that time we knew we would be together and she wanted to be with me."

132

We sit side by side for ages, sometimes talking about Claudine, sometimes silent. We even laugh a little. It's quite comfortable and easy. He seems to need to talk and I feel that maybe I'm the right person at the right time. He tells me about her family, her childhood home and her life in France before she came to live here. He talks a lot about her talent, her plan to go to Art school which fell through and her successful exhibitions. He is clearly very proud of her, very much in love with her. After a while he stands up saying, "Thanks Carly, thanks for that. I didn't realise how good it could feel to sit and chat about her. I haven't been able to do that and I think I needed it."

Smiling I tell him, "I really enjoyed hearing about her. There's so much I didn't know. You are a very lucky man to have known her, to have had all those years getting close to her." My words are tinged with just the slightest hint of jealousy, resentment even.

"I don't think I had admitted to myself how hard this is all going to be," he continues. "I think I just planned to carry on as normal…only without Claudine. Now I know it will never be like that. I'm going to have to carve out a new role for myself…somehow. I can't just pick up where I left off before she… and of course I need to get through tomorrow. Carly, I honestly don't know how I'm going to do that. How will I survive the funeral?"

Instinctively I squeeze his hand. "You feel like this because you loved her, because what you had, everything that you shared was so good. The pain you feel is a reflection of how happy you were together. Some people, most people never have that. And if you knew, right back at the beginning if you knew it would end like this; you would still have gone for it wouldn't you? You want more because what you had was so good, but you get what you get, some more and some less. I reckon you had everything. You only had it for a short time, but what you had was…"

"Perfect," he finishes for me. "For someone so young you are very wise, Carly. Thank you again." He makes as if to leave then turns back, "I'm glad you're coming tomorrow. I'll draw strength from you."

I smile in response and watch him walk away. It was brilliant to hear so much about Claudine, but there are still big gaps. I didn't expect him to talk so freely and yet part of me wants the missing pieces of the jigsaw now. Of course he may not even know! I was warned about that possibility when I started out on this thing and now I see why. I could be on the verge of tearing the lid off something hugely volatile, something that's been successfully contained all these years.

## SEBASTIAN

This is the last thing I feel like doing today. I'm conscious that I've made no effort with my appearance, I'm not trying to impress anyone and frankly the exertion just seemed too great. She doesn't like it when I'm unshaven and maybe part of me also wants to annoy her a bit. I hesitate outside the door and wonder why it feels so awkward. It's my place after all. I built it up into the business it is today. I struggled in the early days with too little money and no staff and working every hour God sent. The success of Café Helene is down to my commitment and my graft. I'm not being egotistical, just stating the facts. Helen wouldn't argue with that either. She knows it was down to me. I threw my heart and soul into this venture in the beginning. I had to; it gave me something to live for. Sadly now it doesn't seem to be enough. I open the door gingerly, expectantly, listening for the predictable jingle that so infuriates me. There it is. Even though I know it's coming it still makes my skin crawl to hear it. The girls look up at me and their embarrassment is obvious. Does everyone know I wonder? I guess it's been clear that things haven't been right recently, but I'm still somewhat surprised at their reaction. I've never been the kind of boss who is all pals with my employees, but neither did I think there was a gulf between us. I kind of thought they might understand, take my side even. Then again I suppose they have to consider who their next manager will be and keep sides with them. "How's things?" I ask trying to strike up a pretence of normality.

"Good, yes pretty good," the expected reply.

Then bustling away, everyone becomes suddenly very busy, consumed in their tasks. I help myself to a jug of water and lifting two tumblers from the worktop move round to the front and sit down in the corner. This is the table that the staff normally uses for breaks, it's out of the way enough not to intrude on the customers or get in the way of the waitresses. Pouring the drink, I wish I had thought of ice before I sat down, but now can't be bothered going back for it. The lukewarm liquid lacks the refreshment I crave, but I settle for it nonetheless. Glancing at my watch I wonder where she is. I am irritated already because I'm sure she's doing this on purpose. She knows exactly how to rile me and seems to take pleasure in doing so. When did it get like this I ask myself? The truth is I don't know. It happened without me even noticing. I mean we were never the perfect match or anything, but things were okay at first. Gradually, I suppose, the lack of love just proved to be insufficient to sustain the relationship. We started to tolerate each other, then as time went on and that became increasingly difficult, to resent the other. Now it is all I can do to keep myself in this room knowing she is coming to meet me. Every time the door opens I lift my eyes resignedly toward it, anticipating her arrival with each new customer who enters.

Another look at my watch tells me she's twenty minutes late. It tells me lots more too; that she's not caring that I'll be in a lousy mood when she eventually does turn up, that she's under no illusions about us getting back together. In a way that's good, though. I really don't want to be dealing with tears and promises. I'd much rather we both remain angry and handle it all in a more detached way. I decide I'll give her five more minutes. Half an hour has got to be the limit of being late without making a phone call to explain, surely. If she doesn't show it might actually be a relief, because then I'm excused this conversation. The only problem being that we probably need to have it at some point and to do it today would put it behind us. I wonder momentarily if I will have to see her again after this. Could this be the last time I am required to endure her company? Is that too simplistic? Anyway if she doesn't turn up soon I'm going to head. In spite of myself I wait on past the thirty minute mark because I really want to get this over with. I want her to come, to be bitter and indignant, but to face up to the reality of our situation. I want to be sure that she accepts we are finished, that there will be no going back. We talk, we tie up loose ends, we make a few decisions, we part. That's as much as I'm prepared to give. Of course if she doesn't come, then I need to do this all over again another day. She doesn't come.

## LEN


Returning home it seems like I've been away for days. The house has a sense of nothingness about it as if there's no air inside. I wonder if it will always have this oppressive feel to it now. No sooner am I in the door than I yearn to go back out somewhere, anywhere that isn't here. I don't expect to see Claudine anymore when I come in, but I know instead I'll be greeted with the absence of her and it's so painful.

Throwing my keys onto the table I decide that I'll probably move. I won't do anything straightaway, but I realise I won't be able to continue like this, here, without Claudine. It's so strange how every aspect of my life has been affected by Claudine's death, not just the things we shared. I don't suppose it's something you ever give any thought to until it happens. Take this house, for instance, we would not have imagined moving any time soon. This house is just what we wanted. We've taken years making it our own and what we achieved was pretty close to perfect. We've been so happy living here, but now, now it all feels so different. It looks the same, sure, give or take a few damages caused by outbursts of emotion over the last few days. But it doesn't feel like the same house at all. It doesn't feel like home. Work's another thing that's changed. Claudine had really no involvement with my work at all. We tended to keep our professional lives separate. Not intentionally, I don't think, but it's just the way we were. Our time together was time that we enjoyed each other, not going over all the moans and groans of the day. I was always too excited to see her. I can honestly say that I thought we had the happiest relationship of any of the couples I know. The initial delight in each other, expected to fade with the monotony of years spent together never did. Maybe it would have, who knows what was around the corner. Like with Sebastian and Helen, I'm not saying that I thought they were made for each other, but I guess having been together this long I just kind of assumed they would last the distance. Carly was right, had I known things would end like this I would have still gone for it, wouldn't have hesitated. Every minute spent loving Claudine was special and worth all this pain. I would do it all again. It's funny how it can take a child to show you the way. How can someone so young have insight like that? It comes through in her work too, that sensitivity. I'm so glad we talked today. It made a big difference to how I feel about tomorrow. Oh I know it's going to be hell, but I can rationalise why. I know it's because what Claudine and I had was so good and I have to focus on that in order to give meaning to these feelings.

Carly, she was a sweetheart to take the time with me today, especially when I was so mean to her. I feel really bad about that now, particularly since it was done so publicly. I don't care what people think, but maybe she does. I hope I haven't made things difficult for her. If I ever get through this I will try to sort it if I can. At the moment it's really all I can do to stay standing. I don't want to eat or sleep. I don't want to see anyone or do anything. I just want it all to go away. I want to switch channel and find something more appealing to live. Facing this head on is hard, really hard. Wasn't I stupid to think I could cope with being back at work? I thought if I could absorb myself in someone else's problems it might help me to handle my own. How wrong could I be? That was obvious I guess when it all came crashing down around us this morning. I thought I could, not over-ride my feelings, but maybe just push them to one side for a while. I don't have any precedents for how to do this, though. My pain is proving to be difficult to handle.

Wandering into the kitchen I carelessly switch on the kettle without any intention of actually making tea. Gazing absently around the room I wonder what I'm supposed to do with myself now. How do widowers spend their time? How do I get through the day? This is impossible I think. If I can't work then I can't do it. I'm prevented from sinking deeper into this morose state by an annoying knocking on the door. How long it's been going on I don't know; it seems to have been there in the background for some time. I really don't want to see anyone. Making conversation is beyond me tonight. I've allowed myself to retreat into myself, in amongst the warm, safe memories that Claudine and I created. I don't want them disturbed. I hold out a little longer, but my too polite nature is unable to leave a visitor stranded on the doorstep and reluctantly I drag myself round to the front door and pull it slowly open.

"Oh my boy, my poor boy!"

I am engulfed in a rough embrace and struggling for breath, pull myself away. "How are you, my boy?" the deeper but just as loud voice of my father pushing past me, on into my living room. I turn, close the door and cautiously follow my parents into the house.

"I didn't realize you were coming," I say simply.

"What! Not come?" We wouldn't miss this for the world."

My mother has a way with words also. This is not what I need right now.

"Well, just so long as you know I'm not much company at the moment. You can stay of course, but don't expect anything of me." She stares at me disapprovingly. I'm waiting for chastisement and know that I won't be able to hold my tongue. We surely can't be on the brink of a row already! That would be a record even for us. I glance at my watch out of habit more than anything else, but it's not lost on my mother.

"Don't tell me we've outstayed our welcome already, Lennon." I shake my head and wonder why I didn't anticipate this. Of course they would come, why didn't I think of it?

"Right do you want tea or something?"

"Oh Lennon, honey we don't drink tea! Coffees would be lovely, though. Milk, two sugars." She settles herself on the couch and pats the seat beside her, gesturing my father to join her. Coffee. Right. I'll do it, I think, but then it's down to them. I know they've travelled a long way and maybe another son would be grateful for the effort they've made. The truth is, though, I suspect there's an ulterior motive. There must be. They never even met Claudine! Why now? That's all I can think as I go through the motions of fixing their drinks. Why pick now to appear out of nowhere and force themselves upon me? If I was close to breaking point before this then I don't know where I am now.

I wonder momentarily what happens to a person when they're pushed over the edge. I remember seeing psychiatric patients in my Dad's ward. We used to have to visit every Christmas while Dad did his rounds. How I hated it: trailing round after him, being introduced to all these mad people. I used to feel so self-conscious, didn't know how to act or respond to them. Funny now to think of it: all these patients acted so inappropriately, shouting, swearing, talking to things or people who weren't there and yet I worried about how I was behaving. I'm thinking now that maybe all those burnt-out schizophrenics were just ordinary people who had one way or another been pushed too far. Will I go the same way? At this moment it doesn't seem beyond the realms of possibility. I wonder do you know when you've lost all your sensibilities. Do you know, but don't care? Maybe there's something appealing there after all. I can't imagine living anything like a normal life now. Maybe one where you no longer have to make any effort, where nothing is expected of you and anything is acceptable would suit me in my current state.

Again my thoughts are interrupted by my mother's shrill, affected voice screeching through from the next room: "Like what you've done to the place, son!" This is just what I mean. I don't want to be interrupted when I'm trying to think. It's taking a concerted effort to get my mind onto anything and her nonsensical remarks haul me back to the present for no reason. How long before I bite back I wonder?

Carrying their coffees through to them I become aware of the phone ringing in the distance. Where is it I wonder? It feels so long since I was last in the house that I can't even remember where I was when I last used it. It doesn't matter anyway, there's no one I want to talk to.

"Where's Mom?" I ask as I hand my father a mug.

"Gone to look for your phone I think"

Oh no! This is the kind of thing I can't take: interfering. Why can't she just leave it? Re-entering the room she hands me the retrieved phone. "It's some of those French relations I think. Can't understand a word he's saying!" She's clearly disappointed not to be able to get into a discussion about my welfare, but that'll come I'm sure. With the funeral tomorrow there's bound to be countless opportunities for people to speculate on my state of mind! Tomorrow it's open season. Taking the receiver from her I'm confused as to why she can't understand him speaking French. She's from Montreal, born and bred!

"Hello?"

It's Luc, Claudine's youngest brother checking that I'm alright and inviting me round to be with them, as he puts it, tonight. Had he phoned half an hour ago I would have sent apologies but now it's a whole different scenario. I need to get out of here and for that reason alone I tell him I'll be there. Turning to my mother as I replace the phone, I can't help myself asking the most ridiculous of questions.

"Why couldn't you understand him? He was speaking French. You speak French better than I do!"

"Oh Lennon…" the way she keeps calling me this is getting on my nerves. No one calls me that anymore and it sounds so pretentious coming from her. "Lennon, we don't speak French anymore. Your father and I are New Yorkers now. We live in the Big Apple remember? We have no need to speak French and so we've actually forgotten how. Haven't we honey?" She doesn't wait for a response from Dad and instead ploughs on like an out-of-control lawn mower wreaking further havoc with every syllable uttered. "In fact I'd say we're more American now than Canadian. We think like Americans if you know what I mean."

I don't, but I don't want her to talk anymore so I say nothing. This has got to stop. I'm not going to be able to take much more of it.

Maybe I'll feel better when I get back, when I've had a bit of a breather from them. Unlikely I suppose, considering they've only been in my house for forty-three minutes and we're careering headfirst into a collision zone. The only thing I want to know is why they're really here, because I don't believe for a minute that it's got anything whatsoever to do with Claudine.

# CARLY

I wonder why I didn't hear from Shane today. I kind of expected to see him too, because he's been home for a couple of days and usually has had enough by that stage. I find the holidays a bit of a strain what with everyone else going back to their respective families. Everyone seems to have somewhere to go, someone to go to. Most of the time I don't mind; I actually quite like having the place to myself and space to think. But from time to time I really wish I had the option of returning home to my family for a few days. I see other students loading up their washing before transporting it back to Mum, returning a few days or weeks later with it clean and pressed and packed lovingly into a bag along with parcels of food and other essential provisions. I think if I had a child I would enjoy this labour of love. It's a very natural role, that of mother hen and despite their protestations to the contrary I suspect most people really appreciate the clucking.

I enjoyed Prof's company today. Well not the row obviously, but later on when we talked in the park. It felt really easy and I liked the way he seemed able to open up to me on a deeper level than before. I'm going to make a go of this dissertation even if I don't manage it. His optimism has encouraged me to at least try. I realise that he doesn't know my present circumstances and if he did he might not be so positive, but that aside he clearly believes in my ability. I'm happy about that. It's nice to feel that I've pleased him.

He seems to be okay about me going to the funeral tomorrow too. I'm glad his friend, what was his name again… something French

144

but it escapes me right now. My memory sometimes is terrible! I wonder if it's a sign of stress. I must look it up when I get a chance. Anyway I'm glad Prof's friend sort of let him know about it. I wouldn't have wanted to turn up if he didn't know. It's funny, I want to go and I don't. I want to pay my respects and to be involved in this very personal occasion, but it also seems wrong given that I never actually got the opportunity to have a frank discussion with her. I feel in a way that I've been cheated out of something. Anyway it's by the by, because I've told them I'll be there, so now not to go would maybe appear rude. Laying out my formal clothes, a nice charcoal grey trouser suit, I hope it will be suitable. I don't have anyone to ask unless Shane starts answering his calls. He must be out of range somewhere, because he always phones me back when I leave a message.

Sometimes I think it's maybe not very healthy that Shane and I spend so much of our time together. I know I've excluded my other friends now for so long that they wouldn't be interested in hearing from me. I feel bad about that. I used to be really close to a few of the girls, but when I met Shane he didn't like me going out with them instead of him. He said he worried that some boy would start chatting me up and he felt quite jealous even thinking about it. It's just because he cares so much about me that the idea of sharing me is hard for him. Anyway I think that's kind of nice. It makes me feel special. To begin with the girls used to put pressure on me to still hang out with them and I did miss our nights out. They were always fun. But that was my life before I met Shane and as he reminded me, I didn't need them anymore because I had him now. Things had changed. I decide the suit will do alright. It's the same suit that got me through my interview for Uni so maybe it'll make me feel better about things if I'm wearing it.

I've only been to a couple of funerals ever so it's going to be quite a strange experience for me. When I was very young, perhaps five or six, my Granny died but I wasn't allowed to go to the funeral. I stayed at home with a neighbour, but I watched with close scrutiny the preparations for the event. Everyone dressed in their smartest clothes, almost all of them in black. People spoke in hushed tones, breaking off abruptly whenever I came into a room. It was something secretive, hidden behind black veils and mystery. At the age of fifteen my second encounter with death, that same neighbour fell from his rooftop where he had been repairing a broken chimney pot, smashing his skull on the patio below. That time we all went together. It was the last family excursion we had.

I knew that as soon as I turned sixteen I would be moving out. It had been discussed for as long as I could remember. Mum and Dad had three young children by this time and had never had a chance to just be together as a family, the five of them. At that time I didn't blame them. The way they explained it all to me it seemed reasonable. When they adopted me they had been told they couldn't have kids of their own. Then of course Ava came along and they were blown away by the miracle they had been blessed with. I was taken to chapel regularly and made to give thanks for the precious blessing that had been given to our family. I was delighted with Ava too. It wasn't really until a year later when Eliza was born that I noticed any difference. I felt it in many ways, but all of them were quite subtle and easy enough to rationalise. Mum and Dad couldn't do stuff with me because they were busy with the babies. They couldn't be expected to come to my dance display because they didn't want to leave the babies with other people. And when they forgot about parents' night, the night my teacher had said she was going to tell them I was a gifted pupil, well who could blame them? They hadn't had a night to themselves since the arrival of little demanding Eliza. It was when Lily was born just two years on that my Dad decided it was time for a little chat. I remember it as if it were yesterday. My Dad thought that now I was twelve I was really quite grown up and I'd be able to understand what he was saying. I wasn't a little girl anymore and I was to start acting more mature and recognize my place in the house. He explained that when they adopted me it was really a last resort. Mum desperately wanted a baby and believing that it was never going to happen naturally they acted in good faith when they brought me into their family. The thing was it had never really taken away Mum's desire for her own child. They had thought it would be just the same seeing how I was so young when I came to live with them. They thought I would become their own even though biologically I wasn't. It wasn't like that and they couldn't have foreseen how differently they would feel when their own baby was born. I felt horrible. I knew I wasn't wanted and I felt I was in the way. I thought about running away but I was frightened. I had nowhere to go and didn't know what to do. I just carried on and tried not to get involved in too much.

The birth of the other babies made things markedly worse. My mum more or less stopped speaking to me. I was clearly a total inconvenience. The family would go on holiday together but always arranged for me to stay with someone, saying that I wouldn't enjoy doing all the kiddies' things with them. I was at that age, they would explain to my babysitter and they weren't going to force me to go with them. My dad, well, he was quite hard on me. I think he resented me most. Now I think it's maybe because I was a constant reminder of what he had been unable, for so many years, to deliver to my mum. Either that or maybe he genuinely felt I was an imposter, there under false pretences. While my mum ignored me, he chipped away at my self-esteem, constantly critical. He told me all the time how useless I was. He put me down, it felt at every opportunity. Only one time did he actually hit me and I think he frightened himself at that. He was furious because I had asked for money for a school trip and he launched into an assault on how much I had already had from them and was I trying to bleed them dry? In an instant I think he just lost control and spinning round caught me on the side of my face with his watch buckle. It stung like crazy and I remember wanting to go to the toilet to see if it was bleeding, but he made me stand there while he excused what he'd done. He told me how I'd made him do it, how I was so difficult, had such a surly nature and pushed him to his limits. He said any man would have reacted in the same way. If I told anyone what had happened he would see that I was sent away. It never happened again, but he kept his distance from me after that. I think he probably hated me and couldn't actually trust himself to be around me. After that I was under no illusions about their feelings toward me. I just kept my head down and tried to keep out of their way. When I was fifteen I met Shane and he really helped me to get a handle on it all.

He has been such a help to me over the years and I don't know where I'd be without him. It occurs to me again as strange that I haven't had a call from him and I check my phone once more, just in case I've missed something.

# LEN

Sebastian's place is much quieter tonight. The boys have clearly slept off last night's alcohol-fuelled revelry and are now facing their grief with clearer heads. Luc opens the door to me and my parents follow us inside. I didn't feel I could leave them as it turned out and so they have happily accompanied me. Obviously they have never been introduced to any of Claudine's family. They never really showed any inkling of interest in my marriage so in a way I'm surprised that they wanted to come. It occurs to me that this meeting of in-laws is the sort of thing that takes place usually before a wedding and not, as in this situation, a funeral. My parents settle down for a long heart to heart with Cecile and Antoine. It irks me greatly. They never knew her because they never took the time to come and meet her and yet now they're here in the thick of things, acting as if they'll never recover from their loss.

I could allow myself to get wound up by them. It would be easy for us all to fall out tonight, but I have reservations about letting that happen. First of all, I don't have the energy for a full-scale argument and subtle snide remarks aren't my style. I prefer to tell it how it is and get everything off my chest if I'm going down the road of confrontation. Secondly, I'm very aware that, whatever their reasons, they've travelled a great distance and they're not as young as they used to be, so I tend to grant them a bit more slack than I might normally. Thirdly and perhaps most importantly, I don't want Claudine's funeral to turn into a circus. I'd like to keep some semblance of dignity about things if I possibly can.

I decide to leave them to it and accompany Luc into the kitchen, where the rest of the boys are watching a soccer game on TV. It's more a distraction than anything else. Their spirit is muted. They are preoccupied despite the commentators' excitement. Luc offers me a drink. It's funny how the youngest has taken on the role of host, making sure that the right things are being done and said. He seems to have some idea about how we should be doing all this, so I'm grateful that he's seen fit to take the lead. He tells me that the undertaker was in earlier confirming arrangements, which incidentally, all seem to be in order. He informs me that Mum, his Mum, had a very bad day today, culminating in a panic-attack and the local doctor having to be called. A sedative later and she seems to have slept off her agitation. I know this must be really hard for her, losing her only daughter so prematurely, but I'm only able to try to cope with my own pain. I don't have it in me to see if anyone else is needing help. I'm unable to offer support of any kind.

Sebastian sits comfortably between the twins, Christophe and Dominic, occasionally commenting on the soccer. He is completely at ease in their company. I know they go back a long way, since they were children, so I suppose it's more natural for him. I like the boys, but I just don't know any of them all that well. It's more of an effort for me to converse with them. It was thoughtful, though, of Luc to have called and included me tonight. I've no idea what kind of state I'd have been in if I'd been left alone with my parents.

I remember the first time I met Claudine's brothers. It was a shameful experience for me. It was the night I finished my thesis. I had been cooped up for weeks trying to pull it all together, barely seeing the light of day. Everything else had been put on the back-burner while I devoted all my attentions to my work. I had hardly seen Claudine in all that time either. So when I finished it and Sebastian suggested we go out to celebrate, I was definitely up for it. We went to a local club; a place frequented by students and met up with a pile of his mates. I knew most of them too, having been out with them several times before. A few drinks into the night and we spotted Claudine across the floor. She was with another girl and these two boys, gathered cosily around a table. The lads got me worked up, riling me that she was out with another guy and kind of pushed me into confronting her and dealing with it. I was totally humiliated when I discovered they were her brothers! As she explained indignantly what the situation was, I could see them across the room laughing. The thing is I was quite insecure about our relationship at that time. I didn't think it would last because she was so perfect, so much what I wanted. I was sure that the cruel hand of fate would interfere and destroy my happiness at any time. For me it wouldn't have been surprising if one day Claudine had met someone else, someone more deserving of her attentions and so I guess I was really an easy target for their fooling.

"You haven't heard a word I've said, have you?" Luc's words drag me back to the present and I realise I have missed something. He looks mildly irritated and I quickly apologise. "You were miles away!"

"Yeah I was. Back in France actually."

All eyes are instantly upon me as if they expect me to launch into reminiscing about how good it all was. I think we've all probably done enough of that over the past few days. The way I feel right now I don't even want to speak her name. This afternoon with Carly was different, I'm not entirely sure why, but I found it easy to open up to her. Here amongst others, who are all struggling for self-preservation in their own individual ways, it just doesn't seem right. I suspect the boys feel the same since there's been virtually no mention of Claudine since I arrived. We don't need to talk endlessly about her, because she pervades every aspect of everything we do. She is everywhere. We are all focussed completely on Claudine all the time, so speaking of her is, in some ways, unnecessary. In the next room I overhear my mother in her high-pitched, too-loud voice dishing out platitudes and I recognise that as being the difference. If you're feeling the loss, if you're actually experiencing the rawness of it then words need to really be the right words. Anything else falls short of being acceptable.

"I said we're going to go and see her."

Turning my attention back to Luc, I stare blankly at him. I have no idea what he's talking about. A look of frustration crosses his face and I realise that he's already explained all this to me.

151

"I'm sorry, Luc. Go on, I'm listening."

He speaks slowly, articulating every word carefully, as if he thinks maybe the language is the problem and informs me that they've all decided they want to go visit Claudine tonight to say goodbye. She is still in the little Chapel of Rest, where she was taken by the undertaker when he collected her from the hospital mortuary. I am horrified at the suggestion. I can't imagine anything more inappropriate. She's been dead for days now, will be buried tomorrow and they want to go gaze upon her cold, lifeless body tonight! My initial reaction is why can't they leave her alone? I really don't think Claudine would like the idea of a crowd of spectators scrutinising her corpse. It must be obvious to them that I don't like it; the twins are looking at their feet, avoiding any eye contact with me. Luc holds out, maintaining his focus on me, waiting for my reply. I don't know what to say. I am absolutely dumbfounded! The embarrassing silence lasts for ages. In the end it is Sebastian who comes to the rescue.

"We feel we never got a chance to say goodbye," he explains. "You saw her the day she died, but for us our last memories are of her alive and well. We think it might help a little to come to terms with it, you know."

So it's not a case of callous voyeurism after all. I guess when I think about it rationally, it does make sense. In fact I have heard of people doing this kind of thing before. Did I find it helpful to look on my darling wife's deadness? Who actually knows? Maybe, I suppose.

Sebastian continues "You know in France it's common practice to have the body at home in the house in the days leading up to the funeral. The coffin is left open and people wishing to pay their respects can come to see the person before the burial or whatever."

I'm afraid this is too much information for me. This is my Claudine they're talking about, not an abstract debate about nameless individuals. I won't try to stop them however, if this is how they want to deal with it. It's not for me though.

Given the choice it's not an easy decision to make. Go with the guys to see Claudine for a last time or stay home with the parents. I decide in the end to go over to the chapel, but not to go in. How's that for a compromise? I've never been here before, but I was quite sure there would be a garden of some sort, you know for thinking in? Sure enough, the Garden of Remembrance it's called. I push through the miniature metal gate and enter the deserted sanctuary. It's a very restful place after all and I almost feel glad I've come. The brothers and Sebastian have all gone inside and for the first time for days I feel quite tranquil. I'm enjoying the stillness of this place. It is a haven, detached from the real world, existing outside of time. It occurs to me as quite ironic that Claudine and I first met in a *jardin*. It wasn't the same as this one, but nevertheless it feels right to be here. I decide that this is a place I might return to on occasion when I need to escape.

I've tried not to think too much about the funeral up till now. I know it will be terrible and somehow I just have to get through it. I can't believe it's tomorrow, though. In some ways it feels like ages ago that I got that awful phone call summoning me to the hospital just a little too late. In other ways it feels that this is something which is happening to someone else, or something quite unreal. Tomorrow will be very real, there's no getting away from that. I wonder if there's any way I could avoid being there. I'm unable, though, to think of any reason in the world that could possibly justify that. I'll be there and somehow I'll do it, though how is a matter of some concern to me right now.

# LUC

I can't believe I'm doing this. I find this place completely oppressive, everything in me is screaming to be out of here. From the dimly-lit table-lamps to the ghastly arrangements of artificial flowers, the whole thing has a macabre feel to it. It's like something out of a cheap horror film. I wouldn't have believed it if I wasn't standing in the midst of it. What on earth possessed Len to let them bring her to such a dingy resting place? Or was it Sebastian? I vaguely remember someone mentioning that Sebastian had taken charge of the details for the funeral. Seemed a bit strange to me, but no one else batted an eyelid, so who was I to question it? Anyway, she's here and I'm absolutely hating this. The twins have left already, crying like babies. I think they take their cue from each other. I don't blame them really; none of us know quite how to act at the moment. I had a look in the coffin and saw a face very like my sister's. Paler though. Very still. I've never seen a dead body before and for some reason I was surprised to find that she still looked like Claudine. I think in my imagination I expected her to look completely different. Dead Claudine shouldn't be just the same as live Claudine to my mind. I am amazed at the hugeness of this. She lies there, to all intents and purposes the same old Claudine and yet dead. I had thought she would look like she was sleeping, I'm sure that's what my parents said when they came back from here yesterday. That she was very peaceful and just looked as if she'd closed her eyes for a moment. She doesn't. She looks dead. Len had the right idea not coming in. I'm really glad for his sake that he didn't. It isn't nice. I'm not sure that he could handle it

154

in fact. I don't know Len well, but this past few days I've really admired how he's coping. He seems like a really genuine guy. In a way I wish now that I'd got to know him better when Claudine was alive. I did visit a few times and often saw them when Claudine came home, but I wonder if I didn't really give him a chance. Mum was always furious with him and I think her impression perhaps tainted my own. She never got over him taking her little girl away from her, away to another country to live. I wish now I'd let myself be the judge of him, because I think the three of us would have had a lot of good times.

I'd really like to get out of here now. The whole place is starting to give me the creeps. The only thing is I don't want to leave Sebastian on his own. I think he's gonna need some company when he eventually tears himself away. He is absolutely stricken, his face creased with pain. I don't think I've ever seen grief so overtly manifest. It occurs to me that he might climb in beside her and die himself. I sneak a brief glance at my watch. We've been in here thirty-five minutes now. I hope the others have all gone, especially Len. This could take some explaining. I particularly hope Len doesn't come in to find out what's happened to us, because I suspect he'd find more than he bargained for. I've discovered a few things tonight, made a few connections.

"You loved her didn't you?" My voice sounds too loud within the silence of the parlour. At first I think my words haven't reached him. He's in another place altogether, far, far away. I'm staring at the back of his head and he doesn't flinch, there's no reaction at all. I shouldn't have said anything. Why did I? Maybe because I just feel so sorry for him, his pain is so obviously tearing him apart. The rest of the time he's put on a pretty good front, although I've noticed the odd flicker suggesting a more-than-just-good-friends scenario. Nobody else seems to have picked up on it. We artists are good at this kind of thing though. We notice things; small things. We see the detail in life. In here it's a different story. Perhaps he feels safe in the darkness and privacy of this awful place. Anyway it's good in a way that he didn't hear me; it's not really for me to delve too deeply. I study my shoes and wonder how long he will want to stay. I'll need to get him out of here eventually. I don't want to be out all night.

A sudden movement startles me. I'm not easily spooked but the whole environment is geared to it so it's not surprising that I almost jump out of my skin. He's turned to face me and raising my eyes from the close inspection of my footwear, I find him staring straight at me.

"I loved her, yes… a long time ago."

Calm, even words, carefully constructed. It's a statement of fact. He isn't asking for a response. Of course I remember how he loved her. I was only a little boy, but my sister's boyfriend made a big impression on me, on all of us. I thought he was great. He was so much older than me, I being the baby of the family, but he took a lot of time with me. He took me to see my first football match and used to bring me tickets and programmes from other games that he saw. I was the envy of my friends being associated with him He was so cool. Everyone thought they made a perfect pair. I know my mother had them married off in her head. I think that's why she took it so hard when he dumped Claudine for that other girl. None of us could believe it. One minute he seemed completely besotted by her, you could see it in his eyes. You could see it in his eyes then and I see the same thing now. I nod but don't push it. It's his thing after all, to deal with as he wishes.

"Ready to go?" he says as if he's been waiting all night for me to make a move. Stepping out into the bright evening my eyes take a moment to readjust to normal light. He obviously thinks I'm crying and puts an arm comfortingly around my shoulder. He's always treated me as if he was my big brother and I must admit I always quite liked it. "You alright?" he asks now, looking intently at me. I wonder for a moment if I got it all wrong. Did the awfulness of that place make my mind run riot? He's back in control now that we're out, anyway.

"It's just the light…my eyes…" I mutter and know he doesn't believe me. When did this role reversal take place I wonder? He was in bits just moments ago. Did he let his guard down in there and now needs to work harder to cover the wounds again? I feel for him, I really do. This perpetual act must be exhausting. However, I gave him an opportunity which he has chosen not to take. If he's gonna confide in anyone, I don't think it's gonna be me. Not tonight anyway.

# LEN

Why is it that when you know you need to sleep, it proves more evasive than ever? I must get some rest tonight or I don't think I'll be able to stand up tomorrow and tomorrow's such a big day. It will become one of the important dates of my life.

IMPORTANT DATES
1. Claudine's birthday April 5th
2. My birthday August 10th
3. Our wedding Anniversary August 30th
4. Claudine's deathday (there must be another word for it) February 5th
5. Claudine's funeral February 10th

I am so restless, I wonder if I should just get up. Maybe it's this bed. Of course it is. How can I sleep here where I last saw my darling wife? I don't know if I'm going to be able to shake off the guilt of not actually seeing Claudine the day she died. I slept in and she was already in the shower. Why didn't I slide the screen back when I spoke to her? Why didn't I take a few minutes to say goodbye before I left, to give her a kiss? I was already late, so it would have made no difference. If I had known it would be my last opportunity I would have done things so differently. How many people have ever felt this way I wonder? Regret is such a difficult thing to live with. The last time I saw her, actually looked at her was when I said goodnight the night before the accident, the night that turned out to be her last. She curled up in this bed beside me, curled up within my arms, kissed me gently, rested her head on my shoulder and slept. I can picture it so clearly, in such detail. I see the way her curls swept across the pillow like a fan. I feel her warm breath brush my cheek, the smoothness of her skin against mine. I can recreate the image, but I can't make it real. I see her so clearly, but as soon as I reach out to touch her, she disappears. I'm chasing a dream now. It was all once mine and now...

This is agony. I can't lie here like this. Sitting up in the darkness I have a sudden thought. The bag of stuff given back to me by the hospital! It was her clothes, the clothes she'd been wearing that day. It suddenly seems really important to me to know what she was wearing, what she looked like. I haven't even unpacked the bag yet; just dumped it inside the back door. I'm wary of waking my parents, though. I really don't want them to know I'm having trouble sleeping. I don't want to give them any reason to stay longer than they planned, as if maybe they might be able to help me.

Cautiously I open my bedroom door. Everything's quiet. I can hear steady, deep breathing from the room across the hall. They're sound. Carefully I tread on the stairs, avoiding the areas known to creak underfoot. I am driven now. This has become like a mission. I must know what she was wearing. The bag has been tied really tightly, was that me? I need to tear the plastic to open it and tipping it upside down, watch her things slide degradingly onto the floor. It feels so surreal. I can almost observe myself going through this scene in my life. A pink sweatshirt, yes, I remember it. Lifting it to my face, I allow its softness to flood me with memories. It takes on massive importance now, being the last garment to be worn by her, the last thing to cover her beautiful body. There are no other clothes, only a pair of trainers. Where is everything else? I feel annoyed that some things are so obviously missing. Could they be still at the hospital? If they are I know I will never go back to collect them. I'll never go back to that place as long as I live, the place where they tried and failed to keep my wife alive. What's missing anyway? Well jeans, she probably wore jeans ... and underwear, there's no underwear. Why would anyone want to keep a dead woman's clothes? With a jolt the penny drops. The rest of her stuff must have been in too bad a state. I don't

159

suppose they give you home blood-stained clothing, do they? I actually have no idea, but it seems a plausible explanation. Wrapping her sweatshirt around my shoulders, I lift a smaller paper bag from inside one of the trainers: jewellery. Carefully I lift out the gold chain she always wore. A chain given to her by me many years ago with a gold St Christopher pendant attached. The St Christopher, a gift from her brother Christophe when she moved over here with me. It was supposed to keep her safe from harm. How ironic that it survives her. I allow the chain to run through my fingers, then catching it in the other hand, repeat the process. It feels very calming, the repetition, therapeutic. I wonder is this an action similar to the incessant rocking back and forth which I witnessed many times in my Dad's wards. It is comforting in a strange kind of way. Emptying out the bag, I catch her wedding ring in my free hand. This is the final sign that it's all gone. She almost never wore her engagement ring, because it invariably got paint stuck in around the diamond and after two very expensive repair jobs, she decided it wasn't worth it. The wedding band, though, took whatever came its way and proved more resilient. Glancing at my own ring I wonder if I should still be wearing mine. Do you stop being married when your wife dies? Technically I suppose you do. Legally even. I don't feel unmarried though. I don't want to take it off. In fact if it wasn't so small I would wear Claudine's as well. That would be nice, to keep them side by side. I finger the smoothness of the gold, bring it to my lips. This is breaking my heart. Why am I doing it? I think it must be a desperate attempt to bring her close again. I miss her so much! I'm about to get up off the floor when the light catches something on the underside of the ring. Looks like tiny writing, an inscription. I don't remember us doing that. Holding it up to the light I can see more clearly and make out the words, "Forever, Sebastian." What? That doesn't make sense! Why would it say "Forever, Sebastian"? I blink a few times and hold the ring against the light again. I must be mistaken. The light or grief is playing tricks on my eyes. But no, there it is, plain as day, "Forever, Sebastian," glaring defiantly at me from the inside of my wife's wedding ring. The ring which signifies the endless love we share. My head is spinning. I make it to the toilet just in time to be sick, violently sick. I feel as if my insides are tearing apart.

My heart thunders within my chest; sweat and tears pore down my face. My feet pummel the pavements, disturbing the night's quiet. On I run, pushing past the physical ache in my muscles, forcing my lungs to gulp shallow breaths of freezing air despite the pain in my throat. I tell myself I'm going there to talk, just to talk. I need to find out what's going on. There have been too many questions lately and not enough answers. Tonight I need some answers. The streets are deserted. I haven't passed a single person since I left. No surprise I guess at this time of night. I should be asleep like the rest of the world right now. Instead I'm running through the streets like a madman. Part of me wonders where this burst of energy has come from. I thought my reserves had more or less run out and yet here I am notching up miles in an effort to get to the bottom of this. It occurs to me that by the time I reach his house I may have burnt up all my anger. I envisage myself collapsing in a useless pile of sweating limbs within his doorway. And then I feel it again, scorching in my heart, brimming up within my soul, screaming to get out: fury.

I don't know how long it's taken me to cross the city. It doesn't seem long, but I've never attempted it on foot before. Pausing for a few minutes, gasping in a vain attempt to regulate my breathing, I glance up at the darkened windows. They're all asleep. This is crazy. What do I hope to achieve here? I should be at home, trying to rest. I should be trying to sort myself out for tomorrow. I almost buckle; almost change my mind and then an image sweeps fleetingly across my mind. I see so clearly the inscription, those grotesque words daring me to accept or excuse them. My head is thumping, I can hardly think straight. Leaning the palm of my hand heavily on the buzzer I press hard, holding it down, listening to the constant noise resonating around the apartment above me. It seems to take ages, but I don't suppose it really is. My perception of time may be somewhat altered at present.

161

Eventually a tired voice answers, "Oui? Qui est-il?" He must revert to French when he's been sleeping. I never knew that. It seems I'm learning more and more about my oldest friend by the minute.

"You bastard," I hear my voice hiss.

Silence. I stand there for a few seconds wondering what he's going to do. Waiting out here is messing with my head. I feel impatient; I don't want to be kept waiting. Without warning I hear the familiar click of the door unlocking and a flat, even tone speaking through the intercom,

"Come in, Len".

I push open the door and am propelled up the stairs two at a time. It occurs to me momentarily how absurd this must look, like something out of a cartoon, but it all feels out of control now. In moments I'm at the top of the steps and staring at Sebastian. He's standing inside the open door still buttoning his jeans. Hatred fills my being. My mouth is dry from breathing so rapidly. I can feel the blood pumping through my whole body, pulses in my neck, my temples, my arms throbbing viciously. Every nerve ending has a heightened sensitivity. I am alert, ready, desperate. He looks me in the eye. I watch him stumble, fall backwards. I see his head crash off the doorframe, his body slide down the wall. Did I hit him? I don't think so, I'm sure I would feel better than this if I had. He looks even more pathetic lying there on the floor, like a wounded animal. There is nothing covering his top and I can see the outline of his muscular torso, see the precise spot just below his rib-cage where I want my boot to make contact, again and again and again: repeatedly, savagely, cruelly; harder and harder: as hard as I possibly can. There is no relief so I keep going. Tension continues building within me. My field of vision has become a blank. Around me, distantly I hear voices, screams. They are distracting and annoy me. They're increasing my agitation. Then one becoming clearer, louder than the rest, the voice of authority, commanding me to stop, "Enough."

The sound tears through my head shattering the compulsion. Gradually I become aware of myself, gasping for breath, soaking with sweat. My surroundings start to come into focus; a crowd of people, frightened, upset; one of them reaching out to me, gesturing me to enter. It's the boy. "Come in if you're going to talk, Len. Otherwise go home." I'm startled by the power in his tone. His ability to influence me is undeniable. Taking his hand I step over the miserable wretch lying still at my feet, curled in agony, holding his side. I resist the urge to wipe my feet on his face, but do stick a final boot in before following Luc inside. I am guided to a seat in the kitchen, the only room where no-one is sleeping, and pressure on my shoulders forces me to sit. Moments later I hear instructions being barked for everyone else to return to their beds, that this is a private matter. Luc re-enters the room, his arm around Sebastian who appears to need assistance walking. I smile in satisfaction as he lifts his beaten face to look at me.

# LUC

"Do you need something on that?"

He shakes his head, but from where I'm standing it looks pretty bad, so I run a cloth under the tap and press it against the wound on the side of his face. He winces with the pressure, but holds it anyway. Len looks on, taking it all in, saying nothing. I decide to take the lead, someone's got to.

"Right who's first?"

Nobody speaks; they're both sitting eyeing each other cautiously. Neither wants to make the first move, do anything which might leave them vulnerable to the other.

"Len, why are you here? What's this about?"

As if I didn't know! These things have a habit of resurfacing eventually. I'm surprised in a way that Sebastian has managed to keep it under wraps this long. He thinks for a bit. Sebastian's eyes never once move from Len's face. Then in a tone I don't recognise from Len he all but spits out, "I came here to find out what's been going on between this bastard and my wife...and also to let him know what I think of him."

Silence as he waits for Sebastian's response. There is nothing forthcoming from him at all. He's watching Len's every move pacing up and down the kitchen, but says nothing. I can see this is beginning to irritate Len and I wish he wouldn't do it.

"So then, how about some answers, Casanova?" Len's tension is starting to build again and I'm becoming concerned. Sebastian made no attempt to fight back earlier, more than that he didn't even try to defend himself. I guess that's why he's so badly hurt. It's almost as if he thought he deserved it. I hate to think what further damage Len could do if he got started again. Part of me wonders if Sebastian would actually let Len kill him if he set about it. Len continues, "How long's it been going on?" We both look to Sebastian for a reaction, anything. Still nothing. I need to do something, Len's gonna explode if Sebastian keeps this up.

"Sebastian?" I'm almost pleading, "Just tell him what you told me. Tell him it was a long time ago." I don't know if Sebastian would have taken my bait, but he doesn't get a chance. Len turns on me yelling at the top of his voice, "You're kidding me! You knew? You knew about this too?" I've made it worse. Shit!

"No... it's not like that." I'm digging myself...ourselves... deeper and deeper into this, but now I've started I'm compelled to continue. "No, Len. Well... we knew because we were there... It was before you... Sebastian *tell* him!" I'm mad with Sebastian too now, leaving me to muddle through like this.

"Well Sebastian?" Len has approached him and is now too close really for comfort. The two men stare at each other for what feels like an age. Len is waiting. Drawing a deep breath Sebastian finally speaks, "What is it that you want to know?"

"Bloody hell, Sebastian, what's the matter with you? I think it's clear I want to know if you were having an affair with my wife."

The answer comes quickly, decisively, "No."

I breathe a sigh of relief.

Len looks shocked. "Fucking liar!"

There is no further reaction from Sebastian, just the constant eye-contact that he has maintained throughout.

"What was he talking about then, about it being a long time ago?" Len's eyes dart from mine to Sebastian's and back as if he doesn't know who to trust.

As ever, Sebastian when he does speak chooses his words thoughtfully, "A long time ago... when we were kids... Claudine and I were... involved. Luc knows, the family knows, because there was no reason to hide it. We were in love. Everybody knew."

Okay, I'm glad that at last he's engaging with Len, but maybe he doesn't need to go into so much detail. There's no point in antagonising him is there?

"You mean it was all in the past, a thing from long ago? I don't believe you!" Len is really agitated. He can't sit down. His voice remains raised. I'm sure the whole house must be able to hear at least his side of things.

Sebastian, much more softly spoken is keeping himself under control. "What is it that you're asking me exactly?" he asks.

Len looks as if he's going to scream. Speaking slowly, loudly as if Sebastian is having trouble understanding him, "I'm asking you, Monsieur fucking Charpentier, if you were in love with my wife. It's a simple question, requiring only a simple answer."

Sebastian shifts in his seat, grimacing and holding his side as he does. "I loved her, yes…a long time ago." I'm pleased. He's said what I hoped he would. Now if we can just get rid of Len, maybe we'll all manage to survive this episode. Maybe it won't all seem this bad in the morning.

But Len, he won't let it be, he's pushing for more. This is dangerous. "And now?" The question is a demand really. It's a demand for the truth and he isn't going to be palmed off on this one. I look over at Sebastian and for the first time he averts his eyes from Len to return my gaze. I beseech him with my whole being to lie. Seconds pass. I become aware that I'm holding my breath waiting for his reply. Turning back to Len he hesitates before speaking. "Now…? Do I love her now…? Yes… I love her now… I never stopped loving her." My heart sinks. That was the wrong thing to say, most definitely.

Leaning over Sebastian so close their faces almost touch, Len hisses, "You'd better not show your bastard face tomorrow. Do you understand me? Keep away from her funeral! Keep away from me!" His parting shot lunges deep through smashed ribs. Striding out of the apartment, he leaves Sebastian clenching his teeth in agony.

## LEN

I sleep late, but feel as if I've only just put my head down. I hear the sounds of breakfast being prepared downstairs, television noises radiating up from the sitting room. My parents are up, hopefully oblivious to my late night excursion. Thinking back over it I groan audibly, sinking back amongst the pillows. I don't want to get up. I don't want to face this day. I honestly can't be sure that I'll make it. Where do you get the strength to bury your wife? The final goodbye looms and I dread it.

A pool of sunlight has gathered on the floor beside the bed and for some reason this makes me smile. It's a beautiful day. I'm glad. I want a beautiful day for her. Rising, showering, dressing: it's all automatic. My thoughts are empty, my feelings numb. Maybe I used them all up last night. Last night! Now that was quite something wasn't it? I don't know that I am much clearer about what was actually going on between them, but I feel a hell of a lot better knowing that I hurt him. It's a bit scary, all the same, to feel so completely out of control. I wonder how far I'd have gone if Luc hadn't stopped me. I wasn't caring about consequences. All I could think was Claudine and him. I try to push his battered image out of my mind. It's no more than he deserved. Anyone would have reacted in the same way. He put his hands up and took it! If you ask me he knew he had it coming, probably expected it. You don't mess with another man's wife and expect to get away with it. Everyone knows that. Anyway, what about me? My heart is broken. Claudine was the love of my life. I thought we were happy together. I loved her with all my being and I thought she felt the same.

I need to push these thoughts out of my head. How am I going to face this day if I doubt my darling wife? In my mind, Sebastian is unquestionably the villain of the piece. I haven't quite formalised how this fits with Claudine wearing that bloody ring, but that's as far as I've got. I desperately need to stop thinking. This is really, really bad.

# SEBASTIAN

I feel absolutely terrible. Everything I do is so much more difficult. The shower this morning was an experience I'll never forget. Excruciating pain in my side as the jets of water bounced off the open wound. I know it needs dressed. I suspect I have broken ribs also, but this is not the day for treatment. Every movement is painful. He did a pretty impressive job on me, I'll give him that. I can hardly blame him either. His wife and me, it must have come as a shock. I still don't know how he found out. It's funny because I've imagined so many times how Len would react if he knew Claudine and I had a past, but you know I never thought he would take it quite so badly. After all, there's been nothing between us for years. I hate to think what he would have done if Claudine had been unfaithful to him within their marriage. I thought at one point last night that he would keep going till he killed me. Surely anger like that doesn't come from discovering your wife had a relationship with your best friend before she even met you? It doesn't add up. He genuinely seemed to have the impression that there was still something going on. Maybe I should have done more to dispel that idea. I don't know. It was all so awful. Claudine's memory being dragged through the mud like that was unforgivable. She was not the person being depicted last night. I truly believe she would not have cheated on Len. Why can't he have more faith in her? I would not have doubted her had she been mine. Not for the first time I bristle as I consider how I would have cherished her, trusted her.

Wincing with pain I struggle to put my shirt on. I'm going to need some painkillers. Raking through the bathroom cabinet I find a cocktail of paracetamol and dihydrocodeine. I'm not even sure who they belong to, but I need something to take the edge off this. I wash a couple of both down with some water and resume dressing. This is taking me so long. I glance at the clock on the chest of drawers and feel relief that I woke so early. I say woke, but with less than an hour's sleep it sounds a bit exaggerated.

Turning to the mirror to start shaving I am startled to see the face staring back at me. I am a complete mess. I look like I haven't slept for weeks; the shadows under my eyes are unbelievable. The gash on my face does nothing to enhance my appearance either mind you. It must have been his watch or something. I'm sure he didn't have a knife. He wouldn't have had a knife! The beginnings of a black eye are also taking shape to complement the whole effect. I look bloody awful. Who cares? What difference does it make? I guess it's just kind of funny to be putting on my smartest clothes when my body and face are so wrecked. I'll do my best, that's all I can do. I'm going for Claudine after all, no one else. I'm going to mark my respect for all that she was. What was he thinking of warning me off turning up? Not go to the funeral? I'd rather die.

Stumbling through to the kitchen (that's the only word for it, I can hardly call it walking) I meet Luc heading the same way. "How're you feeling?" he asks "Did you sleep?" He sounds concerned. He's a good guy, setting himself apart last night to try to help us. I'm not sure that he managed, but I appreciate what he tried to do. I nod in reply because I don't know what to say. "You don't look too good," he continues.

"I've felt better," I reply, forcing a smile. In the kitchen he closes the door then turns and asks, "Can I have a look?" Shrugging my shoulders, I lift my shirt revealing the wound in all its horror. Shaking his head he repeats, "That doesn't look good, Sebastian. I think you need to see a doctor."

I gaze at him in surprise, "Today? Are you kidding? I'm going to your sister's funeral! I don't have time to hang around hospitals…Anyway it's not as bad as it looks." I start making coffee, select two mugs from the shelf, pour and offer one to Luc.

"What are you staring at?" I ask "I know I look like shit, but you don't need to go overboard."

"No, it's not that. I just…"

Impatiently I pressure him, "Just what?"

He's shaking his head again. "It's just I didn't think you'd be going. Not after last night…I'm surprised, that's all."

Ignoring the implications of his words I sip my coffee and wait for him to look at me. "I'm going, Luc. Nothing will stop me."

Nodding, he accepts what I'm saying, but I know he has reservations. Of course he does, he's young. Things are still simplistic to him. He doesn't understand the complexities of love. Maybe one day he will, but now I know he thinks I'm mad. I'm not afraid of Len. Of course I'm not. When you've lost everything then nothing can touch you can it? What I think they're both forgetting is how futile it is to threaten a man who's got nothing left to lose.

"Can I ask you something?" his voice interrupting my thoughts.

"Of course you can. What is it?" He seems nervous and I wonder what on earth he wants to know. I hope earnestly he doesn't want details about me and Claudine, because even thinking about her this morning is unbearable never mind going over the past.

"I just wondered…why did you tell him you still love her? I really think if you'd said it was all in the past then in time he would have come to terms with it. But now…well now he's going to feel a betrayal of your friendship, isn't he and how will you repair that?"

He's right of course. I could have lied. I know they both wanted me to. The correct answer to his question was that it was history. The trouble is they don't understand. I loved her so much, loved her with my whole heart. Nothing, nobody, has ever touched me in the same way. It's an emotion unparalleled in my experience. I couldn't deny my love for her, especially not now. Not now when I can offer her nothing else. I could no more deny her than I could live without breathing. It's as simple as that. She was the very essence of my life. She was everything I ever wanted. That's why I'll be at this funeral if it's the last thing I do. There's nothing else I can do for

Claudine. I have no way of making it up to her. All I can do is be there and do my best to survive it. I'd be surprised if Len didn't realise this himself. The boy is standing, still waiting for my reply,

"Why did I do it? Why did I tell him I still love her? Because it's true, Luc. It's the truth, that's why."

## LEN

I want to go on my own, so I tell my folks to leave without me. They're reluctant. I think maybe they wonder if I'll show up at all and that wouldn't be the done thing would it. I manage to convince them anyway and am left with the space I crave this morning. If I had my way it would be just me and Claudine. How much better that would be, just the two of us and I could say goodbye in my own time, without the inevitable rituals of death all around. Sighing, I pull the door shut behind me, the door to the home we shared. Today is about saying goodbye not only to Claudine the person, but also it's goodbye to the life we had, it's goodbye to me too, the person I was with Claudine. I'm no longer a husband, partner, lover. My most meaningful roles in life have vanished overnight. I am not the person I was, will never be again.

The day has turned out to be truly lovely. I feel the sun's warmth on my hair and back as I walk towards the chapel. The sky, deep blue, dotted here and there with clouds. I want to go back for Claudine. I want to show her what she's missing. My steps begin to slow as I near the entrance to the churchyard. I have a strategy for getting through today. Of course I have. What I'm going to do is just try not to think about her. I'm not going to allow myself to become absorbed in memories. I plan to shove them away each in turn. I've pushed down the shutters and no one is going to get anything out of me today. I will not break down. I will not allow emotion to take over. Perhaps later, in privacy, but not as a spectacle for everyone else's benefit. I want this to be respectful and dignified.

173

Turning in at the main gate, I find that I am not as prepared as I thought. The first indication that things may not go as planned. There are hoards of people streaming up the path before me, milling around outside and entering the side-entrance. So many people I can't take it in. All these people are here to pay their respects to Claudine! What was I expecting? I guess I had an idea that the family and a few friends would turn up, but not this. I feel suddenly very vulnerable. All eyes are going to be on me, the grieving widower and I don't know how I'm supposed to act! I continue up the path, but in my mind I have already turned and fled. I feel so uncomfortable. I'm sweating within this suit. My hands are shaking, so I force them down into my trouser pockets and urge my feet to keep moving, my legs to hold me up.

No one speaks as I reach the doorway and I'm so glad. A number of people nod in my direction or smile sympathetically, but no one speaks. So far so good, I think and climb the steps up and into the vestibule. I am met by the priest. He must have been standing here waiting for me. He shakes my hand, holds it a moment longer than necessary and assures me of his prayers. I nod, because I can't trust myself to say anything and because it seems to be acceptable not to talk. He leads me into the chapel itself, down the aisle past a sea of faces, many familiar, down to the front and indicates where I should sit. I am the husband. There will be no slinking in at the back and sneaking away early. I am here.

I feel very alone sitting up at the front like this. The rest of the church is packed tight and yet I sit here in a pew all by myself. Fidgeting with my fingers, I have a desperate need for a cigarette. I should have had one before I came in. I don't even think I brought any with me. How stupid was that! I start to look around the chapel and recognise people (are they called guests at a funeral?) sitting in groups. There's a group of colleagues from the University and scattered around them a large number of my students. For the first time I feel touched. There's no reason for them to have come. They didn't know Claudine, most of them. They've come to support me. A lump forms in my throat and I realise this is going to be even harder than I imagined. There are faces I don't recognise too and I guess these to be friends and associates of Claudine. I'm pleased for her. Pleased at this visual display of affection and regard for her precious life. Claudine's brothers are seated already across the aisle from me. They nod, affirming they've seen me arrive, as my eyes survey the scene taking place around me. Turning, I find both sets of parents immediately behind. Cecile reaches out, pats my arm. It's strange, I see her do it, but I can't feel the physical contact. There is no comfort received from the gesture at all.

It's really cold in here and I notice I'm shivering. The bright sunlight is banished behind the sanctuary walls. How appropriate I think. All of a sudden there is a burst of music and the choirboys fill the air with their haunting, angelic sound. My heart is stirred by the soulful strains of Ave Maria rising through this place, filling it. The familiar scent of incense also reaches me and it's all becoming much harder. I need to keep on top of this. I need to stay in control. It feels as if all my senses are reacting to the grief pouring out around me. I hear crying nearby and someone further away blowing their nose. You're alright I tell myself. You're alright.

People continue to come. They must be standing at the back by now; the place was already pretty full when I entered. I half-turn to get a better look and my eye catches sight of them, a little group of their own, huddled close together surrounded by strangers. It makes me feel lonelier than ever to see them; sitting in a row, Carly, Luc and Sebastian. They notice me, but there's no reaction from any of them. I'm pleased that Carly came. She did it for me, I think. And Luc, so young, so smart, Claudine would be proud of him. And Sebastian. All I can think is how terrible he looks. Stoned is how he looks.

I turn back to face the front. The priest has taken his place and stands beside the coffin. The coffin. It has been placed centre-stage so everyone can see it. Flowers are draped around and on top of it. In fact there are flowers everywhere. Every window ledge, every available surface it seems, has been decorated with tasteful white flowers. She would have liked that, I think. She loved flowers.

"We are gathered here today to give thanks for the life of Claudine Rousseau…" the words begin to blur as one. Keep it together, I think. Keep breathing.

Everyone stands and I realise that we're going to sing. I'm not used to the patterns of worship. I haven't been in a chapel for years, wasn't brought up with it and don't have the ingrained habits of a lifetime which Claudine's family could carry out in their sleep. We sit. We stand again. We pray. All of a sudden I can't take it any longer. I'm not even sure what triggers it. Was it the choir or something that was said? I don't know, but I feel as if a switch has just clicked in my head. I want to stand up and scream "That's Claudine in there. That's my darling wife. I love her. I love her so much I can't live without her. How am I expected to live without her?" The rituals of the mass begin and I reach my limit. I can't do it! I was wrong. I thought I could get through this, but I can't. I feel my balance go and reach out to hold onto the pew in front. My knees give way and I need to sit down. The choir resume their plaintive cry for mercy and I feel my emotions bubbling up to the surface. I try to push them back down again. I try to overcome the pain that is rising within me, pleading for escape. It's too hard. I have nothing left to fight with. Looking on the coffin all I can see is my beautiful, smiling Claudine stuffed into a box. I know she's there and after today there won't be anything left at all. No. No. No. My whole body shakes as tears flood down my face, pouring down as if they'll never stop. The grief has taken hold and I no longer control it. I feel someone sit down beside me, an arm around my shoulder. Instinctively I lean into it, sobbing within the refuge of love. Her warmth is soothing, her hand as it strokes my face comforting. I know without looking who it is. A son knows his mother's touch wherever he finds it.

# LUC

I wasn't sure who the girl was when she came up to us outside the chapel. Sebastian introduced her as Carly; I suspect he doesn't know her last name. She seemed awkward, shy perhaps, but nice. I'm not sure how she knew Claudine; we didn't talk much, just sort of got the formalities out of the way and came inside. The place was really full and we had trouble finding seats together. I've always hated the inside of a chapel. It feels so oppressive, suffocating almost. I remember as a small boy imagining it was the inside of a cave, dingy and cold. I created all sorts of adventures in my mind to while away the boredom of the Sunday morning tradition and as soon as I was old enough to realise I had a choice in the matter, didn't darken the doorway. Until now: funny how times of desperation take us back.

We struggle to fit in at the end of a row. I don't know most of these people, the family all seem to be nearer the front. I guess I should be too, but to move now would be difficult. Anyway, I came with Sebastian and he could hardly sit up there with us. Not now at any rate. My decision to accompany Sebastian was not one I took lightly and I think he was genuinely surprised when I suggested it. The way I see it, though, he hasn't really done anything wrong has he? I mean no man likes to hear that anyone else is interested in their wife, but the point is he never did anything about it. I feel quite sorry for him in a way. He blew his chance with Claudine and has been paying for it all these years. I doubt if that kicking last night achieved anything at all, except maybe to make Len feel a bit better. I don't think Sebastian deserved it, not to that extent anyway. Talking of which he must be in agony sitting squashed up against me like this. I try to shuffle slightly further down, but now I'm leaning too close to Carly and I don't want her to feel uncomfortable either.

Oh how I wish this was over. I'm doing everything I can not to think about what we're actually doing here. That's no disrespect to Claudine. I just know that if I let myself indulge in feeling the sorrow that's been looking over my shoulder these past few days, it might overwhelm me. I'm scared of the strength of my emotions, the depth of the pain. Pushing away these thoughts I concentrate hard on detaching myself. I refuse to look at the coffin. I mean I know it's there, of course I do; my eyes sought it out like heat-seeking missiles the moment we came in. I just won't acknowledge to myself what it is. Gazing around the chapel I search for something to focus on. I notice Len scanning the crowd. Is he looking for someone? Our eyes meet and for a second I'm embarrassed, because I know it looks like I've taken sides with Sebastian and it isn't really like that. Anyway, he turns away after a minute and the tension lifts.

I think I'm doing pretty well. Avoiding looking at people is helping. I'm aware of the inevitable outpouring of grief all around. I can hear the sound of sobbing, but because I can't put stricken faces to the sound I manage to remain detached. I'm wondering how much longer we have to endure this, but afraid to look at my watch in case anybody notices. My eyes keep straying towards my wrist though and it becomes like an irresistible itch. Eventually I draw my sleeve up a little, casually as I can, and allow my gaze to land on the watch-face. It tells me nothing because I've no idea how long a funeral lasts.

Something at the front attracts my attention, a scuffle of some kind, people getting up and moving. I see Len looking really bad and his mum (is that his mum?) going to him. Oh Len. How are you going to manage without her? Then suddenly my attention is completely diverted. The girl crushed into my right-hand side leans over, whispering, "I don't feel so good. I think I'll need to go." I'm not particularly observant, but looking down at her small, white face I think, "No, you don't look too good either." I'm wondering if she'll maybe last until this thing's over when she obviously decides that she won't and standing without warning shuffles out of the pew and heads on out to the back door. I can't let her go alone can I and so I quickly rise too and follow her out. As I reach the exit I'm aware of Sebastian close behind.

Once out in the safety of the churchyard he asks, "Are you alright?"

"I'm fine," I say "It's her that isn't," turning to indicate Carly slightly ahead of me up the walk.

Carly, by this time, is lying flat out on her face, her body twitching uncontrollably in the shadows. I panic. I've never seen anything like this before.

"What's wrong with her?" I shout.

Sebastian doesn't answer and I turn round to find him speaking on his phone, calling for an ambulance. He's really calm. The next thing he's crouched down beside her, wincing himself at the movement. She looks absolutely terrible. I'm worried that she might be dying on us. Please no! She's been sick and her poor little face is smeared with vomit. Her colour has changed to a blue-grey which seems like a pretty bad thing. The worst though is the sound of her breathing; hoarse, laboured, as if every breath might be her last. I can't take my eyes off her and yet stand rooted to the spot, unable to move.

After a bit, I don't know how long; it starts to subside, the shaking. It's still there a little bit, but the power has gone out of it. When eventually it stops I wonder if she is dead. Sebastian has his jacket off and is wiping her face and hair with it. The colour is slowly, ever so slowly, seeping back into her cheeks. She still doesn't look good, but at least she doesn't look dead anymore. He asks me for my jacket and somehow I manage to take it off, still without moving. He uses it as a blanket, tucks her up like a child in bed. I'm struck by the gentleness with which he treats her. She lies now sleeping.

"What happened?" I stammer, only too aware that I was no help at all. I know I'll be eternally grateful that Sebastian followed us out of the church. What if he hadn't?

"She's had a seizure of some kind," he says.

"Why? What causes that?" I'm totally shocked by the sight I've just witnessed.

"I don't know. Maybe she's taken something."

"You mean drugs?"

"Yeah, maybe. Well, I don't know. Anyway she's going to be okay. Ambulance is coming."

We can hear it in the distance, the siren growing louder by the second as it hurries to help us.

They park the van and jump out, immediately in control. They take over responsibility and start giving her oxygen, dig needles into her arm. Decisions are taken instantly, there's no discussion or wondering who'll do what. They come, they get on with it and before we know it she's in the back of the ambulance and they're asking us if we're alright.

"Now, which one of you gentlemen is going to accompany this young lady in her chariot?" We look at each other. I remain paralysed, incapacitated. Sebastian steps up and sits beside her now-still body lying strapped onto the makeshift bed.

"You look as if you could do with some treatment too." The paramedic indicates Sebastian's obvious pain as he clambers in. "We'll get you patched up once the girl's sorted, okay?" I listen as he radios the control centre that they're bringing her in and watch as the heavy doors clash closed.

"I'll come over as soon as I can," I shout to the retreating rear of the ambulance and stand helplessly by as it manoeuvres awkwardly around the chapel. Picking up speed the siren sounds again, heralding the urgency of its mission. I watch it disappear from sight, then turn and slowly take my place again at my sister's funeral mass.

# LEN

It's one of those situations where you're surrounded by people you know, yet feel completely alone. I'm no longer on the point of collapse, neither am I back in control though. I've managed to pull back from the brink, but in doing so have lost all sensation. I can carry out basic functions; I can make my body move around, shake hands, I've even managed to speak to some people, but inside I'm paralysed of feeling. I'm stone cold, flat, robotic even. I don't recognise myself.

I lost it in church, I know I did. I can't really remember what happened, but I must have let my grip slip for a moment, and everything came crashing down. The churchyard was not as bad. I'm surprised in a way. I'd envisaged that as being the worst part of this ordeal. I think, maybe by then, I had frozen everything out and was operating in detachment. Not for the first time I have the strange experience of watching my life unfold before my eyes, as if I were someone else looking on. I'm powerless in this role. I have no control over events or outcomes. All my interactions happen without will.

Somebody is keeping me stocked with cigarettes and whisky. Every time I look down I seem to have both in my hands. This is the bit where I'm supposed to be thanking people for their trouble, showing appreciation for their good wishes. I haven't done any of that. I'm completely self-absorbed. My tired spirit rattles around within an empty shell. I don't feel as if I have any life left in me.

A woman approaches me, hidden behind dark glasses and I am forced to acknowledge her, because I know she can't see me. "Helen," I whisper. My voice seems to have lost all strength, all character. She

181

takes my hands and I don't resist. I have no wish for her to touch me, but I also don't have the will to stop her. Fleetingly I wonder what all I could be made to do in this half-living, half-dead state in which I'm existing.

"Len, I'm so sorry."

I nod in the acceptable fashion.

"I... don't know what to say..."

I squeeze her hand and pull mine back. She stands there for a few seconds, waiting for her prompt to depart. I suppose, being blind, it's harder for her to pick up what everyone else can see, that I'm wrecked and acting inappropriately. I'm not working on social cues at all. She's making as if to leave when a voice from nowhere startles us both, "Did you know?"

Turning slowly back to face me she speaks, "Did I know what, Len?" Her reply is soft, hesitant. I can't say it. I can't seem to make my mouth open again to answer her. I stand there like an idiot, unable to formulate any kind of coherent thought, never mind articulate one.

"Did I know about...? Claudine and...Sebastian?"

I think I nod. How ridiculous is that, nodding a response to someone blind? It doesn't seem to matter. She turns and leaves, her unintentional answer revealing everything.

I wonder what happened to him. I saw him in the church with Luc and Carly. I didn't like that, seeing him with some kind of an alliance around him. I knew he would come. Of course he would come. Luc surprised me. He could easily have sat with the rest of the family, should really have. I wonder what he's thinking. Maybe he feels Sebastian has a case. Oh I don't have the energy for this anymore. I spot Luc in the distance, making his way through the crowd. I hope he isn't coming over to speak to me. I haven't really decided how to react. He is coming over.

"Len... Are you alright?"

What kind of a question is that? I know I'm being hard on the boy. Nobody knows what to say. Anyway, he's just lost his big sister, so I guess it's the same for him. I make eye contact and nod. I still don't really trust myself to speak. He embraces me in the way that

French people seem to do so easily, but I'm not quite comfortable with it. My guess is he senses this and pulls away to arm's length.

"Can I get you anything?"

I glance down at my still full glass and he mutters, embarrassed, "Oh I see you have one already."

No one lasts long in my company. It must be difficult for them when I'm so hard to reach. I see it all, but have no means of changing things. It's as if I'm trapped inside my body.

Then again, as suddenly as before, a thought transposes itself to speech and I find I have spoken, "Where is he then?"

A momentary look of bewilderment sweeps his face, before his expression settles into realisation. "Sebastian?"

What would happen I wonder if people weren't able to fill in the gaps for themselves? Would these interactions deteriorate into a game of charades as they tried to work out what the hell I mean?

"Yes," I manage, almost choking on the word.

"He was here earlier. I thought you saw him in chapel."

I nod to let him know that I did. I can't get over this inability to talk. I seem to have lost all my words. Strange isn't it? It's almost like grief hits you where you're most vulnerable. I work with words, I live with them and without them…I struggle to function.

"He went with Carly, before the burial."

For a second I'm puzzled. I didn't even know that he knew Carly. Oh yes that's right they met the other day, she was round my house. I feel uncomfortable with this. I need to try to make sense of it, but my mind, it won't work properly. I'm struggling and I wish Luc would spell it out, but he just stares back at me as if he's expecting a reaction of some kind. I try to think methodically. He left. Well that's good. I didn't want him here anyway. He left before the end, even better. It means he didn't stand around receiving condolences and so on. Maybe he was even showing me a bit of respect, clearing out so I didn't have to look at him. He left with Carly. Yes, that's the bit I don't like. Why leave with her? I know people react in different ways, but she's just a child. What age is she, nineteen… twenty? What does he think he's doing? I feel sick to the stomach. I wish I had looked out for Carly better. I didn't see this coming though, why would I? If I'm honest I didn't see any of it. I'm starting to wonder if I ever knew him at all.

## LUC

Things seem to be settling down a bit. People are beginning to move off in their own directions. It's all over as far as I'm concerned. I did it. I survived my sister's funeral - somehow. Suddenly I'm much more aware of my own mortality. I guess I never really thought about it before, but to find my sister dead at such a young age, well, anything's possible now isn't it? I go in search of my brothers. They're both travelling straight back to Paris this afternoon. Wives and families await them and I suppose they'll go back to work in the next few days too. Life will return to some sort of normality. It'll never really be the same though will it? Not now. A precious piece of our lives has died and we will never be the same again either. There's no big goodbye for Christophe and Dominic. I'll be seeing them both in a few days when I head home, so I just check they're okay and take my leave.

I'm quite keen to get over to the hospital. After all I told Sebastian I would follow on and that was a number of hours ago now. I truly hope the girl's alright. Surely she will be. There couldn't be another tragedy today! Life's not like that. She looked terrible though and I admit I was terrified watching her helpless body writhing uncontrollably; poor girl.

I hate hospitals. There's something about them that's quite chilling. I suppose it's to do with the reasons people come here. How someone can work in an environment like this is beyond me. Imagine coming to work each day wondering what state you're going to find your patients in when you get there. I feel uncomfortable the minute I walk through the automatic door. Vulnerable is how I feel, like I don't have a role here and I don't know how to act. Nurses bustle about all around me, no one takes any notice.

I've come to the casualty department because I guessed that's where the ambulance would have brought them. I've no idea where else within this metropolis to look. It's really busy, there are people everywhere and at first I don't see him. Mothers sit with crying infants on their knees. Children run riot around the waiting area. An old man lies across three seats, moaning. A woman approaches me, looks through me with such ease that I feel completely invisible. She must, in fact, see me because she asks me if I'm her husband. Managing to shrug her off, I wander aimlessly around searching for someone to ask about Sebastian and Carly. It's not possible to speak to a nurse or doctor. They don't seem to stand still long enough to be accosted with enquiries. There is a desk with a sign above it indicating a reception, but the queue in front of it trails around the room in a double loop. I don't join the end. Instead I decide to search myself.

A door at the far end of the room opens and I see Sebastian being escorted over to a seat. The nurse pauses to talk with him a moment. She laughs at something he says. Even from this distance I can tell she's flirting with him. It comes so easily to Sebastian. I honestly don't think he even tries, but women love him wherever he goes. Like now, look at him. His face is a mess with cuts and bruising. He doesn't appear to have slept in a long time. I would say he's a wreck right now and yet this nurse is clearly very taken with him.

It was always like that as I remember. Bagging Claudine was a coup in anybody's book, but it wasn't really a surprise to anyone that she fell for Sebastian. They made a good couple. I could only have been about five or six at the time, but I know I admired him, wanted to be like him when I grew up. I wonder for a moment at how differently it might all have worked out. I'll never understand why he ditched Claudine when he obviously still loved her. I wonder how he's managed to live with it all these years. Maybe he even feels relieved now it's all out in the open. He spots me and signals to me to come over. The young nurse takes her leave of him and scurries back through the revolving door as I approach.

"How's it going?" I ask him.

"Yeah, okay. The damage isn't too bad, couple of broken ribs, bit of internal bruising. Could be worse I guess."

"They've put some stitches in your face I see."

"Yes, they think it'll scar but who cares. Don't suppose Len's ever going to look at me again, so it'll be a pretty useless reminder won't it?"

"Did they ask you what happened to you?"

"I told them I walked into a door."

"What did they say?"

"Nothing much…they asked if I wanted to press charges."

"What about Carly?"

"Now she's another story. She was rushed right through this place. I don't know what's wrong, but it looked pretty bad. We need to find someone to tell us what's going on with her."

This place is a maze. We tramp the corridors searching for an enquiries desk. There must be somewhere for visitors to find out information, but it feels like we're going around in circles. Sebastian is quiet. A couple of times I've given him a sideways glance, but as ever he gives nothing away. I don't think I've seen much emotion from Sebastian in all the time I've known him, the only exception being last night at the funeral home. I guess that's why I was so unnerved then. Watching this very private person letting go, even briefly, felt like an intrusion: most of the time he remains a closed book.

I wonder how he feels having missed Claudine's funeral. I was grateful to him for allowing me to go back in, while he took his place with Carly. I needed to see that through. I've no doubt about that. For me, it was really important to say goodbye properly and to be with my brothers while doing so. There is something comforting in collective grief. Perhaps, though, Sebastian would have felt the same. He was a bit short-changed when it came to the funeral. In fact, thinking about it he's been short-changed throughout.

I wonder at him in a way. I mean, part of me really respects him, holding on to that love for so long, especially with no sign of reciprocal feelings. And then another part of me thinks how stupid. He could obviously have had his pick of girls wherever he went. That's true even today and yet he still held on to Claudine, still kept the place of honour for her. It makes you think that maybe they did have something going…and yet that's harsh. He's adamant that they weren't having an affair. I don't believe he would lie about it. He's seemed brutally honest about the whole thing in fact.

"You holding up okay?"

His words breaking through this last thought make me feel embarrassed. He's looking at me with concern in his eyes. I don't really know what to say. I mean I'm here and I'm walking and talking. I appear to have survived the funeral and yet I know nothing will be the same again.

We weren't particularly close, Claudine and I. The age-gap was I guess the main contributor to that. Mum lost a baby a few years after Claudine was born and it was many years later before she could face the thought of another. I really loved Claudine though. I was always very proud of her. I thought she was perfect. Of course, I know now she wasn't, but it doesn't mar my impression of her. She taught me so much, how to draw and paint, how to look at the world and really see it; things that I'll never forget my whole life. It's gonna be really weird having life carry on without her. Even in here, in the hospital I can't get my head round the fact that people seem to be going about their business as usual. Claudine's death, so huge for us, means absolutely nothing to any of them.

"Luc?" Oh, he's still waiting for an answer.

"Yeah, I'm okay. It's all just a bit hard to take in isn't it?"

We turn down a corridor and find it opening out into a broad expanse of foyer. This looks promising. Sure enough, a desk sits majestically in the middle of the floor. Above it a plastic sign dangles suspended from the ceiling indicating it's a place for INFORMATION. Sebastian gestures for me to take a seat. There are many lined neatly in rows around the circumference of the area. It's busy with patients and visitors and the noise level is irritating. I'd give anything for some peace and quiet right now, somewhere to think and try to sort my head out. I watch as Sebastian works his magic with the girl on reception. It occurs to me that I should have let him sit; he's clearly still in a considerable amount of pain. As usual he's adopted the big brother role with me though, and I'm so used to this I just go along with it. Anyway, he's doing a much better job getting that girl onside than I would have. I can't hear what they're saying, but the body language is clear. She's doing a lot of smiling and blushing. She drops her pen and appears a bit flustered. Then lifting the phone I know she's making a call on his behalf. Some guys just have it don't they?

## SEBASTIAN

How long are they going to leave us waiting out here? The girl down at the main entrance said they told her to send us up and someone would come and talk to us. I glance at my watch and am shocked to find it so late. I must have spent most of the day in this place. Luc is tired. Guiding him over to the obligatory plastic seats, he more or less falls into one. "You should go home," I tell him.

"And leave you here? No we'll wait and see how she is and then go together."

My own exhaustion prevents me from arguing. It's easier just to let it be; I desperately long to be home in bed, though. My body aches everywhere, weariness is crippling me and the painkillers they gave me down in casualty have long worn off, but I need to know about the girl. I was terrified back there at the chapel. I really thought she was going to die right in front of us. Poor Luc was on the verge of collapse himself. I don't suppose he's ever seen anyone have a seizure. The only time I did, it was a friend having a bad experience on ecstasy. He was okay though. I'm sure she will be too. Of course she will be. I just need to see it for myself before I go.

She seems a nice girl. I felt sorry for her arriving at the church on her own. I got the feeling she was pleased to see a face she recognised. I mean I realise she knows Len but he was no use to anyone today. I wonder how he's going to be. His pain was so visible, so raw. None of us will be the same after today, I'm sure of that. I wonder how or if we'll all fit together again. Will Len even speak to me? It may be that I've lost two important people today; the two most important people.

The door opens and a young nurse appears. "You're here about Carly Adams?"

We nod in tandem.

"Are you relatives?"

We shake our heads. Realising how foolish we must look I make an attempt at explanation, but it's hard and I'm tired. However long I've lived in this country I've always struggled to translate to English when I'm tired. It becomes a real effort. Right now it takes every ounce of energy I have left.

"Not family... no. I came here in the ambulance with her this morning. We were at a funeral." This last piece of information I realise to be irrelevant.

"You know we can't really give out information if you're not family." She's quite decisive in her speech, but I detect a gentleness in her voice and I suspect she could be won over. Do I have the strength though, that's the question? I could take the easy option and leave now. After all, we tried and we're being told we've no business here. And yet I don't want that last image of Carly lying so helpless, so frail in the back of the ambulance to come with me.

"I'd like to see her," I say "I don't like to leave without seeing her." She's swithering. "Please? Just a few minutes?"

She hesitates "It's not normal practice, but..." I watch her carefully, afraid to speak, to break her train of thought. She's almost there. I maintain eye contact, pleading.

"Okay, since you brought her in, but it isn't standard procedure. Don't expect to get in again. And just you. He can wait out here."

She leads me through a door which swings closed behind us. I follow trying not to look into the rows of open cubicles which we pass en route to Carly's room. We pass through a central area containing several beds, each one with a single nurse in attendance at the patient. It occurs to me for the first time what intensive care actually means. Really bad is what it means. Really bad and needing a nurse watching you all the time. We turn left into a short corridor and she ushers me into a side room. Another nurse is sitting on a stool at the far end of the room fiddling with some dials on a machine. Pages of notes are spread out on the counter in front of her. She glances up as I come in and nods in greeting.

A screen catches my eye almost as soon as I enter, numbers and patterns dance across in a haphazard pattern. The nurse checks the screen too, records her findings amongst the screeds of papers. "Try not to be too alarmed," she says, her voice soft and reassuring, "This is all to help me keep a close eye on her," a sweep of the hand indicating the many pieces of equipment around the room. In the centre of the floor is a trolley, I wouldn't call it a bed, and lying on top of it, Carly. At least I think it's Carly. There is very little resemblance to the girl I met this morning. As if reading my thoughts, the nurse again interjects, "Don't be put off by the machines. It's still her underneath it all." I look from Carly to her in amazement. This feels like something out of a science fiction movie. Put off? I am horrified by what I see.

"What's it all for?" I manage to stutter. I am absolutely out of my depth here. I don't know how to process all this, how to make sense of it. She stands and comes round to my side of the room, "Well, this here is something we are using to assist her with breathing," she points to a tube pushed into her mouth, taped onto her pale cheeks, which seems to be connected in some way to a machine behind her. I realise this is where the noise which fills the room is coming from; a rhythmic, regular whooshing sound. This machine is making her breathe. "It's called a ventilator". The named machine fills me with fear. Isn't that the thing which you hear about doctors switching off when there's no more they can do?

"Is that the same thing as a life-support machine?" I stammer.

"Yes …it is. She's a very sick girl right now. She needs this machine to help her to breathe." I nod to let her know I've understood, but truly I'm having difficulty taking it in. She looks so pale, so delicate lying there. Her hair is matted against her sweating face. Her eyes are closed. She's sleeping or sedated or something, but she looks like she's dead. If it wasn't for the artificial rise and fall of her chest in time with the whoosh from the ventilator she would be. This thought is too big for me. My head is spinning trying to make sense of it. The ventilator continues to pump life into her.

"I'm afraid you can't stay in here." The nurse is kind but insistent. Clearly this is not a place for visitors. They need to focus, to concentrate all their attention on the patients in front of them. I understand that.

"Is she going to be alright?" I'm terrified of her reply and yet I need to know. How can I go home with this picture of Carly in my head and not have asked the question.

"She's very ill, but we're doing everything we can for her," the non-committal reply.

"Is there anything *I* can do for her?" the words are out before I can stop them. How could there possibly be anything that I could do for her? Look at her. She's at death's door.

"Well, maybe there is." I'm startled at the unexpected reply, but grateful for the possibility of perhaps being able to turn these turbulent emotions into useful actions.

"We've been having difficulty contacting her next of kin, a Mr Shane Robertson. Do you happen to know him or how we might get in touch with him?" I shake my head and feel instantly the disappointment of being unable to offer her anything after all. I sense she recognises my need to be of some help as she tries again, "Well maybe you could bring her up a few things, you know nightclothes, toiletries etc. She could be here for a considerable length of time. Once we get her over this rocky patch that is." I nod again. I'm getting good at translating this medic-speak. What she means is that if she survives this, she's got a long haul ahead of her. "I'm going to have to ask you to leave, I'm afraid, Mr ...?"

"Charpentier... Sebastian Charpentier." She escorts me to the door.

"Can you find your way back out? I'm afraid I can't leave Carly here on her own."

I assure her that I can, thank her for letting me in, hope I haven't been a nuisance. She understands that I needed to see her, tells

193

me I can come back again if I want to, "She doesn't seem to have anyone much in her life. I've only ever known Shane to visit her and like I said we can't track him down right now."

I pause a moment in the doorway, "Are you saying you know Carly already? She's been here before?"

"Oh yes, Carly's been in before. Not quite in this state though. Listen, I'll make a note that you were here, that you visited so you'll be allowed in if you come back. Usually it's only relatives, but like I said she doesn't have anyone much…"

Stumbling out, back out to reality, I'm thinking how unlikely it is that I'll ever want to re-visit the horror that I've witnessed tonight in this place. I'm also thinking how much of what I've just seen do I want to share with Luc who's waiting patiently for me beyond these walls.

## LUC

Knocking on the door I suddenly have reservations. Maybe it's too early, maybe it's too soon. His mother answers and I sense she feels the same. She's polite, but firm. He's sleeping. It seems he had a terrible night, up and down, pacing the floor, unable to settle. Now that he's getting some rest, she's clearly reluctant to wake him. Fair enough. I'm taking my leave, apologising for disturbing them, when I hear his voice from somewhere inside wondering who it is. She looks annoyed, calls to him that I'm just going, that it's not important. He appears at the door before I get any further though.

"Luc! Come in."

I'm really embarrassed. His mother has made it perfectly clear this is a bad time. I kind of knew that myself as soon as I got here, but by then it was too late. The only thing is he seems genuinely pleased to see me. "Come in" he urges as I hesitate on the doorstep. He looks absolutely awful. I can see that he hasn't slept, that he's been crying. "How're you doing?" he asks and I don't know what to say so I kind of shrug. He leads me into the living room, while his mother heads for the kitchen. I hear the sounds of pans clattering, water running from beyond the closed door. He smiles, "Mom's spring cleaning." I nod as if it's a normal thing to be doing at this time on a Sunday morning. "You want a drink or something?" I shake my head. He's watching me patiently and it dawns on me that he has no idea why I'm here. The thing is he's not the only one who's exhausted. I did sleep last night, but not for nearly long enough. Sebastian was up and about at dawn. I guess he woke me and as soon as I ventured through to see what was going on he was desperate to share his great idea with me. I never got back to bed, although I did try to wait until a more sociable hour before actually coming over. I've no idea if he got any sleep at all or if he sat all night hatching this plan of his. He didn't say much when he came out from visiting Carly. He wasn't in there long, but I could tell he was shocked by whatever he'd seen. I gather that she's ill, really ill. Funny thing is he didn't ask them what was wrong with her. I think that's the first question I'd be asking if it was me in there. It makes me wonder if he's keeping things from me. He just said she was very ill and they were having trouble getting hold of this guy. Putting two and two together I reckon it must all be pretty bad if they're looking for relatives. They call the family in when things are bad, don't they? Sometimes it annoys me the way Sebastian tries to protect me from stuff. I know why he does and I know it's with the right motives and all that, but sometimes I wish he'd just be straight with me.

"Len, I'm really sorry to come over like this."

"It's good to see you, Luc. I'm glad you've come."

"Well, I know I'm disturbing you. Your mum said…"

He smiles again, "Never mind my mom. I said it's good to see you… By the way, thanks for coming yesterday… she'd have been really proud of you, you know… looking so smart, looking after Se…" He can't say it and I understand. "Anyway, how're you doing?" he begins again.

"Well the thing is I… we've… got kind of a problem and Seb…I…we thought maybe you could help."

He flinches slightly and I know he's disliking my alignment with Sebastian. I plough on, because I've started now and I feel I'm making a bit of a mess of it. Maybe if I can get to the point I might be able to explain myself better. "The thing is… Carly…you know the girl who was with us at the funeral?" He's staring at me, saying nothing. I go on. "Well, she's in intensive care and the hospital…they can't get hold of…" I stop because he's holding his hand up, urging me to halt. His eyes are narrowed; he's trying to make sense of this. I wish he would let me finish. I know what I've said so far doesn't make sense. He needs to let me get to the point.

196

"Wait a minute." He's got the wrong end of the stick. I know already before he says anything else. I feel so frustrated, but am forced to let him say his piece. "What has he done to her?" Now I'm confused. I have no idea what he's talking about.

"Who?"

"Sebastian." He more or less spits out the name. "What has Sebastian done to Carly? Has he hurt her? Has he done something?" I am speechless at the venom in his words. I can't believe what he's saying. Utter amazement sweeps right through me. This is Sebastian he's talking about; his friend. This is a man he's known for years, would have trusted with his life. He seems not to know him at all now. After what seems like an age, I manage to find some words to put together.

"No of course he hasn't!" I'm really indignant. I'm actually quite annoyed with Len for conjuring up this image of Sebastian which is so skewed it makes him barely recognisable. I'm aware of course that this makes it sound all the more like I've taken sides with him, but it's so unfair. "Len, Sebastian did a good thing. He took care of her when she had that… that seizure outside the chapel. He called an ambulance and went with her to hospital. He missed the funeral himself and I think we both know it was important to him to be there too. He spent half the night at that bloody hospital and even now he's trying to help the girl, which is why he sent me over here. Give him some credit!"

I'm shocked at myself. Len is staring at me and I think I've blown it. Shit. He's going to throw me out and this whole thing will have been a waste of time. I should have kept it together. I shouldn't have let him rile me like that. We stand in silence and I wonder if maybe I should just go. Yes I'll just go. I turn towards the door, but he stops me "Luc, I don't understand. I thought you said yesterday that Sebastian and Carly left together."

"Yeah, in the back of an ambulance… You didn't think…?" He looks at the floor. I wonder if it's occurred to him that maybe it's not the only thing he's got wrong.

197

"I'm sorry… I've been stupid… I guess I was quick to think the worst because of… well, you know…" I do. I decide to make the most of his apology though. Maybe he'll be more accommodating now.

"What we want to know is where she lives. We could maybe get hold of this guy for her. At least we would feel we hadn't just abandoned her up there." I hesitate before adding "You know she might not make it."

Len looks totally stricken. "She's that bad?"

I nod and wait to see if he's going to rouse himself to action or remain in this helpless state which so doesn't suit him. He doesn't let me down. "Give me ten minutes. Let me get washed. I know where she lives. I was over there the other day; down Haymarket way. Let's see…Morrison Street. I'll need to check the number. I have it on computer. Ten minutes… I'll be right with you." He disappears upstairs and I smile to myself thinking how quickly things turn full circle.


I told him I was happy to go myself, but I guess he was right, I probably would have struggled to find it on my own. I don't know this city well at all and although I was planning to pick up a map, it'll be much easier with Len. I got the impression he was kind of glad to have something to busy himself with anyway. He's worried about the girl, spoke very highly of her; clearly likes her. He said he's known her this past three years and she's undoubtedly the most gifted student he's ever had. "Do you know this boy they're so keen to get hold of?" I ask him as we walk. He thinks a minute "Not sure. The name rings a bell. She mentioned him the other day, but I don't think that's why. Shane? Yeah, I think maybe I taught him in first year; fairly unremarkable as I remember. She could do a lot better." I consider what he's said. It occurs to me as slightly odd that he's given this any thought. Why would he care who she sees? On the other hand, he does seem to have invested a great deal into this girl. Maybe that's the sign of a good Professor, one who actually cares about his students. At any rate he believes her to have a great future ahead of her. At this moment I'm wondering if she has any future at all.

# SEBASTIAN

I think I might leave town for a bit. Not for any particular reason other than I can't think of any to stay. I don't think I'm running away. Would it be such a bad thing if I was? I just don't feel there's anything here for me now. I know that begs the question was she the only thing that kept me here? The strange thing is I wouldn't have said so until now. I honestly didn't realise that she was the only reason I stayed. I considered a couple of times before, heading back home, leaving it all behind, but I always managed to come up with several excuses to put it off. Now, it feels like all meaning has gone. It used to be that the restaurant held some importance for me and the apartment, I loved this apartment. Helen was a hold for a while, although at some point, I don't even know when, I just stopped caring. And of course, Len is here. Only now he can't bear to be in the same room as me. Little by little it's all slipped away. Oh Claudine, were you the meaning behind it all? Were you the meaning behind me? It's just that now with you gone; I can't find a reason to get up in the morning. I still love you so much. Even now, with all hope finally lost, I can't let go of you. It's going to send me crazy. I know it is. I can't live like this, I can't live without you. I didn't sleep much last night. When I eventually got to bed I realised I had hardly begun to say goodbye when I left the funeral yesterday. You're so real to me when I lie in the darkness. It's then that I feel closest to you. This is madness. Claudine is dead and I'm talking like she's still attainable. I wonder if years of acceptance of living without you have made it more difficult to recognise that this time it's different. I keep hoping to wake up, to find

200

it's one of those terrible dreams where you leave me, but really you're not far away. Did I live in hope that we would one day be together again? Absolutely! How else could I live watching you so close but so out of reach? Don't get me wrong, I wasn't about to move in on my best friend's wife, and this is where he doesn't understand. I don't blame him, I'm not sure I understand either. But I do know I wasn't planning to steal his wife from him. I don't know what I was waiting for, but yes I did feel that we would have our day, one day. Now I need to find something else to live for and I don't think I'm going to find it here.

# LEN

"Is this definitely the right place?" Luc sounds annoyed.

"Of course it's the right place. I was here only a couple of days ago!" What does he think that I've traipsed all this way across town with him and I wasn't sure where we were going? It's hardly my fault there's no answer. Maybe Shane's gone home for a while. Lots of the students haven't returned to campus yet. If that's the case we'll never track him down. He's registered as living here with her on our university records, but with students that doesn't always mean much. I do think it's slightly strange that he's down as her next of kin. They're not married. Maybe she's had some kind of fall-out with her family. This whole thing is a bit weird actually. I mean the way we're kind of getting ourselves involved in something that doesn't really concern us. I feel if anyone should be looking out for Carly it should be me. Sebastian met her once. Once! And even then it was by accident, she was actually round my house at the time. He just happened to drop by. I'm aware that I sound like a jealous schoolboy, but I can't help it. I don't want him anywhere near any part of my life and I consider Carly to be part of my life. At any rate she's more a part of mine than she is theirs. Which brings me to Luc. I like Luc. I've always liked him. But what's this all about? He's making it crystal clear whose side he's on and I can't imagine why. I guess in a way I'm disappointed in him. I don't think Sebastian deserves the chance Luc's giving him. Do they not realise how much it hurts?

So here we are, me and Sebastian's new best mate, searching for the elusive boyfriend… for what? Is this an attempt at easing

Sebastian's conscience? I sound so hard-hearted. Of course I *care* about Carly, it's just I think my emotions are so messed up I don't really know how to *feel* anymore. Everything I do feel is so bloody painful. It's actually easier to put up barriers and try to keep the feelings away. "Okay, there's no-one home. Let's go."

Luc is more hesitant, "Should we leave a note or something?"

Sometimes I'm amazed at the naivety around me. "And what exactly would we say? Please get in touch, Carly's in intensive care? Give me a break Luc. Let's just go. You can't save the world single-handed you know." Why am I being so hard on him? Probably if I'm honest it all comes down to his teaming up with Sebastian. I'm shocked at my reaction. I'm so self-absorbed right now I can only see how everything affects me. And everything does seem to affect me. I know I'm putting the blame for my hurt firmly at Sebastian's door. I haven't begun to consider Claudine's part in it all. I can't. Not yet. I feel like I'm trying to protect her. I don't want to uncover any dark secrets, any hidden past. I just want to preserve what we had. What I thought we had.

I start back down the stairs, sure that if I just set off, Luc will follow me. I'm only a few steps down when I hear voices rising up through the stairwell. A loud bang and the main door is well and truly closed. Laughter, giggling resonates around the close. Rounding a bend in the stairs I come face to face with the boy in question. He glances at me without recognition and turns back to the girl whose arms are draped around his neck.

"Well if it isn't the mysterious Mr Robertson?"

He looks at me, a puzzled expression on his face. "Oh it's you. I didn't realise who it was at first. What are you doing here? Are you looking for Carly?"

"No, as it happens I'm looking for you."

Reaching the door, he fumbles with his keys, a task made more difficult because of the appendage he still has wrapped all round him. He drops the bunch of keys on the floor. Reaching down I scoop them up and suggest, "Shall I?" He nods and I turn the key in the lock and holding it open wait for them to enter. Flicking lights on in every room, he sets to work quickly. Pulling out a holdall and a large rucksack from under a bed, he begins systematically dragging clothes out of drawers and stuffing them in. Into the bathroom and he empties the contents of a cabinet into the bag without a thought. After a couple of minutes he turns to me, "She doesn't seem to be in. Looks like you've had a wasted trip. Keep the keys; you can give them to her when you see her." And with that they start to leave. I catch Luc's eye and he's shaking his head. Before I can say a word, he's stepped up.

"Just a minute… Before you go, I think maybe you might want to know where Carly is."

Shane looks from Luc to me. "What is this, some kind of double-act? Can't you see I'm busy? I don't really want to know where Carly is. I'm actually at this very moment leaving her, in case it's escaped your attention. So if you don't mind, au revoir."

Luc isn't having it. Moving in front of them, he blocks their passage, forces them to listen to him. "She's in hospital. She's very ill. They asked us to contact you." Shane glances at his watch and I see the irritation sweep across Luc's normally placid face. "You don't bloody care do you?" Shane smirks, perhaps for the benefit of the girl in his arms who's soaking up his every move. At any rate, it's the wrong thing to do, because Luc's becoming more and more furious. "Why don't you do the right thing and get down to that hospital and see for yourself? You may not get another chance." He's working really hard at controlling himself. I decide to leave him to it. I'm impressed. He's dealing with this idiot better than I could myself.

I step past them and head on through the flat. What things will she need? Reaching the bedroom I suddenly feel that I'm invading her privacy. The other day when I was round I didn't even see in this room and yet here I am stamping around as if I've every right. It feels really inappropriate and I'm about to go and ask Shane to do it when I hear their voices, raised in the next room.

"What kind of a guy leaves his girlfriend when she's lying sick in a hospital bed?"

Shane isn't taking it though. "And who do you think you are coming in here telling me what I should and shouldn't be doing?"

I'd better just get on with it. Shane isn't going to budge, I can see that. Maybe Luc should save his breath. He seems to have taken Carly on, though, and isn't making this easy for Shane. I smile. I so recognise myself in the boy. I would have been the same at his age. Righteous anger is a strong emotion. Opening the wardrobe I find a small travel-bag. I put it on the floor beside me and start opening drawers. Carefully my fingers push clothes aside, selecting nightclothes. I don't want her to think I was raking through her stuff. What else should I put in? Underwear? This is actually a bit embarrassing. I feel I shouldn't be doing this and standing straight, once again decide to call on the services of Shane. Once again the tone of the ever more heated conversation, if you could call it that, prevents me. Taking a deep breath, I gingerly lift out some underwear, trying not to look too closely at it as I do. Turning to lift the bag, I must brush against the chest of drawers and a bundle of papers scatter at my feet. It occurs to me as I bend to pick them up that maybe she would want some reading material too. I gather what I suppose to be lecture notes; well she's a student isn't she? They'll all be out of order, but she can fix that herself. Stacking them carefully back on top of the drawers, my eye is drawn to a name on the front page. I wasn't trying to look at them, I honestly wasn't, but what I read there sends a shiver down my spine. In black and white typeface, the name James Harris stares boldly back at me. I can hardly believe my eyes. A name unknown to me until a few days ago has now turned up twice without explanation. How does Carly know this man? How did this man know Claudine? I feel myself begin to sink again; deep, deep into the darkness of despair. I lift the letter with the intention, I admit it, of reading every word. It's as if I think it might shed some light on the unanswered questions which Claudine has left behind. Before I have a chance, though, I am interrupted by Luc entering the room. "Can you believe that guy? He's gone without a care in the world! Even had the audacity to ask me to pass on his apologies to Carly!" I fold the paper in half and add it to the bag. As an afterthought I lift the remaining papers and put them in also "Have you got everything?" he asks. I reply that I think so and lead the way out into the sitting room.

205

"Wow!" he lets out a low whistle "Is this her stuff?" He's gazing at her paintings, clearly impressed.

"Are they that good Luc?"

He turns to me, genuine surprise on his face: "Surely even you can see that they're good. They're brilliant!"

I knew she was gifted in literature, but I had no idea she was a talented artist also. Claudine would have been proud of her. I blanch at this thought. Claudine and I shared Carly in common and never even knew it. If Luc is this excited about her work, then Claudine would have been too. I desperately try to remember if she ever mentioned a student who might have been Carly, but if she did, I don't.

"Hey, look at this." Luc's words interrupt my train of thought and jolt me back to the present. I wander over to the row of books which have attracted his attention "Professor Lennon Thomas! Is that you?"

"Well, however many other Professor Lennon Thomas's do you know?"

"Did you write all these books, Len? One, two, three?" he counts along the row.

"Actually there's a fourth. She mustn't have it; must speak to her about that!" He smiles back at me and for a moment things are okay. We're standing here in this ridiculous situation and we're managing to laugh. I feel able to breathe for the first time in days. "I never knew you had written books," he says, lifting a volume down from the shelf. "Lennon Thomas," he reads aloud. "The world-renowned authority on Modern American Poetry…"

"So you thought I was just some two-bit teacher did you?" The moment I've uttered the words I wish I could take them back. "I didn't mean…" He pushes the book back onto the shelf in amongst the others. The moment's gone. He's hurt and trying not to show it. "Luc it was a joke." I never meant to put Luc down. I know teaching high-school art is not an easy option and I know how proud Claudine was of him. I shouldn't have said that. How patronising of me. I just don't seem to be able to choose the right words anymore.

206

The road home is quiet. We're both absorbed in our own thoughts. This seems to be what it's like now: a few minutes of reprieve from the pain and you pay for it big-style afterwards. It almost feels worse to have momentarily taken my eye off my grief to then have it come crashing down around me again. He comes in with me and I'm glad. My mother and father have gone to visit friends up north for a few days and although I was desperate for them to go, I don't really want to be left alone right now. I'm in the kitchen making a drink and Luc's flicking the channels searching for some soccer when the doorbell goes. "Want me to get that?" he calls and I hear him making his way to the front door. Low voices in the hall, I can't make them out. Wandering through to the living room I see Luc heading back through and following him, Sebastian. It's so hard to explain how this makes me feel. Seeing him, it's like a switch inside me flicks on, filling me with anger, rising steadily, steadily. I know that once full I will explode. I can't help it. I can't control it. This feeling, it's so much bigger than me, it's all-consuming. I hate him. Before I can say a word, he's holding his hand up as if to stop me. I find this action massively annoying. Who does he think he is marching in to my house like this? I wish Luc hadn't let him in. But Luc, ever the peacemaker, he doesn't understand that some damage is permanent. This isn't something that can be fixed.

"Len," his voice is soft, appealing to me. "I want to talk, just talk, that's all. I didn't come here to fight, but…"

I interrupt "Well that was a mistake then wasn't it, because fight is what we'll end up doing. I don't want to talk to you. I don't have anything to say." This is true. I'm having such difficulty with words right now that speech is really hard for me, expressing myself properly almost impossible.

"Okay Len, then don't you talk. Just listen. Let me talk. I'm going to go away. I'm going home, but I wanted to speak to you first. I wanted to explain some things." In my heart of hearts I realise this must be hugely difficult for Sebastian, but it hurts so much to look at him. All I can see is Claudine gazing into those piercing blue eyes and it's killing me. I turn my back on him, walk into the kitchen.

Luc mutters something and I hear them making for the door. In a second I reach it, breaking point. I don't even know what triggered it this time, but I'm there and once again there's no going back. I shout to him to come back and he does. He stands there so calm, so controlled, so every bloody thing that I'm not. Is that what she liked about him, that he was all the things that I never was? "I've got something of yours." I toss the ring into the air and watch as it tumbles in slow-motion. I see him catch it, the bewilderment on his face as he looks from the ring to me and back to the ring again.

"What's this?" and the audacity of the question makes me want to strangle him. Who is this show of innocence for, I wonder. Surely he realises we're not buying it.

"It's the ring you gave Claudine. Surely you remember giving her a ring?" I ask sarcastically "I would have thought you would remember giving another man's wife a wedding ring! What was it, a small token of your appreciation?"

He looks angry now, but he takes a deep breath and keeps his cool. For a moment I think I could get some pleasure out of making him mad, forcing him to react. I'd love to see him lose it the way he's made me recently. Everyone has their limit, I know that and if I pushed the right buttons Mr Cool would rise to the bait. That could be quite satisfying. And then without warning, the energy deserts me and I lose all will for anything. I want him to go now. I don't want to have to look at him anymore.

"Where did you get this?" His voice is almost a whisper.

How dare he ask anything of me? He should be out of here by now. I need to finish it. I need to make him go and never come back.

"Where did I find it? My darling wife was wearing it, as if you didn't know. Did you really think I wouldn't find out?" I turn to Luc who is staring at the pair of us clearly confused "Yes Luc, Claudine, my wife who I loved with all my heart was wearing this ring in place of her wedding ring. The ring which this bastard gave her, inscribed with his love. And he tells me there was nothing going on! And he thinks he can come round here and talk!"

Sebastian is speechless. I know I've got the upper hand at last, but it doesn't make me feel any better.

"Take the ring Sebastian. Take it and fuck off out of my life. I don't want to see you again." I'm pointing to the door. He looks at me and then at Luc and finally, oh finally he is gone. Standing in silence my feelings so knocked about, I hardly know who I am anymore. I loved her. That's all I can think. I loved her, I loved her, *I* loved her. My legs can't hold me up any more. Falling to my knees I feel as if my heart will break. My whole world cracks and splinters, bits fall off all over the place. There is nothing left to say, nothing left to do. There is nothing left.

# SEBASTIAN

Travelling by plane is always a very calming experience for me. I guess there's something soothing about being caught in-between places. I like the whole concept of leaving somewhere and not quite being at the destination. It feels as if time has stopped, as if there is no future or past and existence is entirely for the moment. How I wish it could stay like this; to be unable to look back and for it to be unnecessary to look forward. That would be my ideal state. Glancing out of the window, candyfloss clouds decorate an unblemished sky. It's always amazed me how deceiving the soft, fluffy appearance of these clouds can be. The turbulence through which we're presently travelling is testament to this. All too soon this plane will land and I'll be wrenched back to reality. I'm going home.

# LUC

I feel really worried about leaving Len alone today. Yesterday was so bad. After Sebastian left, he just crumbled before my eyes. To be honest I don't think I was really taking in what was going on; not at first anyway. Things had seemed okay. Len and I were talking when we were over at Carly's place and even had a bit of a laugh at her stupid boyfriend when he appeared. Then when Sebastian showed up the whole atmosphere changed. Len's obviously struggling with the idea of Claudine and Sebastian having a past and I don't suppose this is helped much by Sebastian's admission of still carrying a torch for her. And yet by anyone's standards his reaction was so over the top. I felt quite proud of Sebastian coming over on his way to the airport. He didn't have to do that. He could have taken the easy option and just cleared out, but he really seemed to want to sort things with Len first. I believe he truly values their friendship and is having trouble accepting that Len doesn't want to know anymore. Then this ring appears and an already difficult situation becomes really messy. From what I could gather, it appears that Sebastian had given Claudine a wedding ring and she was wearing it when she died! Wow! I can see Len's issues a bit more clearly now. What I can't get my head round is the fact that Sebastian swears he wasn't involved with Claudine. He categorically said they had separated after Helen's accident and that had been the end. That was years ago! Anyway it's caused a lot of damage.

Sebastian asked me to fly back with him, but to be honest I think Len needs keeping an eye on at the moment. His folks are away and I didn't want to leave him on his own. I think he felt it a bit himself. He even let me stay with him last night; I don't think he wanted to be on his own. This morning I left him sleeping. I heard him wandering around throughout the night, talking to himself and crying. It's quite scary to see such a strong person fragmenting like this. I wonder how he's going to pull it together. He has to, he just has to.

And then of course there's Carly. What with Sebastian taking off and Len so out of it the only person left to do anything for her is me. I'm beginning to feel like a bit of a saint carrying out all these good deeds. I don't really mind, though. Carly seemed like a nice girl that day when we met. The fact that she was also very easy on the eye doesn't do any harm either. I'd like to see her okay, so I'm happy to take her stuff up to the hospital. And now that I know the boyfriend is out of the picture it could maybe be quite interesting. I must admit I still hate the whole feel of this place. Having been here just a few nights ago does nothing to dispel the anxiety which starts building up in me as I approach the ITU entrance.

"Are you family?" The inquisition starts all over again. I shake my head. "Well then I'm sorry but we can't allow you access. Hospital policy." How I despise policy for policy's sake.

"Why can't you make an exception? It's not as if she's being pestered by droves of visitors is it?"

Apparently that's not the point. And what precisely is the point? Well, it seems to be that someone has bothered to make up this rule and if they start breaking it for some people then where will it stop? Where indeed? Reluctantly I hand over the bag of clothes and wait as instructed while the nurse disappears behind the hallowed doors. I stand for a couple of minutes thinking they must be discussing it and she'll surely come back and let me in. I wonder how Sebastian would have handled this. One thing I'm pretty sure of is that he would be getting access by now. Where do I go wrong? She reappears, but instead of holding the door open for me to enter, maybe apologising a little, she simply hands over a white plastic bag and heads back into

212

the ward. Washing! She's giving me the washing to do! Great! Trudging dejectedly out of the hospital I realise that if Shane were to show up in the middle of the night he would be welcomed in to visit. Sebastian managed to wangle his way in the other evening. And now even when there's only me left, I still can't convince them to let me in! It's just great isn't it? The only good thing being that if I do this washing then I'll need to take it back, so maybe I'll have more luck tomorrow. This thought cheers me a little and I stride a bit more chirpily towards the bus-stop.

# SEBASTIAN

Isn't it strange? Now that I'm back here I'm not sure why I came. Am I running away? Maybe. Yes, maybe. I guess I thought getting out of town, away from Len and all the memories associated with our lives in Edinburgh might help to distance my feelings from Claudine. It was important for me to put some space between me and Len anyway. I'm not at all sure how to handle all that's been going on with us recently. I'm well aware he can't stand the sight of me, can't even look at me. I tried to talk to him before I left. I wanted to put things right if I could. I hate all this. Len and I have been friends for so long. We've been through so much, good times mostly, but some hard times too. It hurts to have him push me away like this and yet I understand. Of course I understand. I suppose that's part of the problem. I understand so well because I loved her too. I know what it feels like to be so jealous you think your head will explode and your heart break. He realises this too and that's exactly why he can't share his grief with me. He can't share her memory, just like he could never have shared her. The thing is neither could I!

Arriving home feels good. It always does. I miss living here where I grew up. Life in Edinburgh has been so different from the life I imagined I would live. I feel we made a fairly good go of it, Helen and me. I don't think anyone could say I didn't try to make things work. I left everything to settle over there. It's just that now it's all different. There isn't enough to hold me there now. I know that this sounds as if Claudine was the real reason I stayed put and now without her I'm gone. I don't know if that's true or not. It sounds too simple for what was a very complex situation, but maybe it's the truth. I honestly couldn't say for sure. What I do know is that coming home to escape memories of Claudine would be a huge mistake. I have more memories of her here than anywhere else. This was our world. This is where we were together, openly in love. There will be no ghosts put to rest here. So is this why I've returned? Is it because here I can allow myself the luxury of reminiscing without fear of being misunderstood? Again, maybe! I can't be sure of anything, it seems. I'm having difficulty thinking straight, getting my head round it all. I still can't believe she's gone. Maybe I came back to prove to myself she's not still here.

Paris is beautiful on a spring morning like this. Is it spring? I guess technically it isn't. Too early still, but the air is warm and the sun high and the feel of the place is like spring. I get off the bus a couple of stops early so I can take a walk through the park. I feel myself unwinding surrounded by the familiar beauty. This is what I need; time to think. I need time to bask in our memories, time to miss her.

I find a bench close to the pond where I have an unobstructed view of a family of ducks tracing their way effortlessly across the water. Such sights are gentle on the mind. I wonder if maybe there could be some healing to be found eventually in this place. I can't sit here though. My side is aching with a gnawing, unforgiving pain and sitting in one position for too long seems to aggravate it. Rising to my feet, I stumble slightly and wonder if I give the appearance of being the wreck which I feel. Running my fingers down my cheek I realise he's given me a permanent reminder of the pain I've caused him. It seems fitting.

Instinctively I lift some pebbles, feel their smoothness in my palm, skim them one by one across the pond. I'm taken back to childhood days. Carefree days when the world was spread out before us, waiting to be grasped, savoured. Has it all been a waste? Has it all been for nothing? I misdirect a stone and the ducks, startled, take flight in a frightened frenzy. I watch the ripples caused by their disturbance pool wider and wider, creating eventually a wave-effect which spreads over the full surface of the water. Reaching the edge, the wave laps softly at my feet and I think, "I did that."

I take the long route home, the same road we used to walk back from school along L'Avenue des Arbres and am struck with a real deep sense of sadness. Where did all those years go? What happened to all that time we thought we had stretching out in front of us? We were going to do everything. It was all there for the taking. Not for the first time, I am hit with the feeling that maybe life's chances are offered only once, dangled temptingly before us, waiting to be grasped. If you hesitate, take a little time to be sure, maybe you make the right choice. Then again, maybe you miss out altogether. What's sure is you never get it back, not the same anyway.

I stop at the bakery on the corner. I've been coming here all my life. I remember Papa carrying me on his shoulders to collect the morning baguettes. I must have been only three or four. I remember the smell of soap wafting round me as I hunched around his head, knees squeezed tightly together, holding on for dear life. The funny thing is, although I was scared, I knew he would never drop me; knew with a certainty that I haven't had about anything else since. I buy some patisserie for my sister and continue round to the last bend in the street. My steps slow as I approach. I know that as soon as I'm on the cusp of the turn in the road, I'll be able to see my house. I anticipate it with a craving that unsettles me. I desperately want the reassurance of that predictable scene. In a moment it's upon me and my heart soars and aches at the same time. Home. I long for my home, my mother, my father. I know they won't be rushing out to meet me on the veranda, hugging me as if I were the fulfilment of all their hopes. Maman and Papa are gone and this place of unparalleled happiness has become a painful reminder of how empty life has become.

This bag is really heavy and my shoulders hurt under the weight. Maybe the long walk home wasn't such a great idea. My house is in full view now. It could do with a bit of a tidy-up I think, noticing the flaking paintwork around the windows, the garden overgrown with bushes and wild roses. It was never like this when my father was alive. Maybe I can do some stuff while I'm here.

And now the hard bit. Passing Claudine's house my eyes wander, against my will, all over the front garden, up the walls, seeking a face at a window. This was the place of so many firsts. The first time we held hands we sat on that rickety swing-seat on the front porch. I still remember the softness of her fingers, the lightness of her touch. I thought I was in heaven. Maybe this wasn't such a good plan. Immersing myself in the past can't be productive can it? And yet the pull is so strong. I force my feet to keep moving. It takes all my conscious will to move forward and turn in at my own gate, up the path. Finally, it seems I reach the front door. I am drenched with sweat, breathing far too quickly. Before I get a chance to gather myself, the door opens and Monique throws herself upon me. Disentangling herself she steps back to look at me and the shock sweeping her face is all too apparent.

"That bad then?" I attempt a smile.

"Sad." That's all she says, nodding to herself as if it's an acceptable state to be in. Standing aside I am ushered in. Home at last.

## LUC

This has become a familiar path over the past two weeks. I'm sure I could find my way up to the hospital blindfolded now. I'm a bit puzzled as to how I got into all this. Before Claudine's funeral I had never met the girl, hadn't even clapped eyes on her. Now I appear to have somehow become Carly's significant other. Responsibility seems to have inadvertently fallen to me on account of there being no-one else. That asshole Shane has yet to make an appearance and judging by his attitude the other night I wouldn't hold my breath. The odd thing is I don't mind taking on this role. I don't mind at all. If anything I feel pleased to have been given it. I want to help her, do stuff for her. More than anything I want to see her again. I haven't been able to get her out of my mind since she left in the back of that ambulance. She looked so small and lifeless. I was willing her to live with everything I had. Now I know she's much better. They told me yesterday she would be transferred to a ward today and then I'd be able to get in to visit. I feel like a child I'm so looking forward to seeing her. I have the customary bag of washing with me and I've also brought her a book this time; A History of Art Revisited. I hope she likes it.

I'm starting to feel a bit nervous the nearer I get. What if she doesn't want to see me? What if she doesn't even remember me? I have to ask myself why it would matter so much to me if that was the reaction I was greeted with. Sure I fancy her a bit. Who wouldn't? It's more than that though; a whole lot more. I guess I feel kind of connected to her. Whatever it is, I do know I want to see her again.

They told me she'd be in ward twenty-one by this afternoon. It was becoming quite amusing, the daily snapshot of information from the nurse as washing bags were exchanged over the threshold of ITU. They never relented and granted me admission, not once. I had thought that perhaps my perseverance coupled with her apparent lack of any other visitor would have signalled a change in their strict policy, you know the policy which allowed Sebastian in the night she was admitted. They should have a sign up really, one which reads that no-one except relatives will be permitted entry, unless of course they happen to be particularly good-looking, charming and charismatic, in which case the rules may be slackened. Maybe I looked too desperate. Anyway, now that I know I can see her today I'm feeling increasingly worried. What if she doesn't want to see me? What if she tells me to stop coming up? Again I chastise myself that it shouldn't matter so much. Like I said, I hardly know her. In truth I don't know her at all. I'd very much like to though. Is that the reason I'm still here? I was telling myself I was staying for Len. I mean I *was* staying for Len, but Len, well he's really hard to reach right now. He's retreated deep down into himself. He hasn't once asked about Carly. He hasn't asked about Sebastian either. Not that I know much of what's going on with him, now that he's done a runner. Normally my folks would be able to fill me in on whatever was going on next door, but they went away too, almost as soon as they returned home. It seems like everyone else is falling to bits. I wonder if there's something wrong with me that I'm managing to function more-or-less normally. I smile to myself as I consider how this would appear anything but normal to an onlooker. I've left my home, I appear to have left my job and I'm spending my time chasing a girl who, as far as I know, doesn't even realise I exist. Yeah, I'm functioning normally aren't I? Maybe I'm just diverting my thoughts elsewhere. It sounds plausible and yet I don't really believe it. I think the truth is I care about Carly and I just need to be near her if I can.

The entrance to the ward is locked. I can't believe it! What kind of hospital locks the doors? There is a security entrance with an intercom and after buzzing a couple of times, someone orders me to push the door open. I am taken to a single room and told I may go in if I like. Standing in the doorway I see her sitting on her bed. She's reading a magazine or something, wearing the pink and white pyjamas which I washed and ironed for her yesterday morning. She's completely absorbed and I'm glad because for a moment I can watch her unnoticed. She looks thin and very pale, but I guess she's been really ill so no wonder. Her hair is pinned up somehow on top of her head, but several blonde curls have freed themselves and hang loosely down around her neck and tousled over her face. A slender hand sweeps them away from her eyes, tucking the wispy tendrils neatly behind her ear. I am mesmerised, thinking how beautiful she looks, when she glances suddenly up and I find her staring right at me. Perhaps she sensed the intensity of my gaze, I don't know, but right now I realise how intrusive I must have seemed.

"Who are you?" Her voice is quite sharp, shattering my mood. Clearly she doesn't remember me. I begin to speak, to introduce myself, but my mouth is dry and the sound which comes out is rasping and faint. Clearing my throat I start again. "I'm Luc… Luc Rousseau, I was with you at the funeral…before you came in here." She continues to stare at me in what can only be described as a rather rude manner. I remain standing, feeling awkward. Of all the scenarios I had imagined, her not remembering me was the one I feared most. Then again, as suddenly as before, her voice breaks in without warning. She is very direct, very to the point. She's quite unlike any girl I've come across and I'm both irritated and intrigued at the same time.

"Have you been visiting me?"

This is such an odd situation. I explain that while I've been coming up to the hospital each day, taking the washing, getting an update I haven't actually seen her until now. She smiles and her whole face softens.

"What's so funny?" I ask.

220

Shaking her head she replies "It's not that funny. It's just I thought it was the other guy. They told me someone had been visiting every day while I was out of it downstairs, but they didn't know a name. They said he was French and very good-looking, very charming. I don't know why but in my mind I pictured the other guy who was at the funeral with us. I don't remember his name."

"Sebastian," I remind her with a frostiness to my tone that I didn't intend.

"Are you going to stand there all day or are you coming in?" She manages to make her invitation sound like an imposition rather than a welcome. And yet despite her curt manner and sharp words, she is softly-spoken, her voice gentle and interesting. I feel drawn to her in spite of myself.

"I'm sorry if you're disappointed," I say and seat myself in the only available chair in the room.

"No, no. It's not that at all. Please don't think that. I just didn't think of you, that's all." She's making it worse and doesn't realise it.

"I brought you a book." I attempt to change the subject to something more comfortable, less personal. Handing over the weighty volume, I hope earnestly that I've got it right. This isn't going well and I don't want to mess up any more than I already have. She takes it from me, her fingers lightly brushing mine as she does. My heart skips a beat, but she continues to be unfazed, unaware of what she's doing to me. She's quiet for a minute or two, silently leafing through the book, studying some pages closely with an expert's scrutiny. Looking up, I see her eyes shining, a smile spreading across her face. "Thank you. It's perfect. How did you know?"

"I saw your work in your apartment, you know, when I was round getting your stuff. Your paintings are amazing."

"You know about art?" Suddenly she wants to talk, is interested in what I have to say.

"Yeah, I teach art back home. I guess I know a bit."

"I'm glad you like my paintings. Claudine taught me, you see." She's watching for my reaction. I wonder does she think she's said something wrong. Maybe she wonders if mentioning Claudine is taboo.

"She taught me too," I tell her and she visibly relaxes in front of me.

# LEN

Standing barefoot in the kitchen, the tiles are cold and rough underfoot. I'm peering at the calendar on the wall counting. Twenty days. Three weeks tomorrow. That's how long it's been. I'm surprised. It feels much longer, it feels like months since I last saw her, last heard her voice. I don't think I'm doing very well. I'm not sure really how I'm meant to be doing, but I sense that people around me are concerned. Mom keeps on at me to go to the doctor. Why? Surely what's happening to me is normal in the circumstances. My wife has died and left me here to carry on without her. Why can't people understand that it's just really hard? Doing normal things, behaving normally, it's all much harder now. I haven't been back to work. I just don't think I could handle it. I'm actually wondering if I'll ever be able to do all the things I used to. Without work I'm lost, I know this. It's always been my focus, but nothing's been untouched by Claudine's death. I feel as if every aspect of my life is crumbling around me and I'm powerless to stop it.

I've been thinking about Sebastian a fair bit. I know he's gone back to France. Part of me is glad that I don't have to worry about seeing him, but another part of me wonders if maybe I *should* have talked to him before he left. I wasn't in any kind of state to speak to him rationally at the time, I know, but there are still so many unanswered questions and I realise he may have been able to fill in some of the blanks. The problem is I haven't decided yet how much I want to know. I'm thinking about it all the time, I barely think about anything else. Claudine and Sebastian. It's driving me crazy and I wonder if it would help to understand how it all happened, what was actually going on. I get so far piecing it all together and then I can't go any further. I feel as if I will go mad left in this half-knowing state, but then I wonder if the full picture might be too much for me to handle. I'm seriously messed up. Maybe I do need to see a doctor.

I'm wandering aimlessly back through to the living room when the phone starts ringing, interrupting my thoughts. I listen for someone else to answer it upstairs, while it continues to annoy with its unrelenting ring. Glancing out the window I see the hire car has gone and realise my parents must have gone out. I don't know what to do. I no longer have the skills required to make a conscious decision. I listen to the repetition of the ring until I can stand it no longer. I feel like I'm going to explode, it's annoying me so much. Grabbing it from the receiver I more or less shout into it, "Yes?" Silence on the other end and I begin to catch my breath again. It's stopped ringing. I did that. I made that happen. I can control some things. I'm about to hang up when a voice startles me. So soft, so soothing I only just register she's spoken and the content is lost completely on me. I listen for more. I want to hear that lovely sound again, so gentle, so easy to hear.

"Prof, is that you?"

Who calls me that? The voice is reaching in from another life, rousing me back to a world I feel so unfamiliar with.

"Prof... It's Carly. Are you alright?"

A huge effort is required to answer her. I don't want to. I don't want to have to think about words, what to say. But I do want her to keep talking, because she's reminding me of who I am, or at least who I was. "Carly." I repeat back to her. I have no words of my own.

# LUC

The art book was definitely a good idea. At last we found some common ground and she actually appeared to be interested in what I had to say. I was a bit worried she might be annoyed that I'd been up to her apartment. Of course she must have known. How else would I have been able to get her clothes and things for her? Even so, it's not the same as looking at her paintings, her private world, without permission. She seems okay about it, though. I think she's flattered that I'm so impressed. So we sat for a while, discussing mosaics and it felt really comfortable. I was starting to loosen up a little and thinking that, despite a shaky start, we were beginning to get on quite well, when out of the blue she jumps up and says why doesn't she show me round? It was so bizarre, like we were sitting in her apartment or something, not in a hospital ward. Anyway I said okay because I didn't really know what to say and the next moment we're wandering around together and she's pointing things out to me. It was like I'd just moved in or something. I was gonna say to her how weird it was, but I was afraid she might take it the wrong way. I don't know her well enough to really know how she'll take things. I guess that's making me extra cautious. This is a strange situation for me. I feel like a complete novice, as if I have no experience of girls and that's not really the case. Even at this moment, there's a girl back home who thinks we have something. We did have until I came over here; until I met Carly anyway. I push this thought consciously out of my head. I don't want to cloud my mind at the moment. This feels right, that's all I know. Carly feels more right than anything has for a long time.

So, anyway, I find myself being escorted around, shown the treatment rooms, the sitting room, the would-you-believe-it entertainment room complete with television, DVD player, play station, computer. She explains that this is the young people's unit, which is why it's so nice. There's even a kitchen where she can prepare her own food if she wants to. There are six single rooms, all of them occupied. She waves casually to the individuals in each one, or shouts a hello. They all seem to know each other. I just can't get over how odd it all is. It's like they're flatmates, not patients. There's one thing that stands out though, more than anything else, and it's the thing which reminds me that all these people are sick in hospital. They're not friends gathered together. This is not a normal situation. Apart from Carly, none of the other five patients I meet have any hair! As we return to her room, I realise that this is possibly the reason she took me on the guided tour; to allow me to see them and so to work up to telling me. Sure enough it turns out I am beginning to read her. "I guess you noticed that everyone here is bald." She starts back toward her bed, gesturing to me to sit again in the chair. I don't like the set-up of the room. She's too far away from me. I don't like sitting across here, away from her, but it feels too much to start moving the furniture, so I sit as instructed. She doesn't seem to be waiting for a reply, so I say nothing and let her go on. "This ward is for people who have cancer. Specifically it's for young people who have cancer. That means if you're between the ages of fifteen and twenty. Younger than that and you go to the paediatric ward and older you go to the adult ward. I guess you could say this is the best age to get cancer if you're going to get it." She smiles but I know that neither of us is finding this funny. I don't know what to say. Part of me is wondering did I hear her right. Cancer? She can't have cancer. Young people don't get cancer. And yet from what she's just shown me, clearly they do; six of them at a time: Carly.

I realise that she's sitting looking at me. I wonder did she ask me something. Have I missed something? Is she waiting for me to answer her? I'm so shocked I don't know how to react. What should I say? It's unbelievable. I guess I hadn't given much thought to what was actually wrong with her. For some reason I had got it into my head that she had taken some drugs and had a nasty reaction. That's what I really thought had happened. But cancer? Never, never in a million years would I have thought it.

"I know what you're thinking," she interrupts my thoughts. I hope in all earnestness that she doesn't, but today nothing would surprise me. "You're thinking that I look older than twenty so why am I here?" Not quite the foremost thought in my mind, but I let her think she's right. I nod weakly and wait for her explanation. "Well, I am twenty as it turns out. When I turn twenty-one in a few months I'll move on to the adult ward. It's horrendous, so I better get well soon. It's a good incentive isn't it?" Again her warped sense of humour unsettles me slightly. "How old are you?" This is getting more surreal by the minute. How old am I? How can that possibly have anything to do with all of this? Who cares how old I am? Carly has cancer! That's what this is all about. That's what she's telling me. Once more her steady gaze reminds me she's waiting for a response. She must think I'm really slow.

"Twenty-eight," I manage to reply. She nods simply and averts her eyes. A silence follows and I'm not entirely sure it's a comfortable one. She obviously decides it isn't and announces, "You can go now if you want to," that sharp tone creeping back in. I don't want to go though. I want to know everything. I want her to know me. I don't say anything, but I stay where I am. She pretends to read her magazine again, the book I brought lying forgotten on the floor. I know she's not really absorbed in it though, she's flicking through the pages too quickly, too deliberately.

"How come you still have hair then?" I hear the words and can't believe I've just uttered them. It feels like I was thinking and suddenly the words were out there. This could be make or break. How dare I ask such a personal question? I would never normally say such a thing. I guess it felt like she was pushing for a reaction and suddenly there was one. Looking up, she speaks slowly, softly, "Well, that's the million dollar question, Luc." I love the way she says my name. "Either it means I'm lucky and don't have to suffer the humiliation that my fellow patients do, or..." she hesitates, thinks a moment. I wonder if she's choosing her words or just deciding whether or not to tell me, "...or, maybe it means that my chemo hasn't worked properly."

"I don't understand"

"Well, the way it works is I have leukaemia right? That means my bone marrow is making abnormal blood cells...blasts they're called. The chemo kills off the blasts to get rid of the leukaemia. The trouble is it also kills off all the other rapidly-dividing cells in my body. It doesn't discriminate properly. So as well as doing what it's meant to i.e. eradicating the disease, it also affects the mucous membranes and the hair follicles. The other fairly major thing it does is wipe out the white blood cells too so I can't fight infection. That's why I got so ill. My counts were down and I'm not really meant to mix in public places in case I catch something. Even something minor like a cold, can make me really sick. That's what happened the day of the funeral. I had an infection and it got a grip. I should have come up here as soon as I started feeling ill, but I wanted... I needed to go to Claudine's funeral. Anyway, the rest you know. By the time I got here I was in septic shock. That's why it was such a battle to get well again. I'm sorry I sound like a medical text-book don't I, prattling on? What was it you asked me? Oh yes, my hair. Well mine didn't fall out, so I don't know if that's good or if it means the chemo didn't do its job right."

"And how will you know?"

"I'll know next week when I have a bone marrow aspirate done."

I'm confused now. Up till this point I've been following her, she's very articulate, very precise. I remember that she is Len's prize student and think I can see why. Her eye for detail, her way with words is obvious. Recognising that she's lost me she goes on to explain, "That just means that they take a sample out of my bone marrow here," indicating her lower back "and they take a look at it in the lab to see if there are still blast cells there or not."

This feels like a dream, it's all so difficult to take in. I still can't leave her. I wonder if they'll need to throw me out. Everything I've heard, every moment I've spent with her has left me longing for more; I want to know every detail about her, bad and good. I want to know her whole life, her thoughts and her dreams. I want to be a part of her.

"I think maybe you should go now." She doesn't mince her words. Perhaps she doesn't feel the same way, I realise. Perhaps she thinks I've overstepped the mark, made her feel uncomfortable with all these questions.

I rise to leave and feel an overwhelming desire to hold her, to try to make her feel better.

"You don't need to take my washing anymore," she adds "Now that I'm up here I can do it myself. There's a laundry." She looks away, out of the window and I feel as if I've been dismissed. I start to leave, head for the door when suddenly I understand that this is it. This is probably my only chance. When will I see her again? Without thinking of how she'll take it the words are out before I can stop them.

"Do you think you might like to go out sometime…with me?"

For a long moment, nothing: no answer, no response. She continues looking out of the window. Then slowly, turning to face me she smiles and I feel myself melt in her gaze. Our eyes lock for the briefest of moments and I am in heaven.

"I'd like that…When I get out of here…Are you going to be staying long?"

I scribble down my number on a paper towel and hand it to her. "Depends."

"Depends on what…your work…commitments?" Her fingers brush mine again as she takes it from me and I wonder fleetingly if it's deliberate.

"How long I stay depends on whether you call me or not."

She smiles and I smile back. Go now I have to tell myself. Go and leave it with her. See what happens.

229

## LEN

I tell my mother I'm going out and she can't hide her surprise. I don't know what's shocked her most, that I've actually showered, shaved and dressed or that I'm venturing outside for the first time in weeks. It's difficult to describe even to myself how I feel. Words fail me more often than not these days, but expressing my own emotions is hard. I feel like I've been grabbed forcefully and shaken vigorously. Everything is all mixed up, my own hurts merge seamlessly into thoughts of Carly and the news she's just given me. Leukaemia.

I feel so very, very selfish when I think of the time I've spent indulging my own problems. She doesn't realise what she's asking me, though. But I also know that she needs me and I have to get it together enough to try to help her. I allowed myself to get ready really without thinking, just moving through the motions of washing, picking clothes and so on. I'm well aware this is not the way most people function, running on automatic, following ingrained habits in preference to actually thinking, but it's working for me at the moment and it's got me moving. I barely recognise myself anymore. The shave helped a bit. I've never looked good with that unshaven appearance, but long hair! Well not long exactly, but longer than I've ever worn it. I wonder if I've turned into a complete recluse, not caring about the way I look. The thing is I do care really. This is where everything gets so confused. I do care about things and people I just seem to lack the will to actually carry out the actions. Anyway, this is a good morning. I'm going to go out, I'm getting ready. Mom looks ready to applaud.

230

Maybe I'll get a haircut sometime, an attempt at least to *look* normal again.

Into the study, I am a bit taken aback at how strange it all feels. This seems like someone else's room. It's all so familiar and yet so distant. It was a lifetime ago that I felt at home in here. This part of my life feels detached from anything I now am. Reading, writing, speaking; all my language-associated skills are gone. And yet, this is the bit she wants from me. I don't know how I'm going to pull this off. Scanning the shelves, I select the appropriate books. I'm really relying on her own literary talent to carry her through this, because I know I'm not up to it. Maybe she'll be able to read it in my eyes. I hope so, because I'm not looking forward to telling her I think she needs a different tutor. It's amazing really that she's going through all this and yet still wants to work, to achieve what she's capable of. How can she draw on such strength in the middle of it all? Why can't I? I feel so shallow in comparison; so weak and shallow. In truth, almost empty.

I thought I would never have to come back here again. I'd decided that I wouldn't and yet it is me who consciously pushes open the heavy door in response to the intercom release. I hate this place more than anywhere in the world. Claudine's last breath was taken within this building, her spirit left her here. And yet the other rational part of me understands that beyond these doors someone else is fighting to hold on to her life and she wants me to help her. Is it any surprise that I'm so messed up, with my emotions swinging like this? A nurse guides me to the appropriate doorway, tells me she'll be pleased to see me. I would have liked a minute to get my bearings, get my head together. I'm not sure what I'm going to say to her. What do you say to a twenty year old who has her whole life ahead of her, when she calls to say she's got leukaemia? I don't get the luxury of a few minutes breathing space, though. She looks up almost as soon as I arrive. I wonder if she's been waiting for me.

"I knew you'd come!" her face lighting up with joy at the sight of me. I can barely believe that my presence could possibly bring someone happiness. Moving on into the room I tell her, "You knew more than me then. I hardly know what I'm doing these days."

"Is that why you didn't come sooner?" I wonder for a moment why didn't I come sooner? "Carly, I'm sorry." It's enough. I don't need lengthy explanations with Carly. Leaning forward I scoop her up into my arms and hold her close. She feels so small, weighs so little. I'm astonished that I never noticed before. "Are you okay?" I ask, my voice muffled by her hair. I feel her head nodding against my shoulder. Releasing her gently, I hold her at arm's length so I can look at her properly. Her eyes fill with tears.

"Oh Carly…" my words are a whisper. I glance behind me and spot a chair a few feet away. Dragging it over, I position it in front of her and sit down, our knees touching and try to read her expression. For a minute or two she doesn't say anything and then, swallowing hard, "I'm so sorry. I didn't mean to cry. I'm just so pleased to see you. You're the first person to hug me since I got sick. Sometimes a hug is what you need isn't it?" Nodding slowly I feel glad that my instinctive, if some-would-say inappropriate gesture was well received. "People will be talking about us," she says. "First that oh-so-public row in the student union and then embracing!"

"I don't care if you don't." I shudder as I remember the row, kicking over my chair. And why? Because she wouldn't eat her breakfast, because she wouldn't concentrate on what I was saying? "You weren't well that day were you?" She shakes her head in reply. "How can I ever apologise Carly?"

"Well," she smiles, "as it happens I have an idea." I wait for her to continue. It's refreshing being in her company, she's so upbeat. She really does make me feel guilty for wallowing so long in self-pity. "I think you should do your duty as my tutor and start coaching me through my dissertation. That ought to do it."

"You want to go ahead with it?"

"Why not? Do you think there's no point?" Her words are cutting, designed to hurt. She's good at that, but I'm beginning to understand it's a response to her own pain.

232

"No, of course I don't think that. What I mean is I don't know if I'm up to it. I'm absolutely sure you are. I wondered if you might be better with another tutor, instead of going ahead with me." A decisive shake of the head tells me what I already knew.

"No. I can only do it with you. You know that Prof. It's a long-shot as it is. None of the others can get me through it. If you won't help me then I might as well give up now." It's emotional blackmail and we both know it. On the other hand, I do agree with her that my colleagues probably wouldn't put in enough graft to get her there. The question is can I still do it?

"Okay, I'll help you as far as I'm able, but I must warn you that I'm struggling a bit myself right now."

She's nodding as I speak "So we'll struggle together then."

I smile in agreement, but inside I don't share her conviction.

Reaching down, I pick up a crumpled piece of paper from the floor. Without thinking I smooth it across my knee. "Well, I've brought you your texts," I tell her.

"Great. Let's see." Passing the volumes across to her, she looks delighted. "What do you want me to do first?"

"Well the first thing is I want you to read everything Sylvia Plath ever wrote. You still happy to go with Plath?"

"Yes, yes, but Prof I've already read everything she ever wrote!" I knew this. My best student, of course she's read all the texts. This is to give me some time to work out how I'm going to teach her when I feel I've lost all my communication skills.

"Just read them, Carly. The best place to start is always at the beginning." My eyes drop down to the paper on my knee. It's a paper towel with some writing on it. Realising it's a phone number I am mildly embarrassed. "Oh sorry, Carly. I didn't realise this was anything."

"It's not," she says curtly. I pass it over to her but can't help noticing Luc's name scrawled across it. I don't suppose there's more than one Luc Rousseau around here.

"I take it Luc's not your type then." She hesitates, a trick I think she might have learned from me, while gathering her thoughts, selecting her words.

"Luc is lovely but… it doesn't matter…"

"So you're not going to call him then?"

"No. I don't think so."

"Better put that in the bin then. In case you change your mind!"

# SEBASTIAN

I'm doing everything I can to try to chill and yet, inside I'm so tightly wound, I don't know what would happen if I started to unravel. Sitting in the garden, listening to the breeze gently brushing through the trees, feeling the sun's warmth on my face, what could be more relaxing? This place is so beautiful and so calming. I was right to come home. If anywhere is going to offer me some healing then this is the place. Nothing is expected of me here. Monique gives me all the space I need, but at the same time she's looking out for me very well. In a way I feel like a fraud. Why should she look after me? I'm a grown man who's run away from his life. I should be able to take responsibility for that. I guess the difficulty is I haven't decided how to move forward yet. I realise that my life can't continue as it was. I need to find a new role for myself, one which doesn't involve Helen or Claudine or Len. The hard part is accepting that those three people really were my life. Maybe I need some therapy of some kind. This can't be normal can it, after a bereavement to have to completely reassemble your whole entire life. I feel as if I have no direction, no future. There's nothing that I can look ahead to or plan for. I need to find something to live for again. Everyone needs something to live for.

Claudine's parents still aren't back. I've been watching for signs of life from next door, but so far nothing. I believe they went away with Christophe and his wife for a break. There's also been no word of Luc. Could he still be holed up in my apartment in Edinburgh? I don't understand why he hasn't come home yet. He must have a good arrangement with the school, because they aren't on holiday and he's had quite a bit of compassionate leave now. I'm actually getting a bit concerned for him. Maybe I shouldn't have left without him. In actual fact, I was pretty sure he would come with me when he heard I was going, or at least that he would follow me over soon after. I hope he's alright. There isn't really anyone over there to watch out for him and I know he thought the world of Claudine. Didn't we all? I suppose I left in such a hurry simply because I had made the decision to go and there didn't seem any point in hanging around. I also felt this urgent need to do something, to take some kind of action and this was really all I could think of. I don't suppose it's all that surprising. Many species have a homing instinct when they have wounds to lick don't they?

I've been trying these past few days to face some of the issues which caused me to take flight so hurriedly. I guess the main one is obvious and yet so difficult to bring out into the open. I spoke to Monique about it last night. I think it's the first time in my life that I've opened my heart to my big sister and yet she made it feel so natural. We were eating dinner out here on the patio, enjoying the last of the sun's warmth before it dipped down behind the horizon for the night. Monique is not a cook, but her fresh salads teamed with good wine make each meal very palatable. Out of the blue she suddenly announced something about me missing Claudine. Maybe she saw me gazing into her garden as I think I am inclined at the moment. I have so many memories, good memories of our time together growing up here. I can't help allowing myself to absorb these and other thoughts as I sit in this spot. I hesitated of course. I'm never too sure about pouring things out to people who don't really need to know. Sometimes I think it's just better to keep a lid on things. That way you know you're still in control. So, last night, well I don't know why. Maybe it was because she was letting me see that she already understood, that it was no surprise to her to see the state I was in when I arrived. I don't really know, but for some reason we did talk and I did open up to her and it felt really good. She didn't criticise me or take sides. She didn't pontificate about the rights and wrongs of it. She simply accepted what I told her, that I had loved Claudine all my life, that I never stopped loving her. I stopped short of telling her about the ring though and I'm not sure why; maybe because I haven't got my head around that at all yet. Or maybe because it seems like such a clear betrayal of Len that I doubt if she would believe there was really nothing going on between us.

That was such a shock. That day when Len was kicking off and I felt truly hurt at his rebuffs. I thought I was doing the right thing coming to speak to him before I left town. I didn't want him to think I was running away and not being up front with him. I had told him, assured him there was no affair, that our relationship was in the past. Yes I did admit my own feelings for Claudine had never changed, but then I had no idea. The ring threw me completely as it has him. I understand his problem with me more clearly now. The question is why was she wearing my ring? He said surely I remembered giving her a ring. Of course I do. It seems such a long time ago now. It feels like another world. I loved her so much. I wanted to be with her all my life. Yes, I asked her to marry me and she accepted. I had bought her the ring - she didn't want an engagement ring, just the *main event,* as she called it. But that night, when we parted after the accident, I distinctly recall throwing the ring into the air and we both watched as it twirled its glittering way down through the space between us and burrowed itself into the sand. That was it, the end. I turned and walked away. Each step killing me, but I didn't look back. I couldn't bring myself to look back at my darling Claudine's stricken face as I left her for a life with a girl I didn't love. If only I had turned round! What would I have seen? Did she bend down and scrabble through the sand with her beautiful fingers, did she retrieve the ring there and then or was it later? I'll never know, just as I'll never know why she was wearing it the day she died. I've been trying to come up with different explanations, but the only convincing one involves the idea that she still loved me. The idea of Claudine loving me without her ever realising my true feelings is almost unbearable. That's one of the reasons I would like to produce another plausible story for it. But I can't. In my heart of hearts I now believe that she did love me; that she loved me all along. The tragedy of course is that neither of us knew. She died not knowing how I felt about her. I think my heart might break under the strain of this knowledge. The life not lived appears to me in dreams and haunts me by day. Things could have been so different, but now the chance is gone. Regret is such an awful thing.

## CARLY

I'm so glad he came. I felt maybe I was overstepping the mark calling him up like that, but then when Luc said how he was having such a hard time of it, I just had to. Prof Thomas has always been so good to me. He's believed in me when I couldn't myself and I know if anyone can help me through this then he's the one. He did look a bit rough, but nothing like I'd imagined. He said it was good to get out. He was pleased I'd phoned, so it was the right thing to do after all. I hope he can get back to work soon. He really seems to doubt his ability to teach anymore. He's by far the most gifted tutor I ever came across. You only have to look at all he's accomplished at such a young age to know that he's good. Apart from that, though, he really cares about his students. I doubt if I would have ever done anything of any worth had I not had him encouraging me. That's why I know that he'll make the difference now. This is an uphill struggle, I'm well aware. I've a lot of ground to make up even to achieve an average result. He tells me I'm worth more than average and I need to hold onto that. I'm going to need to focus on something to try and deal with all that's been happening in my life lately anyway.

Lifting one of the volumes of poetry from the side table where he left it, I stroke the well-worn cover and opening it at the first page see his name scribbled in black marker pen, large, deliberate letters taking up the whole page. I'm glad he came and I'm so glad he's willing to take me on. I guess there's a part of me that also wants to open up to him, to tell him everything, but my inner radar is frantically signalling to me how dangerous that could be. He needs to find out for himself. If I dive in now I could be creating waves too large for either of us to cope with. I did wonder if he had read the papers which he packed in my bag along with my clothes when I first came in here. Luc told me that Prof had selected all the things which he brought in. At first I was sure it was a sign. I was certain he was trying to tell me that he knew. Today's conversation, however has clarified that. He thought they were lecture notes and I might appreciate some reading matter now that I'm feeling better. Never mind. It's just as well I didn't go blurting out anything today. He would have been taken pretty off-guard. He did say one strange thing though, and it's something I haven't been able to get my head round. He asked me if I knew someone called James Harris. Why would he ask me that? I told him that I did and waited for an explanation, but none came and he didn't mention it again. I think that's when he started trying to persuade me to give Luc a chance.

Luc, now there's another thing. No wonder I'm so exhausted with all this going on. It's probably nothing to do with needing a blood transfusion, but that would be too simplistic for these doctors wouldn't it? It couldn't be that I'm just so stressed out trying to make sense of my life. Luc doesn't understand. How could he? This situation is not right, it's all wrong in fact. Maybe in another life, but not now... I have thrown his number away, because Prof's absolutely right, I would be tempted to call him. Part of me thinks why not? I could just call, it's just talking. Maybe we could meet and become friends, but I already know it's more than that for me and I'm thinking he feels the same. It's too dangerous. It needs to stop before it begins. I just hope with all my heart that he leaves it now. I'm not sure I'll be able to keep this strong if he shows up again.

# LEN

It's now or never. I'm going to get this thing thrashed out if it kills me. The need to know has become the most over-riding feeling, it's all-consuming. I cannot carry on without knowing, it's that simple. I'm aware that I'm fragile right now and that timing could perhaps be better, but the endless questioning is screwing my head. I can't sleep and I can't concentrate when I'm awake. My thoughts are filled with possibilities and now I just need to know. I'm also dealing with a new emotion and it's one which is really scaring me. For the first time, I think ever in my life, I am really angry with you Claudine. I'm so angry that you've left me here like this. I'm angry that you've made me doubt you and I'm angry at all the questions you've raised. I won't be able to rest if I don't find out for sure. The thing which worries me is whether or not I'll be able to cope with the truth. I've thought about the implications, of course. I've been doing practically nothing else these past few weeks. I've tried to imagine the worst possible scenario and only hope I've covered everything. I need to know. Whatever happens, I need to know and deal with the consequences later.

Approaching the dismal building once again I wonder why I'm so sure that this guy is wrapped up in it all. Maybe I'm wrong. Maybe he'll just take the letter and leave me with nothing. I need to try to stay calm. I didn't get anywhere last time when I lost my temper and walked away with it unopened. If I lose control again I won't even get to talk to him. Breathe deeply, I tell myself. Try to keep it together. The difference this time, of course is that now I know the contents of the letter. I'm not sure at which point exactly I decided that protecting

241

Claudine's privacy was no longer paramount. Was it around the time I found the ring? I actually don't remember, but that would make sense. I guess I realised then that she had kept secrets from me, had betrayed me. Suddenly it didn't matter whether I read a letter addressed to someone else. The funny thing is that once I'd torn it open and allowed the light of day to shine on what I anticipated to be sordid contents, I understood that she had expected me to open it. She knew I would. It seems she knew me better than I know myself. Her words are ingrained on my mind. I've read and re-read the letter so often I no longer need to look at it to remember what it says. In Claudine's beautiful, inspired hand she tells James Harris to talk to me. It feels like a cruel game. I feel like my emotions are being toyed with and yet I'm unable to resist. I feel compelled to uncover it all. I want to empty the box, tip the contents out and then see if I can bear to look on them or not.

The reception area is not as shabby as I had remembered: strange how our inner turmoil can so influence our perceptions of everything around us. I'm absolutely petrified standing here. I hope he doesn't keep me waiting because I'm close to walking out. I'm actually shaking. Get a grip, I tell myself, but my body refuses to listen to me anymore. I'm told he'll be with me in a moment. I wonder how we measure a moment. I'm sure theirs is far longer than mine. I already feel I've been standing here too long. I'm invited to sit, but I can't. I need to keep moving. Pacing up and down the lobby I know I must look really distressed. Perhaps they won't let me see him. Maybe they'll think I'm too unbalanced to be allowed a private meeting. Maybe they're right. Again I tell myself to try to relax, to breathe more deeply. It's not working, nothing is. Perhaps if I go outside and have a smoke, that might help. It might at least regulate my breathing a bit. I decide to do this and am heading over to the desk to let them know, when a door opens and the man I spoke with before says my name. I open my mouth to reply, but no sound escapes. This is really starting to get to me. Inside I'm screaming and yet nothing will come out. I feel like a prisoner trapped inside this stupid body. He recognises me and offers a handshake. Mine won't comply. I'm not being rude; I'm not making a point of principle. I just can't will my arm to move to reciprocate the gesture of civility.

"Are you alright?" he asks me as we enter his office. "It's just you look…"

I nod to let him know I agree. "I think I need a cigarette," I attempt to explain my disturbed state.

Lifting his jacket from a hook on the back of the door he turns to me, "Then we better go someplace else. This building is non-smoking and I think we're both going to need a bit of sustenance. There's a pub at the bottom of the road. That okay with you?"

"Fine," I say and am starting to think, maybe this guy's okay after all. He's not going to force me to sit in this stuffy office and go through this ordeal without a smoke. Then I think maybe things are about to get so bad, he wants me out of here in case I explode. As we make our way down the stairs, a colleague calls to him, asking if he wants some company. He waves them away. I suspect they think he might need some backup in case things get ugly again. Reaching the front door a dreadful thought comes into my head, reminding me that I haven't in fact covered all bases in my let's-imagine-the-worst-possible-case-and-see-if-I-can-handle-it state. I suddenly wonder if he's going to tell me that he too was in love with my wife. Please don't let him tell me they were having an affair. I'm not sure I could take that. I glance over at him as we stride side by side in the direction of the pub. Is he good-looking? I wouldn't have said so, but then I don't know what girls go for. The female mind is beyond male understanding as far as I'm concerned. Take Carly, for instance. There she is, on the one hand telling me she fancies Luc and then chucks his phone number in the bin. I mean what's that all about? I don't think this guy is attractive, but who's to say what Claudine would have made of him? After all she married me. I'm starting to wonder about that too, mind you. Why did she marry me? Why did she stay with me if she didn't love me? Did she love me? This is so painful. My head is thumping, my heart too. They're out of synch though and it's making me feel a bit sick. Calm down. I need to get back in control, get on top of things. I need to be able to think clearly.

A pint appears in front of me, then an ashtray. Finally James Harris pulls up a chair opposite me and lights his own cigar. I see. A smile slips out as I realise that the change of venue was, at least in part, for his own benefit. Somehow that makes him a bit more likeable. He seems more down to earth than I had imagined.

"So," he says slowly exhaling smoke over his shoulder.

"So," I repeat.

It's like one of those sad sitcoms where the predictable bad news is about to be broached. I wonder if he's going to pretend he doesn't know what this is about. Is he going to make me go through it all, explaining why I've come back. I'll do it if I need to, but it will irritate the hell out of me. He doesn't. "I know why you're here." I'm liking him more each tentative moment we spend in each other's company. "I'm glad you came back. I realise the last time…it was a particularly bad time for you."

I nod and wait for him to go on.

Taking another deep draw on his cigar he says, "I always hoped we would never have this conversation. I was prepared, yes, but it's not something I've looked forward to."

I don't know what to say. What's new! I feel so tense I can't understand how other people are able to carry on as normal. A momentary look around the room shows people sitting at tables, chatting, laughing. A couple of guys lean against the bar, sipping their pints in companionable silence. No one else is affected. The pub is fairly drab, the furniture worn and tired. How apt I think. I fit in well here. Perhaps people think I am part of the furnishings, I so lack life.

"What did Claudine's letter say?"

I'm taken aback at this question. He's obviously not even going to ask to see it, just wants to know what she's told me. I clear my throat and carefully, slowly, because it commands a great effort from me to think and speak at the same time, tell him she asked me to come see him, to talk. He nods and shifts uncomfortably in his seat. I wonder how old he is. I've never been good at assessing ages, but I would put him around ages with me. This does nothing to settle the fears rising within my head.

"I take it Claudine never mentioned me. The first you knew of me was the letter you found... the letter you were obviously meant to find."

I look steadily at him, "Were you having an affair with my wife?" It's out, before I even realised the thought had formed in my mind. What am I playing at? It was going okay. Why can't I just leave things and let him tell me?

"What?" The shocked expression tells me everything. I'm way off beam. I'm relieved of course, but at the same time wonder how we're going to manage this conversation when my interpretation of cues is so awry. "No...No...You mustn't think that...Please...I wouldn't...I didn't..."

"It's okay," I interject before he starts to grovel. "I'm sorry. I just don't know how to handle this, you know? I'm scared if the truth be known." I seem to have smoothed the waters again. He heads back to the bar for a refill. My own drink remains in front of me, untouched.

# CARLY

"Okay, Carly. We'll have you hooked up in a moment. You'll feel a lot better after this." The nurse is pleasant enough and I know she's doing her best, but nobody really knows how to relate to me. How does she know how I feel or how much better I'll feel after this blood transfusion? I doubt if she's ever had one herself. Still I smile and sit patiently as she flushes my cannula and primes the blood giving set. "Haven't seen your boyfriend for a while?" She says it like it's a question, as if I'm meant to explain the lack of boyfriend. I think for a second of asking the whereabouts of her own boyfriend, but of course I don't say it aloud. There's no need for me to be rude. I suppose she's just trying to be friendly. I find it all so false, though and I don't really have the patience for it. "Where did you meet him then?" For a moment I haven't a clue what she's talking about. I'm so immersed in my own thoughts I hardly realise she's still speaking to me. Clearly she doesn't know when to just leave it.

"Meet who?"

"Oh don't be coy Carly, the dishy French guy who's been visiting. What's his name again?"

"Oh… Luc. That's Luc. Except he's not really my…" I tail off as a movement by the doorway catches my eye. He's standing there, watching this whole bizarre scene. He looks a bit uncomfortable and I wonder if he made a conscious effort to interrupt before I buried myself too deep. The nurse follows my gaze and smiling says, "That's us now. Let me know if you feel unwell, okay? I'll leave you two

246

lovebirds in peace." And she closes the door very deliberately behind her.

"That was a bit awkward," he says shyly. He looks lovely and I'm so pleased to see him.

"Are you going to sit down or stand there all day?" My barking words sound alien. I speak to him so abruptly, but I can't seem to help it. It's almost like I want him to stop liking me. It would certainly make things a lot simpler. The more he gives, the greater the will required of me to resist. It would be much simpler if he just lost interest or got fed up with me and left it before it goes any further. He's making life very difficult. I'd love to sit and chat to him properly, spend time getting to know him, getting close to him. But I know nothing good would come out of it. I'll have to be really careful.

He sits in the seat vacated by the nurse, which on account of her working on my line is way too close for comfort. I wonder if he'll shift it back a bit, put a more respectable distance between us, but he doesn't. "How are you?" He stares at me so intently I wonder that he can't see into my very soul. I hadn't noticed how deep and dark his eyes were until now. Maybe I haven't been looking properly. Maybe I haven't allowed myself to get near enough to see. Anybody else would think I was crazy passing up on this. Maybe I am. He's making it difficult to see things clearly. "Okay," my voice emerges as a whisper. Where is the strong person that I'm meant to be? I sound so insecure and wary. He says nothing for a while and we sit, looking around, looking out the window, looking everywhere but at each other.

"I hope you don't mind me coming by." I don't answer him. I don't trust myself to speak. "I wanted to see you again," he goes on. Once more I let the silence take care of it. I can probably do sufficient damage to this opportunity by saying nothing anyway. "I shouldn't have come," he says and rises from his chair. I've obviously given him the vibes that he isn't wanted, that I'm not interested. He heads toward the door, muttering an apology and suddenly I feel desperate. I don't know what to do. I know I don't want him to go. If he leaves now will he ever come back? Would I? No. No matter how keen I was if I was standing in his shoes right now, I'd give up. He's getting nothing back,

247

no encouragement, nothing. The right thing to do would be to let him go now. Watch him walk out the door and never see him again. Problem solved. And I think that maybe that's the best plan, let him go. If I can just hold my tongue, say nothing, allow him a way out, it'll all be over. And it's happening, in front of me I'm seeing enacted the very scenario I've anticipated and I think I would actually have been able to follow it through if he hadn't turned at the door. He turns to look at me and he looks so sad, so disappointed. I see in his face the hurt I'm causing him and I know I can do something to ease it. "Luc!" I say it quietly, perhaps still hoping that he'll go anyway, maybe he won't hear me. He does hear me and he waits. I realise I'm going to have to give him a clear indication if I want him to stay. I've confused him and he now doesn't know what to do. Once again, I hesitate. I understand that if I say nothing more he'll go. I'm not sure about anything, but I know I want him to stay. Perhaps it wouldn't do any harm for us to spend a little time together, just talking. How could that be wrong? As long as I keep in control of my feelings, we could maybe become friends. And I do like him. "Please don't go." This time it's Luc who hesitates. He probably thinks he's setting himself up for a fall. I know he doesn't understand, but it's not as if I can explain it to him is it? How did I get into this mess anyway? "I've been reading the book you brought me." He smiles and the moment of departure begins to dissipate. He still doesn't come back in, but I see him relax a little. "I wanted to ask you something," I say and reach over to lift the book from the bedside locker. I can't stretch that far though. The blood line restricts my arm and he has to come over to pass it to me. Things are back on course. I leaf through the pages till I find the right one then turning it round toward him ask, "What do you think of that?" Taking the book from me, he sits again and begins to examine the painting I'm showing him. I'm longing to hear his opinion, to listen to his smooth, gentle voice. He is such a calming person to have around when I let him. If I could stop fighting him, I would probably find him very therapeutic company. I smile to myself. I can come up with a lot of reasons to excuse this relationship. It still doesn't make it right, though.

## SEBASTIAN

It was good talking to Luc on the phone last night. Strange though, too, because I've been so detached from my real life since I got here. It's like a retreat really. I've had space and company when I want it. I've been well nourished, enjoyed the sunshine and the tranquillity of the garden. Most of all I've had time to think, to go over things, to try to come to terms with things. Coming home has definitely had a cathartic effect. So when Monique told me Luc was on the phone I didn't actually know if I wanted to talk to him. It felt a bit intrusive. I've created or I'm in the process of creating a self-indulgent island for myself, where the real world doesn't impact. Reconnecting with Luc was like building a bridge back to the life I've run from. I took the call, more out of politeness than anything, but I'm so glad I did. It was great for a few minutes to think about someone else. He's such a refreshing guy anyway, always showing interest, continually seeing new things. I guess that's the artist in him. Consciously I push away the thought which is bound to surface, that of Claudine and her creativity. But then that's good. It's good that I'm able to do that even just for a moment. He sounded great. I'm pleased he's there actually, looking after the apartment. Again that's given me a bit of breathing space till I sort out what I'm doing with it. I'm not ready to make any big decisions, but I feel the natural thing would be to stay here. Not here exactly. Not next door to Claudine's place, but France, Paris probably. The hows and ifs are not things I've yet sorted out and I imagine I might need to make contact with Helen at some point. Luc was able to tell me the restaurant's ticking over fine. He's been helping Helen out a bit and so keeping an eye on things. It's funny how I'm able to think of Helen and our marriage without any sense of sadness at all. It all feels a blur in actual fact. It's like a wind that's swept me through almost twenty years and landed me here without really understanding how.

So Luc is staying put, for now anyway. I must have sounded so stupid. I couldn't grasp why on earth he was still there. His whole life is here, so what reason could he have to stay. At first I thought it was something to do with Len, but he tells me Len doesn't return calls, doesn't see anyone. Then he mentioned Carly, mentioned her quite a few times actually and the penny started to drop. It sounds like early days, but he must be really taken with her, to risk his job and everything else for her. I hope he knows what he's doing. I wouldn't like to see him make a mess of his life over a girl. How ironic I think and can't help smiling bitterly to myself. I was shocked to hear the girl's still in hospital. I had no idea she was so ill. He's taking a lot on and I hope he realises things could get really tough. The last thing she needs is to start a relationship now that's not going to last the distance. Anyway I thought there was a boyfriend on the scene already. What am I doing? None of this is any of my concern. I'm the last person to be dishing out advice on relationships. Look at the disaster I've made of every relationship I've ever had. No, I think I'll let the kids sort this one out themselves. Be happy for them, I tell myself. Let them do what they think is right. No-one can do any more.

# LEN

I need to do this tonight. "Can't it wait till tomorrow Len, whatever it is? It's a dreadful night out there." My mother doesn't understand.

"No, Mom. This is something I have to deal with tonight. Anyway, I need some air." The wind catches the door as I step outside banging it violently closed behind me. She probably thinks I did that on purpose. Never mind. Head down against the driving rain I am buffeted backwards as I lean into another gust. It feels strangely exhilarating, battling against the elements like this. At least I feel alive. For the first time in weeks I actually feel alive. The numbness has lifted. My feelings are once again acute and painful and real. This is a better state to be in.

It seems appropriate to be out in this tonight. The storm inside my head continues to rage and in some ways this mirroring of my emotions is reassuring. The rain streaming down my face soothes the heat of my anger. I think I've experienced every conceivable emotion today. Leaving James I was upset and disappointed. I know it wasn't easy for him either. Rarely have I seen someone quite so uncomfortable in a conversation. I'm sure he'd have given anything to have delegated that particular job. As ever though Claudine seems to have drawn people in, made them emotionally involved, so I guess he felt obliged to see it through, for her sake as much as anything. Upset merged into anger, the all too familiar feeling of these days and on through frustration and maybe a bit of denial as well. Now? What do I feel now? Now I guess I feel moved to action. Not motivated exactly, but something like it. Most of all I feel I have purpose. Pushing on through the wind and beating rain, I can almost feel the adrenaline pumping around my body. A can clatters along the sidewalk behind me, tracking my path. A little way ahead of me a trashcan is lifted by the wind and rammed unforgivingly into the side of a parked car. I'm impressed by its power, by the idea of something bigger than myself and all my problems. It allows me to look out, albeit for just a moment, lessening the intensity of my introversion.

I glance at my watch as I arrive outside the door. Ten thirty. Is that too late? I hesitate for a minute wondering if my impulsiveness was a bit rash, but hearing sounds within am prompted to rap the door. An inner door swishes open and I make out the light tread of footsteps making their way across the hall. Holding the door wide, a look of surprise on his face and I too share the sentiment. I didn't expect to see Luc here! Now I think about it I don't suppose I even considered she might have company, but Luc?

"Len! What a surprise. Come in." I follow his gesture through to the sitting room, while he closes up behind me. The room is warm and cosy, a stark contrast to the wild weather outside. Carly is curled up on the couch and Luc resumes his position beside her. They look like a couple, I think as I watch her head nestle instinctively against his shoulder. When did this all happen I ask myself? I feel like I've blinked and missed something. Surely it hasn't been that long since I last saw them? A few weeks at most. Then again, I've been so self-absorbed lately, the world could have fallen down around me and I might not have noticed. Life has been passing me by. This is evidence enough of that.

"Prof!" she looks happy to see me and my heart swells with pleasure. "You're soaking. Look at you. What possessed you to come out in this rain?" Looking down at my dripping clothes I become aware for the first time that I am completely drenched. A puddle is gathering around my wet feet, my sodden clothes are sticking to me. I start to shiver. Strange that I only realise how cold I am now that I've entered the warmth of this place. "Luc, have you got some dry clothes he could wear? He's soaked through." Rising once more, Luc leaves the room for a few minutes returning with a neat bundle of clothes.

"Thanks," I say and am shown to the bathroom to change. He's given me a pair of jeans and a sweatshirt and replacing my wet clothing with these feels like heaven. I rub my hair dry with a towel and remind myself that long hair really doesn't suit me. As soon as I can drum up sufficient effort I will get it cut. Back in the sitting room the cosy atmosphere is welcoming. It's nice here I think; comfortable.

"What brings you all this way tonight then, Prof?" she asks me innocently. Part of me hates to interrupt their quiet evening. I know I'm about to turn her world upside down and I consider saying nothing. Could I just leave things as they are? She would be none the wiser. What is it that compels me to open up to her? I guess I want her in my life and I want what should have been.

"I came to speak to you," I tell her and wish in a way that she could read it in my expression to save me from ill-chosen words.

"Shall I make tea?" Luc, ever the gentleman, giving us privacy. I'm sure he's wondering what the hell's going on here, but he sees I have something to say and goes out of his way to accommodate me. Closing the door softly behind him we are left in silence.

"What is it Prof?" I think for a minute, trying to decide how exactly to put it. I'm slightly taken aback by Luc's presence here. It's kind of altered the way I envisaged this and now I'm not so sure how good an idea it is. "Prof, say something. You're making me nervous." She does indeed look worried and I'm still struggling for words. I shouldn't have come. I should have planned this better. Luc returns with three mugs of tea and I feel mildly irritated. I haven't even raised the subject yet and we're interrupted again.

"Luc, I could do with speaking to Carly alone for a minute. Would that be okay?" He glances over at Carly who looks from me to him and nods.

"Sure," he says and stooping to pick up his jacket from the back of a seat whispers a kiss gently on her forehead. "I'll go play some pool across the road. See you in a while."

"He's a good kid," I say for no real reason the moment he leaves the apartment. She nods again. "I didn't realise you two were…together," I tell her. Once more, the nod and I wonder if she's suffering from the same debilitating lack of communication skills as me. Go for it I urge myself. Just go for it. You'll never know if you don't. Taking a deep breath, I do. "I went to see James Harris today," I blurt out. She pales visibly in front of me. "How is it that you know him, Carly?" I ask her.

Virtually inaudible, I have to strain to make out what she says, "He's…He was…my social worker."

Now it's my turn to nod. "Carly, I know. I know it all. He told me everything." I wait for a response, a confirmation of understanding. She's staring intently at me, not moving, not speaking. Suddenly, silently a tear breaks free and she blinks it away. Another follows, and another. We sit for what seems like eternity, looking at each other until I realise that I can feel her hot tears running down my own cheeks. I reach out to her and she falls into my arms. Holding her close the tears come faster. I stroke her soft hair as she sobs into my embrace and I can no longer hold back; weeping hopelessly for a lost love, a lost wife, a lost mother.

After a while she leans back and stares up at me with those impenetrable eyes. I look and look but I cannot see Claudine in her at all. There isn't the slightest resemblance. That's perhaps a good thing I think. She was Carly, my student before she was Carly, Claudine's daughter. At least she was to me. I knew her and admired her, liked her even before all this and I'm glad of that. We're not standing here forcing a relationship. We already have the foundations. I don't know her story yet. I don't know her background or how she came to discover her roots. I don't even know if she wants me in her life. I know I want to be something to her though. All I can think is that something good has come out of all this mess. If things had been different, maybe I'd have had the opportunity to be a proper father to her. I'd like to make things up to her if she'll let me.

"What are you thinking?" she asks.

"I'm thinking that I need to be by myself for a bit. You know, think about things." Her face clouds over with disappointment. "Carly, this is good…isn't it? It's all good as far as I'm concerned. I guess this makes you kind of my step-daughter."

"Oh." Once again a glimpse of unhappiness filters through her closed expression.

"It's all been a shock to me that's all. I'm not running out on you, if that's what you think. I just have to work through some issues. Not stuff about you specifically. More to do with my wife having a life I knew nothing about. Can you understand that?"

"Yes I understand. I'm just being silly. I think I had this fairytale idea of how everything would work out for me once I found my real family, that's all. Anyway, you're right, a bit of breathing space would be good. I've got Luc to think of after all." The mention of Luc sends a shiver down my back. She reads the horror in my eyes. "I know. I know. I tried not to get involved. Honestly. You don't… you can't understand what it was like. For the first time in my life I felt truly wanted, loved even. I tried to stop it, but it was so hard. I never meant to get involved, I promise." The tears are welling up once more and my heart goes out to her.

"Hey, don't cry. It'll be okay…You do need to sort things with Luc though…quickly. You can't allow this to go any further, you realise that?"

"Yes, yes I realise that. I'll fix it…tonight…when he comes home."

"Home?" I query. She blushes and turns away.

"We never had that tea," I say gathering the now-cold drinks. "Tell you what. Why don't I make us a fresh pot and then I'll go? Give me a chance to get my head together then I'll meet you tomorrow and we can talk all you want."

"Okay…There's so much I want to ask you, but you're right, we still have tomorrow." Heading through to the kitchen, she follows me, watches me re-fill the kettle, rinse out the cups. "There's just one thing…" I turn, waiting for the unfinished sentence. "Well…it's just I

255

need to know something." I'm waiting expectantly, but she's cautious. "Go on…" I try to encourage her to say what's on her mind.

"Well…I was just wondering…have been wondering, actually…if…well… if you're my dad…you know, my real dad?" Poor Carly! My heart aches for her. She's so young and she seems so lonely, so unloved. I don't know all that's happened in her life, but she appears to me to be really lost.

"Oh Carly! I wish more than anything in this world that I was. For more than one reason I wish I was. But no…I'm not your real dad. I'll have a pretty good go of being your step-dad, though…if you'll let me." A half-smile wavers around her mouth. "I just needed to know. I'm a bit embarrassed now, having asked you."

"No, no. It's okay. It's a reasonable question. It's just…well… you know there are obvious implications for my marriage…" She starts to apologise in a clumsy kind of a way when we're interrupted by the sound of a key turning in the lock. He has a key? Things seem to have progressed pretty quickly between the two of them. I try to remember how long ago it was that she was telling me she wasn't going to call him. It doesn't feel like much time at all. I guess it could have been four or five weeks, but I'm not altogether sure. Time has kind of lost meaning for me.

He wanders through, smiling warmly, clearly happy to be *home.* "Hi guys. Did you have a good chat?" I feel sorry for Luc now: poor ignorant Luc. He has no idea what he's got involved with and he's about to be let down rather unexpectedly I fear. I hope she handles this with the sensitivity I know she's capable of. "What's the matter?" He looks from Carly to me and back again to Carly. Leading him by the hand she says, "Let's go through. We need to talk." A worried look appears on his face, but he goes with her. I try to busy myself with the tea making, but it's a pretty simple process and it's hard to spin it out forever. Unfortunately I can also hear every word and it makes for very uncomfortable listening.

"Luc, I'm so sorry…" she begins.

"Sorry for what? What's going on Carly?"

A moment's silence.

"Luc, I can't see you anymore."

Again, silence.

"What are you talking about? Can't see me anymore?"

"This isn't working for me. I don't think we should see each other again."

"This is a joke right? Just like that...out of the blue...you're finishing it?" She speaks, but her voice has become so quiet I don't hear her reply. "What's happened? Has Len said something about me?" I suppose that's the obvious conclusion to reach. They're getting on great, then I drop by, ask to speak to Carly alone and she drops this bombshell. She's going to have to tell him. She must realise that, surely. Footsteps in the hall and he comes back into the kitchen. "What's going on, Len? What did you say to her?"

I shake my head. "I'm not getting involved in this Luc. This is between you and Carly."

He turns to look at her and she stares right through him. "You expect me to just gather my stuff and go? No explanation? Nothing?" She doesn't answer him. I can see her closing up in front of my eyes. She's detaching herself from the situation, numbing herself from feeling. I've done it myself in the past. He can't reach her and he's becoming increasingly frustrated. "I don't know what's going on, but this isn't over. You owe me more than this." Anger isn't going to get him anywhere, but I understand his reaction. I can't help feeling it would be better if she was just straight with him. At least then he would have the explanation he so badly needs. "Carly?" His voice is pleading with her, but she shows no emotion. Cold as ice she says simply, "I think you better go now, Luc."

He stands for a moment or two, complete bewilderment sweeping his face. "Je ne comprends pas. Je ne comprends pas que se passé-t-il!"

Carly looks over at me: "What did he say?"

Oh great, now we have complete communication breakdown. Luc's retreating into his own world, shutting her out. This is getting really bad. "He said he doesn't understand any of this." She nods, reassured perhaps that it wasn't anything worse, but doesn't reply. He glances over at her, waits for her to speak. Silence. He turns and in seconds is gone. He doesn't stop to collect his stuff. Maybe he thinks it'll blow over and he'll be back. Who knows? I don't think she made a very good job of handling that, but who am I to say what she should have done. Luc's gutted though, that much is clear and Carly, poor Carly looks ready to collapse.

"Hey, you're going to be alright, you know. That was a hard thing to do, but it was the right thing." Nodding, she tries to speak, but only sobs escape. There's been so much crying in this house tonight I'm worried she'll make herself ill. "Come on. Drink your tea and then get to bed. You need some rest." She drinks as instructed.

"He took that really badly," she says finally. "I've hurt him." She's right of course, but I don't want her to get any more upset tonight, so I try to think carefully what to say next.

"Why don't you just tell him the truth? Then he at least would understand. That might help."

"Oh yeah…telling him he's been seeing his niece would be better! You think? How do you imagine that would make him feel? No. I don't want him to know. He doesn't need to know. He'll go back to France now. He'll pick up his old life and he'll be able to forget all about me. If I told him the truth he wouldn't be able to do that would he?" She's determined and I know her mind's made up. "Maybe you should go after him, though. See he's okay."

"Luc will be okay, Carly. He's a big boy. This won't be the first time his heart's been broken. I'm more worried about you. Do you want me to stay?" She smiles, but it's a sarcastic kind of expression.

"Yeah. That would look really good wouldn't it? Everything's great then you come round and I call it all off with Luc and then you stay over! No I'll be fine. I'm just going to go to bed and try to sleep. Maybe tomorrow things will seem clearer." She's right of course.

"Okay then I'll go. Here are my numbers, though" I say scribbling them on a notepad. Various words are scrawled across the page in Luc's elaborate hand. He must have been teaching her French. "If you want anything…anything at all…no matter what time of day or night…you call. Okay? I want you to call me."

"Thanks, Prof. I appreciate it… Will I see you tomorrow?"

"You bet!" I'm a bit unsure of the etiquette of farewells to step-daughters and I don't know whether to hug her or not. She maybe senses my awkwardness and makes it easy for me. Holding the door ajar she gives me a little wave then gently closes it. I set off for home, still wearing, I realise, Luc's clothes.

I'm just turning out of the close when a hand touches my shoulder. I swing round defensively I'm so taken by surprise.

"Hey…easy Len. It's just me." He's obviously waited for me to come out.

"Luc!"

"Mind if I walk with you? I didn't want to go back on my own just yet."

"You gave me a fright there. No I don't mind," though of course I do. I desperately want to spend some time on my own. I need to think, to sort this all out in my head. Was it only this morning my life became so inextricably linked with Carly? I'm also really tired and my head is pounding. Stress I decide. We walk together in silence for a bit, both absorbed in our own thoughts. Maybe he just wanted some company, not necessarily a listening ear. I feel relieved - relieved and a bit guilty. I don't seem to have enough to give emotionally anymore. It's all used up on me and there's very little left for anyone else. Maybe that's why I ask if he wants to stay at my place tonight. I'm not totally sure, but for one reason or another I invite him. He would like to stay, but not for the reasons I've deduced. He left Carly's place without any of his stuff. He has no money, no phone and no keys. Obviously he doesn't want to go back there tonight, so coming back with me is a good option. Most of the way back we don't speak. I dart a sideways glance at him from time to time, but it's pretty dark and I can't read his expression at all. "You okay?" I ask on one such occasion when he catches me looking at him.

"No, not really. Think I'll maybe try to speak to her tomorrow. See if I can clear this up."

"You think that's such a good idea?" I ask.

"You tell me, Len. You seem to know more about this than me." Is he annoyed with me, I wonder? Does he blame me for this? How I wish she would just open up to him, give him it straight. But then, that's because it would make things easier for me isn't it? I must try to stop thinking so much of myself. After all, I have a daughter to think of now, don't I?

## LUC

I shift the weight of my bag to the other shoulder. It's not that it's so heavy, just a bit awkward to be carrying it all this way. It occurs to me that I could head straight to the airport from here. I could probably get a taxi really easily. Hospital entrances seem to be a favoured spot for waiting taxis. I want to see her though. I just can't get my head around all this. I don't understand what's going through her mind at all. Maybe if I see her today we'll be able to sort it out. Things were going great. At least I thought things were great. I've been racking my brain all night trying to see what I've missed. Did she seem unhappy? I didn't think so, but could I have misread the whole situation? I need to try to fix this. I don't know what I'll do if she doesn't want to talk to me.

I see her before she sees me. She's sitting with her back to the door, reading a text book, probably something Len's given her. The sunlight streaming in through the closed window dances over her fair hair. I know how soft that would feel to the touch, but I daren't reach out to her. What happened to us that I now am unable to connect with her in any way? I need to know what changed between us. Beside her the steady drip of the blood transfusion tracks passing time. I don't know if I disturb her or if she just senses someone standing behind her, but she turns and maybe forgetting herself for a moment smiles a beautiful smile. I'm filled with warmth and drawn to her side.

"Are you leaving?" she asks, presumably referring to the bag.

"Well that depends really." She knows what it depends on, but says nothing to reassure me.

261

"You've been over to the flat then?"

Nodding I tell her, "Yeah...I've got everything right here...Not much to speak of is it?" Ignoring the question, dumb question anyway, she holds her hand out. At first I mistake the gesture and thinking she wants to hold my hand, I place my fingers around hers. She pulls abruptly away from me and I'm left apologising clumsily. I wonder if I've misjudged this whole relationship. Maybe there was never anything between us. Was it all my own hopes and dreams?

"You better give me back the key," she spells out to me and again offers her open palm to receive it. This is so bad.

"Carly, what have I done?" I try to read her eyes because her face is giving nothing away. She isn't able to hold my gaze though and quickly looks away from me. Her eyes dart around the room, out of the window focussing on anything rather than look at me. "I just wish I understood...What happened? What changed?" Nothing. She's done this to me before and I hate it. I hate the way she's able to close down completely, shutting me out. I feel so helpless. If I could just get her to speak to me... "Carly, please...please talk to me. Let me back in." I'm virtually pleading with her and aware how vulnerable I'm making myself, but I'm getting desperate. She's scaring me with her total control of this situation. "Do you want me to go?" She nods without lifting her eyes to look at me. "I mean, d'you want me to go back? France?" I almost can't believe my eyes as she shrugs her shoulders. Can it really be that she couldn't care less what I do? Taking a deep breath I rummage in my pocket for the keys to her flat and set them down carefully on the table beside her. She glances at them, but doesn't move, doesn't lift her gaze to meet my frightened eyes. "So this is it then?" How many opportunities am I going to give her? I've got the message. It's not something I understand, but she doesn't want me around. That couldn't be clearer. "I've left my drawing gear at your place. You can have it. I've got masses of the stuff back home." She nods. The reference to leaving for France hasn't had the desired effect. "There's nothing I can say is there?" At last she looks at me "No, Luc. There isn't."

"Even if I was to suggest slowing things down a bit? I know we've moved pretty fast, maybe too fast, but I can back off, give you more space if you thought that would help?"

"No Luc. There's nothing you can say…" she repeats.

"I just wish I understood that's all. It seemed to me one minute things were brilliant between us. You were planning to come over to Paris with me. We were looking forward to so much and then suddenly, without any warning at all, it's over." There's a long silence. I mean a really long one and I wonder if maybe she's not even going to bother to answer me. After all, she's made her feelings pretty clear. Perhaps even my presence here is unwelcome, never mind the demands I'm putting on her for explanations. A couple of times a nurse has looked in, maybe concerned that I'm upsetting her. Chance would be a fine thing. She seems hard as nails right now. She's so different. I stand. Am I about to leave? I'm not even sure myself what I'm doing. This feels so final, so definite. Pushing my hands into my pockets, needing to have somewhere to put them, I feel the bracelet I had bought her. It seems so inappropriate now, but I'm reaching the end of the line and I know it. Picking it carefully out of my pocket I allow the fine silver to run through my fingers before setting it down on the table next to the keys. "This is for you… I got it a few days ago…Maybe you don't want it now…Just bin it if you like." She glances at it, looks up at me and I see tears in her eyes. "Carly, you know I love you. We can work this out," I say helplessly. I've laid everything on the line now. I need something back.

"Luc…" she says carefully, decisively. "This is not about you. It's me." Here we go, I think. I didn't expect platitudes from Carly. Maybe even the excruciating silences would be better than this meaningless rubbish. "I'm still involved with Shane, you see." My heart sinks. I can't believe what she's saying. "I'm sorry. There isn't a future for you and me, because I still love Shane." She looks away now and I'm glad because I feel the anger rising inside me and I really, really don't want to shout at her. She looks so frail, so helpless sitting there. I long to hold her, to make this all go away.

"Shane?" I force myself to say his name. "Shane doesn't care about you. He treats you like shit. How can you throw away everything we are for him? We're perfect together. He's…he's…" She interrupts me with a shake of her head.

"I'm sorry, Luc. That's it. Please go now." She turns away again, staring at something far away. That's it then. Lifting my bag once more onto my back, my eyes plead with her to look at me. She doesn't. There's nothing more to do, so I turn and leave. My heart broken, my hopes trashed. It's over, over before it really began.

# LEN

This morning a few momentous things happened. My folks left town; that was the first thing. They've actually been great while they've been here. I never would have imagined it. I mean we're not a close family. I haven't even seen them for years. But I have to say it did help having some company around the house this last couple of months. I feel quite guilty now that I presumed they had an ulterior motive in coming across for the funeral. I half-expected them to be looking for money at some point during their visit. But no, I was wrong. It was all for me. Guess I'm not such a good judge of character as I thought. So today they left and, get this, they left because they think I'm managing so much better now that they don't feel the need to stay! That must be a good thing. Maybe I'm handling things better than I feel. I must admit Carly has made a huge difference. I've been kept pretty busy too trying to sort the house out a bit and so on, but just knowing that Carly's there really helps. I feel that there's a part of Claudine still here and it's all the good parts; none of the secrecy or the lies, just a talented, beautiful and loving daughter. The fact that she desperately wants me to be her father is another big plus. It would be a very different story if she wanted to go it alone, but she seems to need me and the feeling is mutual.

The second momentous thing of today is that I tried to do some work. I actually went into my office, switched on my P.C. and attempted to create a study pathway for Carly. It was a struggle mind you. It doesn't seem to come naturally anymore and I'm not sure I'd survive a day at Uni, but it's a start and the way things have been lately, it feels pretty huge to me. Carly's pretty keen for me to get back there. I don't know why exactly. Maybe she thinks it will signify things getting back to normal. The way her life has been this past while, that's not a word that instantly jumps to mind. I really admire how she's handling everything. She's such a strange and intriguing combination of qualities. On the one hand so fragile, my instinct is to try and take care of her, protect her and on the other an extremely strong young woman. It's unbelievable the way she was treated by her adoptive parents. It makes me really angry that they couldn't see what they had in her. When she told me of her upbringing I felt so sad. I guess all I could think was how different it would have been if she'd been with Claudine and me. That's something else that's changed. It's becoming more and more difficult for me to think of Claudine without getting angry. Of course I don't let Carly know this. She's placed her mother on a pedestal and there shouldn't be any real surprise there. We all did it, didn't we? Claudine was perfect. Maybe it's my fault she's fallen so short of my expectations. Maybe I shouldn't have elevated her to such an unsustainable status. Or maybe it's just that I didn't really know her after all.

Carly's been really down lately, since Luc left to be precise, so I thought it would be good to give her a treat. I wasn't sure if she would go for it or not, though. I guess it still feels a bit strange getting used to these new roles. It's not awkwardness exactly, but it's just not completely natural yet either. I suppose that's no surprise. One minute I'm her teacher and nothing else, the next I'm also a father-figure of some kind as well. That's the thing, trying to combine the two, because I still am her teacher. It's also a bit difficult to know how hard to push her with her work. In the past, before I knew all that I do about her circumstances and before I became directly involved myself I'd have been asking a lot more of her. In my heart of hearts I feel she's going to have to step up the pace a good bit if we're going to pull this off. Oh, I still think she's capable of first class honours, but I was anticipating a heavier workload than this to get her there. On the other hand, I don't want her to overdo it. She's really very ill and part of me does think it's madness even aiming so high. Having set the standard though, it's difficult to now lower it without her thinking I've given up on her.

So when I suggested that maybe we go away for a few days, just leave everything behind and give ourselves some space I didn't know what she'd say. That's the thing with someone becoming your daughter at twenty years of age; you don't get the chance to grow together. I'm supposed to know how she'll react to things, what she'll like and dislike, but of course I don't. In many ways I don't know her at all. Anyway it turned out great, because she was so delighted at the suggestion. I can't seem to help myself from searching for a trace of Claudine in her, either in appearance or in character, but so far I've failed to identify anything at all. She could be anybody's child, but of course the fact that she's Claudine's is what makes all the difference.

I glance at my watch. I'll need to keep an eye on the time. I said I'd meet her at Outpatients after her transfusion and we'd go straight to the station. She seems to be needing more and more of these blood and platelet transfusions. I don't know if that's significant or not. I wish I knew more about her condition and treatment. I feel I'm trying to keep her positive and upbeat, but it's hard without any real facts on which to base my optimism. Anyway, we'll go away and hopefully recharge and spend some time getting to know one another better.

## LUC

It's strange how easily I seem to have taken on my old life again. I had thought things were going to be different. I was preparing for a completely different future to the one which is panning out for me here. How can everything change so quickly? When I was young, my parents told me I could do anything, be anyone. They were like that. They believed in each one of us so much and we believed it too. We felt we could each carve our own path, make life what we wanted it to be. What happened? When did these dreams start slipping away? Here we are now, Claudine dead, Dominic under the thumb of an ego-inflated domineering tyrant of a wife and Christophe stumbling from one university course to another, clearly afraid of committing to anything at all. And what about me? I took a leap of faith, decided to uproot and take my chances on a new life with a girl I hardly knew. And here I am back home, back in my old job, back with someone I now know I don't love. If I didn't have my painting I think I'd be really struggling through this. I don't have anyone to talk to, there's no-one who would understand. How could they? I can barely make sense of it myself. At least when I paint I can escape from thinking. I can clear my head and stop going round in circles all the time. Most days after school I set off somewhere quiet and spend a couple of hours drawing, getting some sketches together so I can take them home and use them as bases for the watercolours I'm working on. I've never really been one to throw myself into my work, but at the moment it's what's keeping me going. I know some pretty major decisions need to be made and soon, especially where Elise is concerned, but for now I'm burying my head in the sand.

I have my students working in themes this session. It's something I haven't tried with them before, but it's going pretty well. They're an enthusiastic bunch anyway though. I guess that's what comes of teaching a subject that no-one has to study unless they choose. Unfortunately, there's also no evidence of any real talent amongst them either. I'll always wonder if Carly makes anything of her natural aptitude. Then again there are a lot of things about Carly which I think I'll always wonder about. I try not to think about her to be honest. I find it messes with my head and stops me from getting on. Sometimes though an unchecked memory does manage to flutter through to my consciousness and for a moment I allow myself to indulge in the sweetest of contemplations. Two months without her has done nothing to ease the pain of rejection inflicted on me before I left Edinburgh. All the preoccupations I've created around me don't stop me from yearning for another glimpse, another touch. I loved her and can't seem to stop.

Rooftops: that's the theme we're working on right now in school. I force my mind back onto the job in hand. This is what I need to do. So often I find my thoughts wandering and I have to make a concerted effort to drag myself away from these agonising memories, or worse, the thoughts of what might have been. So I haul my psyche back to the view before me and forcibly concentrate on recreating the image I see. This is a café I've come to the last few days. The view is amazing from up here. It's a real find and I can think of countless versions of the drawing I'm working on today, so it'll be a while before I've saturated this scene in my work. I love this little patio veranda on which I've set up my stuff and being so high above the city I get an excellent view of the rooftops layered out below me - orange, brown, terracotta; row upon row upon row graduating downwards in tiers, down through the trees.

Another good thing is that a cute waitress keeps bringing me coffee, so I don't feel in any hurry to move on even though I've already been parked here a couple of hours. If the truth be told, I'm not in any hurry to go home at all. I know I should and I know there'll be another row about me not telling her where I'm going and what I'm doing. It's a shame for Elise really. She feels she can't trust me now and doubts my every move. I can't really blame her, it's natural I know, after what's happened. The ironic thing is that in my mind we're already so far apart I doubt it would bother me if we broke up, but she...she still thinks there's something to save. She's so out of touch with my feelings, she has no idea what's going on in my head.

I'm vaguely aware of approaching footsteps, but sitting so close to the stairway people are coming and going continually, so I don't bother to look up. "Not bad, but I doubt you'll ever make a living out of it!" The voice startles me back to time and place and turning around the familiar smile dispels my daydream.

"Sebastian!" I'm enveloped in his warm embrace, a kiss on both cheeks. My heart leaps at the sight of him, looking so well, so strong again.

"The sun's been doing you good," I tell him "You look great: much better than when I last saw you."

"I'm getting there," his reply typically loose.

"What are you doing up here?" I ask.

"I'm working. Had to get some shifts to bring in a bit of cash. I've realised I was maybe slightly rash in walking away from my livelihood without any alternatives. Anyway, for the time being I'm working in here."

"What, in the kitchens?"

"No, nothing so glamorous," he says sarcastically. "I'm waiting tables."

"Sebastian! You can't be. You're a successful businessman. Don't they know?"

"And why do you think they would care exactly, Luc? They need a waiter, I do the job. They pay me and I go home. That's it."

I'm shaking my head. It's not right. He worked so hard to build up that restaurant. He should have left all this kind of stuff behind him by now. Instead it looks like he's back at square one. My mind is reeling. How does this kind of thing happen to people? Is life really so out of control that stuff just happens to you and that's it?

"What're you doing now? Fancy a beer?" For the first time since I got back I realise there's something I could do because I actually want to do it.

"Sure." And I begin packing up my gear.

There's a bustle of movement and people heading for the stairs and a voice calls over to Sebastian, "Are you joining us for a drink? We're going to Sabine's." It's the cute waitress. She hangs back from the others, waiting to see if he'll take up the offer. It's clear she likes him and I wonder if maybe he's managed to move on there too. He shakes his head and she quickly conceals the look of disappointment crossing her sweet face.

"You're too old for her!" I murmur light-heartedly.

"She doesn't think so," he replies. Raising my eyebrows questioningly I wonder if he's going to fill me in, but he doesn't. When did Sebastian ever share his private life? Not until it was laid bare in the wake of Claudine's death anyway. "Come on then. Let's go," he urges and I resume my efforts to gather up my belongings.

"Shall we just go home?" he says "I mean rather than go on to a bar? If we go home I could make you something to eat, we could sit in the garden…" It sounds so appealing, but I wonder that he can be bothered having slaved all day in that café.

"If you're sure…I don't mind if you're tired…we could find somewhere else…or we could join your friends."

He's shaking his head again. "No, I'd rather spend time with you. I'd like to cook for you. I don't get much opportunity these days and I need to keep my hand in." So we stroll leisurely along an oh-so-familiar route toward my childhood home and his. I feel so relaxed, so comfortable in his company. It makes me realise just how tense the rest of my life must be. The evening is warm, the streets quiet. I love this time of day in Paris, when the busyness of the day has passed and the nightlife hasn't yet started up. It's a very restful time when you get a chance to gather yourself after a hard day. I'm also realising how much I've missed Sebastian. I felt we got quite close again while I was staying with him and when he left it was very unsettling.

"It's a bit weird us both being back here again," I tell him.

"You know I was just thinking that," he agrees. "I guess it's not us both being back in Paris that's weird though, but being back with everything so different." Yes, I think. There's no getting away from it. Claudine has influenced us all so massively and her death has changed everything. Coming home will never be the same, because the memories of our life here as children are amongst the little we have left of her. To be honest I've avoided coming here since my return. There's been no need anyway, because the folks are away helping Dominic and Marie-Therese settle in to their new house down south, so the place has been empty for weeks. I guess if I'd thought about it I might have wondered if Sebastian was staying next door, but as I say I've been shying away from a lot of stuff lately.

"How are you?" I ask him directly as we enter the house.

"It's been hard," he says simply. "And you?"

"You mean you haven't heard? I've more or less turned my life upside down and yet somehow I manage to remain in exactly the same situation I started off in."

He looks confused, but he's smiling. "Tell you what, grab a drink from the fridge and get comfortable. I'll fix some food and join you and you can tell me all about it." I follow his instructions, basking in the luxury of not having to decide anything for myself. I settle down on the veranda and absorb the tranquillity around me.

The kitchen windows are pushed ajar and I can hear him clattering pans, opening and closing cupboards as he sets to work, doing what he does best. It's so easy to relax in such restful surroundings. Each of my senses is bathed in the familiar reminiscence of home. Pots of lavender and jasmine permeate the air with their sugary perfume. A scent I always associate with this place. A gentle breeze lifts the leaves in the trees and the soft rustle provides accompaniment to the chattering birds hidden within. I breathe deeply enjoying the sensation of drawing fresh air into my body. It feels good to be alive. I lie back in my seat and raise my eyes to the heavens. The sky is clothed in a deep blue robe, a vastness of colour uninterrupted by cloud. As far as the eye can see, a blueness so pure and clear I wonder if it's something that can be recreated anywhere else in this imperfect world. I close my eyes, allowing the last of the sun's warmth to wash over my face. Idyllic, I'm thinking when Sebastian appears with a basket of bread and bottles of water. "Couple of minutes…" he says. He looks so much better. I try to think what's different about him. His hair's a lot shorter, he always wore it slightly too long I felt, but it's not that. He's more tanned too, but again I don't think it's that either. More something about the way he looks, not exactly how. I can't put my finger on it. I don't have the energy to think long about anything so I abandon my efforts and retreat into the therapy of peace and quiet once more.

In the distance somewhere I hear a cuckoo's distinctive call echoing through the woods. I haven't heard that sound for years. It takes me back to my childhood, camping trips down south with my brothers. That was one of the benefits of having brothers so much older than me; I got to do all kinds of stuff which made me the envy of my friends: camping without tent or sleeping bags, stretched out under the stars, smoking around a campfire. These were memories in the making. What a pity we don't realise how precious these moments are till they're long gone. If I ever have kids I'm gonna really try to give them a childhood to remember, filled with opportunities and experiences that they can take with them through their lives. This thought leaves me suddenly feeling very sad. Sad for the life lost now to me; my boyhood, my hopes, dreams, all the things I was gonna do or be. I'm sad too, thinking about the future. Where will I be in five years' time…ten? I haven't a clue what I want to do or where I want to go. I'm stuck in this idea of being with Carly, a notion which will never become reality. I wish I could get over her. I think maybe that's why I came back, moved back in with Elise. Okay I didn't have anywhere else to go, but that wasn't the reason. I hate to admit it but neither was making another go of it with her. I think I hoped she might distract me from my preoccupation with Carly, but it hasn't worked.

Sebastian reappears, setting a plate of risotto on the table in front of me and pulling over a seat for himself. It smells fantastic and suddenly I'm starving. "No wonder you look so healthy," I say "If this is your idea of fast-food." He laughs, clearly enjoying watching me eat with such enthusiasm for his handiwork.

"So what's been going on with you then?" he asks. "How have you turned your life upside down?" I think for a minute. Do I want to spill it all out? Is there any point? I'd be better to just hook up with Sebastian again and move forward. No real reason to go over it all again is there? He obviously picks up on my hesitation and doesn't wait for a response. He tries a fresh approach, "How's Elise?" This is worse. I can't lie to him. I've known Sebastian as long as I can remember and never, I think, have I told him anything that wasn't true. He's that kind of person. Trusting, I think. Trusting is the word I'm looking for. "You want me to mind my own business?" he asks astutely.

"No, no. I'm just not sure what to say. I don't want to pour out all my problems, you know?"

He's looking at me intently in that way that he does. A way that makes you understand he's really interested in what you're thinking and feeling. I've seen that blue before I think, as his eyes scrutinise mine. Funny I never noticed before.

"Do you remember the girl, Carly? You met her back in Edinburgh?"

"I remember," he says. "And I remember you speaking about her on the phone. You sounded quite keen."

I smile as I realise how transparent I must be at times. "Yes, I liked her…I thought we had something and then…she pushed me away, told me to leave…that's why I came back." He's finished eating and stacks our plates, pours some more water.

"Is she the reason you stayed over there so long after I came home?" I nod in affirmation. "When you say you liked her…?"

"Yeah I mean I'd fallen for her…like never before. I thought she was the one, you know? If there's such a thing as *the one*."

"There is," he replies flatly. We sit in silence for a few minutes. I know what he's thinking about and I'm reluctant to bring the conversation insensitively back round to me. "So what are you doing way over here, then, if she's *the one?*"

"I told you, she wanted me out. She got back with her old boyfriend. It was finished."

"And if it hadn't you'd have stayed, made a life for yourselves… given up everything that's here?"

"I was in the process of doing that," I say decisively.

"So let me get this straight, cause I'm kind of struggling with it a bit. You love this girl, right? And you would gladly give up everything for her; your job, your home, your let's-face-it girlfriend? And yet, the first hint of trouble and you hot-foot it right back to the safety of those same things? I don't get it!"

"It's more complicated than that. You make it sound more simple than it is."

"You love her, what's complicated about that? I'll tell you something. If I had my time again I would fight with every breath in my body for the girl I loved. Forever's a long time to live with missed opportunities." I look up at him, wondering if he's deliberately drawing a comparison to him and Claudine. "The question is," he continues, "Is she worth it? Is she *the one*, as you put it?" I think about what he's just said. The way he says it, it all sounds so easy. She didn't want me, I remind myself. She told me to go. Then I consider how unsatisfactory her explanations were, how her feelings for me appeared to change overnight. I'm so confused. Sebastian's telling me if I want her bad enough to go after her, to give it my best shot. "Do remember, though," he interrupts my runaway thoughts, "it's me who's giving you advice and I messed up my own love-life more completely and more absolutely than anyone else I ever met. So you may want to disregard everything I've just said. On the other hand, I wouldn't like to see you make the same mistakes I did."

"What if I did as you suggest? What if I went back and fought for her, as you put it, and she made it clear that she didn't feel the same. What if she doesn't feel the same way?"

"Well then you'd know you gave it every chance. Maybe it won't work out, Luc, but if you feel as strongly about her as you're telling me, then you need to live with yourself in the knowledge that you tried your damndest. Believe me, regret is a difficult thing to live with."

I'm suddenly aware of how dark it's become. Without our noticing the sun has ducked out of sight and left behind a cooler evening. Sebastian shivers and standing, suggests we go indoors. This would be a good time to leave, I think. Head back now and face the music. But instead I find myself getting comfortable in Sebastian's kitchen.

"Help yourself to another drink," he says, lifting over another bottle of water for himself. I reach into the fridge and lift out another beer. Tomorrow, I decide, I'm going to start sorting out my life, but tonight I set about getting shamefully, utterly drunk.

I wake to an unfamiliar sound. Voices, or rather voice. One side of a telephone call I realise, someone speaking, shouting in English. I feel completely disorientated. Glancing around the room, I'm aware that I recognise things but I just can't put my finger on where I am. The voice again, moving around the house, more raised now. Sebastian. That's right I came back here with him last night. I must have crashed out on the couch. Swinging my legs around, I drag myself to a sitting position, but feel that I left my head behind on the cushions. The room is spinning, my head thumping: must have had too much to drink last night. I hardly remember anything after coming inside after dinner. I'm aware that the sound of conversation has ceased. A door slams loudly and the walls shake in recognition of a displaced temper. A moment later and he strides into the room.

"Oh, sorry Luc... I forgot you were in here. Helen's driving me mad. Did I wake you?" I shake my head and immediately wish I hadn't. "What's the matter? Did you overdo it last night?" My mouth is so dry I can hardly get the words out to reply.

"Just a bit," I eventually manage.

He laughs and ruffles my hair. "You look like shit! What do you want first, coffee or a shower?" Coffee... definitely! I stumble through behind him and follow him out onto the veranda. The day is hot already. Slumping into a chair, I allow him to prepare the drink and bring it to me. "I'm afraid I can't join you," he says "Need to get to work. The boss is a real taskmaster; makes me feel sorry for my staff now when I think what I expected of them!" He sits though and lights a cigarette, while I begin the tentative business of facing up to the day ahead. "I enjoyed talking to you last night," he goes on "You gave me a lot to think about." I look at him with surprise. I can't remember what I might have said to him, but doubt very much it would be anything life-changing. Turns out I'm wrong. "I think I probably will go back to Scotland after all." Where did this come from I wonder? Surely not instigated by me? "You're right, Luc. It's too late to start everything from scratch again. I've got a thriving business in Edinburgh and there's too much to lose by walking away from it now. Maybe in time I'll be able to expand and move back. Maybe I could open another place here in Paris, but that would be building on what I already have rather than abandoning it. It's either that or I wait on tables the rest of my life." I gaze at him somewhat relieved. I have no recollection of this discussion whatsoever, but fortunately what he's saying does indeed reflect my opinion. His eyes narrow as he inhales deeply on his cigarette.

"You won't be able to do that so freely when you get back over there." I say.

"Why's that?" he asks.

"New legislation...you can't smoke in public buildings anywhere in Scotland now."

"I didn't know that. So the restaurant will be a non-smoking area now? I should know these things. I need to get back there and get on top of it all again." As long as I've known Sebastian, that's what twenty odd years? However long it is, he's always smoked. I can't imagine him getting on very well not being able to light up within his own restaurant. He seems to know what I'm thinking, because smiling again he tells me he's thinking of giving up anyway. "I should really start taking better care of myself. I've been smoking for too long now." Despite this, I think, he appears to be enjoying the cigarette he's having in front of me right now. Smokers always talk like this when they're actually smoking don't they? Make plans for giving up. It's easiest to do that when you're not actually craving one at the time. It's good to see him like this, though; maybe he's getting his life back together. At least he's looking ahead. At least he can imagine there being a future.

"What about your cute waitress?" I ask him as he rises to leave.

"Who?" he looks momentarily confused. "Oh, Isabelle?" he laughs, "You're right about her as well...too young!"
Setting off down the path, he turns suddenly and calls back to me, "Hey, Luc. When do you get your holidays from school?" I shout back that they start in two weeks' time. "Think about coming with me then. See what happens?"

## CARLY

This has got to be one of the most beautiful places on earth. Prof obviously put a lot of thought into this trip and I'm so grateful to him. It's just what I needed; a chance to get away, space to think. He says he's never been here before either. At first I thought maybe this was a hideaway that he and Claudine escaped to when they wanted to get out of the city, and I must admit I kind of liked that idea. He said no, though, that it's just a place he'd always wanted to spend some time and thought this was the perfect opportunity. I suppose I like to think I could share some of the Len – Claudine life, the way it might have been if I'd found them sooner. Maybe I'd have been a part of some of their trips; maybe I'd have had some memories of times spent together as a family. It sounds as if I don't appreciate all that Prof's doing for me and that's not right. I do, I really do. I'm so glad we've got things out in the open. It means that we're able to move on together. I guess it's just a bit disappointing that I never really got to know her as my mother. I would have so loved the chance to call someone Mum and to know that she really was. The other thing is that I got so close. If I had managed to get together the courage a week earlier I might have found her when I called round to the house. As it was, fate had stepped in while I was busy going over in my head all the different possibilities and scenarios which might greet me when that front door was opened. How ironic, I think, that Claudine was already dead and yet I was worrying about how she would react to my visit.

I could have spoken up sooner, of course. I mean I had known for ages. When I decided that I wanted to find my real family, it actually wasn't that hard. I'm not sure why I waited so long to look for them. Maybe I was scared of further disappointment. I had felt so rejected for so long, but at least I had the dream of a future filled with possibility. To find them and to not be wanted, well I wasn't sure I was strong enough to cope with that again. Coupled with the fact, as Shane often reminded me, that my biological parents had given me up already, I couldn't be sure of a warm reception. Shane was good for that. He kept my feet on the ground, stopped me from aiming too high. So it wasn't a decision I took lightly. When my eighteenth birthday came around, I think I decided it was now or never. I wanted to know for the sake of knowing, not because I imagined there would be a great family reunion. I guess I thought that perhaps my parents would have given me a thought on that memorable birthday. It's such a milestone, I figured that maybe I'd have been in their thoughts and so it might not come as a complete shock if I managed to trace them. I'd read lots of stuff in magazines about people trying to find their real family, so I always thought it would be really difficult, taking years of researching and travelling the length and breadth of the country, following false trails and so on. I think Shane was really surprised too at how straightforward it was. The only place I could think of to start was to make an appointment with my social worker. Strictly speaking he wasn't my social worker once I turned sixteen, but I knew him so well that I didn't think he'd mind and I suppose I thought he'd be able to point me in the right direction as I worked out how to go about it. As it turned out that was all I had to do. He knew the whole story and was able to help me straightaway. I've always liked James. He treated me really nicely whenever he came to see me. I hadn't had a lot to do with him in recent times though. He was very busy and once my adoption had gone through there wasn't any real need for social services to stay involved to the same extent. I think he stayed in touch as I was growing up more because he felt personally involved than anything else, although of course I didn't realise this at the time.

Anyway, once I made that appointment with him my mind went into overdrive. I imagined all sorts of things. Some of these depicted the best possible outcome, others a dreadful one. The only thing I knew for sure was that not knowing was beginning to be a problem for me. I felt that I didn't really know who I was. I had never really felt that I belonged anywhere and I needed to understand how I fitted in to the world around me. So the visit to James, the same visit which Prof made a few months back, marked the opening of a story which I had been part of but didn't know about.

When I think of Prof, finding out all that I did, I feel so sorry for him. He didn't know anything about it. He didn't know Claudine had had a baby and everything. He didn't know about me. James was able to tell me immediately that he knew who my mother was. He didn't just know where to find out or even what her name was. He actually knew her personally. That was what made it all so easy. I was really taken aback of course. I didn't go into that meeting expecting to come out knowing who she was. I thought it would be the beginning of a long journey which might never yield the truth. He said that he could certainly help me and would tell me all I wanted to know. At that precise moment I wasn't sure what I wanted to know. As I say I hadn't expected to find out any hard facts at all that day, so I was somewhat taken off guard. He was really understanding, though. I remember him telling me to take my time, making me tea and saying I could come back another day if I felt it was all happening too fast. I did want to know, though, and so slowly he started to tell me the story of my life. He told me that she, my mother lived nearby and that she knew me. I almost fell over when he told me that bit. She knew who I was and I didn't know her. At first it seemed a bit creepy. I felt like someone had been watching me and I wasn't sure I felt totally comfortable with that. He seemed to realise what I was thinking, because he explained that the agreement had been that when I was adopted she would have no contact with me. My adoptive parents had been adamant about that and so she knew she mustn't get in touch with me. He told me how hard it was for her to know I was there and yet to be unable to be part of my life. She had told him that if I was ever to try to find out about her she wanted him to tell me and if I wanted to meet her it was to be permitted. I left that day knowing there was a whole lot more, but I wasn't really ready to cope with every detail. I had her name and address and that was what I really wanted. At last I had a name, Rousseau. And I had the name of my mum, Claudine Rousseau. And best of all I had a face to match the name. My art teacher, Claudine Rousseau was my mother and she knew who I was. I felt exhilarated and petrified at the same time. I wondered how she could meet with me week in and week out and never say anything, never show any inkling of her knowledge. Now I understand that she was waiting for me. She was waiting for me to want to find her, to be ready to find her.

Once I had her name and address it was enough for me for a bit. I didn't immediately feel the need to run up to her and blurt it all out. I savoured just knowing for a while. If I'm honest there was a bit of me which was enjoying knowing without her realising. It meant that I could watch her in presumably the same kind of way that she was watching me. I hoped that one day there would be a re-connecting, but I was also scared to upset the status quo. I didn't want her disappearing from my life again. At least this way I knew where she was. I had also been warned right at the start that sometimes when people start searching for their real family that they stumble across some unpleasant truths. The example that was given was that of a family established without any knowledge of the adopted child. For all I knew she might have another family who didn't know a thing about me and I might not be welcome into it. How ironic then that Prof and I are sitting here in this peaceful haven, totally at ease with each other, forging a relationship even in the absence of our mutual tie. I missed my chance with Claudine. It upsets me to think about that, but I'm also quite philosophical about it. It wasn't to be. What I've gained, though, is far exceeding any hopes I had of my family. I have a father who loves me and respects me and seems to enjoy being with me. I always was fond of Prof, but now I'm able to see a really caring, tender, loving side to him and I feel so lucky to have him in my life. He's everything I ever would have wanted in a dad and more. I would find it difficult now to imagine life without him.

"Do you want another cup? You've let that go cold." His voice startles me and I realise I must have been away in a dream for a while. I look down at the cup of tea in my hands and wonder how long he's been sitting there watching me.

"I'm sorry. I was miles away there," I tell him.

"Somewhere nice?" he asks gently. I'm never too sure how much to say to him about Claudine. I think it really upsets him talking about her. I understand he was completely besotted with her; she was his everything and then I come into his life and I represent a completely different side to her. He doesn't blame me though, not at all. As I said, he seems to like me and likes being with me. It's not a case of him tolerating me, he has welcomed me into his life and I love him so much for it.

"Just dreaming," I reply.

"Shall I make more tea or would you like to be left to your dreams?"

I stand and collect in the cups and plates left over from a leisurely meal of bread and cheese. "I'll make some. You sit a while." He lets me do it, but I know he's itching to jump up and take over. I'm beginning to read him quite well. He's worried about me. I understand that, but he doesn't want me to know. He would run around doing everything for me, only he knows then that I would realise how concerned he is about my health. What he does instead is he lets me do stuff, not much granted, but he's watching the whole time to make sure I'm alright. It's very sweet of him, but it can make things just a little awkward.

"You make great tea," he says as I hand him a mug.

"You just think that because you're foreign. The British are the only people who can make decent tea!" I tease and settle down beside him again.

"Foreign?" he almost chokes on a mouthful of his drink. "I'm not foreign!" It occurs to me that I don't actually know all that much about Prof. He's filled me in on lots about Claudine, but he hasn't told me all that much about himself. This is a classic example. I don't even know where he's from.

"Where are you from exactly, Prof? You have a very interesting accent. Are you American?"

He pales visibly in front of my eyes and I realise I've said something wrong. In the silence that lies between us I replay the last few lines of our conversation and I can't identify the problem. Occasionally he does this, kind of disappears into an inner world where I can't reach him and I don't understand why. I don't know whether to say something or to just leave it. It's hard when you don't know what you've done wrong to know how to react or how best to fix it. Surely he knows I didn't mean any harm, that I was only joking. His words are a whisper, "I'm Canadian," he says. "I speak French, but I'm more comfortable with English."

I nod still wondering what the problem is but not daring to upset him more by asking. I decide to just leave it, it's not important after all and I know grief can do funny things to people. He has more to say though. "I'm sorry, Carly. It's just such a strange thing. You don't resemble Claudine in any way and yet your words have just tumbled down across years and I see her so clearly in you." I don't know whether this is a good thing or not. I'm so aware that he's having difficulty with the issues around Claudine and I sometimes wonder if I make it all worse. "No it's me who should be sorry," I say, "I make it all much harder for you don't I?" He turns to look at me, "What do you mean?" Maybe I should leave it. I never know when to just leave it, do I? He wants an answer though, is waiting for one. "Me being here…it makes it much harder for you." I state it as a simple matter of fact, so that he doesn't feel the need to make a big discussion out of it. "No. It makes it better for me. Living without Claudine, of course that's hard. Living with you is what makes my life worthwhile." He's staring very intently at me. His eyes are so serious. I wonder when was the last time they laughed. Despite what he says, I know it's hard having me around. Okay, maybe he likes being my dad and likes *me* even, but I know I'm a constant reminder of his wife's infidelity and that can't be easy to live with.

As well as that there's this stupid illness to contend with. Now I can totally see that living with someone who has cancer must be a nightmare. Shane struggled and struggled. Shane eventually gave up. I don't blame him at all because I can understand how awful it must be. Prof hasn't even seen me really sick either. By the time he got involved with things I was picking up again, so he hasn't seen any of the really nasty episodes. When I start chemo again, that'll be the testing time. It's so strange. Everyone knows someone who has cancer, but very few people really understand what it's like. Growing up, I sometimes got to know of someone or other who had it, a neighbour perhaps or a friend's uncle or someone like that. It's all so distant though. It's easy to be sympathetic when the disease is kept at arm's length. It's perhaps even a bit exciting to know someone first-hand who has such a sensational condition. The reality is very different. I don't doubt that Prof will last the distance with me. I know I can depend on him; it's just that I'm not sure I want to put him through it. He's had such a difficult time and I sense he's still pretty fragile. I don't want to set him back farther. I feel he's come a long way these past few months. What I'd like to see now is him getting back to work. He's so gifted and it'll be a real waste if he throws it all away. He's talked about it, not much, but the odd suggestion that maybe his time in teaching is up. I'd hate to see that happen. I feel I'll need to be careful not to lean too heavily on him. That's easier said than done though; especially when your whole world is threatened, especially when you're frightened, especially when it's your dad.

# LEN

Looking over at Carly, I still can't believe she's here with me. This holiday was such a good idea. I really felt we needed to escape the pressure for a little while, to take the chance to get away and just spend time with each other. It's not difficult though. I enjoy her company so much. She's such an inspiring young girl and she gives so much. I hope I don't fall short of her expectations of a father, though. I'm not very good at this sort of thing. I wonder who would be mind you, discovering her as I did at twenty years of age. She asked me if I find it hard having her around, presumably a reference to reminding me of Claudine. The funny thing is that she doesn't actually remind me of her. Of course I'm always aware of the connection, but she's a very different girl to the one Claudine was when I met her or to the woman she became. Claudine was much more self-assured, more confident and perhaps even more able. Carly is very insecure, anxious to please and way, way more sensitive. Neither is there any physical resemblance. I find that bit the strangest of all. I guess you just sort of expect a daughter to look like her mother, but Carly doesn't. So having her around me isn't a reminder in the way that she thinks it is. What she does represent is something good which Claudine left behind and in that I suppose I think of her as part of our life.

This place is so beautiful. I think she has enjoyed being here, getting some rest. She's been busy this past month, painting and drawing every day. There hasn't been so much reading and writing as I might have hoped for from an Honours student, but I've tried not to say too much. I don't want her getting in a state about it and, to be honest, I'm no longer sure she's going to manage what we've been aiming for. If she's happy with her art then that's fine with me. I just want her to be happy. My main concern is the condition of her health. She's told me not to worry, that she's convinced she's going to beat this thing, but her words don't match her expression when she thinks I'm not looking. I know she's worried and I'm guessing she's trying to protect me in some way. I've been doing a bit of research and I'm aware she's far from out of the woods yet. It's so wrong. I just can't get my head round the idea of her having cancer. She's so young, has her whole life stretching out before her, has so much to offer the world and yet here she is struggling to hold onto life itself.

It's starting to get chilly. I should suggest we move inside, but raising my head to speak I see she is absorbed watching a fishing boat steaming its way out to sea. The water looks cold and a strengthening wind is whipping the waves around the boat in a froth of foam. The gentle monotony of the engine provides a background noise which both soothes and disturbs at the same time. A flock of hopeful seagulls are gathered around the vessel as it motors its course through the salty waters.

"They're brave men to head out on a night like this." she states.

"Yeah, it's starting to get quite choppy out there. I guess they have to go, it's their livelihood isn't it?"

She's quiet again, her eyes straining to see the now-tiny boat as it continues on its path. "It makes me feel really safe in comparison," she says.

"I know what you mean," I tell her and putting my arm around her shoulder guide her gently into the warmth of the cottage.

"Do you think there will be a storm tonight? The forecast said so earlier."

I don't want her to worry, but it looks pretty clear to me that it's getting wild outside. The wind is picking up strength and heavy, dark clouds are descending over the bay. "They know what they're doing, Carly. These men go out in all weathers to fish. If anyone knows the changing weather and what it can do, it's fishermen. Try not to worry." I set about making a warm drink. This has become a bedtime ritual for us. I prepare some supper and we sit together reading or talking, sometimes listening to music, occasionally in comfortable silence. For me it's the nicest time of the day, when we're both tired, but happy just to be in each other's company. Whatever did I do without her? The thought which follows instinctively on from that one is so awful I can't bring myself to contemplate it. Whatever will I do without her should anything happen? And by anything, of course I mean Cancer. I'll admit it to myself, but never to her. I'm absolutely terrified of this disease and what it's capable of doing to my precious girl.

We've only had one trip back to Outpatients since we came away and I'm really glad for Carly that that's all. I think she badly needed to get away from that place for a decent length of time. They took blood that day as they seem to at every visit. I wonder she hasn't turned into a pincushion with all the needles they punch into her. We were forced to hang around for several hours while she got a top-up of blood, but we just came straight back afterwards. It was amazing mind you, the difference in her after the transfusion. She was so full of energy that night, sitting up late chatting about anything and everything. She looked much better too, her colour much healthier.

Tonight she's pale again and tired. I've noticed her becoming increasingly tired over the course of this week. Maybe it's not such a bad thing that we're returning to Edinburgh on Friday. I hate to leave because it's been such a retreat being here, but I'm not really happy with how she is. My gut reaction tells me something isn't right. It's hard to know though, because she will never admit to feeling bad. The most she'll say is that she's a little tired. From that I read absolutely exhausted, but they're my words not hers. Yes, Friday's a big day for her. We'll go back in the morning and we meet with the consultant in the afternoon. She's hoping to hear that she's in remission. I can't help thinking she should be better than this if that's the case. However, my job is to keep her positive and upbeat. At least that's the role I've assigned myself. Focus on Carly and how she's doing and the rest of my life assumes a far less significant status. After all, any father will tell you his child's life is far more valuable than his own, won't he?

# SEBASTIAN

I'm wakened from fitful sleep by the glare of headlights illuminating the room as a car slows and stops outside my window. The engine continues its pulsating throb as voices disturb the quiet night air. Reaching across the bed I tug back the curtain and see two shapes moving about in the dark, unloading bags from a taxi. Still half-asleep I pull on my jeans and head downstairs. Monique calls to me from her room, wondering what's going on. I tell her it's fine and to go back to sleep. A glance at my watch says it's two-thirty. It could be any time really, I feel like I've only been asleep five minutes although I came to bed hours ago. I've never been a good sleeper, but this is definitely something which has been getting worse over the years, increasingly so recently. Opening the front door I find Luc standing on the doorstep, a sheepish expression on his face. "I'm really sorry to turn up like this, unannounced," he begins.

"Luc, it's the middle of the night! Is something wrong?"

"No…yes…well…"

A quick glance around at the heap of baggage on the road and the penny drops: "She's thrown you out hasn't she?"

"Well, I've left, yes…by mutual agreement…she's…yes, she's thrown me out."

Shaking my head, I can't help smiling at the unhappy boy standing there looking so forlorn. "Well, you better come in before you wake the entire neighbourhood." He hesitates, glances back at the waiting taxi. "What is it?" I'm getting impatient. It's freezing out here and I want to go back to the warmth of my bed.

290

"Well, it's just that…"

"What the hell is it Luc?"

"My stuff!" he explains lamely, indicating the car still sitting there with its engine humming into the still air. Oh no, I think. This is all I need in the middle of the night.

"Right let's get it then," I say and start to help him empty the boot of the taxi. She's thrown him out all right. This must be every last possession he owns packed in here. We set to work quickly and soon the pavement is laden with his "stuff" and the taxi finally beetles its way down the street. Just as well it's not raining or this would all be ruined. Closer examination shows me that a lot of it is. Broken easels, torn canvases and bashed boxes demonstrate the extent of the fight that obviously took place tonight a few miles down the road.

"I really am sorry, Sebastian," he says, "I didn't know where else to go." I guess your options are limited at this time of night. In a way I'm pleased he felt he could come to me when he found himself in trouble.

"A tip from an expert," I tell him, "Don't get into a heavy discussion with a girl after ten o'clock at night. In fact, don't even talk to her after that time: that way if you have a row, at least it's daylight when you have to move out!"

"Very funny," he says and starts dragging bags into the hall.

"What about all this?" I say indicating the pile of broken pictures and equipment.

"She wasn't pleased," he says simply.

"I mean do you want it?" A shake of the head is all he gives, so preoccupied is he with unloading the pavement of its unexpected booty. It's a shame so much has been spoiled. I can see hours and hours of work ruined in a moment's rage. "So what did you do to deserve this?" I ask once we're finally indoors surrounded by boxes and bags.

"I told her the truth."

That explains it. "I see!"

The poor boy's shattered. I suggest we leave it all where it is till morning and show him to the spare room. He collapses onto the bed and I'm sure he's asleep before I even switch off the light and pull the door closed. I know I won't get back to sleep now and rather than lie awake troubled by thoughts, I head back down and start stacking his worldly goods neatly in the living room. Tomorrow he can go through it all himself. I wonder what he'll do now. Maybe a trip to Scotland is on the cards after all. I do hope the girl is worth all this, for Luc's sake.

## LEN

I'm woken by sobbing; heart-rending, frightening sobbing coming from the end of my bed. For a moment I don't know where I am. Sitting up I desperately try to force my eyes to focus in the dark, to put a name to the shadow that is the source of this terror. A flash of lightning plunges a fork of brightness across the room and for a moment Carly is bathed in light. She is distraught. Leaping from the bed I gather her into my arms, holding her close. Her slight body heaves with the effort of crying. The intensity of her distress is really scary and I'm not sure what to do. Outside the thunder continues to roll ever closer, the wind gusting with increasing ferocity. Something somewhere in the distance clatters, clearly powerless in the face of the storm. Another flash of lightning and I realise we look like we're standing in the middle of a horror film set. I need to calm her down. This can't be good for her. I wonder if she's ill, has something happened. Setting her gently on the bed, I pull some clothes on, every now and then catching a glimpse of her stricken face in the half-light. Leading her through to the kitchen, I flick a light switch as I pass, but there's no response to the empty click. "Power must be down," I say and my voice sounds far too loud in the silence of the house. I sit her down on the couch. She seems to have no will of her own, her body moving only at my insistence. Kneeling in front of her on the floor, I can't think of anything to do to break into her pain, so I hold her in my arms and will her to feel some comfort from my touch. We sit like this for what seems ages. I've no idea; the only measure of time, the nearing storm until finally a crash of thunder right overhead. We both jump at the viciousness of its rage. It feels like something to be feared and I have to remind myself it's only a storm. Gradually, gradually the thunder travels on, becoming more distant, less threatening. Now the rain comes; battering cruelly against the windows, bouncing off the flat tin roof sheltering us within. The storm continues to whip debris around the house, occasionally smashing something savagely against the door. The letter box rattles as the wind forces its way in, snaking through the narrow space, whistling its unwelcome presence.

Little by little the gasping sobs start to ease. She feels like a doll in my arms, lacking resolve or spirit. She's worrying me, but at least the dreadfulness of her cries has ceased. Eventually she pulls away, fumbles in her pyjamas for a tissue. She's exhausted, her pale face gleaming white in the dim light of the room. "Okay?" I ask.

She looks at me, deep, deep into my eyes, "I'm scared." She says it simply, as if it requires no explanation.

"You're okay," I assure her, "It's just a storm. It's passing."

"No, not that. I'm not scared of the storm, at least not this one. I'm scared of dying. Prof, I don't want to die." Her eyes well up with tears again, but she doesn't have the energy to display the distress she feels. Instead the tears trickle softly, silently down her cheeks; terrible in their simplicity.

"Carly…Carly. We're going to do this. We're going to fight it. With everything that we have we're going to fight it."

She shakes her head. "I don't think I can. I don't think I can go through another round of chemo. I don't want it. I don't want to fight it anymore." I hold her arms steadily so she's forced to face me and I stare at her until she lifts her gaze to meet mine. "You don't have to. I'm strong enough for the two of us. I'll give you all the fight you need. Carly, you can lean on me. I can take it." Averting her eyes, she appears unconvinced.

"I can't expect you to go through all this with me. Your life's been shattered already. I think it's asking too much of you, of anyone. You don't understand. You don't know how bad it could get. I might die, you know. I might." I release her arms and stand in front of her. "Carly, I'm scared of dying too."

She looks up, confused. "Yes, but you don't have leukaemia."

"No, I don't. Neither did Claudine."

"I know what you're saying. It doesn't make me feel any better though."

"That's just it, Carly. You don't have to feel better. You just have to believe. Trust me. I'm here for the duration. I'm not going anywhere. You are my life now." She's quiet. I wonder if I've made things worse. The last thing I want to do is let her down. After a while, she yawns. "You're shattered. Do you want to go back to bed?"

She shakes her head. "I don't want to be on my own," her voice a whisper.

"Okay," I reply. Heading back through to her room I set about stripping covers off the bed and drag them into the kitchen. She's lying on the couch now, so I squeeze in at the end and rest her head gently onto my lap. Tucking her in, she looks like a child, warming to the security of the blankets. "Okay like that?" I ask her, stroking her soft hair off her face. There's no answer. After a minute or two, I hear the steady breathing that is characteristic of sleep. Leaning my head back against the couch I watch her closed eyes, her chest rise and dip, and finally, finally allow my own tears to fall.

# LUC

I wish Sebastian would hurry. They've called our flight and there's no sign of him. I appreciate he's nervous about returning to Edinburgh, going back to all the things he's run from. On the other hand it seems like he's really got himself together since he's been back home. All morning, though he's been pacing around restlessly and I know he's having second thoughts. I'm not sure that the many phone calls to and from Helen this past week have done much to persuade him this is a good idea either. He doesn't talk much, but living in the same house it's difficult to ignore the raised voice, the door slamming that seems to accompany each of these conversations. Despite this he's packed his stuff and here we are. Or at least here I am. I'm still not sure where he's got to. I'm starting to get a bit anxious myself. If he doesn't show then I can't really go by myself. The plan is I stay with Sebastian for a few weeks over the summer and try to get myself sorted out, see Carly, see what's happening. It felt like the right thing the way he put it. I know he's trying to help me by suggesting I accompany him and have a bit of a break away from here. It means I can give things another go with Carly, but without the pressure of having given up everything. It's school holidays so my job isn't in jeopardy while I'm away; to be honest though, that's the only thing I have left here now. I would chuck it in a minute too if I thought Carly wanted me to stay. Where the hell is he? Our flight is boarding now.

This is all I need; to be left here after all the soul-searching it's taken to bring me this far. I really don't want to stand here and watch that flight take off, but without Sebastian... I'm starting to get pretty

296

agitated. I need to make a decision. Will I go anyway? Will I just go by myself? Lifting my bag onto my shoulder I realise I'm going for it. Glancing around the bustling airport lounge one last time I almost don't see him. I do a double-take and spot him in the distance, ambling along as if he had all the time in the world. He's chatting to someone, an air stewardess I see as they get nearer. She's laughing, clearly animated by whatever he's saying to her. What kind of a time is this, I think, to be chatting up a girl? Can he really not help himself? I'm absolutely furious that he's put me through this and clearly for no good reason. As they near, she gives him a little wave and continues on her way. He comes over to me, still smiling, looking relaxed and unperturbed by my anguish. "Ready to go?" he asks. "I think they've called our flight." I'm so annoyed I can't even think of a reply. Angrily I head off in front of him, leaving him to catch me up.

"What's up, Luc? You seem a bit stressed."

Shaking my head I continue on. My sole aim now is to get myself on this plane. Is he really so self-centred that he can't see what he just put me through? He knows what this trip means to me. When we finally settle down in our seats, he turns to me, "Come on Luc. We can't set off like this. What is it? Is it because I went off like that?"

Ignoring him, I gaze out of the window. He sounds so reasonable I'm starting to wonder if it's me that's the one with the problem. Sebastian kind of does this to you though. He does something and you're mad as hell with him for it and then he talks to you and you realise he never meant anything by it and you end up feeling like shit. "I thought we were going to miss the flight," I eventually reply curtly.

"Well, we made it okay didn't we?" he says gently.

He's right of course and it would be silly to keep up this animosity throughout the entire journey. As I said, I know he didn't mean anything by it. "Yeah, I guess I'm just a bit tense, you know."

He nods, "Me too."

# LEN

I'm really not looking forward to the appointment this afternoon. Last week was bad enough, coming home from our vacation and meeting with that doctor was an unbelievably bad experience. I know Carly's really stressed out too. She's been difficult this week and it's not like her. She wants to talk and then she doesn't want to talk and it's hard to know exactly how to respond to her. Of course, I'm not surprised at her reaction. After the news we got last week I'm amazed actually at just how well she is coping. Still it doesn't make the prospect of this afternoon's appointment any easier. I'm just so glad she wants me with her at these things. Terrible as it is for me to sit and listen I would hate to think of her having to endure it all by herself.

The doctor last week was really very good with her and I was so grateful to him for showing her such warmth and sensitivity. I can't stand those who seem to treat her like she's just another case. She's not just another case, she's my Carly and I want her treated with care and respect. When we arrived last time, Carly was ushered away to have her blood sample taken as is the custom at practically every visit. I was shown through a door labelled Interview Room to wait for her to come back and for the doctor to arrive. Immediately my antenna was engaged. I recognised it as a bad news room instantly, but tried to tell myself it can't be only used for that. If they need to meet with relatives they have to go somewhere quiet where they won't be disturbed every five minutes. I should have trusted my instincts, though, prepared myself better. I sat for a couple of minutes on my own and then the door opened and this guy walked in offering his hand to me in introduction, "I'm Dr Armstrong. I appreciate you coming in this afternoon." I took his hand, shook it firmly. He was about ages with me I would say and my first thought was, I hope he knows what he's doing. How ironic I think, I would go crazy if I heard anyone doubting my abilities as Professor on account of my age and here I am casting aspersions on this guy for precisely that reason.

"We haven't met before, I'm Carly's Consultant Haematologist," he said, gesturing me to sit again, "I understand you're her step-father is that right?" I nodded that I was, at the same time wondering what was keeping Carly.

"She's just gone to have her finger-prick done. I'm sure she won't be long," I told him and thought how foolish, as if he didn't know where she was. He probably wrote the protocol which sends her dutifully off to the labs on every visit to have the sample retrieved. My nerves were showing. I tried consciously to get it together before Carly got back.

"Actually I was hoping to have a word with you before Carly comes in on this, if that's alright with you?" I was getting rattled by this time. I didn't like the tone that was being set here. He seemed to take my lack of response as a cue to continue. "There's no easy way to say this…" He glanced at the sheet of paper in front of him, presumably searching for a name, "… Professor Thomas… I'm afraid I don't have good news for Carly today." He paused. I wondered if this was deliberate, an opportunity to see if I'd taken in what he'd said so far. I held his gaze. I was thinking, tell me, just tell me. Imagined words are always worse than the reality aren't they? Not so in this case. In those few moments I had the chance for a few fleeting thoughts to pass through my worried mind, none of them as bad as the scenario he was about to portray for me. "Professor, Carly's disease is proving difficult to manage with conventional chemotherapy. She's had three pulses now and so far we haven't been able to get on top of it for any length of time." Go on, I thought. Keep talking and tell me what you're going to do for her. You can't leave me with this thought, that what you've done so far isn't working. I wondered if he thought I hadn't understood. He was looking at me very intently. It occurred to

299

me that maybe he wanted some kind of a response so I opened my mouth to speak, "Right," is all I managed. It was enough and he continued. "I wanted to speak with you before Carly came in, because I'm going to tell it to her with a slightly different slant. I'm sure you'll understand my need to do that. It's hugely important, though, that you appreciate just how ill she is. I'm going to need your help in supporting Carly through this. I think you need to be fully in the picture."

I was starting to feel sick, my head was spinning. "What are you saying Dr Armstrong?" I asked.

"Okay, Professor…"

"Len," I interrupted. This Professor thing was starting to bug me. "It's Len."

He nodded, "Len…This is how it is. Carly is really sick. Ideally her chemo would have dealt with things, but as I said it hasn't been as effective as I might have hoped. Carly's leukaemia will require much more aggressive treatment to eradicate it. We need to give her much stronger drugs in much higher doses." I saw the logic, but not the problem. There was definitely a 'but' coming. "That should do the job of wiping out the cancer cells. The trouble is these drugs cannot discriminate. What I mean is they don't just target the abnormal cells, they will also kill off her normal blood cells." I was lost. I didn't get it. I thought that's how all chemotherapy worked.

"What does that mean to Carly then?" I asked, feeling increasingly out of my depth, but determined to keep up.

"What it means is that she'll have her entire bone marrow wiped out by the treatment she needs."

The penny dropped; a bone marrow transplant! I wasn't even entirely sure what that was, but I'd heard of them and it was becoming clear this is what he was alluding to. Sure enough, he continued, "She'll need to have a transplant. Because her own bone marrow will be scrapped, it needs to be replaced by healthy bone marrow from a donor. It's a common sense procedure, give intensive chemo, wipe out bone marrow containing cancer cells and replace with healthy bone

300

marrow. Unfortunately common sense doesn't mean easy. This is a big deal, Professor Thomas. It's a high-risk course of action."

I was struggling to take this in. Of all the things I thought might be discussed that day this was not one of them. I had been taken completely by surprise. That will teach me, I thought, to let my guard down for even a short time. The shock is made so much worse when it does come. "What are the risks?" I managed to stutter.

"Well, she'll be at very high risk of infection. That's the first big risk. Without any white blood cells at all she won't have any means of fighting infection. Even a fairly minor thing could …well it could kill her. I apologise for being so blunt. I just don't want you to be under any illusions about the gravity of the situation."

I realised then why he didn't want Carly in on this. I can't imagine what this would do to her if she knew all that I do. "Please continue," I told him, "I need you to be straight with me. What are her chances?" I swallowed hard, not entirely sure that I was ready to hear the reply, but needing to all the same.

"As I said a transplant is a high-risk procedure, the risks being primarily from infection or bleeding. There are other risks but these are the big ones. Her chance of survival, though, if she makes it through those difficult weeks and if the donor marrow isn't rejected, is significantly greater than if she doesn't have the transplant at all."

So what have we got, I thought, trying to process this information into some kind of understandable fashion? "Excuse my ignorance," I said as a preamble to the most horrific sentence I think I've ever had to utter, "Are you telling me, Doctor, that if Carly has this transplant it could kill her, but if she doesn't…if she doesn't she'll die anyway?"

He's very patient, I think as he looks on at my troubled eyes. "What I'm saying is that, in my opinion, a transplant is her best chance."

Okay, okay. Keep it together, I told myself. He's not saying there's no hope. He's saying it's risky, but risky doesn't mean impossible. I don't suppose they would bother to do it if there was no reasonable chance of it helping. We need to go for it. I'd already decided. In my mind we were going for it with every ounce of hope we could muster.

"I know this is very difficult to hear, Profe…Len. But as I said I think it's important that you are aware exactly how the land lies. I've been completely honest with you, brutally perhaps. In a few moments you're going to hear me tell Carly the same thing, but as I said before it will have a very different slant to it. She's a young girl. I don't want to scare her. The other thing is I need her to fight this herself. I can do only so much, the rest has to come from her and for her to do that she needs to believe she can." I nodded in agreement. I fully agreed. She mustn't give up. "Would you like a few minutes to get some air before we bring Carly in?" he asked me. Gratefully I stumbled out of the room, seeking out the fresh air which I desperately hoped would clear my head and help me to focus. I can't fall apart this time. I can't. I need to keep myself together. There's no room for any self-pity or wallowing in despair. No time. I must be strong and positive and I must believe totally and absolutely and without any shadow of a doubt that she's going to make it. Any other possibility is unthinkable. Most of all, Carly must never see in my eyes any glimmer of uncertainty, because if she did I think all hope would vanish and she would lie down and let it take hold. No, I decided, I will take control of this here and now and I'll fight with her until we conquer this monster.

Shaking my head I rouse myself back to the present. Horrific, that was a horrific experience, one which no one should have to suffer, never mind a twenty year old girl. She took it well, I thought, all things considered. I mean how are you meant to take news like that? I actually feel she's taking her cues from me, from my response. I've told her it's going to be alright and I think she's doing her best to trust me. Quite a responsibility, mind you, now to make sure it is alright. We came out of that meeting with a plan and I think that focus took away some of the powerlessness, the helplessness I had originally felt. These doctors know what they're doing. Telling me first was a good move. It gave me a chance to absorb the shock and to get one step ahead of Carly. It gave me the chance to come up with something.

That Armstrong guy was very kind to Carly. I sensed that he's really fond of her. Who wouldn't be? She's a treasure. He took his time telling her and as promised delivered the same message with a far more positive approach. Naturally she was devastated, but because of the advance warning I was able to respond quickly to the openings given me by the doctor. So when he asked the question about suitable candidates for tissue-typing I was ready...

"Morning honey, how did you sleep?" I ask her as she enters the kitchen. She looks so young, cuddled up in her fluffy dressing gown. She also looks tired and I'm thinking she didn't sleep much at all. She mutters something incoherent in reply. Smiling to myself I rise and start preparing her tea and toast, a thin scraping of butter, thick of marmalade, the way she likes it. I'm getting used to her morning moods. In actual fact I find them quite endearing. I know not to push it, though and refrain from any further questions, at least until she's had her breakfast, maybe until after her shower. After that she'll be her usual sunny self.

I'm really glad she agreed to move in here. It was going to be very difficult for her if she didn't. With Shane out of the picture and Luc gone, paying the rent on her apartment would be pretty near impossible. Add to that the fact that she's had to give up her part-time job and has lost her bursary since she's not attending Uni and the problem is compounded. At any rate, I'm glad to have her. This should be like home to her. This is the way I've put it to her; that I'm her family now and this is her home as long as she wants it to be. For me it's fantastic to have the company. It also means I can keep a closer eye on her, see that she's looking after herself properly and try to keep her spirits up.

She finishes her breakfast in silence, then rises and takes her dishes to the sink. "I'll do those," I say and make a move towards her. Ignoring me she sets about washing up and feeling slightly embarrassed I leave it. I know I overstep the mark sometimes. It's hard, though, when my every instinct is telling me to take care of her. I force myself to sit again, pushing my hands under my knees to make sure. Resting the clean crockery on the draining board she turns and gazes absently out of the window. I'm longing to ask her how she is, to get her to talk to me about how she feels, but I know this isn't the time so I leave her alone in her thoughts. I've finished reading the paper and folding it in two I toss it across the table and reach for my cigarettes.

"I wish you wouldn't do that." Her voice cuts into the quietness with a sharpness which surprises me.

"Do what?" I ask her, feeling clueless as to what she's talking about. If she's referring to me sitting in silence, I thought that's what she wanted.

"The cigarettes," she says curtly.

I pause, overly conscious of the cigarette between my lips. Removing it, looking at it, looking at her, I'm confused. "I didn't realise it bothered you," I say simply, "you never said." Still I stub it out into the ashtray and wonder what other surprises she's likely to drop today.

"It bothers me," her words still stiff and cold. "They give you cancer, didn't you know?"

I'm not sure she intends to be so harsh, but it cuts deep. Crushing the packet between my fingers, I throw it into the trash as I leave the room. "That was my last then," I tell her. She doesn't acknowledge my words, her uncompromising gaze continuing to be fixed on something far, far away.

## SEBASTIAN

It feels good to be back; strange but good. I wander around the apartment, taking in all the familiar things. It feels like it's been empty. There's an eeriness about the place. Maybe that's just me making associations though. It was such a bad time when I was last here. I couldn't wait to get clear of it, put some distance between myself and the awful memories which haunted me day and night. I move from room to room, lifting books, pens, everything exactly as I left them. I don't think I supposed Helen would have moved back in my absence, but I did think she might have come up even just to collect her own personal things. Nothing's changed though. That's good, I tell myself. It's my place after all and she obviously respects that. I wonder why she's being so difficult about the business in that case. I've spoken to her several times over the past few weeks and it's clear she doesn't want me to come back. Doesn't need me, is what she actually said.

I'm glad Luc's come with me. It's partly selfish because I know it would have been much harder on my own. At least this way I have someone to distract me a bit from myself. Having said that I'm quite relieved he's gone out right now. I need a bit of a breather from him. Oh it's not his fault. In fact I know I'd be exactly the same in his shoes. He's just… well I guess he's just quite high maintenance right now. I don't mean to be hard on the boy, I think he's great and I understand totally, it's just difficult to keep up with his emotions at the moment. I hope for his sake he gets some kind of resolution from this thing he's got going with Carly. He needs to know. I think that's why

305

he's here in actual fact. He just needs to know. That I understand. If I could replay any part of my life that would be the bit I'd want, the bit where I get to know. How *did* she feel about me? Did she love me all her life as I did her?

I stand up, tell myself to give it a rest. Do something, occupy your mind. I didn't come back here to re-live all the painful memories of the past. I need to stay in control or else this isn't going to work out. I thought I'd made good progress while I was home. Things seemed better. Being back here…hmm…it doesn't feel so good, not right now. Okay, put the coffee on, get busy. Maybe Luc will want to eat when he comes back. I could go out and get some stuff in, make him something. On the other hand he may be fed up with my company, might prefer some time on his own. I felt he was pretty exasperated with me on the plane. I know what he was thinking, he's said so often he thinks I'm helplessly flirtatious. I think he gets a bit annoyed or irritated or something. Babe-magnet he called me. How that makes me laugh; a babe-magnet without a babe! Yeah, if I'm that good how come I haven't known love in all these years? Will I ever again, I wonder sadly? It's so hard to imagine. I don't blame Luc. I don't expect him to understand. How could he know that all the time I'm craving love like I knew it once? All these flighty relationships mere attempts to replace the emptiness I feel, the love I lack. My heart aches to be loved - it's a longing that never leaves me. Instinctively I feel that I'll never again experience such a thing, that I've had my chance, but maybe it's human nature to seek it out anyway. I see myself growing old and lonely and the idea fills me with dread. In some ways maybe it would've been better if I'd never met Claudine. My expectations would be lower. I might have been easier to satisfy. And in the next moment I remember it was she who showed me what love really is. It was Claudine who revealed to me a strength and depth of love that I've never known since. It *was* worth it, I decide. It was worth it to know love that good once, even if it means I never do again.

I need to give myself a shake or I'm going to slip back again. I can feel that blanket of despondency drawing over me and I need to stop it. Maybe one day I'll be able to look back and enjoy the memories without feeling completely stripped emotionally afterwards. The day that happens I'll be over her. I doubt if it'll ever happen, but if I could…if I could put Claudine behind me maybe then I'd be able to move forward, maybe then I'd be able to trust my feelings again, maybe I'd allow myself to love again.

Time for a drink, I decide. This is beginning to go wrong. If I can't shake this melancholy off I'll need to go back home. It occurs to me that I might not be able to do this, stay here, carry on as before. I just might not have it in me. Pouring myself a beer, the first I've had in weeks I realise just how fragile I am. I truly thought I was getting on great. I guess the different environment and different people helped. I wasn't known and I didn't have to explain to anyone how I was. Waiting tables, yes it was mind-numbingly dull, but on the other hand it didn't require me to think. I could operate automatically, do a day's work, get paid, go home. Isabelle was a good distraction too. I'm so conscious of how awful that sounds. Just as well there's no one here to listen to my ramblings other than my wretched self. What a mess I am. My head is in turmoil, I don't know who I am anymore. I sometimes think I can see myself acting out a role. All my interactions seem so fake. Whose benefit is it all for? Am I kidding myself that anyone really cares about me anyway?

This is no good. I've finished my drink without tasting a mouthful and am setting about another. How good's this going to look when I turn up to meet Helen tomorrow and I'm obviously wrecked. Part of me wanted to show her I was alright, that I'd got my act together, that I was capable of running the place like I've been telling her. Leaving the drink on the table I pace restlessly around the apartment, opening cupboards, aimlessly lifting things and putting them back. I'm getting agitated. I need to calm down. Picking up my jacket from the chair where I dumped it I rummage in the pockets for my cigarettes. An empty packet! Great, that means I'll need to summon the will to go out for some more. Frustrated, I throw the jacket as hard as I can across the room, where it hits a bewildered Luc smack in the face as he opens the door.

"Hey!" he shouts irritably as soon as he realises what's happened.

"Sorry," I mumble, "didn't see you there."

Lifting the abandoned jacket from the floor, he comes towards me, "What's up?"

I shake my head. I'm not going there. I'm not about to bare my soul to him, tempting though it is right now. It was his sister after all. "Nothing...nothing new anyway."

He sits at the table, opens a newspaper. "You didn't tell me the football season was finished over here!" He scans the back pages and drops the paper on the table. "I was planning to go watch Hibs tomorrow." I'm so glad he's here. His refreshing youth makes everything so straightforward. He just might be able to save me from myself.

"Where did you go?" I ask him, pleased to have someone else to focus on.

"Where do you think?" he says grinning.

I can't believe he's been round to her place already! That's where we're so different. Luc's much more headstrong. He's impulsive, reckless even, but maybe that's where I go wrong. Perhaps I put too much thought into things. I'm maybe too cautious and then once I'm sure what I'm doing I've missed the boat. "What, you've seen her already?" I look at my watch, we've been off the plane four hours exactly.

"No, I haven't seen her. I've been round to her apartment though."

I remember it well, young love, where anything associated with the girl takes on special significance. He's pleased with himself because he feels near to her. It's a beautiful thing, this kind of innocent love, untarnished by mistakes and misunderstandings. Only that's not the case here is it? I remind myself that Luc might have difficult times ahead if this doesn't go to plan. He wants her badly and he's going to take it pretty hard if she doesn't feel the same.

"Nobody home?" I ask him. I can see he wants to talk about her and that suits me fine right now. Anything would be good if it stops me from thinking about myself.

"Oh yeah, somebody home alright. That asshole, Shane was there. Had a pleasant chat with him…got some things out of my system…"

I shake my head, "Have you been fighting Luc?"

He grins, "Yes, Mum. Sorry, Mum!"

# LUC

I'm feeling fantastic. I'm absolutely buzzing. I can't believe I've already managed to achieve one of the things I set out to do by coming over here. I'd only been off the plane two hours, hadn't even touched base and I'd seized the glorious opportunity to give Shane Robertson a doing; should have done that a long time ago. It happened by chance really, well not the kicking, that was deliberate obviously, but stumbling upon him was just by accident. I'd gone round to the apartment; part of me still thinks of it as our place, even though it was only six weeks that I stayed there with her. Clearly Shane still thinks of it as his, though. The door was ajar when I arrived, music blaring from the kitchen. I did call out, I wouldn't have wanted to give her a fright by just barging in, but the music was too loud. I didn't think anyone would be able to hear me, so I pushed the door open and wandered into the hall.

At that precise moment I wasn't sure I'd done the right thing, dropping by without warning. When I think of how things ended, maybe it wasn't so smart to think she'd be pleased to see me. I just couldn't wait though. I'm so desperate for her. As soon as we landed and I knew she was within reach, I couldn't help myself. I guess I would have looked pretty eager, so as it turned out maybe not a bad thing she wasn't home.

I feel like doing something now, going somewhere maybe. My adrenaline's pumping and I can't settle. Wandering around Sebastian's apartment I stop to flick through his music collection. "You've got not

310

bad taste for someone your age," I say, hoping to make him laugh. He does.

"You're on form tonight aren't you? Is this the result of your reunion with the boyfriend... what's his name again?"

I try to sound annoyed, "Shane, he's called...Anyway it turns out he's the ex-boyfriend now."

Sebastian looks surprised, "That's pretty good going is it not, by any girl's standards?"

He doesn't understand. He doesn't realise that this gives me more hope than ever. I knew she didn't really love Shane. I knew going back to him was a safety net. She obviously ditched him once I'd moved on and that shows me she doesn't have any real feelings for him. I'm not sure about this other guy Shane referred to though. It's possible he was just trying to rile me. I kind of got the impression that was what he was doing, but it's hard to tell. I don't actually know the bloke and yet I can't stand the sight of him. The feeling's obviously mutual too. He was more or less laughing in my face when he realised I didn't know she'd moved out; couldn't wait to tell me she'd shacked up with someone else, someone twice her age. Is that what made me hit him? No I don't think so, because I'm not convinced I believe him. I think I just felt this compulsive urge to smack that stupid smile off his face. It was for treating her so badly and it was for taking the piss out of me. At any rate it felt bloody good and now I'm up for a night out. "Fancy going out, getting a few drinks?" I ask Sebastian.

"Not tonight, I'm afraid. I'm meeting Helen tomorrow morning...can't afford to be below par...sorry."

I'm starting to get a bit agitated now. All this energy's being kept bottled up too long. I need some release. "What'll we do then? Want to get something to eat?" I continue my wanderings, looking out the window then back through to the living room. I'm feeling really confined. I'm going to need to get out. "Your ansaphone's got messages," I tell him as I pass it for the second time, the flashing green light catching my eye. He reaches over and presses the button, waits for a voice.

"You have one message...beep... 'Hi...em...It's Len here...em...heard you were heading back over this way...maybe you would give me a call when you get back...em...I'd like us to talk...okay...em...call soon.' End of messages."

Sebastian looks at me questioningly, "What do you make of that?"

I shake my head, "How did he know you were coming back?"

"Don't know...Helen maybe? I don't know how much contact they've had, but who knows? Maybe they've started a Sebastian-hate group. Why do you think he wants to talk to me? D'you think this is good?"

I'm confused. When did Sebastian ever ask my advice or anyone's advice for that matter? He always seems so sure of himself. I'm careful with my words, because I don't think I'm really in any position to give counsel to him, but I don't want him to think I'm not interested. "I'd be cautious. Yeah, maybe with you gone he's had time to think...maybe he's seeing things clearer now...that it wasn't all down to you." He winces at this last remark. I go on anyway, "You don't know though. I wouldn't want you to get your hopes up and think everything's going to be back to normal just because you've been away ...how long? Four months? Five?"

He nods, but now it's he who is restless; his agitation increasing in front of my eyes. "I need to go out for something. Do you want anything?" I ask him to pick up a pizza and when he agrees I know he's not himself. I don't think Sebastian has ever eaten a takeaway pizza, preferring always to make them himself. He heads off into the stairway and at the last moment I decide to go with him. Grabbing my jacket, feeling for my wallet I follow him. We both need some air and a chance to think.

# LEN

She's been in bits since we got home. It's so difficult to be the strong one in this situation. I think she's right to cry; it wouldn't do her any good to bottle up her feelings. And it's right too that she feels this way. What I need to do is give her space enough to experience her pain, but try to help her feel safe enough to get through it. I know this, but it's easier said than done. What I can't do is let myself go to pieces. I need to stay in control. She's looking to me to make it better. I need to do everything I can to reassure her it's all going to be okay. I too was bitterly disappointed today. I think I'd allowed myself to think we might be lucky. Carly's been having such a bad run of luck lately that I really think things have got to change soon. Even the most downward spiral takes a turn for the better eventually doesn't it?

What am I thinking of? Luck's got nothing to do with this. This is about having the most highly skilled experts in charge of Carly's medical care, taking every opportunity to ensure she's getting everything she needs and staying positive. I've done my research. These are the things which will make the difference. Coupled with the fact that her disease was caught early and treatment started immediately and she should have the best chance. Chance! How I hate that word. It suggests we're not really in control after all; that we could do all these things and more and yet somehow it could still all go wrong. I just can't allow that to happen.

She says she's not hungry so I'm not going to make much for supper. We'll just have something light and she can get more later if she wants. I'm learning, ever so slowly, but I'm learning not to put too

313

much pressure on her. She sets the table very methodically. Always it's the same as if it matters how it's done. I guess that's Carly's trademark though, perfection in everything.

"What'll we do now then?" Her voice surprises me breaking through the silence surrounding us since we got back from the hospital. I'm a bit taken off guard. I didn't really expect her to want to talk about it just yet. That's not usually her way. I pause in my preparations, turn to her to give her my full attention. She's standing forlornly as if she has no idea what to do next, her expression expectant.

"Sit down," I tell her. This isn't the kind of chat you have while peeling the potatoes. "I know today was terrible for you," I go on. She wants me to talk her through it. She wants me to fix it. "We'd gotten our hopes up, probably a bit prematurely, but there's still hope."

She looks me squarely in the eye, "Is there?"

I nod with certainty. We've only just begun. This isn't over yet, not by a long chalk. "Listen honey, we still have options. They did tell us it might not be straightforward finding a donor…"

She interrupts me, "Yes but the family were likely to be the best match and none of them are." She's right and her eyes welling up with tears make me feel so helpless in the midst of her pain.

"Yes, it would've been good if one of them had been a match. We knew they might not be, though. It's just something we had to do as part of the process of finding that match. We had to call them and ask them to be tissue-typed so we would know what the possibilities are. Now we know we can move on to other options."

"Like what?"

This is really hard, because I know as well as her that if one of the boys or Claudine's parents, who were tested last week in the American Hospital in Paris, if any one of them had been a match we would be home tonight with a date for transplant. Instead we're still stuck at square one.

"Well…" I'm so conscious that my voice sounds more confident than I feel, "Well, there's still the National Register…something might come out of that…and I think we could do a campaign at the Uni…you know get people who're not already on the Register to come forward and be tested. We could maybe do a national appeal through the press…a gorgeous young girl like you would really capture the media's attention and we could reach more potential donors that way. There are still lots of possibilities. There is a match out there - we just need to find it."

She nods, but she's looking weary. "The words needle and haystack come to mind."

The other factor which she hasn't mentioned is that of time. We need to do this fast. All the time that we spend searching for a donor is time that this disease is being allowed free reign inside Carly's fragile body. We need to get on top of this and quickly. I'm so disappointed that none of Claudine's family was suitable. I was holding out great hopes as I'm sure was Carly. I'm also sure she's been wondering whether Claudine herself would have been a match. That's another of these secrets which, unfortunately, Claudine took with her to her grave.

"There is another possibility," I tell her, "and I think you should give it some thought."

"What's that?" her voice almost a whisper, as if gradually all her fight is dissipating with her tired breath.

"We could look at the possibility of tracing your father."

She sits in silence. I hold my breath. She hasn't shown any inclination to find out about her biological father since I've known her. Once we shared with each other what we knew about Claudine, she was happy to accept me as her dad and obviously that suited me fine. I think she was more than a bit scared to contemplate this as a reasonable possibility, but I feel in the circumstances it's something we have to consider.

"I'm not sure," she says, "What if he doesn't want to know? What if we find him and he refuses to be tissue-typed or worse what if he is a match but refuses to donate? I couldn't bear that, I really couldn't."

"And what makes you think that would happen?" I ask her gently.

"Well he abandoned me once already didn't he?"

"He won't abandon you," I assure her.

"How do you know?"

"I just do."

## LUC

Back at the Sebastian's place, I'm still feeling agitated. Maybe I should go out for a run, burn off the excess energy I seem to have tonight. I could take a turn around the Meadows and get some fresh air into my lungs. It might help me to focus more clearly and settle my mind down a bit. I decide to do it.

Sebastian's not much company anyway. He does this sometimes; kind of disappears deep down into himself and to be honest I'm not sure I want to rouse him out of it. A part of me is scared to uncover the secret depths of Sebastian. He's a private person and in some ways that makes life easier; he's not likely to want to discuss his problems with others. And yet I'm so conscious of how lonely he must feel at times. I wonder does he offload to anyone. He has so many friends, a great social life and girls aplenty when he wants them, but I do wonder if there's anyone amongst them who would give him the support he might need in the wake of Claudine's death. I suppose Len was the closest friend he had and now that relationship is under tremendous strain. I do feel a bit guilty about leaving him, but on the other hand he seems really preoccupied anyway.

"Alright if I go out for a bit?" I ask him once I'm changed.

"Sure, yeah. On you go. I'm thinking maybe I'll give Len a call back, so it might be good to have…you know…some privacy."

I can't be sure if he's just giving me a let-out or if he genuinely wants some space, but I do need to get out of here or I'm not going to be able to calm down.

## CARLY

It's a beautiful evening. Sitting out here on the deck, it feels very therapeutic. I didn't have any appetite for supper so we just brought our drinks outside to enjoy the cooler evening air. The breeze feels lovely on my hot face. I don't know what I'd do without Prof right now. When I try to imagine what it might have been like coping with all this on my own, I really don't think I could have done it. He's so strong and so positive. He believes absolutely that I can beat this thing and sometimes even I am able to catch his vision. I was shocked tonight mind you when he suggested we try to find my dad. Obviously it's something I'd considered, but I had hoped we wouldn't have to go there. Just supposing we did manage to track him down, and let's face it what are the chances, but say we did, what a guilt trip this is to put on someone! I mean I would be a complete stranger to him and yet we'd be asking him to be my donor. It's a big ask, whichever way you want to look at it. I feel uneasy about the whole thing, actually. I just keep coming back to the fact that he didn't want me. He didn't want me then, so why would he want me now? And if he doesn't want me now, can I really deal with having this man's bone marrow transplanted into my body? It's so invasive, so personal. It would also be life-saving I remind myself. Maybe this isn't the time to get all high and mighty about the ethics of it all. If I find someone whose marrow is a match I should just take it and be thankful. I can worry about how I feel afterwards. At least in that event there's more likely to be an afterwards.

"You okay?" His voice is very gentle, as if he's not sure about dragging me back to the present. I try to smile, but I'm not sure he's convinced. I don't trust myself to speak in case I start crying again. There's been so much of that and it doesn't achieve anything. All it does is make Prof feel really bad and leaves me in such a state that I can't think properly. And if there's one thing I need to do right now it's think. The trouble is time isn't going to wait for me to get my head around all these things. I know Prof is keen to move things forward. He's drawn up a list of contacts at Uni and has spoken to someone at the TV studios; he seems to know a lot of people and that could be really useful. I get the impression he's waiting for me to give him the go-ahead to put these plans into action. I need to get myself together sufficiently to do this. I need to.

"Did you give any more thought to what we were talking about?" He's looking at me very intently. I just don't know anymore. I think I'm going to have to trust Prof on this one. He's never let me down before. It occurs to me that he's probably the only person in the world who hasn't.

"I don't know Prof. I think you'll need to help me. I can't even think straight. Whatever you think...that's what we'll do...whatever you think."

He nods. I know he won't push it. He's so sensitive to my feelings. He seems to instinctively know when to encourage me to talk, when I need a shove and when to just leave me. I squeeze his arm, "I wish you were my dad, Prof, you know...my real dad. It would make everything much simpler wouldn't it? You could maybe be my donor and we could sort this all out ourselves without having to become a public spectacle."

He forces a small smile. "There's no point even going down that road. We need to think factually and deal with the situation as it is...But for what it's worth, I wish that too. I'd have been really proud to think you were my daughter."

He's started scribbling on a page torn from a notepad. Leaning over his shoulder I read his spider-like scrawl:

319

PLAN OF ACTION
1. Father
2. Dr Armstrong re - progress with National Register
3. Student rep re - Uni campaign
4. Media: local and national papers, radio stations, news etc.

The way he puts it, it does look as if we still have lots of options. That's good. Maybe it'll be okay after all. I know that's what he wants to hear anyway.

Suddenly I'm starving. "Shall we eat now?" I ask him. It's not an intentional diversion, but it does double-up as one. I am hungry now, though and we try to eat when I feel I can.

"Sure," he says and offers me a hand to stand up. "Do you want to eat out here or are you getting cold?" I'm mulling over what I would prefer when the doorbell goes. Instinctively I glance at my watch. It's seven thirty. Typical, just as we're about to sit down and eat. "Are you expecting anyone?" he asks me.

"No, I'm not. I'll get it though. You start serving up and I'll get rid of them."

He laughs and heads for the kitchen as I make my way through the house to the front door.

# LUC

"Carly!" I can't believe my eyes. After so long planning this moment, yearning for it, now that she's standing in front of me, I can't think of anything to say to her. I know I must look really stupid, standing here like this, not saying anything. All I can think is how much more beautiful she is than I remembered. She's cut her hair really short and it's lovely. She resembles a street urchin with her closely cropped style and I'm thinking it so suits her. Unusual, that's how she looks. For a moment when she opened the door a smile lit up her face as she shared my surprise. It didn't last long though. A few seconds later and the clouds once again chased it across her sweet cheeks, replacing it with the cold stare I'm being subjected to now. Is she going to keep me out here I wonder? Surely she'll ask me in. She must realize I've travelled all this way to see her, to talk to her. It's starting to get a bit awkward now. I need to do something, say something. "You're looking good," the thought which is foremost on my mind. She continues to stare at me, cold hard eyes that I don't recognise. She isn't pleased to see me. This is going so horribly wrong. I didn't plan it well enough. I'm starting to panic; this might be my last chance. I need to do something right or the opportunity's going to pass and it'll all have been for nothing.

I hear a noise behind her and Len appears by her side, "Who is it, honey? Oh, Luc! How're you doing kid?" An outstretched hand welcomes me into the house, but my feet are stuck on the doorstep. Honey? Did I hear him right? And what's with the arm around her shoulder? What's going on here? And in a flash I get it. Another guy…twice her age…that smug smile…This isn't happening. No way is this happening. What have I just walked into? I feel sick to my stomach. I need to get out of here, I need to get away. Turning, I'm face to face with Sebastian standing behind me. He doesn't move, but holds my gaze. Looking me directly in the eye, his face inches away from mine he nods the slightest of gestures. He's telling me to go in. Doesn't he understand? Doesn't he see what I see? Suddenly I realise. He does get it. He wants me to go in and face up to this. I feel trapped, Sebastian on one side blocking my escape, Len and Carly on the other inviting me into their home. Because I feel I have no other choice and for that reason alone, I reach forward and take the outstretched hand and allow him to lead me inside.

We're invited to sit. When I say we, I mean between the two of them they're managing to be civil to both of us. Len has so far completely ignored Sebastian, while seeming genuinely pleased to see me. Carly, on the other hand, is warm and friendly to Sebastian, but freezing me out altogether. What a good team, I think. I can't actually believe what's being played out before me. My sister's husband and one of his students! It's only seven months since Claudine died. I just can't get my head round this. I understand maybe Len's been feeling lonely and so on, but even so…

This feels like such a farce - the four of us sitting round a table together with so much hostility firing around the room in different directions. I feel sorry for Sebastian. I gather he was actually invited round. It seems he called Len back and was asked to come to the house so they could talk. At this rate there's not going to be much talking done between them. Every now and then I catch Len looking at Sebastian, studying him you could say, but still not a word has passed between them.

I glance around the room, more for something to do with my eyes than anything else. Carly refuses to look at me. I've been trying to make eye contact to ascertain whether there's any spark left there at all, but she won't oblige. The place looks different. On the walls there are three new paintings. I recognise them instantly. Last time I saw them they were hanging in our... I mean, Carly's apartment. I'd know her work anywhere. I'd so love to have even one of her canvases. I'm quite sure Len doesn't appreciate them anyway. An uneasy feeling settles upon me as I realise that I'm actually jealous of Len. He's stolen my girl! I can't do this. I can't sit through this. I know Sebastian wanted me along for moral support, but he must realise that this puts an entirely different complexion on things. I think I'm going to be sick. The silence in this room is so uncomfortable, the atmosphere so tense. It's excruciating. I glance over at Sebastian and right on cue see him rise to the occasion. I know he's as uncomfortable as me, but he turns to Carly and starts chatting to her, so casual, so natural. She responds to his charm, smiling again, offering drinks - the perfect hostess all of a sudden. Would I like a drink? Yes a beer would be great. The bottle is slammed down on the table so hard, she spills some of it, but doesn't bother to apologise, doesn't bother to mop it up. It's Len who comes to the rescue, but even he doesn't have a bad word to say to Carly. It's like she's a spoilt brat and everyone's busy tiptoeing around her. I almost can't stand it. She's making me angry the way she expects everyone to accept this unacceptable behaviour.

"So how are you doing? You look much better than you did the last time I saw you." Sebastian looks at ease, really comfortable with her. How come I can't say anything right? I just don't get it.

She smiles at him, "Yes I'm doing okay. I never got a chance to thank you for helping me; you know when I had that fit. I'm so sorry putting you through that. I'm grateful for all you did that day."

Excusing myself I head up to the bathroom. Splashing cold water on my face does nothing to quell the sick feeling I have in the pit of my stomach. We were beautiful together. I truly thought we were forever. I concentrate hard to focus my thoughts. It's difficult with my emotions flying around all over the place like they are. I'm in love with her, but at the same time I'm totally confused by her and angry, yeah angry too. What has happened to us? Things were good, real good and then…then what? All I can remember is Len coming round to talk to her one night and I went out and when I came home it was all over. Suddenly it's all crystal clear. Len! How could he do this to me? How could he? And Carly! What does this mean, that she was already involved or what? Oh, this is agony. Am I really expected to sit here and dine with them; watch them playing happy families? And where does Carly get off treating me like this, as if I'm the one to blame? What did I do? No I'm not going to make this easy for her. She's clearly not happy with me being here, so I'm going to sit it out. If it kills me I'm going to stay and force her to acknowledge that I exist. Surely somewhere within her she must have some idea what she's doing to me, how unfair, how heartless she's being.

Returning to the table, I find Carly and Sebastian sharing a joke, laughter fills the air. Immediately I join them, though, Carly stands and leaves the table, leaves the room. It's all I can do not to shout at her to come back and face me. I've never been treated like this before, ever in my life.

I turn to Sebastian, "So I'm supposed to just sit and take this am I?"

Unbelievably he nods, "Take it easy Luc. Give her a chance." Am I hearing him right? This is turning into a protect-Carly-at-all-costs society.

"She's treating me like shit, surely you can see that?"

He smiles ever so slightly. "She's upset, Luc. Make a bit of an effort and she might soften."

So now we have it. Sebastian, expert on all things concerning women, giving me advice and telling me how to talk to my girlfriend. She was my girlfriend, I remind myself. I can hardly believe that we were once so close. I thought she was my soul mate. I'd never felt so connected to a person as I did to Carly and now… now we can't even manage eye contact. Despite this, I delve deep into my reserves of civility and when she comes back through, accompanied by Len and the food, I change tack.

"You look great Carly, I love your hair like that," I say smiling. Surely she can't find anything wrong with that.

Her reply takes me by surprise, though. "Yeah, it's great isn't it? I thought I should just cut it all off before it falls out completely."

I take a deep breath and try again, "How are you anyway? I've been thinking about you a lot, especially since we got the call about the transplant." Sebastian looks confused and I realise he probably doesn't know that Len contacted us asking us to be tissue-typed as potential donors.

"I'm fabulous. As if you didn't know..." She practically spits the words at me, "The only fly in the ointment being a tiny thing about needing a transplant to stop me from dying. Only thing is of course, I need a donor and some people don't think it's important enough to bother going to be tested for matching." She's standing by this time, her eyes blazing with anger. "Forgot to thank you, Luc." Picking up her glass she drenches my face with water. "Thanks for nothing...and I actually thought I meant something to you!" The next thing she's storming out of the room, slamming the door so hard behind her that the walls shake.

No way, I think. There's no way she's getting away with this. I'm furious by this time too, and I stride across the room, following her steps and I'm shouting now too. I'm vaguely aware of Sebastian and Len protesting, but I'm so angry I don't even hear what they've got to say. She turns to face me and I realise it's the first time we've made eye contact since I arrived. Her eyes glare, their beauty obscured by hatred for me.

"You think I didn't go don't you? You actually think I refused to be tested!"

"Well let's just say there's no record of you having been tested. Now don't you think that's strange? Don't you think it's just a little bit strange that my doctor sat today with a printout of all the blood results and everyone's name was on it, but no Luc? I couldn't believe it myself. I thought you loved me. You claimed to have loved me, but just not enough to try to save my life. It hurts, Luc. It hurts like nothing ever has. What do you expect from me?"

I'm shaking now I'm so furious with her. How could she believe such a thing? "You must really despise me…"

She interrupts, "I do."

I'm speechless. She takes the opportunity to continue her rant against me. "So why did you come back anyway?"

I take a deep breath, "I came back for you…"

She doesn't let me finish, "I heard your girlfriend threw you out. The girlfriend who I understand was waiting for you in Paris, while you were living with me over here. You're something else, you know that…and to think I loved you…I thought you loved me too."

I can't help it; all my emotions are tumbling out now. I'm aware I'm shouting at her and I don't even mean to, but she's got me all wrong, so completely wrong. "I do love you. I've loved you all this time. I didn't know when I came over here that I was going to meet you. I didn't plan to fall for you; that's why I still had a girlfriend."

A voice from behind interjects, "Go easy on her Luc," and I realise we have an audience, but I'm too far gone to take any notice.

Again she raises her voice, "But you went back to her did you not?"

"That's not fair, you kicked me out."

"Best decision I ever made…and while we're on the subject of not fair, having cancer's not fair, depending on someone else's goodwill for a donation of bone marrow isn't fair, dying because you don't have a match isn't fair. You expect me to say it's okay, that I understand you were too busy or that you're a bit scared of needles or whatever feeble excuse you came up with not to be tested?"

"For the last time Carly, I did bloody go to the hospital." I know I shouldn't be swearing at her, but she's got me so mad now.

"I don't know why your doctor didn't have me on the list, but I went. Of course I went. I just can't believe you would think that of me. You must really hate me."

I can't even see her now, my mind's so clouded, my eyes wet with angry tears. Somehow I stumble back through the house, out through the front door, slamming it as hard as I can behind me and finally I'm free of this torture. I feel so bad. I hate myself and I hate her and most of all I hate what we've become.

# SEBASTIAN

I'd better go after him. Lifting my jacket, turning to leave I feel a firm hand on my arm. "Don't go, Sebastian." Looking down at the hand clutching at my sleeve, glancing up at his face, I see he is pleading with me.

"The boy's upset," I say by way of explanation, "I should see if he's okay."

His eyes continue to bore deeply into mine, "Later…you can check on him later. He's upset, you're right, but he probably needs a bit of space right now…I really want to speak with you…tonight…before I change my mind."

I'm really confused. Tonight has been a complete disaster on all counts. I did think Len wanted to talk to me, he said so on the phone, but ever since I got here he's practically ignored me. This turnaround is a bit unnerving. Despite my misgivings, I'm aware that I may not get another chance if I don't take this opportunity. This is my moment to explain things to Len. Maybe we can build some bridges if I stay. Removing my jacket, slipping it over the back of my chair, I resume my place at the table. Len releases a long, slow breath and I sense the tension he's feeling. I'm left alone for a few minutes. I can hear muffled voices in the kitchen and sobbing too. He isn't gone long, though, and when he returns he places a cup of coffee and a large brandy in front of me. We sit in uncomfortable silence, drinking our coffees, eyeing each other nervously.

"I don't think you understand how I feel," he begins suddenly.

"Perhaps not," I reply, cautious to say the least. I'm not sure what's on the agenda here and I feel the need to be careful. Another silence.

"We used to be very close, you and I. This feels strange, this not knowing what to say or how to say it."

I nod in agreement.

"I don't know if you can grasp how painful this has all been for me. I thought Claudine and I were happy. I loved her with all my heart. I thought she felt the same…"

I interrupt him. I need to say it, "I'm positive she did love you, Len. You were good together."

He glares at me, his expression harsh and angry, "Don't patronise me!"

I should just shut up. I'm going to make things worse if I'm not more wary of myself. He takes a large gulp of his brandy and seems to regain his composure. As if nothing had happened, he resumes where he left off, "When Claudine died I uncovered a few unwelcome skeletons in her closet. I've had to face up to some big issues at the same time as trying to come to terms with her death. It's been hard…the thing is…you and her."

Again I feel the need to interject and can't help myself from jumping in, "You never believed it was all in the past. You've made it more difficult for yourself, torturing yourself over something that never happened."

He's shaking his head defiantly. "No, Sebastian I don't think you understand…how I feel …when I look at you…all I see is what Claudine saw. I look at you and I think did she love this about him, or that? I wonder did she look into your eyes and find herself there. I'm jealous, I guess. Yes, I'm jealous because she still loved you after all those years. Even without any glimmer of hope, even without any encouragement from you, she continued to love you until her dying day. That hurts like hell. It's hard to be angry with her, but I am and I'm angry with you, because if it wasn't for you I truly believe I would have been enough for her. I was second best; always I was second best in Claudine's eyes."

I don't know what to say. He doesn't know how much it hurts to hear him say all this. His words bring to life the possibility that was and yet can never be. I sense he's waiting for me to say something. "I'm sorry you got hurt Len, I really am, but I'll never be as sorry as you think I should be. I did love her, yes and I know, even as I say it, how much it's hurting you. The thing is I've spent my whole life living with the sorrow of losing her. I've had to endure watching her make a life with you instead of me. I've been paying for my mistakes all this time. I can't change what happened, nor can I change my feelings for her. I can't ever be as sorry as you think I should be."

He looks down at his feet for what seems like ages. I wonder if we're finished, if I should leave. Eventually he lifts his eyes to meet mine and starts again. "I found a letter after she died…when I was going through her stuff. It was addressed to a guy I'd never heard of, a James Harris. Do you know him?"

I shake my head. I've never heard the name before. I'm wondering what this has got to do with anything, but he appears to want to talk about it so I listen.

"To cut a long story short, I met with this guy a couple of months ago…maybe a bit more than that…since you went back to Paris anyway. He told me some interesting details about Claudine's life…things I didn't know…things a husband should have known…and it makes it all really difficult to handle. The secrecy, the hidden world…I feel like I hardly knew her at all."

He's completely lost me. I'm beginning to wonder if he's maybe had a drink too many. I wait for him to go on. I'm intrigued if not entirely sure what he's talking about. "This man was a friend of Claudine's…also he was her confidante…a listening ear…and he was her social worker."

"Her social worker?" I echo unintentionally. Why would Claudine have had a social worker? Ignoring my obvious surprise he proceeds to explain.

"It seems that Claudine had a child…a daughter…she was put up for adoption at birth…"

He's watching me closely, clearly looking for a reaction. A child? Adoption? How can this be? How could he not have known about this? I need to be careful how I put this, "I take it this was news to you. You didn't know about it?"

His eyes narrow. "It wasn't mine if that's what you're getting at."

I don't actually know if that's what I was getting at or not, but bloody hell, this is so difficult to take in. No wonder Len's been struggling big-time with all this unravelling in the midst of his grief. And I thought I was the source of his problems!

"Sebastian...I..." He tails off. He's having difficulty continuing. If things were different I would reach out to him, offer him some comfort, but there's still too much distance between us. I couldn't possibly touch him. He breathes deeply, appears to be trying to calm himself. "The baby was born at Edinburgh Royal Infirmary...a daughter. Claudine was heavily pregnant when she walked into the social work office asking for help. James, that's the social worker I was telling you about, he was given her case. He described a very attractive, very intelligent young woman who knew exactly what she was doing. She had left her home in France and come over to London and had hooked up with some travellers. They headed up North and by the time they reached Edinburgh she was nearing her due date. He felt sorry for her, he told me. She had no-one to help her. It seems she had given up everything, a promising place at Art College, her family, everything and here she was in a strange country with strange people and pregnant to boot. Are you still with me?"

This last question, the first time since he started his monologue that he's properly registered me. It actually feels like he's thinking aloud and not talking to me at all. I'm starting to get agitated. I don't know where he's going with this, but he seems almost unhinged right now and I'm not even sure that it's wise to let him continue. Stopping him might be another matter mind you. He goes on, without any prompting from me. It's almost as if he's forcing himself to keep going, as if he needs to. "So the baby was born, a girl like I said. She named her Caress and handed her over for adoption the day she was born. Are you getting this yet?"

His question surprises me, but I'm not sure what he means.

"Sebastian, the baby's twenty-one this year. Do the math. It's Carly!"

Twenty-one? Claudine would have been nineteen then. She had a baby and there was no-one to help her. Claudine had a baby after she left Paris. When she went away she was pregnant. I'm struggling to process this. I feel ill; my head's thumping, my heart beating so loudly I'm surprised he can't hear it. Breathing is becoming an effort, something requiring conscious will to keep going. Taking a deep breath I ask him, "What are you saying?" There's no hiding my distress, my voice, almost a whisper, chokes me as I try to speak. He doesn't answer me. Instead he slides a piece of paper across the table towards me. Tentatively I reach out to lift it. "What's this?" again the words of someone else speak from my detached body. He says nothing, but gestures me to read. At first I don't understand. I read but I'm not sure what he's trying to do. It's a birth certificate. Caress Rousseau it says. Mother: Claudine Rousseau, her date of birth, occupation etc. etc. I scan down to the next section. Father: Sebastian Charpentier…The words start to swim in front of my eyes. This is more than I can bear. This is too much. Father: Sebastian Charpentier. Father: Sebastian Charpentier. I think I'm going to pass out. The pain searing within my chest is excruciating. My face is soaked with sweat. Each breath hurts so much. I feel like I'm dying. Father: Sebastian Charpentier. Me - the father of Claudine's baby! My heart feels like it's going to burst out of my body. From somewhere in the depths of my soul a longing so absolute shakes me to my core. Raising my head I see him staring at me, taking in my reaction in all its horror, my eyes awash with stinging tears. Unrelenting, unendurable agony racks my body and spirit and my pain, my suffering must now surely be complete.

A soft click alerts me to the door opening and the girl enters the room. She looks embarrassed, as if she knows she's interrupting something. My eyes are trained on her face, so tired and pale. Wandering over toward Len she speaks, her voice smooth and quiet. "Sorry to barge in like this. I thought I might go to bed, but I need my medication first."

"It's fine, honey," he says gently. "Go right ahead."

She rummages around in the wall cabinet above the bookcase and retrieves a couple of medicine bottles. Carefully she counts out several pills into a little container then, turning, glances over at me. "It was good to see you again, Sebastian. Good night." To Len a peck on the cheek before she heads back out of the room. I'm unable to take my eyes off her the whole time she's present. I'm aware I'm staring at her, drinking in every detail; her face, her expression, her eyes, the way she speaks, the way she moves. Only when she has left us am I able to return my gaze back to Len. He's sitting there, his eyes clamped squarely upon me. I wonder how long he's been watching me. Naturally he's been examining my reaction to her. It occurs to me at this point that Carly doesn't know. Her interactions with me weren't those I would expect from a girl who had just found out I was her father.

"You haven't told her?" I ask him.

He shakes his head. I'm quite sure that it wasn't out of courtesy for me, that he thought I should hear first. Slowly the gradual realisation takes shape in my mind. No, he's told me because he wants to be sure I'll donate the bone marrow and only when that's certain, when there's no alternative will he tell her who I am.

"You weren't going to tell me were you?" I'm annoyed suddenly. Confused, yes and upset, but more and more I feel the anger rising within me. It's not an emotion I'm accustomed to experiencing. Normally I'm a pretty chilled kind of guy, but this has really got to me. I can't believe he blames me like he does. He's never going to let go of this.

"I just did tell you, didn't I?"

Here we go. Len can be so condescending sometimes. He's trying to convince me I've misunderstood, but I know I haven't. How dare he treat me like this? I speak slowly, carefully, emphasising each word. "No, you weren't going to tell me I had a daughter. The only reason you have is because you need me. You need me to be the donor, don't you?" He looks uncomfortable. I suppose when you hear it out loud, like that, it sounds worse than when you quell the little voice of guilt inside your head. "You would have gladly kept her to yourself except this...this situation has forced you into a corner. Am I right?"

He looks away, looks back at me. He must see I'm not going to let him get away with this. "She didn't want to trace her birth father. She was happy with things as they are. You're right, we need you. And yes you're right, that's why I'm telling you."

I shake my head in disbelief. How can he justify this to himself? "Well guess what..." my voice raised by now, "...guess what...you're not going to win this time. I'm not about to let the same thing happen twice. You think you can have her as your daughter and I can go to hell...once I've handed over my marrow of course. Well it's not happening. She's my daughter, not yours. I will not allow you to live the life that is rightfully mine, not this time."

I'm blazing now with pitiless resentment for him. I can't believe he thought this was an option; that he would step up to be the father and leave me in the dark about it. He didn't even tell her! Angry steps lead me to the front door and he makes no move to prevent me from leaving, makes no attempt to excuse himself or give account for his actions. "You're not doing this to me again." I more or less spit the words mercilessly at him.

He stands and raises a hand. "Seb...Sebastian...you will do it won't you? We can depend on you?"

How dare he even ask me the question? "I'll do the right thing, Len. You can be sure of that." I know it's vindictive and I know it's unnecessary, but I want to hurt him. I want him to feel some of the pain he's caused me over the years. Turning within the open doorway I throw my parting shot cruelly back at him, "I'll donate my marrow alright. I'll do for her what you can't!"

## LEN

"What was all that noise about?"

Lifting my head to look at her, I realise I didn't even notice her come into the room.

"How much of that did you hear?" I ask her.

"All the shouting bits," her reply too vague to allow me to assess the damage. She sits herself down opposite me at the table and it occurs to me that this horrific night might just be about to get worse. "Is it true?" she asks.

I'm stupid, so stupid. Did I really think I could keep this from her? I'm not even sure when I decided that I wasn't going to tell her. I wasn't going to tell either of them. Discovering that Sebastian was Carly's father was the final nail in the coffin for me. That revelation marked for me the worst possible scenario. It linked Claudine and him together forever and I found that impossible to bear. The only thing which gave me any kind of a reprieve from the pain was the fact that no-one else knew. When I realised that Carly didn't know and wonder of wonders didn't appear to want to know, I thought maybe everything would be okay. It was wrong. I know it was, but at the time…

Tonight, listening to Sebastian, I couldn't fathom how I thought I would get away with it. Perhaps I didn't really think, maybe that's more like it. Perhaps I brushed it under the carpet in a crude attempt at denial. It didn't really become true to me until I told Sebastian. Only then did the magnitude of the secret I'd uncovered, and almost as quickly hidden again, hit me. Now sitting across from her pale, tired face I feel I've let her down. I misled her. I lied to her. How am I ever going to be able to fix this? I may just have ruined everything.

"Is what true, Carly?" I know I'm stalling. She knows it too. Her gaze is steady. She's a strong girl I think, stronger than she looks.

"Is it true that he's my father?"

Taking my face in my hands because I can't look at her, I frantically try to come up with some words. What do I say? How do I say it? How can I justify what I've done? I can't lose her, I can't let that happen. She's the only thing that gives my life any meaning. She saved me I suddenly realise. Carly coming into my life when she did, embracing me as her father is what brought me back to life. Without her I dread to think where I would be or what would have happened to me. And now I'm on the verge of blowing our whole relationship out of the water.

"Prof..." her voice is so gentle I find it painful to hear. I deserve all that's coming. I know I do and yet at this very moment I would move mountains to prevent it from happening. "Look at me, Prof." Her fingers, reaching across the table, peel my hands from my face, forcing me to engage with her. Her eyes make contact with mine, staring deep into them. I wonder for a moment if she's reading my thoughts. "I just need to know. I need to hear you say it."

Clumsily I start to speak, but I don't know what I'm saying, haven't decided what to say. I'm rambling in a manic fashion; words for the sake of words. Maybe if I talk then she won't and if she doesn't she can't ask me any more questions can she? I'm aware I'm talking rubbish. She's going to think I've lost it completely isn't she? Have I lost it completely? Am I, right here and right now, am I finally cracking up? How do you know if you're having a breakdown? Do you necessarily have the insight to understand or does it just feel like...does it just feel like this?

"Prof." Her voice louder this time, insistent. "Prof...just tell me...I'm asking you...please!" I think maybe it's the please that finally tips me over the edge. I can't bear to hear her pleading with me for the truth. This is my girl. I'd do anything for her. Do I really mean that? If anything means losing her to Sebastian just like I lost Claudine? Can I do this? Do I have any choice?

"Carly, what can I say? I should have told you, I know I should…I was afraid if the truth be known, afraid that once you knew about him you wouldn't have any need for me. Pathetic isn't it? I am really a pitiful character. I almost can't believe what I've done. Yes Carly. Sebastian…Sebastian… is your father. I have a copy of your birth certificate…" Sliding it across the table towards her, I hold my breath waiting for a reaction. She lifts it with trembling fingers, her eyes boring into the page drinking in the truth as it leaps into life. Will she cry, I wonder or will she stand up and scream at me the way she did to Luc? I know she's capable of the most intense emotions and I'm not sure how best to deal with her distress. She reads the page over and over again. Without raising her head she focuses absolutely on the news in front of her, the answer to her question. I decide to make things easy for her. I love her after all. I love her as my own daughter. Besides I don't deserve her and he probably does. He was always the better man, always.

"I understand if you hate me for this," I tell her. "I totally understand…it was unforgivable to find this out and to keep it from you. Whatever you decide to do, I promise I'll support you…I'll never blame you or think badly of you…and I'll always be here for you if you…"

She looks at me with apparent confusion as to what I'm talking about. "Prof…" she interrupts my ramblings, "Prof…I have a name!" Now it's me who's confused. "I mean I have a real name!" Her face is radiant with joy, her eyes shining with laughter. I don't think I've ever seen her look so happy. "Caress…my mother gave me that name. It's the only thing she ever gave me and now I have it back! And Charpentier…my father's name! Oh Prof, thank you, thank you." She jumps up and skipping round to my side of the table, it's the only way to describe it, she hugs me to her, laughing and talking the whole time. I'm in shock. This girl continues to amaze me. Her resilience, her capacity to forgive is unlike anything I've ever encountered. In her I search for and find honesty and compassion and love in abundance. She has thrown me a lifeline, become my salvation.

## LUC

I don't know what to do with myself. These past few days I've immersed myself in coming up with new ways to obliterate the pain I feel. I've lost her that much is clear. I can't deal with it, though. I still don't understand. Why does she hate me so much? All that stuff she was yelling at me, it just doesn't make sense. Today is possibly a day for thinking. I know I need to face up to things; I can't keep clouding my mind with artificial means of escape. Yeah it's very effective, but I know it's a temporary measure. Sooner or later I need to confront reality and decide what I'm going to do about it. Today might be that day. It's so bizarre to think I've spent so many nights this past week partying, living it up with complete strangers and yet deep, deep inside I feel completely broken. Maybe I was a bit naive coming back here. I guess I just kept thinking about how good it was, how close we were, and I couldn't imagine it had all gone. I needed to give it another try. Well, I've done that and where did it get me? What I know now is how much she despises me. I was stunned, I have to admit, absolutely stunned at the strength of her animosity toward me. The thing is, getting my head around it - she seems to have got me all wrong. Maybe that's the part that hurts the most; the fact that I feel it's so unjustified. I'm starting to wonder if she's been told things about me to try to turn her against me. Len? Would he do that? Up until now I'd have said no, but now? I feel I don't really know him anymore either. I cannot believe he's moved her in with him. It's not right, even leaving me out of the picture, it's just not right.

340

And where did she get the idea that I refused to be tissue-typed or whatever they bloody call it? My brain's buzzing, but it's with the over-stimulation of all these unanswered questions. Funny isn't it, I came over here to find resolution and yet I'm left with more questions than I had to start with.

I drag my mind back to the phone call from Len a few weeks ago. What did he say? He told me Carly was really ill. At first I thought she'd asked him to contact me; that she maybe wanted to see me. It wasn't that though. He said she needed a transplant and he was contacting everyone who knew her to see if they'd be interested in being tested in a search for a donor. He was sure I'd want to be involved. Of course I would. I was devastated to hear she'd got so sick, but he was right, I'd do anything for her, absolutely anything. What else did he say? Oh yes, he asked if any of the family could be encouraged to do it too, since she was a friend of mine. I must admit the use of the word friend turned my stomach, but I got his drift. He was trying to spread the net as far as possible in the search for a suitable donor and in the absence of her own family it was a more difficult task. All I said was that he could depend on me and I'd do my best to make sure the boys and maybe even Mum and Dad went for this blood test. It was only a blood test, after all. In actual fact it wasn't difficult to persuade them. I contacted the doctor that Len told me about and he already knew all about it. The groundwork had all been done by Len or the doctors at Carly's hospital or wherever. Anyway I was quite impressed with the setup. They were able to accommodate us all at different times and, like I say, it was only a blood test, took hardly any time at all. My parents have a very strong social conscience and like to be seen to be doing the right thing, so I phoned them first. My mum likes a bit of a drama and I guess it was gonna make a good story; how they were called as a matter of urgency and had to rush down to the local hospital to be tested to help Luc's poor *friend*. I knew that once she was on board the boys would dutifully make the trip, because they'd never hear the end of it from Mum if they didn't. That was it. We'd all been tested within the week and

341

we'd all been told that, unfortunately, we weren't suitable matches. I was so disappointed. I wanted to be the one who could help her. I really did. Maybe it's just as well. I guess partly it was selfish. I suppose I thought she would be grateful to me and it might get us back on course again. I can see, now, how wrong that would have been. Still, to hear the things she said about me and to think she believes that I refused the test, it just doesn't make any sense. I couldn't convince her though. She didn't want to listen to anything I had to say. I guess her mind was already made up, so I didn't really stand a chance. I do wish I'd stayed calm, though. I must have really inflamed the situation by losing my temper like I did. It was bad, but I made it worse. It was just so hard, though, to hear her saying all that stuff and not get mad with her. My feelings for her are so strong; I couldn't just listen and say nothing. I so wanted her to believe me. I desperately wanted for her to see me the way she did before. Where has our relationship gone? What happened to us? I'm as mystified now as I was when I left the last time. The difference now, though, is I don't think there's any going back to what we were. I think it is truly over. Do I want to see her again before I leave? Probably not. Not in these circumstances, not with all the bad feeling that remains between us. It's killing me, but I can't force her to love me back. I'm gonna have to learn, somehow, to let go.

# CARLY

"How are you feeling?"

I like Mary, she's looked after me since I was first diagnosed and she seems to instinctively know how to talk to me. Some of the other nurses don't care as much; it's obvious it's just a job to them and they can go home at night and forget about us. Mary is different. She's one of those people who'll always go the extra mile for you. How am I feeling? Well a week of total body irradiation is no fun, but other than pretty tired, I guess I don't feel as bad as I expected.

"So far, so good," I tell her. She smiles back at me, but I know she's taking me seriously.

"Is there anything you want to ask before we get started on all this? Anything you're not sure about?"

I shake my head. I've been pretty well schooled in what lies ahead. I'll go into isolation tonight, start receiving chemo tomorrow and, all being well, I'll have my bone marrow transplant in a couple of days. I'm really nervous, obviously, but there's nothing I can do but go for this with all I've got.

"You've had a lot happen to you these past few months." She says it matter-of-factly. I recognise the technique. She's offering me an opening if I want to talk, but leaving an opt-out if I don't.

"Yes, massive changes in my life - most of them good... some of them very good."

"You're pleased about your dad?"

I think for a minute. Pleased? Is that the word I'd use? I don't know that it is. "Satisfied more than pleased. It's met my need to know, if you understand what I mean."

She sits with me a while, messing with my charts and documentation. Again I realise she doesn't want to leave me on my own for too long. It occurs to me they might be worried I'm going to change my mind. I know I won't. No matter how scared I get I can't look back. Now that my conditioning has started, my counts will already be starting to drop. Once I get the chemo, I'm going to need that bone marrow to rescue me. There's no opportunity for cold feet or a change of heart. This kind of treatment is all or nothing.

"Where is he?" I ask her, surprising myself a little at the directness of my question.

She looks up from the bundle of papers on her lap, "Who? Your dad?" It thrills me to hear her refer to him so casually as *my dad*, as if it's quite a normal thing for a girl to have a dad. I nod and hope I'm not being too intrusive. I hope I don't look too desperate. "He's in ward seventeen. He's fine. The marrow was harvested this afternoon. It's all systems go now."

It's so surreal to think of him going to theatre and having this procedure done for me, solely for me. I want to see him. I need to see him. I haven't had a chance to even let him know that I know. After that awful night at Prof's, funny how I still think of it as Prof's house, when really it's my home now too…after that night I didn't get an opportunity to speak to him. Prof gave me the number, but there was no reply when I called his flat. Then we found out he'd gone directly to the hospital the next morning for tissue-typing and then Dr Armstrong called us later that day to say the early signs were looking good. They still had a bit of further analysis to do, I don't really understand the technicalities of it, but he was convinced things were looking good. I hardly slept at all that night. Neither did Prof. He was such a help to me, sitting up with me most of the night, making me tea, reassuring me. Where would I be without him? I'd be lost and I'd be desperate, that's for sure. He's changed my life and I owe him so much. He's stood by me when I had no-one else and when I felt I was hitting rock bottom he scooped me up and brought me back to level ground. I love him dearly. I hope he realises that.

Eventually Mary goes for her break. I think she feels a bit awkward about taking her breaks, because it shows that this is her work and she's not just here because she cares about me. Poor Mary! I wonder if she lets herself get emotionally involved with all her patients or is it just me. Anyway, I've really appreciated her company and the time she's spent with me over the last few days. She's given me something to distract myself and stopped the jitters from getting a strong hold on me. Right now, though, I'm quite glad she's gone, because there's something I need to do and I don't think it's something they would allow me to do if I asked them. I need to see him. I need to see him again, whatever happens. Peeping out of my cubicle door, I clock that there's no-one around in the corridor. Half of the staff will be away for tea, so that makes it really busy for the other half. It's a good time to go. I probably won't even be missed. Anyway, I rationalise, as I scurry down the corridor to the exit, it's not as if I'm in isolation yet. I'm not imprisoned in my cubicle, so they shouldn't be surprised that I want to make the most of my last day of freedom.

Ward seventeen she said. Pressing the button for the lift I'm getting impatient. Glancing over my shoulder, I realise I must look pretty suspicious and so I consciously try to relax. Think calm. Act cool. I press the lift-call button again. I'm so aware that at any moment a member of ward staff might come out of the canteen and catch me standing here. They're so protective of me and they want this procedure to go without a hitch. Finally, the familiar ring as the lift lands and opens its doors. I'm inside in an instant and pressing the close-door button repeatedly, trying to hurry the stupid thing up. Slowly I let out my breath as I feel the lift nudging its slow course upwards.

Ward seventeen is easy to find and being an open ward there's a board at the desk indicating who's in which bed. Here, as downstairs, there are few staff around. Suddenly it dawns on me that no-one here will realise I'm a patient. I'm fully dressed. I probably look like a visitor. Why don't I just ask to see him? Approaching me in a brisk, business-like fashion a nurse arrives right on cue to ask if she can help me. She wants to know if I'm a relative and I take great pleasure in saying that I am. He's in a single room, she tells me; they like to take good care of their donors. I'm wondering if she's going to escort me right in and I'm not even sure that I'm planning to go in, so it's a relief to hear her being summoned to help someone else.

In my mind I can't really picture him. I think I've been trying too hard to conjure up his image and now I'm not sure what's real and what's my imagination. There are so many things I wish I'd taken more notice of, but at the time I had no reason to be examining him, so there are a lot of gaps in my memory. I had only met him a couple of times too, so maybe it's no surprise. As I reach the glass windows that run the length of one wall of his room, I'm both excited and petrified at the same time. He's standing over at the window on the far side of the cubicle, staring out at the evening sky. His back is to me, which is good. It means I can stand and watch him a while without him noticing. The name above the door sends a shiver down my spine. Sebastian Charpentier. The name on my birth certificate. My dad.

You can tell he's French just by looking at him. There's something about him, though I'm not sure what. This is the first time I've really looked at him, looked with a scrutinising eye, wanting to notice every detail. I don't know if he's likely to stick around after this, so I want to be able to remember everything. He's casually dressed in jeans and a white tee-shirt. He's very tanned, a feature accentuated by the whiteness of his shirt. In fact he's very handsome, which seems a strange thing to be able to say about your own dad. I guess I'm still able to see him fairly objectively, though. It occurs to me for the first time that my mother and father, both being French, possibly makes me French too. I find that funny. I barely understand a word of the language and have never even visited the country. Suddenly I'm conscious of just how much I've missed out on. It's not just a case of not having known my real parents. It's about a whole different world, a different way of life, language, everything. A sadness sweeps through me as I realise I can never get this back.

346

Finding my parents was only ever going to be a part of the story, I always understood that. I guess I just didn't realise how big it would all turn out to be. The sense of loss is huge.

I should head back downstairs. They might be missing me by now and there's really nothing to be gained from standing around here gazing at a man who, biologically it seems, is my father, but who in essence is a total stranger. I raise my hand to wipe a tear from my cheek and perhaps it's that movement which alerts him to my presence. Whatever the reason, he turns and looks directly at me. His expression is impossible to read; he looks serious though, holding my gaze. I feel uncomfortable. I don't know what to do. Maybe I should just go. Maybe he doesn't want to see me. I turn to go, sorry that it's me that's broken the connection, but I couldn't keep hold of such a steady stare any longer. I'm half-way down the ward when his voice cuts into my heart in a way I never imagined possible. *"Carlee... Carlee*, please stay!" The way he says my name sounds so strange to my ears and yet his words tug at my soul, calling me home. Instinctively I re-trace my steps until I'm standing in front of him, staring up at his beseeching eyes. He pushes open the door and gestures to me to enter. I'm scared but I feel compelled anyway. Inside the room he pulls two chairs together and, shaking, I sit on one of them. A couple of minutes pass and we don't speak. I know he's watching me, waiting for me to speak, but I haven't any idea what I should say. I feel embarrassed by the silence and awkward and stupid. It seems like an age that we sit like this, not moving, not speaking. Eventually he holds an outstretched hand toward me. It's such a simple gesture, but I find it massively symbolic; my father reaching out for me. My own movements are taking place in slow motion without will or intent: my smaller hand within his palm, his trembling fingers clasped tightly around it.

His stare is so intense, his eyes so penetrating. I feel really unnerved, sitting here wondering what he's thinking. Am I a disappointment to him? I know I don't look a bit like Claudine and he maybe wouldn't have expected that. I don't know what to say or do so I just sit and try to maintain eye contact as best I can. Eventually he speaks, but it's not English. I guess it must be French, but I couldn't be sure. Doesn't he realise I don't understand him? Maybe it's difficult to imagine that your own daughter wouldn't understand the language you speak. Maybe he doesn't know anything about me. I shake my head to let him see that I'm not following him and it seems to have the desired effect. He pauses, swallows hard and begins again, "I'm sorry," he says. I smile awkwardly. I didn't mean to make him feel uncomfortable.

Now it's him who's shaking his head and he looks annoyed. He stands and heads back over to the window. Looking beyond him the night sky is settling over the city. He stands staring out as the last glimmers of daylight dip beneath the horizon. Dragging his fingers through his hair he seems agitated. Turning back to me I wonder if he's going to scream. I can sense the tension bottled up inside clamouring for release. I wonder again if I should go, maybe my being here is disturbing him, maybe I should have left well alone. I mutter something quietly about how I shouldn't have come and stand to leave. Before I can take a step, though, he's alongside me, his hand upon my shoulder. I can't stand this. It's too intense for me. These emotions are so powerful I feel like I'm going to explode. My instinct is to run and hide, but where?

Again he speaks, "*Carlee*, I need you to understand that I didn't know…I didn't know about you…anything about you…until Len told me the other night. Claudine never told me. I had no idea." It seems now that he's started to talk he can't stop the words from tumbling out. He's rambling almost, all this stuff about how he didn't know Claudine was pregnant when she left, how he had no idea she'd had a baby. On and on, it feels almost like a confessional. "Things would have been so different…I'd have never left her. Do you believe me? You have to believe me…all I ever wanted was a life with Claudine. I'd have married her in a minute…we'd have brought you up together…It could have been…should have been…" Tears are trickling down his face as the torrent of feelings overspill from his secret world. I get a strong sense of regret and frustration vocalised, perhaps, for the first time. I feel so sorry for him. He looks like his

348

heart is broken and it occurs to me that I'm not the only one to have dreamed of a different path through life. Placing my hand over his, where it still rests on my shoulder, I try to offer him some remnant of comfort.

"I know it's a cliché," I tell him, "but you know life's too short for regrets...I know that only too well. None of us know how much time we've got, but one thing's for sure, it's not long enough to be burdened with thoughts of what might have been...I longed for you all my life. I wanted a dad who loved me and wanted me. I didn't have that, but now...look what I have now..."

He's shaking his head again. "That's very philosophical *Carlee* and very mature, but look at what you've got...nobody. I'm a complete nobody. I've wrecked the lives of everyone who's ever had the misfortune to get close to me. I've messed up my own life unimaginably. Every choice...every decision...what you've got is a dad who's worth nothing to you. I've let you down, like I've let everyone down. I'm sorry, but I know that's not enough. I don't expect anything from you, you realise that don't you? I've donated the marrow because, well because it's the only thing I could do for you, but I don't expect you to want to hang around afterwards. You don't owe me anything if you know what I mean."

How wrong he is. He doesn't get it at all. He thinks I'm looking for superman; the perfect father. All I want is him, the real thing. I speak slowly and carefully to be absolutely sure he understands what I'm saying. I wouldn't want him to be in any doubt about what I'm about to say to him. "I'll be grateful to you forever. I cannot thank you enough for what you've done for me. You gave me life...and now you're giving me the chance of life again. You've done what no-one else could, because only you're my dad. You're my dad! I feel privileged to be given your bone marrow and I also feel very positive about the outcome of this transplant, because it's come from you. Like I said, I'm your flesh and blood and so your marrow in me feels like a very powerful thing. Do you understand me? The past is past...what are we to do? We can allow ourselves to fill to overflowing with regret or we can move on together. I'd like it to be together…I was kind of hoping it might be together."

Have I overstepped the mark? Have I been too presumptuous? Have I lost him completely? I didn't plan any of this. I guess I did intend to thank him, but not in such an outpouring of emotions. He's been listening intently the whole time, concentrating on my words. Quietly he lifts my hands in his, examining them. I look down and see my own small, pale fingers contrasting with his own. "You have your mother's hands," he says, "tiny hands…artist's fingers…" I smile at the thought of being like my mother in some way. I never knew that about her, never noticed. I feel a sense of belonging that I've never experienced before. A love I've never known.

# SEBASTIAN

The door opening provides a diversion and I think it comes at a good moment. I'm concerned that already I've been a bit heavy emotionally with her. It isn't like me to open up so easily, especially to someone I hardly know. Feelings I've kept hidden all these years came bursting out from somewhere deep inside. I surprised myself at the intensity of it all and more so the fact that I let her in on it. There's definitely something between us. I can't explain it, but I can feel it. I guess it's a bond of some kind; an instinctive homing device perhaps. I wouldn't ever have believed in such a thing, but the strength of feeling I have for her is unlike anything I've experienced before. I've only just met her, but already I know I'd do anything for her. Is it parental make-up? Does that exist outside of stories? I don't know the answer to these questions, but I do know that I love her. The worrying thing is that I get the feeling she's expecting me to be a good addition to her life and to be quite honest, I think that's unlikely. I tried to tell her what a wreck I am. I'm sure she could see it, in fact, but she doesn't seem to be taking it on board. I can't imagine that me being a part of her life would benefit her in any way. I haven't a clue how to be a father. I don't even know how to talk to her properly. How do you learn to connect to your daughter when you first meet her as her twenty-first birthday approaches? I'm filled with sadness at all that I've missed, at the times that I can never get back. The life we might have lived...then again, she said herself we shouldn't be looking backwards. I wonder at her. How she can be so resolute, so strong. I drop her hands as the troop of doctors wander into the room.

"Monsieur Charpentier! I see you have a visitor!" Dr Armstrong's announcement breaks the awkwardness of the interruption in his impeccable fashion. Turning to Carly he adds, "They're looking for you downstairs Miss Adams. Hard to believe they didn't think of checking here first isn't it?"

She smiles back at him and I'm astonished at the ease of their relationship. I feel so clumsy, so out of my depth with her. I'm envious of all these people, Dr Armstrong, Len... people who have such a natural rapport with her. I suppose the difference is, maybe, that I just don't know her. I wish I could relax a bit more though. I'm sure she must think I'm really strange, inappropriate even.

"Anyway, Sebastian how are you this evening?"

I smile and tell him I'm not too bad at all; feeling pretty good even. He's visibly pleased. I guess they're all getting quite excited now about the prospect of the impending transplant. In medical terms it's probably very interesting.

"We got a good harvest of bone marrow this morning," he says. "I'm delighted with what we've stored. I'm sure Carly is very grateful to you for doing this. We all are." She's beaming proudly across at me and I feel really humbled. I mean who wouldn't? It's not the big hero act they're all making it out to be. It's just what you do, what anyone would do. "How are these wounds doing?" he continues. Crossing the room to the wash basin he scrubs his hands as if he's about to perform surgery. Everything about this man is meticulous. I decide there and then that Carly's in the best possible hands and feel a small sense of reassurance about what's about to take place for her. "Do you mind if I take a look?" he asks, lifting my shirt to expose my abdomen and chest. Ushering the students, junior doctors, whoever they all are around him, he begins an explanation. "What we have taken from Monsieur Charpentier today is an allogeneic harvest. Bone marrow has been removed from his pelvis here and here via needle punctures. We also went into the sternum here and here in order to get a good enough supply. We withdrew approximately two pints of bone marrow which Monsieur Charpentier will replace naturally within about four weeks. Our donor is more than likely to feel quite sore and bruised this evening. He'll receive a top-up blood transfusion later on and will remain with us for another day or so. Any questions?" Replacing my shirt, he nods a thank you and proceeds to lead the unquestioning entourage out of the room. Stopping beside Carly he whispers something to her. She smiles and says, "I know." The followers traipse out behind their hallowed leader, the last one closing the door decisively behind them. Carly glances over at me and bursts out laughing. It's infectious, her laugh, in its innocence. I can't stop myself from laughing too, although I've no idea what's so funny.

"What did he say to you?" I ask her.

She smiles again, "He asked did I know that all the nurses fancy my dad?"

"He didn't!" I'm so embarrassed. I wish I'd heard him, maybe I could have said something. More than likely I'd have just made it worse though. Anyway, it seems to have lightened the mood a little and it's so nice to see Carly relaxed and at ease again.

Without warning the door swings open once again and the familiar face of authority leans around it. "I hate to be the one to break up the party, Carly but you should really be getting back to the ward. You're going in tonight remember?" Her face falls so suddenly it feels like the world's come crashing down amongst us.

"Oh please," she begs him, "Can't I have just one more night? I've only just found my dad. I need time with him. Please Dr Armstrong!" Her pleas are so heartfelt I wonder how he'll ever resist her. She looks so child-like staring up at him, imploring him with all her might. Perhaps realizing this isn't going to be easy he comes back in the room. This time he closes the door on the masses waiting outside, hanging on his every word.

"Carly, your dad needs some rest. He needs a transfusion and he needs his dressings changed. You need your medication and you need to get your head round going into isolation. I appreciate this is bad timing for a family reunion, but you knew it would be like this."

She's nodding, showing him that she understands, "Yes, but can't it wait until tomorrow? What are my counts anyway?"

He stands for a moment without speaking. He's obviously thinking about it. When he does speak it's deliberately emphatic, "Okay Carly, here's the deal. I'll get a nurse to review your counts. If they're okay...and only if they're okay... you can have until tomorrow...after that there's no discussion. I can't allow you to stay out if you're at risk of infection. You know all this."

She's so pleased she can hardly contain herself. I'm thinking how young she still is, how pure. Without warning she throws herself at him and hugs him. He's taken by surprise, but again responds without reservation, spinning her round and laughing at her impulsiveness. "Okay...Some of us have work to do," he says finally. "You...get yourself back down to your own ward...I'm sure your father will escort you safely there." He gives her a wink as he makes his retreat and she starts to gather herself together.

"How did you manage that?" I ask her. I'm impressed with the way she worked him there.

"I don't know what you mean!" she replies with mock innocence.

"Come on," I tell her, smiling, "Better get you back before they send out a search party." Casually she links her arm through mine as we set off through the ward. I'm astonished by this child. I don't know how she intuitively seems to know how to act. Me, I still feel so self-conscious that I'm allowing her to make all the moves. Everything she does, though, feels so right. I wish I wasn't so uptight about it all. I keep worrying that I'll do or say something wrong and it's making it difficult to be myself. She...well she just seems to be herself...my little girl!

# LEN

I've been sitting here waiting for ages. It's hard to believe they don't know where she is, this hospital's hardly a place she'd get lost in. I'm beginning to wonder if I've got it wrong. Maybe she's not expecting me. I'm sure, though, I said I'd be here. I know I intended to be here for her going into isolation and I doubt I'd have forgotten to tell her. Perhaps she's taken fright at the prospect of what lies ahead. Suddenly I'm quite worried for her. I don't think she'd do anything silly, but on the other hand it's a pretty big deal and who's to say how anyone would react? I can't sit still so I resume my pacing of the ward. The nurses don't like this, they've told me repeatedly to try to relax and I think it's because I'm annoying them. My agitation is proving difficult to hide though. I mean I'm nervous about the whole thing anyway and this disappearance just heightens my fears. The sound of familiar laughter reaches my ears as I round the corner towards the entrance and looking up, I find its source heading in my direction. Arm in arm, looking as if they haven't a care in the world they stroll towards me. Spotting me eventually, Carly smiles, "Hi Prof! How are you?" She's forgotten. I know it instantly.

"I thought we'd arranged that I'd come up tonight."

I'm sharp and abrupt and I don't really mean to be. It's not even her I'm annoyed with, it's him. The very sight of him is enough to upset me. Feelings which I have under control the rest of the time come unchecked to the surface whenever I'm in his company. He hasn't even spoken to me. It's enough to see them together, though. He senses my irritation, I'm sure he does. I can tell by the way he avoids any kind of interaction. He stands beside her, the very fact of it a statement of some kind of alliance. I don't like it and he's bound to realise that. He stares at me for a bit. I'm aware even without looking at him. What's he waiting for, I wonder? Does he expect me to talk to him? I know I'm in the wrong, but it's just too painful to disregard my own feelings. I can't ignore how I feel and I guess I'm not sure how to handle it.

"Oh Prof, I'm sorry. I forgot. I went up to see how things had gone today and I suppose I got a bit side-tracked and everything. Have you been waiting long?"

I shake my head. I should have realised where she would have gone. The thing is I guess I wasn't sure how she'd be with him. I knew she was pleased to have found him, so I should have supposed she would find the courage to make a move toward him. He's her father, of course she would!

"Maybe I'll get going." He's speaking to her, not me. He's uncomfortable with this and looking for a way out.

"Oh don't go...please. I only got the extension so we could spend longer together."

Her words hurt me so badly and she's oblivious to my pain. Funnily enough I don't think he is. He casts me a quick glance, possibly seeking out a reaction to her statement.

"No, listen...I need to. They want to sort out my dressings remember. Maybe I could see you later on...after Len goes." This last mention more pointed a remark than she realises.

Out of sheer politeness I feel the need to ask how he is. "So how did things go today anyway?"

He turns to look at me now, surprised possibly that I've spoken to him, but it's not the apologetic Sebastian I've come to expect. "Things went pretty well, thanks. There was a shaky moment when they weren't sure if they could do it or not. Something about soft tissue damage from broken ribs earlier this year. Fortunately we got over that hurdle though. They got a good harvest it seems. Looks like my little girl will get her transplant after all!"

I know it's designed to hurt and I know I shouldn't let it, but it does. It hurts like hell.

Finally she agrees to him going back to his own ward, but only with the proviso that she can visit again later this evening. He leaves us, but I instantly feel I'm intruding on her time with him and I wish I hadn't come at all. Carly, though, is sunny as ever. It's hard to believe she's got such big problems. I really don't want to add to the burden she's already forced to carry, so I need to find a way of dealing with this.

"Shall we go for dinner?" she asks me. This is better. We had arranged I would come up and take her for a meal before she went into isolation. She has remembered after all.

"Where do you want to go?" I force a smile and consciously try to let go of all the bad feeling within me.

"Well I don't think I'll be allowed out of the hospital. I was pushing it negotiating an extra night before going in. I think it'll have to be the canteen. Is that okay?"

Of course it's okay. All I want is to spend time with her, for things to be the way they were between us. The thing is that she seems absolutely fine with me. She doesn't appear to have harboured any grudges about me keeping Sebastian from her. It's me that the problem lies with. It's about me and him. She decides she better get her medicines and also tell the nurses where she's going this time, so I head off to the canteen on her instruction. She isn't hungry. There's a surprise! I wish she could have put on a bit of weight before coming back in for this treatment. There's so little of her I wonder what will happen if she gets really sick. Coffee; white, one sugar. It occurs to me that Sebastian must know so little about her. I bet he doesn't know how she likes her coffee for instance. Things which come so naturally to me now will still be unknown to him. I don't feel superior in any way though. I don't feel anything except ashamed at how jealous I've become. Joining me she's like a breath of air sweeping into the room. "Oh thank you Prof. Mmmm that's perfect!" It pleases me to do things for her. I love it when she lets me.

"So you've bought yourself some more time have you? What did you do, bribe someone?"

Laughing, she tells me of the conversation with her doctor and how she was grasping at straws really, not for a minute expecting him to go for it and then he did. Almost as suddenly her face clouds over again. "What's wrong, honey?" I ask her. She worries me when she does this. She's obviously allowed some unpleasant thought into her mind. It occurs to me that maybe the rest of the time she's concentrating really hard on being upbeat and positive.

"Well, I'm happy to have delayed my isolation a bit, but I guess it just worries me…"

"What? What worries you?"

She hesitates. "Well I worry that maybe he's given in to me because he knows I might not come out of there…you know, that maybe…"

I interrupt her. I can't let her begin to go down this road. "Stop right there… This is going to work, okay? We have gone for this transplant with a positive focus. You have a good match and things are going to work out fine. Don't you think it's just too strange a coincidence that your father is available right when you need him most? You haven't known him all your life and then at the crucial moment he comes up with the goods."

I can hardly believe it's me saying these words. I desperately need her to believe in herself, though and maybe believing in him will help her to do that. She nods ever so slightly, but says nothing. We drink our coffees in silence. I'm watching her closely. Looking for an indication of what she's feeling now, but she's pretty guarded again. After a moment or two, the change of subject comes.

"Have you seen anything of Luc?"

Tonight does indeed seem to be the night for surprises. It's natural, I suppose. She's on the brink of something huge, so all the important issues in her life are edging their way to the fore.

"Actually, yes… I saw him today…He was looking for Sebastian. He didn't realise he was in hospital, didn't know where he was."

She nods again. I know she's wondering if he asked for her. The truth is he didn't.

"So he's still here then. I thought maybe he might have gone back to Paris," she says sadly.

"He's going." I say it as gently as I can. Poor Carly; she really cared for Luc. "He told me he plans to leave in a couple of days, once he gets himself organised. I think he wants to see Sebastian before he goes."

She can't hide the look of disappointment that flashes over her face. "Oh…I thought perhaps he might have come to see me too."

Did she really? This is one of those occasions when I just can't comprehend the female mind. I don't honestly think there's a man alive who would come back for more after the way she treated him last time they met. I understand why she did, of course, but Luc doesn't.

"Did you tell him about me and…and my…dad?"

I shake my head. She asked me not to say anything. She was adamant she didn't want him to know about their relationship. "You told me not to."

"Yes," she says. "That's right."

We sit another few moments without talking. Sometimes we're good at this; just being together, not feeling the need to speak. Other times it's a bit more uncomfortable, like now. I don't like it when she starts burying her feelings. I don't think it's good for her.

"Talk to me," I say.

I want to be able to comfort her when she feels like this, but unless she tells me what's wrong. I feel powerless to do anything. Stirring her coffee unnecessarily, she hesitates. Without raising her eyes to look at me she asks, "How is he?" Luc, obviously. This one clearly isn't going away.

"He…well he…I guess he's looked better if you know what I mean?"

Shaking her head, "No, I don't know what you mean. How did he seem to you?"

I'm not sure how much to tell her. Is there any real point in this, other than the fact that she clearly wants to talk about him? "Well, to be honest...he looked pretty wrecked. I gather he's been out a lot...like I said he didn't miss Sebastian these past few days. I got the impression it was just this morning he noticed he wasn't there." She's thinking too much about this. I wish I could get her off the subject and on to something more positive. I really don't want her to get depressed, not with so much depending on her frame of mind in the weeks ahead.

"He's not sitting at home wallowing obviously. Where did you meet him?"

"Carly, do you think this is a good idea?"

She shrugs her shoulders and backs off slightly. I can sense her retreating into herself. This is the worst thing that can happen. I need to keep her with me, keep her on top of everything.

"He called round to the house."

She glances up quickly and I know I have to dispel the fragment of hope she's detected in this last statement.

"He knew you wouldn't be there, that you were back in hospital. He called round...didn't come in...said he had stuff to do. He asked about Sebastian...as if I... he did say he was pleased we'd found a donor, hoped it went well..."

I tail off because the child sitting in front of me is crumbling before my eyes. Reaching over to her, I draw her close. Holding her in my arms I'm acutely aware of how fragile she feels; physically and emotionally. It's such a shame about Luc. If things had been different he might have been a real asset in her fight. She would have had something to hold on for and someone else to draw strength from. It's an impossible situation, though. She's fallen in love with the wrong person. Just as I did.

# LUC

It's really strange to be sitting here watching the familiar drip, drip of the blood transfusion and for it not to be Carly that's attached to the end of it.

"So how long do you think they'll keep you in here?"

He's not sure, hopes he'll get out tomorrow. He looks pretty exhausted lying there. I have to be honest, I didn't realise it was such a big deal being a bone marrow donor. It really turned my stomach when he showed me the puncture marks where they took out the marrow. I can't believe it's such a primitive procedure. I mean, I know they took him to theatre and he had an anaesthetic and everything, but when it comes down to it, they ram a huge needle right through the bone and suck out the marrow from inside! It sounds almost barbaric! However, this is the life-saving substance that Carly is relying on, so I'm glad he's done it. It's funny how he, of all people, proved to be the match they were searching for. I wonder if this will put his and Len's relationship under further strain. I can't imagine Len wanting to share Carly with him, not after all that happened with Claudine. "You look pretty tired. Maybe I should go." I stand to leave, but he assures me he's fine. He doesn't seem to have had any other visitors. There are no cards or flowers or anything. "Does Helen know you're doing this? Does she know you're here?" He laughs as if that's answer enough. I guess it is. "What about Len? Obviously he'll know you're a match for Carly. Has he been to see you?" I'm thinking that surely he'll have been able to bring himself to thank Sebastian for doing this. Surely for the sake of his precious Carly!

"I spoke to him briefly this afternoon. I think he's downstairs with her just now."

I'm a bit annoyed. I would have thought Len could have spent a bit of time with Sebastian. "Are they inseparable then?" My words sounding, even to me, filled with bitterness.

He looks at me closely. "I don't think it's that. Carly was up here herself this afternoon. I think it's because she'll be going into isolation soon. Probably just making the most of time together, you know."

"Yeah…I know…at least I did know. What do you think she sees in him anyway? Do you think she's just desperate for attention or what?"

"I'm not sure I follow you. What does she see in him? What makes you think she sees anything in him?" He looks a bit irritated.

"Well she's hooked up with him hasn't she? She left me for him by the look of things." Laughing now, he's shaking his head. "I don't think it's particularly funny Sebastian. I really liked her." He goes on laughing and now he's getting me mad. I'd never be so insensitive. This time I decide I am leaving. I don't care that he's lying in a hospital bed, he's pissing me off now and I don't need to take this.

"Luc…Luc don't go…I didn't mean it."

Swinging round I can hardly contain myself, "And why not? You're laughing at me. I don't find this funny. It hurts in actual fact. It hurts a lot."

He composes himself, although I still detect the faintest trace of a smirk playing around his lips. "Luc, it's not like that…it's not what you think. Len and Carly…they're not a couple…not like that anyway."

I'm confused now. What does he mean? What kind of a couple are they? What's going on? Reluctantly I approach the bed and sit beside him. "What are you saying?" I ask him earnestly.

"Just that: they're not a couple. Carly isn't his girlfriend."

I try to process this information. It's hard to take it in. All week I've been thinking of them as being together. Now it seems I've got it all wrong. But I can't get my head around it. They seemed very close. She's moved in with him. I don't understand.

"I need to explain don't I?" He's speaking much more seriously now. I feel a bit apprehensive as if he's building up to something, but yes I think he does need to explain. I want to know but I don't as well. I'm afraid, now, that it's going to turn out to be worse than I anticipated. He sits himself up so he can look at me properly. I don't like it.

"Well?" I ask impatiently.

Hesitatingly he begins, "Claudine…after Claudine died…some stuff came out…stuff we didn't know before." He stops and seems to be watching to see that I understand. Well I don't. What is he talking about? What stuff? He goes on, I can't help feeling he's a bit reluctant to divulge the details, but he obviously realises he can't leave me in limbo like this, not now he's started. "I don't know if it's my place to be telling you this… on the other hand it would help you understand what's been happening."

"Just bloody tell me! You can't leave me like this."

He puts his hands up in a gesture of surrender. "Okay, okay. I'll tell you…but this isn't easy for me either, you know." He takes a deep breath. "Claudine …she had a baby…none of us knew at the time. I just found out myself."

I'm shocked, no, more than shocked. I'm astounded at what he's saying. My sister had a baby! How can this be? Surely we would all have known? "I don't understand." I manage to choke the words out.

"She had a baby…years ago…it was…it was *our* baby…I haven't told another soul about this, Luc… I didn't know…she didn't tell me she was pregnant…I swear I didn't know…" His eyes are shining and he's having difficulty getting the words out now. I'm still trying to sort out what it is he's saying. Claudine had a baby, *his* baby? No way! I don't believe it. And yet, look at the state of him. I realise that he's struggling to continue. It's obviously true.

"When Sebastian?" Does this explain the animosity between Len and him, I'm wondering? Images of Len kicking the living daylights out of Sebastian flash across my mind. Len had been ranting about Sebastian and her having an affair. But I'm sure Sebastian had sworn blind there had been nothing going on.

"It was...it was twenty years ago...We were nineteen at the time...I didn't know, though. If I'd known do you really think I'd have left her? I loved her...that's all I would have needed to make me stay." There are silent tears now and I'm so confused I don't know what to do. This is Sebastian; strong, independent, needing no-one. The man across from me is not.

"Sebastian...I'm so sorry for you. I'm having trouble getting my head around all this. She was nineteen when she had the baby...so...is that why she went away?"

He nods, wipes his face with his hand, takes a deep breath, starts again. He's getting himself together. He's probably really embarrassed about losing it like that. It's so not Sebastian to open up in that way. He doesn't really show his feelings. My heart goes out to him though. Knowing how much he loved my sister, to find out news like this only after she's died, well I can only imagine how hard that would be to bear. "There's more, Luc." Oh no, I think. Please don't let it be worse. I'm terrified to hear any more. "The baby...Luc...the baby was...it's Carly."

What on earth is he talking about? How can the baby be Carly? I don't get it. I don't understand. The baby was Carly. And suddenly it all makes sense! "So that explains why you're a match for the transplant then." I say. He nods simply. "And Len? He's treating her like family...that's why she's moved in?" Again a nod. "Wow!" I say simply. I mean what do you say to that? At least I understand now. I feel sorry for Sebastian. I realise this revelation has been as big a shock to him as it is to me.

"Does she know about you? Does she know you're her father?" I ask him.

"She does now," he replies.

"Well, you know I'm glad for you. I'm happy, I really am. I hope you're able to make a good go of things. I don't understand the girl and I'm sure you realise things are a bit different for me. I don't think I can stick around now. There's no reason for me to stay. In actual fact it would probably be quite hard for me especially if you're going to be spending a lot of time together."

He looks disappointed. "Why don't you cut her a bit of slack, Luc? She's having a difficult time of things right now."

Now I'm really confused. "Hang on a minute. Am I somehow in the wrong here? Am I missing something?"

He shakes his head, "No, no not at all. I understand where you're coming from. Of course I do. It's just that she's facing some pretty major things, isn't she? Life's hard for her at the moment. I realise you're hurt, but…"

I can't let him continue. I realise, of course I realise she's having a rough time. This would be a nightmare situation for anybody; cancer and all the treatment and everything and then on top of all that all this family stuff. "The thing is though, me and Carly, I thought we were pretty special. I thought she was the one, remember? She's made it clear she's not interested and where does that leave me? Okay, so I got it wrong about her and Len, but even that aside I know she's not interested in me anymore."

He isn't done defending her though, "I don't think you do understand, Luc. I don't think you've got any idea what this is like for her."

He knows how to rile me, how to get me worked up. Why is he doing this? "What is this with everyone around here? Why this constant need to protect her? I'm fully aware she's ill and things are difficult for her right now, but why does that give her carte blanche to treat other people so badly. I don't need it, you know. I don't need her and I don't need all the grief she brings with her. This past week I've done a lot of thinking and, you know, I'm over her. I'm going home but not because I'm running away. I'm going because there's nothing left for me here. There's nothing to stay for. There are plenty other girls out there who're just as much fun, more probably. When we came back, sure I thought maybe there was a chance for me and Carly, but now I see what a mistake that would be. We're completely incompatible, we've nothing in common. I don't even know what I saw in her in the first place."

I stop and am surprised by the silence that's descended over the room. Sebastian is staring at me. His eyes haven't left mine since I began what turned into a tirade against Carly. I know I didn't mean any of it, of course I didn't. It's just so difficult to handle them treating her with kid gloves when she's dishing out so much hurt herself. I think they've forgotten that I haven't actually done anything to deserve the treatment she's given me. What is he looking at? Why has he gone so quiet? I'm sure he must realise I didn't mean it, not the way it all came out anyway. An embarrassed cough from behind prompts me to turn round. Shit! Len and Carly. How long have they been standing there? What have I just said? What have I done?

She doesn't say a word. She looks at me with such sad eyes that I feel my heart will break and before I have a chance to say anything she's gone. I'm still in a state of shock. What just happened here? Glancing round the room I find Len and Sebastian both staring at me. I've blown it, I think. I've just ruined any possibility of any kind of reconciliation. What was I thinking of? I didn't even mean any of what I just said. I need some direction and I look to Sebastian to provide it. "Go after her," he says quietly. Without taking any time to think I'm up and out the door. I see her in the distance, outside the ward following the corridor. She turns a corner and is out of sight. Starting to run, I know I mustn't lose her. If she disappears I might not be able to find her. The hospital is her territory, not mine. I don't know my way around like she does. Reaching the ward entrance I once again catch a glimpse of her, this time making her way down the stairs. I call out to her. She hears me, looks back and carries on her way. I'm sure she's quickening her step now too. She doesn't want me to catch her. I don't blame her. I was pretty callous in my remarks. She doesn't know I didn't mean a word of it. I could shoot myself for being so stupid. Why was I even trying to convince Sebastian I was over her? What difference would it have made to him anyway? Racing down the stairs behind her, I realise I'm gaining on her. Maybe I will manage to reach her. Once on the ground floor she hurries toward the exit. Jumping the last few stairs, I step up my pace once on level ground and find myself striding side by side with her as she leaves the building. She's ignoring me, treating me like I'm a stranger. Taking hold of her arm I force her to slow and stop.

"Carly…please…"

My eyes are pleading with her. Surely she can tell by looking at me how desperately I still love her. She gives no indication, however, of understanding my feelings. Shaking me off, she continues walking outside. As the automatic doors close silently behind us, we step out into a beautiful summer evening. The air is warm in spite of the sun's rapid descent. The world looks bright and appealing. She settles on a small wall overlooking a play area, deserted now of children and parents. The slight breeze catches an empty swing, tugging it gently to and fro. Abandoned spades and buckets litter the sand-pit, a reminder of happy, carefree times. She doesn't turn as I seat myself beside her. She seems resigned to my presence, however unwelcome. I don't know where to begin. Again I reach out to her, placing my hand softly on her shoulder. She remains cold and rigid beneath my touch. I'm embarrassed and quickly drop my hand. We sit like this for a few minutes. Slowly it dawns on me that it's up to me. She doesn't need to do a thing. If I want to make things better, I need to sort it.

Bracing myself for a well-deserved onslaught, I begin, "Carly, those things I said…none of it's true. Please believe me."

She doesn't answer me, doesn't even acknowledge I've spoken.

"I don't know why I said all that stuff. I think maybe I was trying to convince myself. I don't know…"

Still nothing. Okay, I guess she doesn't owe me anything. Still, if there's anything I want her to know, this is my opportunity. I might not get another.

"You really hurt me the other night, you know."

This time she turns to look at me. Silently she's watching me. At least now I know she's listening even if I'm getting nothing back. I feel slightly encouraged, so I go on, "I suppose tonight was about being angry with you. You see when I came back here, to Edinburgh; it was for only one reason. I came back for you. I wanted you...I still do."

She's shaking her head and I'm starting to get scared.

"Carly, I'm so sorry. I didn't mean to upset you. Please believe me when I say I didn't mean it. I'm not over you...no way am I over you. You're all I can think of...you're all that I want."

I know I'm sounding increasingly desperate, but this lack of response is really unnerving me. I need her to know how I feel.

"Carly, please say something."

For a moment I wonder if she's just going to ignore me completely. It's getting cooler now that the sun has finally set and she's starting to shiver. My instinct is to cuddle her close, but I daren't lay a finger on her.

"Carly?"

Eventually she opens her mouth, her words no more than a whisper, "Luc...we're not right for each other. I'm sorry but I can't love you, not the way you want me to."

I don't understand. "What do you mean? Why can't you love me? I don't get what you're saying."

She doesn't explain, but I realise she's finished with me. Slowly she shifts from her position on the wall and walks, it seems in slow motion, back toward the hospital entrance; each deliberate step widening the chasm between us. I ache for her, but still she goes. I'm losing her and there's nothing I can do about it.

# LEN

Poor Carly. She looks terrible. I don't suppose she slept much last night, what with all that carry-on with Luc and of course, her worry about what all lies ahead today. She's in her isolation room now and trying to put on a brave face. Sebastian and I have agreed a kind of shift system for visiting; partly to make sure she doesn't spend any more time on her own than is absolutely necessary, but also, I must admit, to avoid bumping into each other if we can help it. It's more than a bit awkward coming across him so frequently now that we appear, once again, to have a common interest. She's immersed in her books at the moment so told me to go get myself a coffee. I wonder if she truly believes she's going to be able to manage to study while this treatment works on her.

Dr Armstrong has been incredible, spending hours with us going over everything. I can tell Carly's a pretty special patient to him and that reassures me a bit. He'll be doing his best for her at every step, I know that. There's just so much uncertainty associated with this kind of thing. Transplants carry risks, he told me that at the start, but the alternative…well the alternative was unthinkable. Now, however, we're faced with all the possibilities he highlighted at the outset and I feel so powerless to protect her from harm. Watching that first lot of chemo being pumped into her vein was such a horrendous experience. The knowledge that the very substance which will destroy the cancer could potentially kill her is too huge to contemplate. Part of me was willing the toxic liquid to wash through her diseased body and flush out all trace of these dangerous cells. The other part of me wanted to scream at them to stop. She's so frail; what if she can't take this? She'll have this process repeated and a cocktail of other drugs added in for good measure. Once her bone marrow has been stripped bare, she'll be rescued with an infusion of Sebastian's marrow. Dr Armstrong has prepared us for a long haul. I'm aware that nothing dramatic will happen straightaway. She'll carry on, pretty much as before, until the side effects of the chemo start to kick in. Nausea, vomiting, diarrhoea, hair loss; these are all to be expected. The real threat however will come once her blood counts have plummeted and she's unable to fight infection. He anticipates that will be in about two weeks' time. So we wait and watch her gradually get sicker and sicker. In a way it's good to be prepared, to know what to expect. But on the other hand, it's so very hard to look at her right now, apparently so well, reading and writing, occupying her time and to know that she's going to become really ill.

It was her decision to take her books in with her. I had to buy her all new copies so they could go into the isolation room with her. She isn't allowed any of her stuff from home, only things which can either be sterilised or which are brand new. Sebastian was getting home today. He came down this morning to see her. He'd assumed things had gone alright last night with Luc when she didn't return after talking to him. He couldn't have been more wrong. Fortunately I called in here on my way out. She was breaking her heart crying all by herself. It tore me apart to see the state she was in. The poor girl loves him so much. I wish there was something I could do to help, but of course there's nothing. I was at least able to hug her, though and let her know that I care how she's feeling.

Wandering back to the transplant unit, my polystyrene cup of takeaway coffee burning my fingers, I am met by one of the nurses. I don't know this girl's name, but she has seemed nice and very efficient. "How are you getting on?" she asks me "Are you getting used to things?" I nod slightly. I don't feel like a big discussion, but it's good to have the opportunity given me, to know that they're there if we need them. Reaching Carly's room, I sit down in the chair positioned carefully beside the window and lift the walkie-talkie to speak to her. "I'm back," I tell her. She laughs into the other end and informs me she can see that.

"Do you want anything?" I ask her.

She shakes her head, "No I'm fine just now…oh actually there is something. It's a bit of a bother though." I assure her that whatever it is won't be a bother, she just needs to ask. "Well I'm getting on fine with this, but I could do with having a look at one of my essays from last year…you know the one I wrote about Sylvia Plath's private life and its influence on her poetry?" I know the one she means. It was an excellent piece of work, one which I was in the process of putting forward for publication before I embarked on this leave of absence, this extended leave of absence.

"Okay, if you need it I'll get it for you. I could go in to work today if you want it in a hurry."

She does. She must think I'm an idiot. I'm perfectly clued into her and her ways and I realise exactly what she's about. Still, I can't really blame her. She's made no pretence about her desire for me to return to work. Forcing me to go back on campus, into my office is a good first step and one she knows I'll do willingly for her. She doesn't need this essay, we both know that, but I'll get it for her and let her see the lengths I'll go to for her sake, because I care about her.

## LUC

I hardly slept a wink last night; just kept going over everything in my head. Why did I say all that stuff? What possessed me to offload like that to Sebastian? I guess it was something to do with his standing up for her the whole time. I really wanted him to see how much she'd hurt me. How stupid! I've done it this time. She could hardly look at me. I can picture her face: so lovely, so sad. I did that to her. I caused her to be so unhappy. I can't think straight anymore. I've gone over it all so many times now, I'm not even sure I'm remembering accurately what really happened. I need to clear my head somehow and take a long hard look at my life. I know I've lost her. I know that with a certainty I haven't had about anything for a long time. What I don't know is how I continue my life without her. I had based all my plans, all my hopes around Carly and me being together. It felt so right that I couldn't imagine us not making it. Now I have to review everything and how do I do that while my mind is bursting with confusion?

Sebastian's place is starting to feel like a prison. I'm stifled by its lack of colour and character. I understand he likes a minimalist look, but to me this place is so empty it feels dead. I also don't think I can carry on staying here knowing she's lying sick half a mile away and doesn't want me with her. To be unable to see her, to hold her while she's enduring this dreadful treatment, I don't think I can handle it. I need to get away. I'm not ready to go home yet either, wherever home might be. I thought home was right here. I thought home was with Carly. Why can't she let me back in? Part of me feels I shouldn't give up, but how clear does she need to be? She doesn't want me. She said as much. She's said it repeatedly.

Wandering down to the corner shop to buy a paper I know I won't read, I have a sudden inexplicable longing to speak to my father. I guess I need some direction, some guidance, but I don't think I've ever turned to my dad for advice about anything. Who is it that helps me when I'm finding things tough? Who is it that's always been there for me as long as I can remember? Yes, Sebastian.

Years ago when I was a small boy it was Sebastian who had time for me. He explained stuff to me, helped me when I was growing up. I remember very clearly one time when he took me away for the day. I was about seven or eight and the family were all going to a funeral. It was some aunt that I didn't know, don't think I'd ever met her and there had been a democratic decision that I shouldn't attend. I guess I was considered to be too young or something. Anyway, everyone else was going to be there so it fell to Sebastian to look after me that day. I don't know if he offered or if my mother asked him, but it was a natural enough thing. He was always about our house at that time and I was happy to be with him. He was older and cooler and all my mates looked up to him. This day was scorching hot and as the others traipsed away in their best suits, the air was oppressively humid. The sun beat down on us, it was close to unbearable. Inside the house we were roasting, outside it was worse. "What'll we do all day?" I moaned. He had smiled and asked if I'd ever been out of the city before. I hadn't and my curiosity was instantly aroused. He walked me to the station. All the way I was asking where we were going. Excited, boyish chatter was patiently tolerated by him as the train propelled us away from the airless, overpowering heat of the metropolis and out to cooler climes. On we went, past miles and miles of graffitied suburb until eventually we reached the countryside. It was at a small unmanned station in the middle of nowhere that he ushered me to disembark. I hadn't a clue where we were. To this day I couldn't tell you the name of that village. Sebastian had been there before though. He led me with the air of someone who had many times visited this place and I was happy to follow on, wandering across fields, through gates and under a massive canopy of trees until we reached a small brook. This was the place he had intended. The trees provided a welcome shade and the temperature felt instantly cooler as we settled on the bank facing the water. Passing me what I thought was a snooker cue, I felt completely bewildered. All this way he had carried these cues and I had wondered why he hadn't left them at our place. It was only now, unzipping them from their pouches that it dawned on me why we were here. Fishing! We sat there for hours while he showed me how to cast and reel. At first it was frustrating watching fish jump a few yards from us and failing to tempt any onto my hook. Hours passed and with the time my irritation at my own inabilities also waned. He taught me that it wasn't about making the catch. It was about going through the therapeutic motions. The soothing repetitions worked wonders, calmed my hot spirit and helped me to focus on other things. I remember him telling me this was where he came when he had filing to do, when he needed to sort out his head and put problems into workable bundles of thought. I was surprised. I never thought of Sebastian as being someone who would have problems. To me he was omnipotent.

Reaching the newsagents I make my purchase, the single copy of Paris Match on the shelf. I wonder do they stock this for him. Heading back to the apartment, I catch sight of my reflection in a shop window. I'm smiling. I have a plan. Taking the stairs two at a time, my mind is racing. I'll pack my stuff, get a hire car and I'll leave straightaway. There's nothing to stop me; I have no ties. Out of courtesy, I tear a piece of paper from a notepad and scribble a message. After all, the last thing I want him to do is come looking for me. Gathering my things, I drop it by the phone where I know he'll find it.

Gone Fishing!  He'll understand.

# SEBASTIAN

The shower raining down over me is invigorating, bringing me back to life. All these days spent in hospital have unquestionably left me feeling jaded and spiritless. There's nothing like getting back to your home comforts though to hasten the transition to normality. It was such a weird time in there. The first few days I was so bored I thought I would go mad. It was hard, I guess, because there was nothing actually wrong with me. I was only there so they could run all the checks to make sure I was a healthy enough specimen to use as a donor. Then there were all the issues around consent. It didn't appear to be enough that I was there saying "Here I am. Take my bone marrow." I had to be informed. In essence this meant that I had to undergo lengthy conversations with doctors, nurses, anaesthetists, surgeons, everybody it seemed they could think of and almost convince them I was happy to do this. To be fair, a very patient nurse did explain to me why it's such a complicated process. Apparently it's to do with me being fit and well and not actually needing the surgical procedure they wanted to do. In addition, the fact that I won't benefit myself from the bone marrow harvest is significant. I guess the idea is that if anything should happen to a reasonably young, healthy guy on the operating table they would all have some major ethical issues going on. Only by making absolutely sure that I know what I'm doing and having the relevant documentation to prove it can they go ahead with clear consciences. Anyway, it's just the way it is. The main thing is that it's done and Carly can get her transplant. The only bonus of being stuck in there was, of course, having the chance to spend a bit of time with her. She's just so lovely. I can't get enough of her. I want to know everything about her; the past, the present. Most of all I want to be a part of her future. I knew that the moment she walked into my room. The instant she gave me the signal that she wanted me in her life I knew. Coming to find me was the perfect way of doing that. I would never have approached her. Despite the longing I felt to gather my daughter in my arms, I wouldn't have made the first move. I told myself that if she wanted me and only if she wanted me, then I would get involved. If she didn't, I would have given the marrow and walked away. I would never have presumed to take on the role of her father. Having left her for so long to struggle through life without me I couldn't have expected her to suddenly welcome me into her life. I *didn't* expect it. One thing I've discovered already though is how unpredictable a girl Carly is. Unpredictable, beautiful, bright, I could go on forever. I'm so proud of the young woman she's become. In spite of me. In spite of Claudine.

Dressing in fresh clothes, which don't smell of the hospital, I give my uncovered wounds a cursory glance. What a small price to pay for such gratitude. I didn't like her thanking me. I felt really uncomfortable about it. Making out that it was such a heroic thing to have done. It wasn't. Anyone would have done it and gladly. And now, now you would hardly even notice the marks, they're healing so quickly. I wander barefoot through to the kitchen and realise with a smile I can have a decent cup of coffee now. The ansaphone's flashing, speaking to me of hidden messages within. I pick up a scrap of paper lying beside the machine. Laughing out loud, I remember the day he's referring to. Yes, that was a good day. I'm surprised he remembered; he was only a boy at the time. I wonder where he's gone. I guess if he wanted me to know he'd have said. He's being deliberately vague, I decide; probably needs some space. I hope it helps. He seemed pretty screwed up the other night when he went off on that rant about Carly. It was obvious he didn't mean a word of it, although I gather Carly was convinced. What a pair. If they could just see themselves; clearly besotted with each other, clearly made for each other! I wonder why they're making it all so complicated. Don't they understand that it's up to them? Only they can give themselves permission to love each other. It won't come from anywhere else. If they want it, they'll have to go after it. It won't come to them. I know, to my cost I know.

Taking a sip of the first good cup of coffee I've had this week, I start to relax. Lighting a cigarette I enjoy the feeling of being back in control of my life. That was one of the most difficult parts of being in hospital. I appreciate the reasons behind a smoking ban, but on the other hand it's not an ideal time or place for someone to try to quit is it? Luc's been at me for a while about it. I guess I should give it some thought. Maybe once things settle down with Carly; when she's better and home and there's less to worry about.

Heading through to the sitting room, I press the ansaphone to play and listen to four messages, all from Helen. She's been phoning since she heard I was back obviously. In each one she sounds more irritated than the last, wondering where the hell I am, wondering if I'm the least bit interested in the restaurant and finally telling me I know where she is if I can be bothered lifting the phone. I do and am greeted by her voicemail message. Replacing the handset without speaking, I take a long draw on my cigarette and consciously try not to get annoyed. This isn't going to be easy. She didn't want me here and she's clearly working on making life difficult for me. I don't need this from her, not right now. I'm glad she didn't answer. Maybe I'll leave it a bit before calling again.

Glancing at my watch, I feel an irresistible draw back to the hospital. I want to see how Carly's doing. I want to be close to her. It's far too early though. This is Len's time. We agreed. I need to find some way of passing the hours until five o'clock - then we'll swap over. I suppose this way it's better for Carly. She'll have someone there most of the time and hopefully we'll both be able to bring something fresh to her each visit. Outside it's a gorgeous day. Typical! Poor Carly gets cooped up in a goldfish bowl and the weather picks up all of a sudden. I wish she could be here with me right now. What would we do if she was? What would I suggest? I know. I'd take her out down the Mound to see how the Fringe Festival is shaping up. We would take a wander through the Meadows and down towards Princes Street, enjoying the sunshine and fresh air, feeling the buzz of activity from the festival acts. The decision's made in an instant. Pulling on my trainers I set off out. Obviously Carly can't come with me, but if I go then I'll have something to share with her later on when I visit. Everything takes on greater significance now because of Carly. Every aspect of my life, everything I do, everywhere I go, Carly's a part of it. When did this change happen, I ask myself? When did my life take on new meaning? When did it start to have any meaning at all?

I'm halfway across the Meadows when I realise I've forgotten my phone. I seem to be doing that a lot lately; too much on my mind obviously. There are loads of people milling around, vans and lorries negotiating their way tentatively around the park. In the centre, an enormous tent signals the reason behind all the activity. The circus is here. It's an annual event, but I've never been to watch it. This year I'd like to go. This year I'd like to go with Carly. It won't happen of course. There's no way she'll be ready to go out and about in the short time the circus is running, but again I'm conscious of a shift in my outlook. She's changing me. I pause for a few minutes to watch, like everyone else it seems. Standing with my arms folded, I feel suddenly very lonely amongst this crowd of people. Groups of teenagers are gathering in corners, trying to look uninterested behind dark sunglasses. Mothers with pushchairs stop to point out various sights to their wondering offspring. I become aware that I'm straining to see the truck with the decorative painting of the tigers down one side of it. I'm wondering how they offload that lot safely, where they're going to house them for their stay. The young boy in me has wakened up. I feel the excitement filling the fields around me and I long to be a part of it. After a bit I glance absently at the building directly ahead and realise I'm scanning the windows trying to identify Carly's room. I wonder what kind of a view she has. Might she be sitting watching this same scene from the confines of her enclosure?

The interruption to my thoughts lifts me out of my daydream state and I start to move reluctantly on. Once through the Meadows, the bustling sounds of commotion become fainter and I cross the road.

Passing a pub I notice with a new interest the groups of hospital staff making their way inside, marking the change of shift in the infirmary. Do I recognise any of them? I don't but they all look different out of uniform anyway. It's a strange feeling to consider that the same people who are busy looking after Carly all day, looking after such incredibly sick teenagers go home to normal lives once their work is finished. I think we forget that. We assume that our children are the centre of their lives as they are ours. How could someone leave my daughter's bedside and go directly to the pub for a drink? Easy, I think. It's precisely because someone has been at Carly's bedside that they head straight there. How else would you keep a lid on your emotions unless you had some kind of an outlet to vent them?

Down the hill I continue, the increasing slope of the Mound pulling my feet, giving them a momentum of their own. Rounding a bend in the road, the majesty of the Castle rears up on the left, perched high above the city and its people. I cross again and make my way down the Playfair Steps to the foot of the Mound, where most of the throng are gathered. The Fringe is coming to life and I want to immerse myself in its sights and sounds. I want to be able to share it all with Carly when I visit later today. She would love this so much: all the arty people doing their thing, trying not to appear appreciative of the praise and applause from the uneducated masses. Reaching the bottom step, I toss a few coins and a cigarette into the bucket placed carefully by one of Edinburgh's multitude of beggars, as he sits huddled apologetically in the corner.

All around me is a vision of colour. Various groups occupy their own small patch, vying for the attention of the passing crowds. Flyer after flyer is thrust into my hand. Words of commendation urge me I mustn't miss this show or that. One night only, debut performance…the words start to merge together. I'm surrounded by clowns, fire-eaters, men on stilts. Dancers and musicians, comics and street theatre fill the air with sound. The atmosphere bursts with life. I find myself smiling as I pass through. The energy, the enthusiasm has captured me and I'm enjoying the exhilaration I feel. Toward the end of the concourse I spot a row of stands. Getting closer I see an assortment of displays by students from the art school. Paintings and drawings, jewellery, pottery…it goes on. The work looks fabulous. I know I have an untrained eye, but all these creations are so lovely. In an instant I decide I have to get her something. She would so love this. This would be her kind of thing. I find myself pausing at a stall exhibiting a mesmerising collection of necklaces, rings and bracelets. I'm captivated by the colours and textures used to make these beautiful creations. I'm almost able to imagine the love and care which must go into fabricating something out of nothing. On a simpler scale, I guess it's a bit like cooking.

The idea of buying a present for my daughter fills me with delight. It's the first thing I'll ever have bought her and as such takes on huge significance. I want it to be the right thing, though. I want to choose something she'll love. The girl behind the stand is friendly and talkative. She speaks very fast and I'm not really following all that she's saying. I tell her it's for my daughter and feel myself filling with pride as I do so. She lifts several items, gives them to me to hold. Does she have pierced ears? Embarrassed I have to admit that I don't know. Unperturbed she suggests some necklaces. This one I like. It's very plain. A gold chain with a disc pendant attached. It feels nice in my hand; flat and smooth. She tells me I could have it engraved by the guy at the next stand. Looking up I see the boy in question busily absorbed in his work. Yes, this is the thing. I'll buy it. She leads me over to her neighbour and I duly inform him of my requirements. She's still speaking and I can hardly hear a word now. A band has started up somewhere nearby and everyone seems to be shouting. I feel only semi-conscious, as if I've been drugged or something. This sense of over-stimulation is slightly unsettling. I find myself following her out of the crowd and into the Gardens. It's a little quieter here and we find a bench to sit on. Around us picnickers are busy setting up individual and family pitches ready to enjoy a day of relaxation in the sun. She's holding two plastic cups of coffee and hands me one.

"You couldn't hear a word I was saying back there could you?" She's young; twenty maybe, somewhere in the region of Carly's age anyway. Does absolutely everything in my life now have some connection, however loose with Carly? Maybe that's what it's like to be a dad. Maybe it's an all-pervading role. It seems to be for me anyway. "I was trying to ask you for a date," she continues.

"A date?"

How did we get to here? Did I hear her right? She's laughing, her white teeth parted revealing a pierced tongue.

"Am I being too forward for you?" she asks.

It dawns on me that she's flirting with me. How did this happen? I hardly said two words to her back there and here we are sitting together having coffee and she's asking me out.

"I think maybe you're a bit young for me," I finally manage to stammer. Again she laughs, but her expression has changed. She looks disappointed.

"So that's no then?"

I honestly don't know what to say to her. I don't want to hurt her feelings, but I'm not sure how I even got into this conversation.

"It's not a good time for me right now," I begin. She looks up, waits for an explanation. "My daughter…my daughter's ill. She's very ill…in hospital…I couldn't even think of…"

She's nodding. "Hey, it's cool…don't worry about it…It was just a thought…Here I'll give you my number in case you change your mind…"

Smiling she passes me a card decorated with the art school logo and the name Millie. She's scribbled an almost undecipherable phone number across the picture. Then, without warning, she stands and saunters back over to the busy walkway, presumably to take up position again at her stall. She disappears from sight, surrounded by a company of interested individuals swarming in on either side.

As I drain my drink the sound of bagpipes reaches my ears from a distant source. The warmth from the sun is pleasant on my face. The atmosphere is a bit more restful here in the Gardens and less intense than the frivolity of the Fringe a few hundred yards away. I sit for a while, thinking but not about anything in particular. It feels good to be here. It was the right thing to do. Closing my eyes I allow the anonymity of the city to protect me from unwanted conversation or distraction. The sounds of the world around become more and more muffled as I retreat into my inner place. I feel better. I feel a lot better. It's hard to believe that she's been here all this time. All those years when my life had no meaning at all, she was here. Unknown to me, a little girl was growing up alongside me whose very existence had the power to completely change mine. And she has. Carly has changed everything.

Rousing myself from this surreal state of awareness, I glance at my watch and realise I could start heading for the hospital. Stopping to collect my purchase from the engraving guy, I smile as I examine the fine workmanship. It's just what I wanted. The girl with the pierced tongue, Millie, is busy with another customer. Perhaps she senses me watching her, because she lifts her face to mine, but resumes her work without acknowledgement. Clutching my parcel I break into a run. I've waited all day for the time to pass so I could head back to see her and now I'm probably going to be late. It's uphill all the way and I'm starting to feel the strain around my hips, where they operated. I'm forced to slow to a walk. I guess I'm not fully fit just yet. It's frustrating, but I don't want to end up with problems because I've pushed myself. I need to be well so I can be there for Carly. By the time I get into the ward, I'm twenty-five minutes later than I told Len I would be. He's not impressed. I suppose he's been clock-watching to see if I made it on time or not. He'll no doubt add this to his list of things which make me a bad father.

"You've got a watch have you?" he asks me, sarcastically, as I reach him.

"Yeah I'm fine thanks. How are you?" My words are equally loaded.

"What about a cell? You have a cell, yes?"

Of course I have a phone. He knows I do. I must look confused, because he doesn't wait for a reply, but spells it out for me. "I've been trying to reach you. You weren't answering."

Suddenly I feel very frightened. "I forgot it. Why? What's wrong? Is something wrong with Carly?"

He appears to have taken pity on me. Shaking his head, he quickly extinguishes my anguish, "No, she's fine. It's not that. She wants me to go get her some stuff from Uni, that's all. I didn't want to leave her on her own so I was waiting for you to come. The place will be locked up now, it's after five."

I'm relieved it's nothing more, but still feel he can't resist turning the knife at every opportunity. I guess that's why I answer him with a bitterness I don't really feel. "Well, you have a key, don't you?"

He holds my gaze for a moment and I read the hostility in his eyes. Without a word he looks away, gathers his belongings and leaves. I feel like shit. I don't even mean it half the time. I just can't seem to help myself.

## LEN

There's a bus pulling in just as I reach the stop and I'm thankful. I've spent so long waiting around this afternoon, unable to get on and do the thing she's asked me to do. Now, at last I can make myself useful; I can demonstrate to her what she means to me. It's important to me that she realises how loved she is. I guess I feel she's had such a hard time, she deserves a break and I want her to feel strong and safe, knowing there are people around her who care deeply for her. I suppose that's why I'm learning to tolerate Sebastian in her life. It would be foolish not to, though. I mean he's made it clear that he's here for keeps. I'm kind of surprised in a way. I wasn't sure what he would do. Even though I'd tried to imagine all sorts of outcomes to him finding out the truth, I could never make up my mind what he would actually do. I feel I don't know him anymore. So much has changed between us that all the things I used to believe he represented now seem meaningless.

I enjoy the calming motion of the bus as we sail through town. Outside the window images of shop-fronts and hurrying pedestrians are gradually replaced by quieter streets and vast expanses of residential neighbourhoods. On and on; the further we go, the greater the distance from the hospital, the more focussed I become on my mission. I'll probably be able to nip in and back out again without having to actually speak to anyone. In some ways maybe Sebastian has done me a favour turning up so late. I do have keys, yes of course I do, so it shouldn't really be a problem gaining entry and if I can manage to do so without anyone wondering what I'm doing, so much the better.

The familiar landmarks of this habitual journey pop in and out of my field of vision as we spin on towards the University main campus. I tick them off mentally in my head. As my stop approaches I start to feel something close to butterflies in my stomach. Nerves! Me? This is my domain, I remind myself. I'm in charge of all that I do here. I don't have any reason to be nervous about entering my own office. Nevertheless I do feel anxious and I hope against hope that I don't meet anyone. Jumping off the bus along with another two men, I take a look at my watch. It's six-thirty. Good! Hopefully the students will be long gone with classes having finished an hour ago. As for the staff, well there'll be plenty of them still about, but with a bit of luck most will be getting something to eat around about now. I'll just have to keep my fingers crossed. It's as good a time as any to come here if I want to sneak in unnoticed. It's not because I think it might be a problem, it's just that I don't want to get drawn on when I'm coming back to work. I haven't decided if the truth be known. I'm not even sure that I'm capable of doing the job anymore. It's been so many months now and I've given it very little thought in that time. I've shied away, I suppose, from facing up to many things. Anyway, I've got Carly to blame for this. She's a clever girl. I'm quite sure this is a ruse to get me back here and of course it's worked.

Walking the familiar corridors, taking the well-known staircases, I tread a route so routine I could do it with my eyes closed. Turning a corner I spot a group of students hanging around at the end of a row of office doors. Dropping my gaze, I keep my head down, my eyes on the polished floor as I continue my path. I don't know if any of them recognise me as I pass, but if they do no-one speaks. That's the main thing; to avoid conversation with anyone at all if possible, to evade their pity. Another turn in the lengthy passageway and I'm standing directly outside my own office door. Pushing the key clumsily into the lock, I feel suddenly that I shouldn't be here. I feel like an imposter intruding on someone else's private space. The name plate above the door speaks to me reassuringly of my rights, but doesn't make me any more comfortable about it. It's almost with a sense of surprise that the door yields to my touch and I find myself able to push it open. My heart's beating too fast, but I have to admit it's not as bad as the last time I came in to this room. I was a wreck that day. Tonight it's different.

Closing the heavy oak door behind me, I'm enveloped by the peace of the place. The quietness is soothing and I realise I've spent very little time on my own these past few weeks. I move directly to my filing cabinet and locate the correct year group. I file alphabetically so it shouldn't be too difficult to find her papers. Also I have a large record of Carly's work so it stands out anyway. Leafing through the various essays which make up her portfolio I find the one she wants. Skimming through the first page I appreciate, as I have so often, her skill and flair for turning thought into beautiful prose. Yes it's good work, but I still maintain she doesn't need this to help her with what she's doing at the moment.

Wandering over to my desk, I sit myself down and feel comforted that everything is as I had left it. They haven't replaced me then. It doesn't look like anyone's been using my office. I'm pleased about this. Running my hands across the smooth wood of my desk, feeling its warmth beneath my fingers generates emotions that are hard to explain. This is such a difficult journey.

My desk is neat and tidy; my in-tray empty. This is the way I work. I don't leave stuff over till the next day unless there are exceptional circumstances. Always I'd rather stay late to finish up. I don't gather lots of paraphernalia either unlike some of my colleagues. It's just me I guess. I don't like distractions and prefer only to be surrounded by things which are relevant to my work. I wonder what this room says about me. What did Carly make of me when she knew me only as her tutor? Did she come in here and think what a sad guy, there's so little of himself in there?

Face down on my desk the one item which connects me to another place. The photograph of Claudine upturned on my last visit when looking on her beautiful face was too painful to contemplate. Reaching over, I pick it up and turn it slowly over in my hand. Why did I select this picture for public display? I loved it, that's probably why. It's a fairly old photo taken on vacation one year. Only her face is contained within the frame, an absent-minded smile giving her a reflective look. What was she thinking about? There are things I now understand I'll never know. I've had to accept that. She's gone and with her all the explanations which she must have known I would crave. She must have realised that the truth would come out one day, but with only second-hand accounts of what happened and how and why, I'm left only with speculation and probability.

Sebastian loved her, I now know that and he believes she loved him all those years ago. I know he's right. She gave up so much for him. Leaving Paris when she knew she was pregnant meant giving up her place at Art School. She never got that chance again. Sure she did great professionally in spite of that missed opportunity, but still it would have been a big decision for her at the time. She also didn't tell him anything about the baby. Presumably that was to protect him in some way or most likely to allow him to follow his conscience and marry Helen without any additional complications.

I believe she loved him all her life. The ring, I just can't find any other credible explanation as to why she would be wearing his ring in place of mine. It hurts. It really hurts, but I have a driving need to know the truth even if I can't understand it. Did she love me is the next problem preying on my mind. Could she love me if her heart truly belonged to Sebastian? That's the million dollar question isn't it and the one whose answer eludes me. I'll never know for sure. We were happy, yes I think we were. As for love…

Setting the photograph in its rightful position on my desk, I realise that I don't blame her. I'm still stinging from the pain of losing her, but I'm not particularly angry anymore. I certainly don't hate her. She's Carly's mother, perhaps that's one reason why. Carly has become so precious to me that I'm unable to despise where she came from. The best of Claudine exists in her daughter. The daughter she barely knew. Claudine was the loser in this whole mess. Claudine lost it all. Sebastian and I, we both missed out, but Claudine never got the chance to really know Carly. She should have been here for her at this time and she isn't. What I need to do is make sure Carly doesn't miss out. Carly mustn't look back over her life and feel she lost out too. It's up to us, to me and Sebastian and Luc, the people who love her to ensure she is happy.

Reaching into my top drawer I pull out a sheaf of paper. I'm going to jot down a few things that I need to remember. Things I want Carly to know about her mother. If I make a list of bullet points it'll be enough to jog my memory and I'll be able to fill her in on things which she wants to know. The words flow freely as I focus on my task. Images of Claudine flutter in and out of my consciousness; my pen provides the words to describe her. I allow it to move across the page, I give it complete control. I remain in tune with my wife, her beauty, her laughter, her talent. All the good things about Claudine come rushing to the fore. How it felt to hold her in my arms, her breath on my cheek, the warmth of her around me. I see her eyes shining with joy, her perfect skin so smooth to the touch. Her voice reaches me now; the accent pitched beautifully, her exquisite inflections, her odd way with words. My hand moves across the page and back and across again. The memories pour out into words, phrases, poetry; our first days together, a growing love affair, the depth of my feelings for her. Never before have I been able to capture on paper all that she was, all that she meant to me and I can't allow myself to stop. I'm immersed in Claudine and it's so painful I almost can't bear it. Almost, but not quite and it's that fraction of endurance which I'm clinging on to. I don't want her to go away. I don't want to lose this moment. This is as near to her as I've felt since her death and I cannot let her go. Claudine my darling, my beautiful friend, lover, wife: how I admired and respected and marvelled at her. Her presence is so strong I feel I could reach out and touch her. I long to link my fingers with hers and feel joined to her again. The depth of love I felt for her is unlikely to revisit me in my lifetime, I realise this.

The words continue to come. Now that I've started I can't seem to stop, tumbling out one after another, words and more words. The expression to all my emotions takes shape on the paper in front of me. Let it go on, I tell myself. Go with it and go on with it. Time has no meaning. I could stay here for ever. My love for Claudine is everything. Write and write while the words urge themselves forward.

Pushing themselves into my mind, spilling out into my poem, my feelings overflow and are recreated before me. I'm unable to stop myself. I've lost all resistance. I could die right now and I would be complete.

How long I sit at my desk like this, delving deep into buried memories, embracing denied feelings, I don't know. It's a tap on the door which eventually rouses me from my dream-like state. At first I think I've imagined it and continue with my work. Its repetition forces me to acknowledge the existence of someone other than myself, of a world outside my private thoughts. Standing reluctantly, I drag my feet away from the desk where they've been rooted this whole time. Opening the door, it feels like I'm welcoming another into the bizarre scene which I've created on the pages lying strewn across my always tidy desk. It's only when I see the familiar face and hear the well–known voice that I am stirred completely out of my reverie.

"Len! You're back! Sorry to disturb you. I saw the light under the door and was wondering who was in here. I didn't realise it was you. Sorry."

I shake my head, assure him he's not interrupting and open the door wider, inviting him in. "It's good to see you Arthur. How's things?"

I can't help noticing his eyes sweeping the room as he enters, taking in everything, clearly interested in what I've been doing in here.

"It's late, Len. Even for you it's late to be working. Are you doing anything in particular?"

I smile. He's so transparent. He must realise I see right through him. "Yes, actually I've been doing some work on my book."

He's intrigued now. "Oh. I didn't realise you were back writing again. Is it another Criticism?" He's longing to know all the details.

"No… not this time. This is a book of poetry which I started about twenty years ago. The time feels right now. It's flowing for me, if you know what I mean."

I'm wondering now what he's doing still here at nearly midnight. Did he always stay as late as me? The truth is I hardly know anything about Arthur. I've never really shown much interest in his world. I guess I've been pretty self-absorbed most of my life, only concerning myself with things and people which had a direct significance to me. "Do you want a drink?" I ask him, surprising myself at the warmth of the offer. He too looks taken aback, but covers his surprise quickly.

"Yes. Yes, Len… that would be fine."

In all the time I've worked with Arthur I've never invited him in for a drink. He's going to wonder what's wrong with me. *I'm* starting to wonder what's been wrong with me all these years. I must have been a very selfish person. Maybe that's why I've been so successful in my career. Always looking inwards, always thinking of yourself makes you real focussed. So what's changed? What is it that's made me shift that focus and start to reach out to people again? It can only be her can't it? She's changed my life.

Drawing up a seat for him, pouring two glasses of whisky, I go through the mechanical motions of hospitality. This kind of thing doesn't come naturally to me.

"So how have you been?" he asks.

Pausing for a moment I try to decide how much to tell him. "Things are slowly getting better," I tell him. "It's hard. I miss her desperately, but I'm beginning to move on a bit."

He nods as if he has some idea what I'm talking about. "And the Adams girl, is she a part of that?"

I'm completely stunned by his remark. He's staring straight at me and all I can think is how dare he? I'm absolutely astounded by the audacity of the man. For a moment I'm speechless. I wish I hadn't asked him in. I wish I hadn't come. Carefully I reply, "What exactly are you insinuating, Arthur?" He's not the slightest bit embarrassed. I would have expected him to be.

"It's common knowledge, Len. She's moved in with you hasn't she? Don't worry. I don't have a problem with it. I don't think anyone has. After all who's to say how any of us would react if the same tragedy struck us?"

He actually thinks he's reassuring me that it's alright if I'm having a relationship with one of my students seven months after my wife's death.

"Carly Adams is not my girlfriend." I say it plainly so there can be no misunderstanding.

"You don't have to explain…" he begins.

Cutting him off, I wade back in, "Oh yes, clearly I do. Let me explain so that there's no doubt. Carly is Claudine's daughter. I am her step-father, that's the reason she moved in. The history is complicated and frankly none of your business, but there is absolutely nothing untoward in my relationship with Carly Adams. Do you understand?"

He's nodding, but he looks completely baffled. Never mind, once the message sinks in and he's had a chance to relay it a couple of times, I'm sure he'll manage to make sense of it. Draining his glass, he rises to leave. I'm thinking it'll be a while before he calls on my door again in the middle of the night. I guess he got more than he bargained for tonight. He's on the verge of leaving when he turns back, rummages in his briefcase for something and hands me a heavy typed document.

"What's this?" I ask him, flicking it open as I do.

"It's next term's curriculum. You'll be needing it. Welcome back, Len."

He closes the door behind him and it dawns on me, as I stand in the silence, that I've travelled further this evening just by re-entering my old life than I could ever have hoped to anywhere else. I've come full circle in the months since losing Claudine, but it's a very different person who stands here now.

## LUC

This is a beautiful place, but although I can see it, I don't feel it. I can't really explain what's going on with me right now. I'm not mad anymore, or confused. I just feel sad. Oh yeah and empty. It seems like everything I ever wanted, everything I had is gone and I'm left with nothing. I never felt this way about a girl before. I don't like the power she has over me; power to make me feel this bad. I'm starting to think coming away like this was maybe not such a great idea. I think maybe fishing and solitude is more suited to someone in a better frame of mind. It's making me depressed and I need to get over it. A week should surely have been long enough to sort myself out, to have at least ascertained what I'm going to do. I keep coming back to the same thing though. I desperately want to try again. Is that completely stupid? If anyone was asking me, I think I would tell them to give it a miss. Go home, come to terms with it. But somehow, I just feel it must be worth another try. She's got me all wrong. I'm sure she doesn't realise what she means to me. Maybe if I could convince her how much I love her she would come round. It's a crazy suggestion, I know it really, but I just don't know what else to do. Maybe it's time I spoke to someone instead of attempting to fix my head myself. I can't think straight anyway.

My phone's lost its charge so I can't call anyone. It's probably time to go back. Nothing's working for me here. The peace and quiet of this place hasn't done for me what I hoped it would. My mind isn't any clearer, no decisions have been made. All I can think about is Carly. I see her in everything. All the beauty around me I want to share

392

with her. The colours, the images everywhere, they're nothing to me. My paints haven't been out of their box this whole time. What's wrong with me?

# CARLY

"How are you doing, princess?" Dr Armstrong appears in my doorway as bright and cheerful as ever. It's a strange feeling to be visited only by people dressed in theatre attire, gowns and masks included. This I know is to prevent any infection reaching me which my immune system probably wouldn't be able to cope with right now. I smile at him. He's such a caring person and I've really appreciated all the attention he's given me. I actually feel a bit embarrassed that I don't feel better than I do. I want to get well partly to prove him right; to show him that all his efforts haven't been in vain.

"That bad is it?" He's so tuned in to me that I can't fool him. I don't know what to say, so I just sit and wait for him to take the lead. He sits down on the edge of my bed facing me across the room.

"What's going on?" he asks. I'm a bit surprised. Surely he knows everything that's going on with me. I mean it's not as if I have any privacy here is it? My every move is on show for everyone to see. I even have to tell them when I'm going to the toilet. Maybe he decides he's being too heavy with me, because he changes tack when I don't reply.

"What's all this?" he says indicating the stickers covering the window. I smile proudly, I can't help it: "My dad's trying to teach me French."

It's his turn to smile, "Trying?" he asks.

"Yes, well you know how it is. They say you shouldn't let your parents teach you to drive don't they? I think learning a language is probably the same. He can't understand why I don't just get it. I

394

think he expects I should really just know it instinctively and I don't. I'm not much good to be honest."

"What? Something that Carly Adams doesn't excel at? Surely not!"

We're both laughing now and I wonder if that's why he came in, to try to cheer me up. It isn't ward round time so he usually wouldn't even be in the unit at this time of day.

"The thing I don't understand is why is it that when my dad speaks English with a strong, French accent everyone thinks it sounds really sexy. No-one corrects him do they? You don't hear anyone saying to him, 'Now come on Sebastian you've been speaking English for years now, let's hear it sounding a bit more British.' Do you? And yet, he has the nerve to say to me that although I'm using the correct vocabulary, he can't understand me because I have the accent all wrong!"

He's nodding in agreement. "Personally, Carly I think they just pretend they can't understand us so that they can show off their English." He may have a point, I tell him. We sit for a moment or two before he speaks again.

"Are you happy to have him here? Would you prefer a bit of distance between you?"

"Who? My dad?"

He nods.

"No way! I think there's sufficient distance don't you? I mean I can only talk to him through this walkie talkie. I can't touch him at all. I think there's plenty of distance, thanks!"

"You know what I mean, Carly."

He doesn't understand. He thinks I'm down because of Dad. "I'm pleased he's here. I want him here. Why do you ask?"

He looks at me steadily for a while and I start to feel a bit uncomfortable under his scrutiny. Eventually he speaks. This time he's not trying to be funny or make me laugh. "Well, the reason I ask is because you seem to me a very different girl to the one who came in here ten days ago. Things are going well from my point of view. I'm pleased with your progress so far. But you, well you seem to have lost your spark. It's like a light has gone out somewhere and I'm not sure what's going on. I need you to be strong, Carly. We talked about this before. I can't fix you on my own. You need to do your part. If anything your side of the bargain is more important than mine. If you give up, then I might as well give up too."

He's being pretty blunt with me. It's a bit scary in fact. The funny thing is that no-one else has actually asked me how I am. I mean Prof and Dad and the nurses and everyone they all ask me, but they don't mean it like this. They mean am I feeling sick or am I sore or stuff like that. Dr Armstrong wants to know about inside my head. He's taking the time to really talk to me. The trouble is I don't know if I want to pour it all out. I thought I was doing okay, putting on a pretty good face, but apparently not.

"What's this?" he asks me suddenly, breaking the silence. Pointing to the necklace which Dad bought me and hung up outside the window where I can see it, he looks at me questioningly.

"That is the very first present which my dad ever bought me." I say it with pride. I know it's a beautiful thing to have chosen for me and I love it because it's so personal.

"What does C C stand for?"

"They're my initials...at least they will be when I get my name changed back...Carly Charpentier. How does that sound?"

His eyes are smiling again. He looks at me very tenderly, "It sounds great. I think you'd better learn your French, though, with a name like that."

"I need to learn French. My dad wants to take me to Paris when I get out of here. He's going to show me all the wonderful museums...the Louvre, the Picasso Museum...He's going to take me to see Degas' Little Dancer and Monet's Waterlillies and all the magnificent works of art that I've only ever seen in books." He waits and I realise he understands there's a but coming. "The only trouble is he also wants to introduce me to my family. You know... he wants to tell them who I am."

"And you have a problem with that?"

"Yeah…just a bit! They don't even know he has a daughter! It's not just that though. He wants me to become a part of my mother's family too. He wants to tell them all who I am. I think it might be a huge shock for them to discover she had a baby which they knew nothing about."

"So your father is in contact with your mother's family is he?"

I nod. I have the feeling from what Prof and Dad have both told me that Dad would have been Claudine's mum's preferred choice of husband.

"Well, wouldn't he be the best judge then of whether that was an appropriate thing to do?" I see where he's coming from, but unfortunately he doesn't understand it all.

"I'm a bit worried about how Prof will take it all though." I know this is weak. Even as I say it I know he won't be convinced. He isn't.

"Come on Carly. I've met your step-dad a good few times and I know he won't stand in your way over something like that. He's a strong man. He's very like you in many ways, strangely enough."

I could just call a halt now. I could tell him I'm tired. The only thing is I really do want to talk to someone about what's on my mind. Will he think badly of me, though? Will he change his opinion of me?

"The real trouble is…well, you see…there's this boy…"

He smiles at me reassuringly, "Now we're getting somewhere. This boy…would he by any chance be the reason why you're so unhappy?"

I intend to tell him yes, my plan is to simply nod, since I'm having trouble getting the words out, but before I can check myself I realise I'm crying. I'm not wailing or anything embarrassing like that, but tears are welling up in my eyes and I know he's noticed.

"Hey there, princess, don't cry. If he can't see what a treasure you are then he's simply not worth it."

His arm around me feels so protective. I have trusted this man with my life. Surely then he is the one person I can open up to properly.

"It isn't like that. I pushed him away and now I wish I hadn't…It wasn't right and I knew it wasn't…I shouldn't have ever let it happen…And then he hurt me so much…"

I'm aware through my sobs that I'm rambling and it probably doesn't make any sense to him. He looks a bit confused, as if he's frantically attempting to piece things together.

"He hurt you… How?" he asks simply.

"I thought he loved me…he told me he loved me…and then when it came to the tissue typing, he wouldn't…he wouldn't even…" I can't get the words out. Crying uncontrollably, I wish I'd never started this. Dr Armstrong wipes my tears and holds my hands and I feel his compassion, but still I wish he hadn't made me dig this all up. Despite what he thinks, I was doing alright burying my feelings. At least I was managing to keep a lid on things. Now he's forced me to face up to stuff and I'm not sure I'm ready for it.

"How do you know he wouldn't get tested, Carly? Did he tell you he wouldn't do it?" I shake my head. I don't want to talk about it anymore. I want him to go now and leave me. I beg him to leave me. He's such a gentleman I know he won't outstay his welcome. "Okay princess I'll go, but I'm not leaving you like this. I'll tell the nurses to show your dad how to scrub up and he can come in and sit with you for a while. Will that be alright?" Of course it will. I really want a hug from my dad. "The only trouble is I won't get any work out of them once he's dressed up like George Clooney! You do understand this, don't you?"

I can't help but laugh in spite of myself. He smiles gently back and leaves as I requested. Outside I can see the look of surprise on Dad's face as Dr Armstrong obviously tells him he can come in. He's nodding and then the next minute a nurse appears by his side. Dr Armstrong stays too though and I wonder what they're saying about me. This is so horrible. I wish I could hear what was being said. If it wasn't for all these drips that I'm tied up to I think I would just walk out of here. There doesn't feel any point to any of it anymore. I don't think I have it in me to fight like he wants me to. I really don't.

# SEBASTIAN

"So you're saying she's giving up?" I can hardly believe what he's telling me. It's true he was in there a good while and they were obviously having a heart to heart of some kind, but Carly give up? I just can't get my head around it.

"Monsieur Charpentier…"

"Sebastian…it's Sebastian," I interrupt. I don't like all these formalities at the best of times, never mind now.

He nods. "Okay, Sebastian…what you need to understand is the pressure she's under in there. This is a terrible situation for a young girl to find herself in and really she needs a lot of support to help her through it. I know you're doing your bit and having you around means a great deal to Carly. Also the Professor… like it or not, she loves him dearly and he's a very good influence on her. He's also helping her to cope. The two of you are doing a fantastic job. I don't know how you're managing it around the rest of your lives, but what you're doing is good for her."

Well, that's a relief. At first I thought he was going to ask me to clear off, tell me that she didn't want me here. I've felt we were getting somewhere, starting to get to know each other, but then again with this permanent barrier between us it's difficult to really know. What more can we do though? How can we get Carly thinking positively again?

As if reading my thoughts, he continues. "I think she's doing remarkably well. The trouble seems to be this broken heart she's nursing. I have a teenage daughter at home, a little younger than Carly, but twice as much trouble, so I think I understand. You could give Carly the world and it wouldn't be enough if the boy she's in love with doesn't return her feelings. All she wants is him, in that all-consuming, selfish way of young love. Do you know what I'm talking about, Sebastian?"

I do, of course I do. The thing which is puzzling me is if she loved him so much why did she tell him to get lost? I'm unable to get my head round my daughter's thought processes. Again, the doctor pre-empts my questions. "If we could understand the minds of our daughters we would be worth a fortune, believe me. There's not a father alive who completely comprehends his little girl's inner world."

That's reassuring at any rate. He doesn't seem to be blaming me. I feel such a failure as a father. It doesn't take much criticism to knock me off altogether.

"So, this boy…is there any hope there? Is there any possibility of reconciliation or are we dealing with damage limitation here?"

"Luc? Oh he'd be back in a minute if he thought she would have him. She made it pretty clear, though, that she didn't want to know. He took off. I don't know where he went."

He's thinking. After a long pause, he resumes, "Luc you said?"

I nod, "Yeah, Luc Rousseau. I know him well. He's a good kid."

He seems to be thinking. "She said he wouldn't get tissue-typed for her, that was why she was so angry with him…the thing is that name's familiar. Let me check her notes. I'm not convinced she's right about that. You get scrubbed up and go in and I'll join you in a few minutes, okay?"

I'm really glad the nurse is here to guide me through this. I wouldn't have a clue otherwise. She shows me how to wash my hands, my fingers, and my arms right up to the elbows. It takes ages, soaping up and rinsing off. Then she hands me clothes like they wear in the operating theatre to put on. On top of these a sterile gown, plastic overshoes, a hat. It really brings it home to me how sick she is. I can't even be near my own daughter without donning all these preventive measures. Finally when I'm permitted across the door, she greets me with a beaming smile. I'm so pleased. All she has to do is smile at me and my heart skips a beat. How can your child have so much of a hold over your emotions? She has mine so completely under her control, it's a bit disconcerting. I've never experienced anything like this before. I feel as if my sole purpose in life is to make her happy. I would gladly give up everything for her. I wonder if she realises this.

"How're you doing, baby?" I ask her when I'm at last able to reach out and take her hand. Isn't it funny how all my awkwardness disappears when I'm actually with her. There's definitely a natural bond between us, something instinctive which takes over when we're together. She's smiling, but her eyes look really sad.

"I don't think I'm ever going to get out of here," she says simply.

"Hey, of course you are. We're all fighting for you. The doctor thinks you're doing great. He's really pleased with how it's all going. He told me that."

She nods, "Yes, he told me that too. I feel awful though. I feel really down as if there's nothing to aim for anymore. I hope you don't take that the wrong way. I love having you around and you've changed my life...it's just...it's just..."

"Luc?" I finish for her, seeing the struggle she's having to utter his name. Again the nod, this time accompanied by large, soft tears dripping down her cheeks. "Come here, baby. I know how you feel...I truly do. I loved your mother with such a total complete love that I thought it might actually kill me. Living without her was like living without half my soul. But I'm here. I'm still here. And I'm glad, because you've made it all worthwhile." Holding her close, I feel her pain as she sobs against my chest.

"I'm sorry Dad, but I don't want to live the life you did. I don't want to live without him, knowing I'll never love anyone like that again. I don't think I'm as strong as you. I don't think I can do it. I just want him back."

I don't know what to say to her so I just hold her. How can I tell her he never would have gone if she hadn't pushed him? The doctor's right, I don't understand her. Why did she let him leave if she knew he was walking away with her future happiness? Why did I let Claudine go? The parallel is so painful. I don't like the idea of history repeating itself. If there's anything I can do for my girl I need to do it. I need to think.

There's a flurry of activity outside the door and Dr Armstrong reappears, once again scrubbed up ready to enter this germ-free zone. Carly pulls away from me and sits down. She looks really tired and drawn. Her eyes are dark and shadowed; her face really pale. I notice some bruises appearing on her face, presumably from the buttons of my gown pressing against her. She's so fragile, I think. Sitting down on her bed, he gestures me to do the same.

"Right Carly, I think we've got some talking to do. Do you know what I'm on about?" She nods. "Does he?" he points at me. She nods again. What's going on? I don't like it when I feel out of control and that's the very feeling rising inside me now. Whatever it is, please don't let it be bad is all I can think. He continues, "You told me you were angry with Luc because he wouldn't get tested for the transplant, is that right?"

"Yes, he might have been a match, but he wouldn't go to the hospital and I couldn't forgive him for that. "

"Okay, I understand what you're saying Carly, but listen to me, Luc Rousseau *did* get tissue-typed." She starts to interrupt, but he raises his hand to stop her and continues with what he has to say, "Let me speak, Carly. I think you've already rushed in without having the full picture. Let me finish, okay?" She sits back in her chair, looks at him expectantly. "Okay...Luc definitely got tested. I have the results in your notes. I've just checked. He wasn't a match, but that's neither here nor there now, because we've got your dad right here. I can assure you Carly that Luc did go for tissue-typing. Are you clear about that? I don't know if this makes a difference to anything, but I thought we should clear up the discrepancy about it."

She looks confused, really bewildered. Shaking her head, she cries, "No, that's not right! I sat in your office with Prof by my side...go and ask him...ask him, he was there...and you said you had a list of all the results of testing and …and you showed us the printout…I held it in my hand…I specifically looked for his name and it wasn't there…do you hear me, it wasn't there!"

"Carly, Carly calm down. Listen to me, you must calm down. You're getting yourself in a state. Settle down, we'll sort this okay? Give me a minute. Listen I'm going to call a nurse, because you're having a little bleed. Probably because you've got so upset, but I think your platelets must be a bit low. Settle down and we'll talk about it, but I need you to stay calm."

She nods and sits back down. I feel so helpless as I watch him call the nurse, tell her to order platelets and pass in some swabs. Gently he dabs her nose and mops up some of the blood. Turning to me he says, "Don't be alarmed. A little blood goes a long way. It always looks worse than it is. Because her counts are down…remember I told you about this? Her platelets are low too…that means she's not able to clot her blood properly and a bleed is more likely. We'll give her a transfusion and top them up and she'll be right as rain." She does as he tells her. He's so calm, but very authoritative. She does exactly as he instructs her.

"Okay, Carly what are we going to do about your young man. Do you think he would understand if we explained the misunderstanding to him?"

She starts to shake her head, but he gives her a warning look. Holding her head still again, she speaks, "No…you see it's more than that. I never should have got involved with him…It was wrong from the start. I know you're trying to help, but there's nothing you can do, there's nothing anyone can do."

"Right, you've gone all female and cryptic on me again," he replies. "Remember I'm a man. Spell out to me what exactly the problem is."

She hesitates, but must realise she can't really get out of this. We're both sitting here waiting for her explanation. We're not going anywhere. "Well…the thing is, I don't want you to think badly of me…I don't want you to think I'm a terrible person…I couldn't help it, I just loved him so much."

403

"Spell it out, Carly."

"The thing is…Luc…Luc's my mother's brother…he's my uncle!"

I'm shocked by her words, "Carly!" I interject, but she doesn't hear me. With this last statement she has dissolved, her head in her hands, presumably so she doesn't have to look at us, becoming covered with blood as the red liquid flows freely.

Lifting her up, pressing the swabs against her face, he speaks softly to her, "You're alright. Carly, it is alright. You're going to be alright. Hey, look at me."

Turning her face to his, her large eyes plead with him for forgiveness. She looks surprised and stops crying almost abruptly. Looking from her to him I see why. He's smiling! She turns to me and then back to him, "What's so funny?"

"Oh, Carly what a state you've got yourself into and all for nothing. Luc Rousseau isn't your uncle!" Her face crumples with confusion. "I've just been looking at his blood results remember? There's absolutely no way that guy is related to you. It's not a possibility. He was nowhere near a match for you. His blood is completely different. I can only assume the reason I didn't show you his results is because they were so vastly different. He didn't feature on the same printout as your relatives. His results were on a separate page along with your step-dad and the other volunteers. I think you automatically thought the worst of Luc, because you needed an excuse to finish things. At least you thought you did. After all you never doubted the Professor did you and you didn't get to see his results either."

I can hardly believe it. I feel this is all my fault. I had no idea she thought Luc was her uncle. I just assumed because they were involved with each other that she knew all about him. "Carly, I'm so sorry. I feel really responsible. I had no idea you were thinking this. If I'd known…"

She looks up at me now in anticipation, "So this is true then is it? Is this true?"

I nod, "Yes, Carly. I thought you knew. I had no reason to think you didn't know. Luc was adopted too. I guess I thought you had so much in common...I don't know what I thought...Luc was adopted some years after Claudine's mother lost a baby. She never got over it and when she was approved for adoption everyone was delighted for her. The little boy, Luc was about four or five when he came to live with them. His parents had both been killed in a house fire. He'd been staying with a family friend when it happened. I don't think he really remembers them. Oh, Carly, I wish you'd talked to me...told me what was on your mind."

The doctor looks at us both kindly, "Lesson number two, Sebastian. Daughters very rarely tell their father what's going on inside their heads!" We laugh and suddenly the whole situation seems ludicrous. What a lot of pain caused by simple misunderstandings. If only we could turn the clock back... "Okay, I think we've got something to go on now. I suggest Carly that you let your dad start trying to track down your fella and I will let the nurses do their work and get on top of this bleed before you ruin any more of your clothes. How does that sound?"

She nods weakly. She still looks totally miserable, but at least she's stopped crying and even manages a small smile before I reluctantly leave her.

# LUC

I feel I'm even more confused now than when I first came out here. It would probably be a good idea to stay put tonight and head back to the city in the morning. Night's falling and I don't know the road that well. It was very twisting in some places, still if I'm careful and take my time it should be okay. After nearly two weeks of having no-one to talk to I'm craving some company and to be honest, I don't think I could stand another evening on my own. If I get back to Edinburgh tonight I might be able to have a few beers with Sebastian and chill out a bit. That would be nice. He probably thinks I'm crazy coming away like this in the first place. Maybe it was. I just couldn't think what else to do. I feel as if I'm running round in circles, going nowhere.

Pulling out of the driveway, I at least have some resolve. I know where I'm headed and for now that's about as good as it gets. I'm swinging from thinking I'll go straight round to the hospital and give it one last go, to deciding the best course of action would be to book my flight first thing in the morning. I'm really hoping that Sebastian will be able to dispense some of his calm, clear-headed advice on to me. I could do with his help right now.

Large spots of rain are beginning to drop noisily onto the windscreen and I wonder if we're in for a downpour. It's been pretty hot over the last few days so maybe a storm would help to clear the air. I haven't heard a forecast all week and I've no idea what to expect, but a storm if it does come doesn't worry me. Setting off down the dirt track I see heavy dark clouds gathering on the horizon. I attempt to calculate how long it should take me to get back, but I actually don't know the distances. I think it took about three hours on the way down, so hopefully I'll be there around ten. If my phone was working I'd call and let him know I'm on my way, maybe we could have planned to do something. As it is I'll just have to turn up. He won't mind. Nothing fazes Sebastian. An image of him looking very much fazed flashes into my mind, as I remember him the night before Claudine's funeral gazing adoringly upon her lifeless body. I never imagined that I might know such a depth of feeling, such intensity of love. And then I met Carly and my world turned upside down. I haven't felt the same about anything since. She's touched every aspect of my life. It's just got to be right between us. I can't imagine anything so perfect could be so completely destroyed and all for nothing. I'm aware that I'm once again allowing my thoughts free reign and I need to pull it together again. I can't allow myself to become so absorbed thinking about her. It's madness in my mind when I do. Concentrate on the road, I tell myself. Focus only on the task in hand.

The rain's coming heavier now and my wipers are having to work harder. What an awful night to be driving. The only good thing is that now I've started I'm that bit closer to my destination. Glancing at the clock, I estimate I've been on the move about thirty minutes. I'm making good progress. At this rate I might even make it by nine. Switching on the radio, the journey takes on more pleasure. I always enjoy listening to some music while I travel so it doesn't feel so tedious now. A flash of lightning in the distance adds a somewhat gothic, melodramatic mood to the night and I smile, feeling secure and safe within the warmth of my vehicle.

It occurs to me that the storm might already have hit Edinburgh and I wonder how Carly is. She's absolutely terrified of thunder and lightning, so I hope not. A picture of her comes to mind, looking scared and upset and my whole being longs for her. My heart aches as I remember what I've lost. Maybe it's this preoccupying thought or maybe I take my eyes off the road for a split second. I don't know. I really couldn't be sure. All I'm aware of is a car coming towards me, its headlights full on and I can't see a thing. I'm completely blinded and slamming my foot hard on the brake, attempt to bring the car under control. I was probably going a bit fast in my hurry to get back. I can't actually say what happened. The car swerves, yes and swerves again and suddenly I'm conscious of falling. I'm no longer driving the car, but it's still moving. I roll and roll down some kind of embankment or other. The car hits something hard and I hear a deafening crash. The window smashes and I'm covered in glass. I feel myself being rocked back and forth, restrained only by my seat belt. Everything is dark. I can't see anything at all. The taste of blood fills my mouth and an excruciating pain stabs me in the stomach. This is not good. This is potentially awful. I wonder where I am. I can't figure out whereabouts I was, not that that would help me get my bearings now. I wait for the driver of the other car to come and find me. That's probably my best bet. No-one else knows I'm here after all. After a few minutes I realise I'm going to be sick. The taste in my mouth is terrible. And then a chilling thought occurs to me. What if no-one comes? Listening to the silence all around, it dawns on me. No-one is coming.

## LEN

On a night like this I am glad to be surrounded by home comforts, safe in the knowledge that I don't have to venture out. My study has assumed a far warmer, cosier feel than it usually does, presumably just because it's so wild out there tonight. I've been holed up in here for hours now, since I returned from my shift at the hospital this afternoon. As has become our custom, Sebastian and I exchanged only minimal pleasantries as we crossed over. The situation between us isn't improving with the passage of time. If it wasn't for Carly I can only imagine we'd have severed all ties completely. In a way it's sad. I mean we were friends a long time and really good friends at that. If there was one person in this world who I'd have trusted absolutely it was Sebastian. The only other person would have been Claudine. Enough said. I push these thoughts aside, something I'm becoming better at, and focus my energies again on my book.

It's developed into a therapy. Each moment I have free I find myself coming in here and absorbing my mind in my poetry. It's almost a compulsion. Writing, I'm finding is a route to freedom. Within words I can escape the pain, or substitute it or sometimes relish it. Whatever way my thoughts lead me I go with them and allow my creativity to flourish. The satisfaction is total.

I've also managed to do a bit of planning for the future during these spells of rational thought. I intend to return to work at the start of next session. Carly's been the drive behind all of this. She has so much faith in me and encourages me, I would say, every single day. I've already planned for my part of the syllabus on a part-time basis. This is to allow me plenty of time with Carly who, by that stage, will hopefully be recuperating. Despite my small steps of progress, Carly remains my number one priority, the most important thing in my life. She has also been the inspiration for much of my recent writings, including the one I'm working on right now.

The sound of the telephone ring breaks my train of thought abruptly and totally. I can't concentrate with even the slightest outside distraction and I know I've lost it now. Impatiently I lift the handset and without any attempt to conceal my irritation enquire who's calling at this time of night. It's Sebastian. I'm surprised. My first inclination is to panic. "What's wrong? Is something wrong?" No, he assures me Carly was fine when he left about an hour ago. Relief sweeps over me. I glance at the clock on the wall and register he's stayed late with her tonight.

"Are you sure everything's okay?" I demand to know.

"Yeah, she's alright. She was a bit upset though. We talked and a lot of stuff came out, mostly to do with Luc."

"No surprise there," I tell him.

He agrees, but when he goes on to explain about the doctor's concern for her state of mind, I begin to worry once more. "The thing is, it turns out her issues with Luc have all been a bit misguided…You know he *did* get tested for donor status, the doctor checked his records."

"Well that should have settled her somewhat …did it not?" I ask him.

"Yeah, it did, but then she was still holding on to this idea that she was in some way related to him… I take it you were in the dark too?"

Now he's lost me. What does he mean about being in the dark? I hate it when he speaks like this. I feel as if he's got the upper hand in some way, as if he knows something I don't. I'm not sure that he actually enjoys it, but I imagine that he does and of course that makes me feel worse. Curtly, I tell him I don't know what he's talking about.

"I'm talking about Luc not being Carly's uncle like she thought... like I presume you thought... otherwise you would surely have put her right."

Reluctantly I have to confess, "You're right. I haven't a clue what you're talking about. Of course he's her uncle, how could he not be? He's Claudine's brother after all!"

The next few sentences uttered by Sebastian blow me out of the water. I can't believe I wouldn't know this. It's not possible that I wouldn't know this. Unable to accept what I'm hearing I take my frustration, my confusion out on Sebastian.

"You think this is funny? Who do you think you are, fabricating this rubbish? I know you want Carly to be happy, but you can't just lie to let her have what she wants."

There's a silence from his end of the phone and it makes me feel uncomfortable. He's taking his time, gathering his thoughts in a way that I haven't. Finally he replies, his tone measured and without expression. He's far better at hiding his feelings than I am.

"So...something else which Claudine and Len didn't talk about. I wonder if there's anything more."

He hangs up before I can begin to vent my fury on him. How dare he speak to me like that? Frantically I punch in the first few numbers and then decide against calling him back. Slamming the phone down, I'm only too aware that I asked for that. I provoked him and he reacted just as anyone would have. The hard part is that I know he's right. Another mystery concealed by Claudine. This time I don't get it though. Why would she keep something like that from me? It's not as if there was even anything to hide. Maybe the topic of adoption was just too close to home for her, though. Otherwise why not tell me Luc was adopted? So what if he was? I scarcely knew him anyway, just like I hardly knew any of her family. Turns out I barely knew her either.

## LUC

The silence all around is so profound I wonder for a moment if maybe I've just died. The blackness too; I've never seen such a total absence of light, never anywhere. Raising my hand in front of my face I still can't see it, can't even make out a shape or a shadow. The stabbing pain in my stomach, though, is very physical, very real. I decide I must be alive after all or I probably wouldn't feel it, would I?

Moving slightly, more to see if I can than for any other reason, my head starts spinning; it's a strange sensation especially when there's nothing to focus on. I'm wondering what to do. Should I just sit tight and hope someone sends some help? That might be the safest thing to do considering I have no idea where I am and not much of an idea what kind of shape I'm in. The only troubling point about that is I don't know how long I might have to wait. If only I'd called Sebastian before I set off. Then at least someone would be aware that I hadn't shown up. As it is no-one will miss me. No-one even knows to be worried about me. What a horrible thought. I'm lying down here and potentially nobody is even conscious of my predicament.

A clap of thunder nearby signals the proximity of the approaching storm. The rain continues to hammer down on the roof of the car. It's also now raining in on me as the windscreen has all but gone. I'm starting to get really cold. Shivering, I realise my clothes are soaking. My feet, in particular feel like ice. They seem to be sloshing about in water. Another round of thunder is followed by a flash of sheet lightning, illuminating for an instant the whole landscape. In that moment I'm able to see for the first time my surroundings. Fields and trees rise up on my left climbing steeply. That must be the route I took when the car started to roll, all downhill. On my right is a more disturbing sight and one which spurs me to immediate action; water, lots of water. The car seems to have come to a halt, not in a ditch as I first thought, but right on the edge of a loch or a reservoir or something. The front of the vehicle looked in the momentary light to be more raised then the back, leading me to suppose that maybe the car's actually already partially submerged. Unfastening my seat belt I attempt to open the door, but to no avail. I'm conscious now of water pooling around my knees and I know I need to get out. Another flash of light and the natural escape route is exposed for a second - the broken windscreen. Pulling my feet up onto the seat, I lean over the dashboard. In the pitch blackness I cannot avoid the jagged shards of glass protruding daringly from the remnants of the window. Pushing myself through I hear my own voice cry out in the silence as I'm cut on the knees, shoulders, hands, face. Finally I'm through and sliding over the bonnet, landing on marshy grass in a heap. Behind me I hear the car sliding backwards, a wave of water splashing over me, as it sinks slowly without my weight to slow its progress. Now I need to move and be careful as I do. I don't want to inadvertently end up wandering into the bitter waters which I've only just managed to avoid. In this darkness though, knowing I need to get moving and knowing which way to go are very different matters.

# SEBASTIAN

I feel cooped up in this flat. Pacing around is heightening my sense of anxiety rather than relieving it. Why does he always do this to me? It didn't used to be like this. When I think about it, I'm surprised in a way that we got on so well before. In reality what has changed between us? From my point of view not so much; I always knew I loved Claudine. I watched from the side-lines as she married him, carved out a life with him. The revelation has been for him and he can't deal with it. I suppose I'm thinking that if I've been able to handle it all these years, then now it's his turn. Is that really heartless? I guess it is. I can only imagine how I'd feel after fifteen years of marriage to discover that in fact my partner was in love with someone else. Yes, it would feel pretty bad.

My thoughts turn abruptly to Helen and it dawns on me that her situation is a mirror image of Len's. I've hardly given her a moment's attention since this all kicked off and yet she's dealing with a lot of stuff too. Why have I not considered her feelings in all this? How must it be for her to discover that I never really loved her and all the time was longing for Claudine? I feel like a complete bastard. In my defence I think I resented her so much, because if it wasn't for her I would have married Claudine. I felt that it was she who changed the course of history, robbing me of happiness forever.

It occurs to me that she may have been struggling with the business since I left. Again I haven't given it much thought. I've been so preoccupied with my own feelings and with Len and Carly and now Luc. Helen has slipped gradually further and further down my list of

414

priorities. I should address this situation now. I've got the time and I need something to focus on anyway. Lifting the phone I dial, at the same time bracing myself for the likelihood of an onslaught of abuse. Helen clearly feels she is the woman scorned and doesn't hold back in letting me know just what a loser she thinks I am. She's probably right. Her sister answers. This is hardly a better scenario. We've never seen eye to eye and I imagine she's been fuelling Helen's anger with her own version of possible events.

"Harriet! How are you?"

Dismissing the civilities without acknowledgement she replies, "Sebastian. How nice of you to finally ring. It's good of you to squeeze in a call albeit three weeks since you got back to Scotland."

I grit my teeth and tell myself not to rise to it. "I don't know who you've got keeping tabs on me Harriet, but they're not doing a very good job. I've been back here six weeks now."

"Even more of a disgrace!" she says curtly.

I plough on, "Anyway, I'm sorry to disturb you. I was wondering if I could have a word or two with Helen. I believe she's been trying to get hold of me."

"Yes she's been trying to get hold of you. I'm sure she's left any number of messages on your machine. I think she's busy right now. I think she's given up on you actually."

I take a deep breath and try to stay calm, "Harriet, just get her."

She's stubborn though, this woman and she won't be happy till I've danced to her tune. I can see straight through her. I don't like her, never have, but tonight she's starting to really irritate me. I need to keep a lid on things, though. If I allow her to rile me, if I respond to her antagonism, she'll have won. She wants me to get mad and I'm determined that's not going to happen.

"She's in the bath and no I'm not getting her out. Why should I? You've taken this long to bother phoning so now you can wait till it suits her. Any problems she's having with the restaurant can just wait."

She's got me now and she knows it. I can visualise her smiling as she anticipates my reaction. The way to rattle me is, as she well knows, to suggest there's something wrong at the restaurant. I need to know what and I need to know right now. "I'll be over as soon as I can," I tell her and put the phone down. I don't know if she protested or not. I didn't stop to listen.

What a night to have to go out. This storm has been brewing all day, but I don't think anyone anticipated it would be quite so bad. The last weather report I heard told of unexpected flooding across large parts of the country. From the sound of it the rain hasn't let up yet. I can hear it battering angrily against the windows. At least the thunder and lightning side of things has passed, though. Grabbing a jacket, I set off into the wind and rain to face the music. What has she done to my precious restaurant? What have I let her do?

# CARLY

I don't feel too good. I mean I haven't felt good for a few days now, but tonight I think there's definitely something wrong. I buzz for the nurse, something I don't like doing because I know they're really busy, but I'm starting to get a bit scared. My heart feels like it's beating too fast and I'm sweating profusely. I feel a bit shaky too. Looking out the window I wonder if Dad got home okay. This weather is terrible and he would be walking across the Meadows to get back to his flat. I don't like that route at night at the best of times, but tonight it would be horrible. The nurse comes quickly. It's Mary and I'm so glad. She understands.

"What's the matter, pet?" she asks me kindly.

"I don't know. I feel terrible." I tell her simply.

"Okay, I'll come in and we'll get you checked out. Just let me scrub up and I'll be right with you."

She disappears, but I feel reassured. I know she's coming in and she'll help me. I wonder what my counts are doing. They've probably fallen by now. This could be the beginning of my ordeal. I try not to think about all the things which could go wrong. Instead I've been actively concentrating on my studies and Prof and of course on Dad. They've both been such a strong support to me since I came in here. I feel bad about the way I carried on today about Luc. Poor Dad's doing everything he can think of for me and then I go and ask for the impossible. I realise I've put him in a very difficult position. That's one of the maddening things about being stuck in here. I have to rely on other people doing stuff for me, stuff which I should really be dealing with myself. If I wasn't in isolation then I could just call him. I should be speaking to Luc in person. Because that's not possible it's become this big public thing and I hate it.

"Okay pet, let's check your vital signs and see what's going on with you," says Mary, as she enters the room. A thermometer is placed under one arm, a blood pressure cuff wrapped around the other and I sit in silence watching her count each breath I take. After a couple of minutes the machine beeps signalling a complete blood pressure result. Glancing at the monitor I see a normal reading displayed on the screen. Well that's a relief. Whatever's wrong can't be too bad. A moment later and the thermometer indicates time to read and removing it Mary tells me I'm hot.

"How hot?" I ask her.

"Hot enough to need antibiotics," she answers. Preparing to leave she adds, "I'm going to get you some paracetamol to bring your temperature down. I'll also take some blood for culture to see what kind of infection we're dealing with. You know the script, Carly. We'll start IV antibiotics now and add in if we need to once we've got the results from the lab."

I nod. Yes, I've been here before so many times. Being neutropenic means I'm much more likely to catch infections, things which a normal healthy body would shake off easily. Me, they seem to floor in this state. I know it's the predictable pattern with this treatment. After chemo my counts always fall and I always get an infection. Once the antibiotics have kicked in, I'll feel a lot better. For now, though, I'm not in the best condition and to boot I feel a bit sorry for myself. I wish there was someone here. I wish my dad was here. Glancing again out of the window, I toy with the idea of getting them to phone him. He'd come, I'm sure he would. In fact he'd probably want me to call if I need him. He's always saying as much. But look at the weather. I don't think I can drag him out in this. It wouldn't be fair. No, I'll wait and see how I am in a couple of hours when I've had the medicine. I might be okay in a while.

# LUC

This is hard, really hard. For the first time in my life I actually think I might not get out of here alive. This could be it for me. I am completely disoriented. It seems like I've been walking for ages and still have no idea if I've made any headway. I might be using up all my energies trudging around in circles for all I know. Everywhere looks the same when you can't see anything at all. A bizarre thought shoots through my mind, that this must be what it's like for Helen all the time. What a miserable existence. The thing which is keeping me going is the hope that the darkness will lift or daybreak will come or something, which will allow me to see clearly again. To know that was never going to happen! I'm surprised she wasn't suicidal at the prospect of lifelong blindness. I suppose she had Sebastian, though. He must have been a real help to her. It's admirable really the way she's coped and made something worthwhile of her life. It occurs to me then that Sebastian did make the right decision when he said he would stick by her. Yes, he was giving up his chance of happiness with Claudine, but to live like this… I guess it's just because I'm in the middle of it at the moment, but I can imagine few worse experiences.

The rain is unrelenting. The storm itself seems to have passed on, though. I can hear thunder but more distant now and there hasn't been any lightning for ages. It would actually be better for me if the sudden shafts of split-second light were still illuminating the sky. At least I was able to catch a glimpse of the landscape then. It made little difference mind you. It all looked the same; miles and miles of moorland stretching as far as I could see. I didn't manage to register any notable landmarks at all. This rain is terrible. My face smarts with the pummelling it's taking from the battering wind, my eyes stream; my throat is hoarse and dry. There's an ever present pain in my side. It feels as if I still have my seatbelt on and its pulled way too tight. It cuts into me and I'm gripped by a throbbing I've never felt before. In normal circumstances I would be finding it difficult to walk in this condition, but tonight well, tonight there's just no choice. If I stop, if I collapse in a heap, I'm sure I'll die. I don't think I would last the night out here if I stop now. I'm so cold and so wet. My clothes are saturated and cling icily to my frozen body. I need to keep moving. It's my only hope. I need to keep alive because I need to see Carly again. I can't bear the thought that maybe I'll never look on her lovely face again. If the last moments we share turn out to be those angry, bitter, confused minutes when she walked away from me at the hospital…

No! While there's breath left in my body, I will not lie down to this. Pushing myself to keep going, dragging my feet, progress is slow, but at least I'm still here. That's what it's coming down to isn't it? The measure of how well I'm doing has become whether or not I'm still alive.

## SEBASTIAN

"Right, you've got me to trail all the way over here to speak to her, so get her down here."

Harriet, though, continues to wind me up with her procrastinating antics. "I certainly won't be bringing her anywhere near you while you're in such a foul mood."

Shaking my head I really do have to make a conscious effort to contain my anger. If I explode I'll never get to see her and I want to get this over with. This is not like me. I usually am able to remain detached from things and keep a fairly chilled outlook. This is just so maddening. Helen knows me well. She's lived with me all these years, after all. She knows how to upset my internal balance. She knows exactly which buttons to push to make me annoyed.

Harriet is, if anything, worse. She never liked me. I was to blame for her sister's accident and I didn't pay a high enough price in her eyes. She thought I should have gone to jail for what I did. Sometimes I thought so too. Why is she making out now that Helen would be in some way threatened by me if she came down while I'm angry? She knows full well I would never ever lay a finger on her. She's just trying to get me really worked up. Could she be actually enjoying this? Her twisted way of thinking is so beyond my own comprehension. I have absolutely no connection with her so have no idea how her mind works.

Taking a deep breath, I force my voice to sound calmer than I feel. "Okay. Please tell Helen that I'm here and I'd like to speak with her if she can spare me the time."

"You can hold your sarcastic tongue, Sebastian. I'll go and ask her if she wants to see you. That's the best I can do."

She leaves the room and I can't help thinking the whole scene has been stage managed to allow her to flounce out in this state of righteous anger. I'm left for a few minutes with nothing but a ticking clock for company. The house is warm and I'm already starting to dry out. Taking off my soaked jacket, I place it carefully over the back of a chair. I'm hoping not to have to stay too long, so it would be good if my clothes were dry for me leaving. All I want to do is find out what the problem is with the restaurant, hopefully come up with some interim measure to fix it and be on my way again. This is not the forum for addressing all our problems and I hope it doesn't turn out to be a slagging match. I'm not in the mood for that at all. The door opens slowly and Helen nudges her way cautiously into the room. She doesn't know her way around here the way she did at home. She seems more nervous about her movements, appears more vulnerable.

"Did I get you out of the bath?" I say on seeing her wrapped up in a huge dressing gown, presumably something of Harriet's. I've never seen her wear it before.

She shakes her head, "No, I was just sorting out some stuff upstairs. Harriet said you called earlier, that you wanted to speak to me."

"Well, something like that, I guess."

I'm a bit shocked to be standing here with her. She doesn't look too good, very pale and tired. Have I done this to her? I've barely given her a thought over the past few months. Has she been falling apart and I didn't know?

"How are you? How have things been?" I ask her.

"Without you, you mean?" Always to the point, Helen's forte was never sparing your feelings.

"I mean how are you?" I repeat.

"I'm tired," she says simply as if that's explanation enough. Tired? Tired of what? The responsibility of the restaurant? The pressure of running things on a daily basis? Tired of me? I decide to stop shirking the issue and cut to the chase. It's late and I want to be home now.

"You called me several times. You said you needed to talk to me. I'm here. Talk."

She's silent a moment, collecting her thoughts presumably. I'm starting to get impatient. I've crossed the city tonight in the middle of a storm, because I was under the impression she had something to say to me. If she doesn't hurry up and say it, I'm going to be on my way.

"Well, you left me in the lurch with the restaurant. I've had to manage it single-handed and yes, it's been a nightmare. I didn't know if you were coming back or not. I've had to make all kinds of decisions, some of which you probably won't like. I thought when you came back you would be picking up some of the responsibility, but there's been no sign of you. I need to know where I stand."

Fair enough. It's been hard for her and she's done well to carry the burden when I just went off without any warning. The funny thing is I always thought she wanted the restaurant to herself. I thought she'd have revelled in the opportunity to run things without me. Instead here she is saying she wants me to take over again.

"I'm sorry, Helen. I've neglected things, I know and I'm really grateful to you for holding it all together while I've been away. The thing is I've been really preoccupied since I got back. There's been a lot of other stuff I've had to deal with."

I'm not sure how much she knows. She is in contact with Luc and probably Len, but she and I have never had the conversation about Carly. I sense we're about to have it.

"I take it you're talking about the girl... am I right?" she asks me. I'm relieved in a way. At least I don't have to break this to her.

"Carly, she's called Carly," I reply quietly.

She nods. "Pretty name... Did you choose it?"

"No... I didn't know about her Helen. I didn't know until a few weeks ago... Did you really think I'd have kept this from you all this time if I'd known?"

She doesn't have to answer and she doesn't. We both understand that I kept massive secrets from her throughout our entire married life. What difference would this have made?

"What's she like?" Her question surprises me. I wouldn't have thought she'd have been the slightest bit interested.

"Well... she's ...she's beautiful... She's bright, very bright; gifted even... charming... she's lovely. She's everything a father would want his daughter to be."

She flinches at this last remark and I think how careless I've been with my words. For a long time, it seems, we sit without either one of us speaking. I start to feel awkward and wonder whether I should go.

"I want you to start helping out with the restaurant. I can't do it all anymore."

"That's fair. You've done enough, I realise that. I'll start pulling my weight again. I will need to be flexible though... Carly's ill, I don't know if you realise... I need to be with her." She does realise it turns out.

"I'll be taking some time off myself in a few months, so perhaps you can return the favour then?"

"Sure, whatever suits you. Just let me be there when Carly needs me and I'll take over running the place when you want me to. Thanks for being so understanding about her... I thought you would go mad when you found out."

She seems to reflect for a moment on what I've just said before replying. "Despite what I think of you, despite what you've done to me, I do happen to think you'll make a pretty good dad. I always thought that."

Is it my imagination or is the hand, which has instinctively cupped the small rounding of her belly, concealing something more? I gaze at her, but the dressing gown's so oversized I can't make it out.

"You're staring at me," she says. Helen always had this uncanny intuitive sense which defied all logic. I used to say she didn't need her eyes to be able to see. Always she could read me better than anyone else.

424

"Helen are you…you're not…are you?"

"Yes… I'm pregnant Sebastian. Seven months gone… I'd have thought you'd have noticed. The baby is quite small it seems, but not worryingly so."

I can't believe what she's saying. She's sitting there so cool and telling me this. I'm stunned. Eventually I manage to formulate a coherent thought and find some words to express it.

"Is it mine, Helen?"

This was definitely the wrong thing to say. I watch the anger rise up within her. I had to ask though. I mean we haven't been together for so long and I've been out of the country. We were hardly even speaking.

"Of course it's yours," she retorts. "Don't judge me by your own standards. I've been faithful to you from the moment I met you, which is more than I can say for you. Yes, we're having a baby…a boy… I thought I'd call him Peter… I'm due in a couple of months and if it's not too much to ask I'd like some time off from work around then. If that's okay with you, then our business tonight is finished. You can go now."

She rises herself to leave the room. I'm still struck dumb. What's going on? We were together for fifteen years and never any baby. Now we've split up and we're going to have a little boy! Moving toward her, my instinct is to reach out. Stroking her hair, her face I remember other tender moments and think that it wasn't all bad. Our marriage has been fraught with problems, most of them a result of my own betrayal of her feelings for me. But we did have good times too. She's grown with the passing of time, she's turned into a very strong woman; someone who, I now understand, doesn't need me at all. Turning her face upward to mine, I trace the outline of her mouth with my finger. Her voice when she speaks is gentler than I remember it being for a long time. Without animosity or bitterness she whispers, "Perhaps we could call him Pierre…if you'd like that better. It would sound right with Charpentier wouldn't it?"

The softness of her voice throws me. I hesitate before answering her. "Helen, I…I don't know what to say…I'm sorry…I'll help you, of course I will. Having a baby...it's, well it's... it's wonderful news... isn't it? I'll be there for you, don't worry about that...I'll want to be involved...Being a dad is...it's the best thing that ever happened to me. The only thing is...I don't want you to think it means..."

She interrupts, "Don't worry, Sebastian, I don't want you back. I always knew you'd make a wonderful father and you will - by all accounts you are. But you're still a lousy husband."

# LEN

The journey to the hospital has never taken me as long as it has today. The bus has been rerouted three times in order to avoid areas of road blocked by debris from last night's storm. I heard one lady at the bus-stop telling someone that the news this morning reported hurricane winds in some areas overnight. I was aware of the rain and thunder for a few hours, but I must admit I just stayed put the whole night so it didn't really affect me. This morning though, this is a nuisance. Carly will be wondering where I've got to. I'm usually there by breakfast or very shortly afterwards, but today it's already nearing ten and I'm not even in the vicinity yet.

Today of all days it's annoying, because I've been worrying about Carly ever since Sebastian called last night. All the stuff about Luc is emotional turmoil, which I really think she could do without. He said she was alright and I'm quite certain he wouldn't have left her if she wasn't, but I need to see her for myself and this frustratingly slow bus is starting to get to me. Also the fact that it is jam-packed with other impatient travellers doesn't help. I wonder if I'd be quicker getting out. Maybe I'd be able to catch a cab. Then again, not likely, anyone with any sense will be doing just that and the taxis are probably overstretched too. Walking? I decide I can't stand this snail's pace any longer and pushing my way through the standing crowd, I head for the front of the bus and escape from these stifling, sniffing bodies all around me.

## LUC

On waking my first thought is of how cold I am, how desperately, bitterly cold. I can't move my fingers, can't feel my toes. My next thought is how on earth did I manage to sleep out here? I wonder was it sleeping or did I pass out finally from sheer exhaustion? The last thing I remember of the nightmare I've just endured was seeing a light in the distance. The headlights of an approaching car weaving their way in slow motion across the moors, disappearing with dips in the road, reappearing again, each time slightly nearer. Silently I watched, mesmerised, as my answer to prayer drew ever closer. The excitement I felt when it dawned on me that the road must be really close to where I was standing was almost uncontainable. Fixing my eyes on the lights I tried to anticipate where it would pass me, tried to foresee exactly where I should be for the car to drive right by me. I couldn't miss this opportunity. This was the first sign of life I'd come across since the accident and I knew it was my best hope of surviving. Unbelievably the car, taking a final turn about a hundred yards away from me, started moving directly toward me. I must have been standing right by the roadside and had no idea. Still in complete blackness, the landscape was hidden and I had most likely been struggling along the uneven ground which ran alongside the road. It was almost laughable. If anyone could have seen me I would have seemed a really pathetic sight, I'm sure. But the car coming nearer now was raising my spirits. It's going to be fine, I thought; a terrible experience, but one which in the cold light of day would make a good story. The sound of the engine was like music to my ears. I raised both arms in anticipation of its approach. As it neared, I was blinded momentarily by the glare of the headlamps full on my face. Closing my eyes I waved frantically, shouted out expectantly. The brightness passed in a flicker and opening my eyes again I turned to watch the car continue past me, on into the distance and finally out of sight. I stood there, unable to move watching the lights disappearing further and further away from me. Not until it had gone completely did I stop following it with my eyes. Then the utter darkness enveloped me once more. I couldn't believe it. The car went right by me, the lights shone on my face. They must have seen me. They couldn't have failed to see me. Why didn't they stop? Why indeed?

That was the lowest ebb. Right then I told myself that I probably wasn't going to make it. Okay I now knew where the road was and if I followed it I would eventually come to somewhere, but as far as I could see in all directions there was no sign of anything. If I was even within several miles of the city I would expect to see illumination from the street lights reflected in the night sky, but there was nothing. Everywhere a suffocating blanket of dark, closed in on all sides.

I did try to keep going. I walked, stumbled, fell and staggered on again for ages. I had no idea of time, my watch having been smashed at some point, but it felt like a long time. Walking along the road, a route which should have been easier than the rough fields and waterlogged moorland, turned out to be still very challenging. I realised then that the problem was actually with my legs and not so much the terrain. Eventually, though, I just stopped. I couldn't do it anymore. I had no more push. Sitting down by the side of the road, I huddled my arms and legs in as close to my body as possible, shivering violently. The last thing I recall thinking was that at least here I would be found relatively quickly and wouldn't be left to rot out in the wilds somewhere. Someone would find me and Carly would be told. That was preferable to me than having her think I'd run out on her, started a new life without her and was never seen or heard from again. At that point I must have passed out, fallen asleep or whatever.

Waking feels strange. This is not the place I was in before. I mean it is, of course it is, but in the daylight it seems so different. The quiet is also a bit disconcerting and I think that may be what woke me. The wind has died right down, that torrential rain now a gentle drizzle. The power of the storm has been extinguished. I'm aware that it must be still early because there hasn't been to my knowledge any more traffic along this way yet. It'll come though. With each passing hour, the possibility of rescue will increase and it occurs to me that everything's maybe gonna be okay. Dragging myself to my feet, I stand shakily on the road and begin very tentatively to take slow, steady steps. Get moving, I tell myself. Keep moving. Don't let yourself die from hypothermia right when help is at last imminent. My feet are moving but this is the shuffle of an old man. What the hell kind of a state must I be in?

# CARLY

Another morning and the routine remains the same. The ward round hasn't reached me yet. That's a good sign, I always think. I've been part of this set-up for long enough now to have clocked that the sickest patients get seen first and rightly so. I just don't want to be one of them. I'd gladly wait all day to see a doctor if it meant I was doing okay.

I'm wondering where Prof's got to, though. He's usually here by now. I don't want to seem demanding so I haven't asked for him; I know he'll come as soon as he can. It occurs to me that it's maybe not all that easy for him trying to juggle his life to suit me. I kind of forget that other people actually have a life outside of this place. Just because this is all there is for me doesn't mean that's the case for everyone. Having said that the way Prof and Dad are working things I'd be surprised if either one of them had time for anything else. They're probably trying to do too much. I don't want them to start resenting having to visit me and keep me company. I don't suppose I need someone every minute of every day anyway. It's nice, of course to know there's someone there, but it might make life more manageable for them if I asked them to ease off a bit.

I slept not too badly after all last night. I had wondered if I was in for a bad one what with the temperature and everything, but surprisingly once Mary got me organised with my drips and stuff, I was able to settle quite quickly. The storm didn't even disturb me much. Mary was lovely to me, sitting in here with me long after she'd finished all the tasks associated with treating my infection. Perhaps that's why I was able to rest more easily, because I felt safe. This morning I've already had the regular schedule of activities carried out. Each morning it's the same; the drugs are given out, my temperature, pulse and blood pressure are checked, I wash and dress, breakfast is handed in to me and a little while later I hand it back out, then the room is cleaned from top to bottom and my bedding changed. The nurses are kept going all the time. One of them has just been in to take blood to check my counts and a whole pile of other stuff.

I can't believe Prof's still not here, it's so unlike him. He's never been this late before. Normally he comes before I get my breakfast so he's able to moan at me for not eating. He always laughs about it now though, ever since that time in the Student Union when I felt so sick and he was trying to make me eat something. I decide to make a start on the essay he gave me a few days ago. He's been great about this. I don't feel under any pressure, but I know he's worried about me overdoing it. The thing is it's actually really good to have something to do, something to get my teeth into. There are times when I'm so absorbed in my work that I forget where I am and what's happening to me. That can only be a good thing. Maybe I'm not going to have the rough ride which everyone's expecting. I'm supposed to be pretty ill by now, but even though I do have an infection, all things considered, I don't feel too bad. I can't eat, that's true and I've lost weight, but I think that's to be expected.

I notice a bit of movement outside my room, people standing around. At first I assume it's the doctors, but then Prof's concerned face appears at the window and I realise he's being briefed on last night's carry-on. One good thing is that Dr Armstrong now lets him come in to be with me, once he's all scrubbed up of course. Dad's also allowed and what a difference that's made to everything. I can actually have a conversation without the rest of the ward hearing as we shout through these stupid walkie talkie things. I watch him move over to the basin and begin the laborious process of making himself clean enough to share the same space as me. It's times like this that it's really brought home to me how risky this whole procedure is. They don't want me to catch anything in case I can't fight it off.

I'm doing okay, though, I reassure myself. Take it as it comes. For now my Prof's here and I'm so glad, so relieved to see him. I was getting worried for a bit there. I couldn't bear it if anything were to happen to him. He's my constant, the one who drives me and I've come to love him dearly over these past few months.

"Why didn't you get them to phone me last night?"

I smile. I knew he would say this. "It was fine, that's why. I had a temperature and felt a bit funny till it came down again, that's all."

"The nurse said it was really high and they started IV antibiotics."

I nod, "That's just par for the course, Prof. That's how it works. It's not a big deal, really."

He stares at me for a bit. I'm sure he does this when he doesn't really believe me. It's as if he thinks he'll be able to read the truth in my eyes. I don't think I'd ever be able to lie to Prof. So intense is his stare I sometimes think he can see into my very heart. All the hidden places, all the things I try to cover up, I'm sure he knows all about them.

He changes the subject and I'm relieved. I don't want to talk about how frightened I was last night, how I weighed up whether to have someone called or not. I'd rather just leave it behind now. "I brought you some music," he tells me.

"Thanks…we can put it on later. Tell me what you've been doing. What are you writing?"

This is when I enjoy Prof most of all. When he's back in his own territory, doing what he does best. I feel like I'm privy to mini-tutorials on these occasions when I can get him off the subject of me and onto his life's work. I can't wait to get out of here so I can read what he's been doing all this while. I'm not allowed his manuscripts in my room and he's refused to read then out to me through the walkie-talkie. He's quite shy about his poetry really, which is something which I believe would shock everyone who knows him. Shy is not a word you would ever associate with Prof Thomas. Then again, I don't suppose many people know him like I do. Not really.

# SEBASTIAN

This is one morning when a long lie in bed would have probably been a good idea. I'm not someone who's used to that, though; few chefs are, but after such a late night, this early start is particularly difficult. I told Helen I would do as much in the restaurant as I can. I need to take the pressure off her a bit; it's far too much for her now. Showering, dressing hastily, I'm one of the first few to survey the storm damage, as I make my way across town shortly after dawn. I always loved this part of the job, if the truth be known. This quiet time, before the rest of the world comes to life has an almost spiritual feel to it. At times like this, as I watch the early morning sunrise, breathing in the freshness of the new day, it feels good to be alive.

I realise after a little while that I'm whistling as I walk. My heart seems lighter; my mind less troubled than it has been for a long time. I'm a dad and I'm going to be again! It's mind-blowing. I struggled to sleep once I finally got back from Helen's. I was buzzing with excitement. I'm starting to feel as if my life has been worth something after all. First finding Carly and as if that wasn't blessing enough now this new baby to look forward to.

Helen and I talked a long time once she finally broke the news to me. I've been able to come to a better understanding of her and I think the feeling's mutual. She doesn't hate me; she just finds it hard to be around me. It all makes so much sense, but I couldn't get my head around any of it before. There's no future for us as a couple, I'm pretty definite about that. I think we tried for long enough and we

434

couldn't make it work. I don't love her, not the way I should as her husband. I care for her very much and I want to help her if I can, but love, well that's something else.

Helen made it clear to me that she felt at least partly to blame for what happened to us. I think maybe that was the real breakthrough in our conversation. Once we started being honest with each other we seemed able to crack some of the barriers and lose some of our defences. It was difficult for her to admit the things she did and I have to say I actually admire her candour. She opened up in a way she hasn't before. I wonder if that was down to me. Maybe I never gave her the opportunity, maybe I wasn't interested enough. We went way back, back to our first meeting in Paris and covered ground which we haven't discussed in years, maybe ever. She knew how I felt about Claudine even then, she told me. At first I was dismayed to hear her say it, but as she went on and explained things, I was at least able to understand, if not accept, the cards she chose to play. She recognised my feelings for Claudine, but had decided that she would win me over. With Claudine out of the picture I guess she thought it was the perfect opportunity to help me forget about her. I wasn't innocent in this, I realise that, but it did help to feel I wasn't totally to blame either. After the accident, she said, she decided that if her life was not to end right then, she would need me. Fully aware that my heart belonged elsewhere, she knew that guilt would bind me to her and only she would be able to free me from a crushing sense of responsibility. She made up her mind that it was her right to have me by her side for the rest of her life. Everything was ruined. She couldn't work, she doubted she would ever meet anyone else, her life was in tatters. If I stayed with her out of a sense of duty, then that was good enough for her. She also reminded me that although my feelings for her did not run deep, she *was* in love with me. It made sense. Her family agreed. I obliged. The rest is, as they say, history.

We were never meant to be together. It's hardly surprising we had such a tough time of it. Her views on Claudine and me never changed. She said she always could see how we felt about each other. It constantly amazed her that no-one else could. Here was she, the one

435

who was meant to be blind, and yet she could see it clearer than anyone else. Putting all these things to rest was good for us I think. Getting it all out in the open was painful, but I bet it will mark a turning point in our relationship. We'll never be able to live with each other again, neither will there be any romantic involvement, but I do think we'll be able to bring our child up between us, without the bitterness and recriminations of the past constantly haunting us.

Pierre. Wait till Carly hears about this. She's going to be a big sister! I hope she takes it well and realises this is for her too. He'll be part of her family and I want her to be really involved. It'll give her something to look forward to as well, hopefully something to aim for.

Luc's absence hasn't been helping her situation at all. The doctor asks me every time I see him if we're any closer to tracking him down. Personally I'm wondering if he's gone back to France. I know he's not gone home, because I've called Cecile and the other boys and they were under the impression he was here with me. I don't have a number for Elise; it seems she's had it changed since Luc moved out. In a way, I'm glad because that would have been a difficult call to make. Also, I don't want to hear he's gone back there. Imagine what that would do to Carly. It's better not to know where he is than to know that. Len doesn't think he would have, not the way he feels about Carly, but I'm not so sure. He went back to her before didn't he, the last time Carly told him to leave? What would be so different this time? Except that maybe this time Elise wouldn't have him. Anyway, I don't know what else I can do. I can hardly contact Interpol can I and short of that I'm out of ideas. The only thing which surprises me is his phone being off for so long. There's probably a reasonable explanation for that too though. He could have lost it or something. Anyway, sooner or later he'll get in touch. I just hope it's going to be sooner, for Carly's sake; for all our sakes.

# LEN

"So what are you saying, Doctor?" I'm confused. I don't know if this is normal or not. He did say that she would probably be at her lowest ebb around this time, but she doesn't seem too bad to me.

"What I'm saying, though perhaps not terribly well, is that just because she appears to have sailed through things pretty much, so far, that we mustn't become complacent. Yes, it's good she hasn't become too ill, but she still could. Occasionally we do get a lucky person who doesn't fall apart in there, but not often. I cannot emphasise that enough."

I nod. For a moment there he had me worried. I thought maybe he was saying the conditioning hadn't been effective or something, that she wasn't ill enough to show it had wiped everything out. This isn't easy. I knew it wouldn't be, of course I did, but nothing prepared me for the emotional turbulence which I think we're all feeling. Okay, I better get back to her. She gets very suspicious when she knows the medics are having conversations with us which she can't hear. I'm sure I'd be the same myself. Also, Sebastian will be here shortly to take over and I don't want him to think I've deserted her. When did I start caring what people think? I guess I don't generally, but this situation is different to any other. I feel I have to prove myself to him. I suppose it's because he has the upper hand, or at least I feel he has. He's got the actual relationship with her, the biological connection which I haven't. Nothing will sever their bond, whereas I...I feel a lot more vulnerable. She matters more to me than anything else in my whole life. I love her with a depth, a completeness that I've never known and with that comes the fear, the constant threat, I guess, of losing her.

# LUC

At first I don't hear it. It's there in the background, a gentle murmuring, but it doesn't register, doesn't penetrate my consciousness. My eyes are fixed on my feet, watching each step as I laboriously lift and lay, lift and lay. It's almost like I need to keep looking at them to make sure they're still moving. The car's almost upon me when it dawns on me what it is and what it means. Glancing over my shoulder I see it, no more than a few metres away. It's moving at quite a pace, but most cars do along straight stretches of road such as this. In an instant it's passed me and once again I'm looking at the rear of a car travelling away from me. The same feeling of panic begins to well up inside my chest. Raising my arms, opening my mouth to shout, I watch myself as an onlooker, incapable of actually making any sound or movement. In an instant, though dread is replaced with a rising hope. My eyes lock on the tail lights, illuminating bright, indicating the driver is braking. The car slows, stops, eases into reverse. I hear the whine of the engine as it motors steadily backwards and comes to a halt beside me. I don't know quite what's wrong with me. I stand rooted to the spot, staring at the driver returning my gaze from behind the misted window. Opening the door, an elderly gentleman clambers awkwardly out and scrutinising me closely asks if I'm alright. Unable to speak, I open and close my mouth several times with no sound uttered.

"What are you doing out here? You look like you could do with some medical attention."

He speaks in a clipped, military-style fashion. I have a little difficulty with his accent, but I know he's trying to help me. With the greatest of efforts I delve deep into my dulled brain and manage to retrieve some English. I need to communicate with this man. He is my help, my hope. I depend on him.

"I had an accident…car crash…" I'm at last able to mutter. He nods and clearly decides he's taking control of the situation.

"Alright, young man, here's what we're going to do. Get into the car…can you manage? I'm going to drive you straight to hospital…we'll get it all sorted out there… nothing to worry about now."

Opening the passenger door for me, his arm around my shoulders I feel myself being almost lifted into the seat. It all appears to be happening without any effort from me, which is just as well because I think I'm done.

# SEBASTIAN

I'm in good time despite the race I've had to get across town today. This past couple of days has been really hard; getting to the restaurant for six and running around mad in there till four. I head straight to the hospital after that and stay with Carly until around ten. It looks like this will be the pattern for the foreseeable future. It's exhausting but I can't come up with a reasonable alternative. Well I can, but until I get hold of Luc I don't know if it's an option or not. It's starting to concern me a little that I don't know where he is. I know it's none of my business and if it wasn't for Carly's desperation to see him I'd probably be cool about him taking off to clear his head. In these circumstances, though, it is really frustrating to know he feels the same way she does, but I've got no way of contacting him. Poor Carly won't believe it either until she sees him for herself. Only yesterday she asked me to stop playing games with her, said she thought I was just going along with things to try and raise her spirits. Of course I explained to her how cut up Luc was when she sent him packing, explained that the reason he left town was because he was so upset and didn't know what to do with himself. What Carly can't grasp, though, is where is he? If he wants her so badly how come there's been no sign of him? I'm not sure she believes that I haven't been able to reach him. She thinks he just doesn't want to know. I decide to try calling again. I've already tried several times, but his phone's been off for ages.

Glancing at my watch, I reckon I've got time for a cigarette before I head up to the ward. It's a good opportunity to use my mobile too before I have to switch it off inside the building. Wandering over

441

to the wall facing the main entrance I start dialling. Again the network provider informs me that the person I'm calling may have their phone switched off and to try again later. Instead I light up and savour a few minutes of relaxation; time to myself in which I physically and mentally start to unwind.

Len will be waiting. He doesn't miss anything and if I'm even a few minutes late, his more-obvious-than-necessary glance at the clock tells me what he's thinking. It doesn't bother me now. In a way I find it mildly amusing that he thinks he can get to me. Surely he knows me better than that! Anyway, if that's the game he wants to play, I'll allow him the gratification if it grants me time for a smoke before I go in to face him.

The summer evening is very restful. A cooling breeze refreshes my mood and I feel a lot lighter as I watch thin wisps of cloud dance across a beautiful, pale evening sky. The sun still bright, though descending quickly, throws shadows over the playground in front of me. It's quiet there now. I guess all the children have been taken indoors to eat or get ready for bed. I'm contemplating what it will feel like to take a child, *my* child to such a playground. The thought thrills me and I wonder why the solitary figure sitting on a bench within the play area looks so sad. Where is the child I'm wondering? I don't know if he senses me looking at him, feels my eyes upon the back of his head or what, but just at that moment he turns his face to mine and I find myself staring eye to eye with Luc. Luc, who I thought had disappeared off the face of the earth. Luc, who I've been trying fruitlessly to contact for over a week now. I don't understand how he's just turned up like this. I don't understand why he looks so bad. Has something happened? In a moment I'm beside him, berating him for not getting in touch and it's then, only then that I see it.

"Sebastian!" He stands to greet me, throws his arms around me.

"Luc! Where've you been? What happened to you?"

He smiles, but it doesn't look quite right, because his eyes still retain a painfully sad expression which I don't recognise. It's something I don't associate with Luc at all.

"You mean this?" he says indicating a laceration straddling his face from his right temple to almost his upper lip.

I nod. I don't like to mention that the two black eyes and cuts around his neck and head are also a bit of a give-away that something's happened.

"Had an accident...I'm fine though...just cuts and bruises. I was a bit cold too when I came in so they wrapped me in one of those space blanket things for a couple of days to warm me up...felt like a goose waiting for the oven to heat!"

It must have been bad, I'm thinking. "Why didn't you call? I would've come...I'm bloody here anyway aren't I...for Carly?"

"D'you know, I think I must have been a bit out of it when I came in at first, because I don't remember much. I don't think I was quite with it enough to think of calling... Anyway, it's fine. As it happens I just did try phoning your place a few minutes ago. There was no answer."

"I was here, that's why."

"Yeah...of course!" he's laughing. It's good to see, but still it seems as if a light's gone out somewhere deep inside him. I hug him again, but this time he draws back, his hand clutching at his side.

"Sorry... Did I hurt you?"

He shakes his head. "No, it's not you...There's a bit of bruising that's all, from the seat belt...it's not serious, but sore as hell." He looks tired and cold, very cold.

"Why don't we go in? We could find somewhere to talk if you like?"

"Yeah...yeah that would be great. You know it's so good to see you...I think I could do with talking over with someone what happened. I'm fine, it's just...you know I didn't think I was gonna make it...I thought my time had come and all I could think was ...was no, not yet. I never got to see Carly again...never got to tell her how I feel...I thought I was gonna die and she'd never really know..."

Poor Luc. I decide Carly will probably be okay for another hour, and anyway Len's with her. He won't leave her until I get there.

He'll have a field day with this one mind you, I think, as the clock ticks unforgivingly on.

## LEN

Carly's getting bored, I can tell. I don't blame her, mind you. Much as I love her I'm becoming a bit fed-up myself. Seven hours of the same company does start to grate a bit and there's only so much you can think of to talk about. It's not just that, though. It pains me to admit it, but I know she wants to see Sebastian now. We offer her different things and I think she finds that helpful as we try to keep her occupied during these long hospital days. Too much of one means less of the other and her balance is upset. Where is he tonight, though? He should really have been in two hours ago and it's not like him to be this late. I realise he's got a lot on his plate at the moment having taken over running the restaurant again. It can't be easy juggling a business full-time and being here so much as well, but he was adamant that nothing would change. He wouldn't hear of coming in less often or for a shorter time each day. I guess he doesn't want Carly to feel she's being marginalized and I understand that, especially now that the baby's on the way, but even so, he's trying to manage an awful lot single-handed.

It occurs to me that, not so long ago, he might have turned to me for help in a difficult situation. Not so now. I think he would struggle on if it killed him, rather than ask me for support. Again, I can't blame him for feeling that way. I've made my own feelings perfectly clear. Strange isn't it how easy it is to transfer my anger, my disappointment in my wife onto Sebastian. I'm acutely aware he was only one half of the equation, but he still endures the full force of my betrayed feelings.

445

Where can he have got to? Carly's locked herself away listening to music on her iPod. I know she's worried about him, but again she doesn't feel she can talk to me about her dad. Isn't that a shame? We've created something between ourselves, something we can't deal with and Carly's caught up in the middle of it. It's not right. I don't want to look at my watch again, because I know it will draw her attention back to the fact that he hasn't pitched in. I could kill him for putting her through this. No sooner are these harsh thoughts formulated in my mind than I see him sauntering down the corridor. For some reason his casual, unhurried approach sends a wave of intense annoyance through me. Here I've been trying to account for his disappearance and then when he finally deigns to show up he looks as if he has all the time in the world. I have to bite my tongue to stop myself from making some kind of sarcastic remark. Usually I would react, but I don't want to make it into a big deal for Carly.

"Hi," I say simply as he approaches.

He looks surprised, as if maybe he expected me to be ranting and raving about his delay. Am I so predictable?

"Sorry," he says before I can say anything else.

I shrug my shoulders, "It's fine...everything okay?"

He hesitates a moment, looks at Carly, looks back at me. She's engrossed in her music and hasn't noticed yet that he's arrived. It gives us a few minutes.

"Luc's turned up," he tells me.

I'm pleased. Carly will be ecstatic, at least I hope she will. Something about Sebastian's demeanour implies that all is not well though.

"What's wrong?" I ask.

"He's in the hospital...I mean he's a patient in the hospital. He was in a car accident...the night of the bad storm. Seems he wandered around all night in the cold...I think he was in quite a bad way when he finally got picked up...he...he doesn't look too good. I think she'll need a bit of preparation before she sees him."

"Is he okay though?"

"Yes…yes he's okay…or at least he will be. It's not life threatening or anything, but I think he went through quite an ordeal."

Poor kid! At least he's alright. I should go and see him. In fact that's just what I'll do. Sebastian's here now for Carly, so I'll go visit Luc before I go home, see if there's anything I can do for him.

# CARLY

"How're you feeling, baby?"

I love the way he calls me that. Somehow it makes me feel safe and special all at once. Knowing there really is a baby on the way, I suppose it takes on even greater significance that this is his chosen term of endearment for me. He's been fantastic too about that whole business. The way he told me was so sensitive and thoughtful. I realise he's delighted about it, but he didn't allow that to colour his impression of how I might feel. At first I was shocked and quickly after that I was very, very frightened. I could see it all happening again, just as it had before. My adoptive parents losing all interest in me once they had their own children and the awful sense of loss I eventually had to learn to live with; it all came rushing back. I was upset, but the difference this time is that Dad cares. He made me talk to him about it, about how I felt, what I thought. He was genuinely concerned that I might think I would lose him and of course he was absolutely right. Being able to express myself in total honesty, though, was a really important thing for me. I feel that it's actually brought us closer, because now I know I can share my deepest fears with him and he'll still be there. Dad didn't really know all that much about my background up until then. This gave us the opportunity to uncover all the skeletons, which I'd jammed into the closet. Bringing them out into the light and scrutinising them with Dad beside me has helped, finally, to put some of them to rest and it feels good. He says he wants the baby to be as much a part of me as it is him. I take it he means he wants me to feel it's a part of my family; that we're all in it together.

He's also pointed out that this baby will be related to me. I mean biologically we'll share the same dad, so it's a genuine connection between us. Now that feels good too. My family is growing and I think I am too because of it. My Dad, he's wonderful. He knew exactly what to say to assure me that he wasn't going anywhere. I doubt actually if anything else he'd said would have struck home quite so effectively. He cuddled me and stroked my hair, as if I was a little girl again and he told me that I needed to remember that I was Claudine's child too. I was, he reminded me, the result of his one true love and he would always treasure my existence. I felt safe then and loved, very much loved.

"Hello? Is there anyone there?" He's smiling at me, clearly trying to rouse me out of my daydream.

"Sorry... I was busy thinking."

"Oh that worries me. I don't like it when girls start thinking too much. It's always potentially very dangerous in my experience."

I pretend to throw my magazine at him: "You're lucky there's a glass wall between us! Anyway... aren't you coming in?"

He shakes his head. "Not just yet, baby. I want to find someone to give me an update...Find out how your counts are doing and stuff."

"Didn't Prof tell you all that? He was in speaking with the doctor this afternoon for ages."

He looks a bit annoyed and I wonder if I shouldn't have mentioned that. Sometimes it's really tricky walking this tightrope between the two of them. I wish they could just be friends, like they used to be. It would make things really nice for me, not to mention much easier.

"No, Len left in a hurry, which brings me to something else we have to talk about. I've found Luc...or he found me. At any rate he's here, but I need to explain some things. Let me speak to your nurse for a couple of minutes, then I'll come in and tell you all about it...it's nothing to worry about, by the way."

He must be able to read the anxiety in my face. I feel my heart start to pound. It's a weird sensation and something which has been happening on and off over the last few days. Sometimes it's when I'm worried, sometimes it just seems to happen for no reason. I thought about telling the doctor, but then I thought if there was anything wrong they would surely know, after all I'm being pretty well watched 24/7 aren't I? Right now it does feel a bit scary though. It's not normal that's for sure.

"What is it Carly? Is something wrong?" He looks worried now too. Shaking my head, I know he isn't convinced. "Speak to me, baby. Tell me what it is."

"Well… I've been getting this feeling. I don't think it's anything to worry about… it just feels a bit strange… like my heart's beating too fast or something… it's probably my imagination."

He is definitely concerned now. "Has it happened before?"

I nod, "Yes, but only recently. It passes quite quickly. I haven't mentioned it yet to anyone."

He looks at me earnestly. "Don't worry about that. I'll tell them right now. I'll be back in a minute."

With that he disappears and I know he'll return soon accompanied by a nurse. Other people can spend hours attempting to track down someone to speak to, someone who can explain how their loved one is doing. Dad attracts people to him; women mostly and since this ward is laden with female nurses he won't have any trouble getting what he wants. I hope I'm not worrying him though. He's got so much on right now and I don't want to make things worse. I need to get sorted out though. Luc's here. I need to know about him. Where is he? Why isn't he here? Maybe it isn't good news. Oh, I wish I could calm down. This racing heart is a horrible feeling and I don't know if I'm making things worse now by focussing on such big issues in my life.

# SEBASTIAN

I'm pleased Mary's on duty tonight. She often looks after Carly and she's one of the best. She's also really nice and seems to genuinely care about her so, of course, that elevates her even more in my estimation. Another nurse approaches me with her, "Anything I can do to help you?" smile on, but it's really Mary I want to speak to, so I bypass her and wait till I can catch Mary's attention. She looks up from the chart she's reading and asks if there's anything wrong. I'm not sure if what Carly's describing is a worry or not, but then I'm not trained to know. She listens carefully and then tells me they're on to it. Apparently this is something which if not quite common, is certainly not completely unusual. It seems there is a pattern to the increased heart rate and although Carly hasn't noticed a connection, the medics have. It happens when her temperature is either up or on its way up. She tells me that it's a sign that her body has an infection, which, again is something they know about.

"I think I'll come in and check her out though," she tells me and I'm relieved. This is what I want her to do. "She should probably have some more bloods done too if her temperature's still a problem. The antibiotics should have made some impression by now."

Thanking her I return to Carly and start getting myself scrubbed up. I need to be with her now. I have an uncontrollable urge to hold my daughter, to try to protect her. This disease, this treatment is too big to understand. I can't fathom it and the fear of it taking control is so awful I can't begin to imagine what it would mean. I want her close to me, in my arms, safe from harm.

451

# LEN

"Hey Len...it's good to see you." The boy in front of me is barely recognisable as the one I saw just a couple of weeks ago when he dropped by my house looking to say goodbye to Sebastian.

"You too... you've been in the wars by the look of you. Was it really bad?"

He nods slowly. "Yeah, pretty bad...I take it you've seen Sebastian... he's filled you in?"

This time I nod. "It must have been terrible. You'll be alright though. You're here now and things'll get better from here on...Carly'll be pleased to see you."

I notice him shift uncomfortably in his seat at the mention of Carly's name and I hope it doesn't mean bad news for her. Please don't tell me he's changed his mind, moved on like we told him to. I don't think she could take that. She's so in love with him and I was at least partly responsible for her breaking things off.

"What's the matter? Don't tell me you've changed your mind after all this?"

He looks at the floor, avoiding my eyes. Great! Just great, I'm thinking. I thought you were bigger than this, Luc Rousseau. I thought you really loved her.

"Sebastian told me what's been happening...about Carly misunderstanding and everything. I'm cool with that...it's okay...she didn't know. It's just..." He tails off and I feel frustration rising in me like a volatile volcano. I don't control my emotions well. Since I've been more in touch with my feelings through my writings, through

452

Carly, I find they often surprise me, spilling over when I least expect them. Often it's a good thing, but sometimes like now, I could perhaps benefit from a bit more caution.

"You're through with her? Is that it?"

He looks up instantly, his eyes blazing. "No…no, I'm not *through* with her. Do you think for a minute though that a girl like Carly's gonna want to be seen with me now…look at me…look at the state of me!"

Sometimes I feel I could bang their heads together. Playing Cupid really isn't my thing and I can't say I'm totally comfortable with this role. Like I said, though, I feel I'm someway to blame for the situation they find themselves in, so it's harder to leave them to it. As well as all that, I want it sorted for Carly. I want her to be happy and if this is the guy she wants…well, she could do a lot worse.

"You've been in an accident! What do you expect? No one walks away from an ordeal like you've been through looking as if they're just out of a beauty salon!"

"Yeah, but girls…they like you to be fit, you know? Aside from the way I look, my leg's buggered. The doctors think it's likely I'll always have a limp. Carly could have anyone she wants…she's not gonna settle for this!"

I'm getting angry now. How can he be so stupid? I don't get it. "Luc, in a few  days you're going to look a lot more like your old self…the swelling will go down, your eyes will fix up. Okay maybe you're going to have a few scars, but do you really think someone like Carly, someone as intelligent…sensitive…loving…is going to struggle with that?" He knows I'm right, but still there's a hesitancy. "Is there something you're not telling me? Is there something else?"

Another of these awful silences when I long to grab him with both hands and shake him till he speaks. A sudden flash of recognition, though, stills my annoyance as I see myself in his place not so terribly long ago. People couldn't reach me and I had a lot of difficulty socially. Basic communication was a struggle. I wonder if people had felt like this about me. It would have been a gross misjudgement and I realise Luc needs a little more sensitive handling too.

"I'm sorry, Luc. I realise you've had a hard time of it too. It's just…well she's just so in love with you. I thought you felt the same about her. If you don't, though it'll be okay. She's got people around her…she'll survive."

He's shaking his head again: "You and Sebastian…you're so alike. The pair of you come round jumping to the same conclusions without really knowing anything. I do love her…surely you realised that? But it's hard to get my head around the fact that she wants me back…I'm scared if the truth be known…terrified that this time apart has allowed her to build me up into something I'm not. I want her so badly…*I'll* be the one who struggles to come to terms with it if she knocks me back again."

When did love become so complicated? I shudder slightly as it occurs to me that it always was; way back when I first experienced the depths of feeling one person could have for another. It was complicated then and nothing's changed.

"I see what you're saying," I begin as gently as I can. He's clearly in a very fragile place right now and ranting on at him isn't going to help. "Don't you think you should give it a try, though, tell her how you feel? Just maybe things will work out for you and then…well then it's whatever you want it to be, isn't it?"

Finally he gives me eye contact and his expression has softened. He wants her, so I think he could be encouraged, with enough support that is, to give it a go.

"You think I should tell her how I feel?"

I nod.

"See what happens?"

Again I nod.

He smiles: "Exactly what Sebastian told me. You two must rehearse your scripts!"

454

# SEBASTIAN

"No, Monsieur Charpentier......Sebastian...I'm not unduly worried about her. I just want to check things for myself before I go home for the night. Please don't be alarmed, the nurses didn't call me in. I've been keeping a close eye on Carly's condition over the last few days, as I'm sure you're aware. This is not unusual."

I know he's trying to placate my fears but, although I have tremendous faith in this man and respect him greatly, I find his presence here at this time of night quite unnerving. Whatever he says, I know it isn't customary for him to "look in on her" as he puts it, not at this time. I'm concerned. The nurses are concerned. He's concerned, it's obvious. I suppose I should be glad he's here and let him do his work. Nodding, I consciously try to relax, or at least to feign an impression of relaxing, but it's hard. There's something wrong with Carly. I can feel it and I sense they all do too.

"I'll pop in and see her for a few minutes and then we'll talk some more, okay?"

"Thanks, doctor. I appreciate your time..." I'm about to apologise, to explain that I'm just worried about her, that I'm probably over-reacting when I notice a familiar figure stumbling down the corridor towards us. "Luc!" I call out. Spotting me, he heads in our direction.

"So...you're the famous Luc Rousseau are you?" Dr Armstrong asks Luc as he nears.

Confused, Luc glances at me. I smile in reassurance and introduce the two men. Holding out his hand, Dr Armstrong continues,

455

"This is encouraging…my secret weapon has turned up with perfect timing. I take it you're here to see the beautiful Carly…and to hopefully make her day?"

Luc smiles shyly. I guess he's a bit embarrassed at all the attention he's getting over this increasingly public relationship.

"I tell you what…I need to see her too, but I'll give you ten minutes with her before I do, okay? Ten minutes and then she's mine…I need to check her out." Luc's happy with that and we indicate to him the cubicle she's in at the end of the ward. "Oh and Luc…you know you can't go in don't you?" The doctor's not taking any chances at the moment so poor Luc won't be allowed into the room with her, while she's still spiking these temperatures. He knows. Len's obviously spent some time with him going over it all and I find myself feeling a sense of gratitude to him for not going straight home tonight. Although it's difficult for me to admit, even to myself, I know that Len's made all the difference. I couldn't get Luc to come over to see her, despite trying every trick I know. Len's succeeded where I failed. The irony isn't lost on me.

All eyes are on the poor boy as he continues slowly on down the ward. Passing the nurses' station, several heads raise and glance back at us questioningly. The doctor lifts a hand in approval and they resume their various activities. Reaching the isolation room where Carly's been cooped up since he left, he stops. Staring into the room, saying nothing, he stands there…just stands…and stares. I can't take it; it's too uncomfortable. Presumably the doctor feels the same, because at the same moment we both start hurrying down to join him. He needs some help. We can't just leave him there. Maybe he's shocked by what he sees. She's lost a lot of weight and of course, her hair… maybe we should have prepared Luc a bit, too, for this reunion.

As we approach the room, we're stopped, prevented you could say, from proceeding any further, by an action so simple and yet so intimate, I almost wish I hadn't been there to observe it. Without a word being uttered between them, Luc lifts his finger to his lips then presses it firmly against the glass. In a reciprocal action, Carly too kisses her finger and aligns it alongside his on the other side of the window. The passion within this most private of moments is beyond description. The unspoken word, the unsung song, the unfelt touch - it's all here in the simplicity of this kiss. Love is here; pure and deep, transcending any physical domain. I've witnessed something tonight I didn't think existed anymore. Love so intense, so strong they've become halves of a whole and now need the other to complete themselves. Tonight, here in the most unlikely of places, without any of the usual trappings of romance, feelings are stripped to the barest of emotions and love exposed in its rawest, most fragile state. Their eyes lock and in that moment they're bound by a promise which overcomes any partition between them, visible or otherwise; the simplest of kisses sealing their togetherness, forever.

# CARLY

"Sorry to break up the party like that…you know I wouldn't if it wasn't absolutely necessary." Dr Armstrong's such a decent guy. How could I object when he's come in to examine me at this time of night? He says he hasn't been home yet, so it was no problem to come and take a look at what's been going on with me.

"Okay, princess…let's have a listen to your chest…" He places the cold metal of the stethoscope against my skin. "Breathe for me…and again…" I operate on automatic, obediently following his instructions. "So, you're pleased to see your boyfriend…is he your boyfriend now?"

I smile because I like the sound of that. In actual fact I don't know what you would call it. Are we a couple? We didn't get a chance to talk about anything. Dr Armstrong only allowed us a few minutes before interrupting, but I guess that's alright. He's got a job to do and it's all for my benefit isn't it? So, are we a couple? Well, he came back. That's a good sign. And he kissed me; also a good sign I would say. I feel so happy I can hardly contain myself. How I wish I wasn't stuck in this stupid room. I want to go to him, find out what happened. Dad said he was in a car smash, but didn't really know much of the details. Thank goodness he's alright. Imagine if something had happened to him and we never got the chance…

"Well, he seems to have done the trick. You're brighter tonight than I've seen you in weeks!" Again I just smile. I probably look really stupid, but I can't seem to do anything about the grin which I know is plastered across my face. "Your chest sounds a bit clearer tonight.

That's good. I think we'll just carry on with the antibiotics you're already on. In the morning we'll get an x-ray and compare it with your last one. Okay?" I nod.

"Anything you want to ask me, Carly?"

"Yes. Can Luc come in here next time?"

He shakes his head without hesitation. "No princess, absolutely not...these rules are for your protection, remember? Don't look so disappointed! You make me feel so bad! How am I going to sleep tonight knowing I've left you with that sad face?"

I can't help it. I knew he wouldn't let him. I just thought it was worth a try. I am very disappointed though.

"Listen, Carly...work with me...I know what I'm doing...it's better if he doesn't come in the room."

I nod to show him I'm accepting of the situation, if not entirely in agreement. "Do you think I'll be out of here in time for my twenty-first then?"

He thinks a moment, "That would be in what, a week's time...less?"

"Six days!"

Slowly he shakes his head. "I won't say it's a complete impossibility...but I have to tell you, Carly I think it's unlikely. You still don't have any counts at all...you're completely flat. That's not to say things won't change over the week and once they do, improvement could be quite rapid. However faced with the clinical picture we have today, I would have to say don't get your hopes up."

Now *that* is a disappointment. When I first came in here that was my goal: to be better and out of isolation by my birthday. It wasn't totally off the mark either, because that was giving me six weeks and Dr Armstrong said six to eight weeks depending on how fast my counts came up. I think he's wrong about this though.

"I'm going to prove you wrong. I bet you my counts are good by next weekend."

He smiles kindly, but I know full well he doesn't agree. "Talking of birthdays...I take it your dad knows it's your twenty-first coming up?"

459

I don't actually know. "Probably not," I answer, "Prof won't know either. Great! I'm going to have a fab birthday all round…stuck in here and nobody even remembering!"

"Hey now, don't go feeling all sorry for yourself over this. You can't exactly blame them. It is a slightly unusual way that they've come into your life. It's not like they've forgotten or anything…they just never knew. Anyway I'll soon sort that."

"Thanks Doc…I do appreciate all this, even though I probably seem like an ungrateful brat most of the time."

Smiling he tells me, "You're never that. Now if it's alright with you I think I'll go home and see if I can remember what my wife looks like. I'm tired so behave yourself tonight, okay?"

A quick wink and he's gone and at last I'm left to my thoughts. I'm so excited to have seen Luc again. Everything we had, it all came pouring back. I could actually feel myself filling up with love for him. It feels so right, I don't ever want to lose him again. Now I'm impatient to see him and to get the chance to talk. There's so much I want to ask him, to tell him. I never want us to let anything get in the way again. I need to get myself well and out of here so we can get on with our lives. For the first time I feel like my life is really going somewhere and there's nowhere I'd rather be heading.

# LEN

Luc's return has signalled a change to our routine and one which is taking me a while to get used to. I now practically never see Sebastian, that's the main difference I guess, as far as I'm concerned. Luc comes in every morning and sits with Carly for hours. He takes a wander around lunchtime and she often has a sleep then. When he comes back I'm getting ready to leave. Sebastian's able to come in a bit later because Luc's here when I'm away and I imagine that's making life a lot more manageable for him. He really only does an evening shift here at the hospital now, in order to let him keep the restaurant going in Helen's absence. The result is we rarely cross paths. I suppose this is what it would be like if we didn't have Carly in common. We just hardly see each other and when we do it's by accident and basic pleasantries suffice as conversation. I never ask him how he is, or about Helen or preparations for the baby or the restaurant or indeed anything to do with his life other than Carly. Even at that, it's often me that knows more about what's going on with Carly because I'm here during the day when the doctors do their rounds, so I get updated regularly.

Luc coming back has made a huge difference to her mood too. She was becoming quite low right before he showed up. Now she's on cloud nine and desperate to get out of there. She still has no counts, though and still has this infection kicking around, so I guess her escape might be a way off yet. She was aiming for her twenty-first. Poor thing, that's on Saturday so it's not looking like it. Other girls are able to plan their twenty-first birthday in meticulous detail and have everything just the way they want it. I hear them around the Uni chatting about which club they're going to and who's all going. Carly doesn't have that luxury. She'll be here with the three of us standing around raising glasses to the future. She will have a cake. Sebastian's baking specially for her. He's cleaned his whole kitchen scrupulously so that he can cook for her without any risk of introducing infection through the food. He's been instructed how to prepare her food separately from anything else he might be cooking and to wrap and store it carefully so that it's free from germs when it reaches her. So she'll have her cake and a few other bits and pieces to eat. She doesn't manage much in the way of food anyway, but we decided we had to have something for her. The nurses are decorating the cubicle with balloons and paper garlands and Luc's put together some music for her. That's about it! I hope it's going to be okay. She will have a proper party when she comes home, but all the same I don't want her to be disappointed. I am a bit worried that it's all going to feel second-rate, as if we're having a party at all costs, no matter how pathetic an event it turns out to be. As for presents; well it seems we've all gone for jewellery. This is one occasion where it would have been nice for her to have her mother around to advise us. There are lots of these times, mind you, when I'm sure having Claudine here would have been a help to the girl.

Claudine would have chosen the perfect gift. She was great like that, always knew just the right thing for someone. Never in our marriage did she ask me what I wanted for my birthday. She always chose something herself and it turned out to be perfect, without fail. But in the absence of female direction I've somehow managed to select a delicate gold bracelet for her. It's very fine and I guess reminded me of her in its fragility. I might have chosen a necklace for her, but Sebastian got there first with his hand-crafted piece with her initials inscribed. Now that was a shock to me. She hadn't told me she planned to change her name back to Charpentier, so I was really taken aback when I saw it. I'm trying so hard to swallow my pride though, so as not to hurt her feelings. Personally I thought it was pretty distasteful, but Carly was so excited about it I had to pretend I thought it the loveliest thing I ever saw. I haven't seen the present he's picked for her birthday - a watch he tells me. Chances are it will be equally vulgar, but she'll love it all the same. Her father can do no wrong. I guess that's how it should be, though.

And Luc, well I suspect Luc's planning to propose to Carly on her birthday. He's been vague about his gift, but I did spot him slipping a ring-sized box into his jacket pocket the other day when he heard me coming, so I wouldn't be surprised. It would certainly fit with the speed their relationship is developing. I realise they do have a bit of history, so maybe it's been a case of picking up where they left off. In a matter of days they've passed through "Missing you," to "Let's get a place together," and even as far as "Paris or Edinburgh?" I'm staying out of it. Whatever decisions she makes have to be the right ones for her and I don't want her to be influenced by me. Having said that I was greatly relieved to overhear them discussing how they would most likely set up home in Edinburgh. Carly told him she didn't want to leave me or Sebastian having just found us and Luc, bless him, agreed, saying there was nothing for him in France now anyway. He's such a good kid. I know he'd do anything for Carly and that reassures me of her deepening involvement with him.

When I left her this afternoon she was happily lying on her bed watching him sketching through the window. He was busy drawing the house he grew up in back home in Paris so she could see what it was like. His pad is full of sketches such as this, all drawn meticulously, beautifully in order to please Carly. Sometimes, like today, it's a scene from his past which he wants to show her. Sometimes it's a place he's just been or something he passed on his way in to the hospital. He draws the way some people speak or some people write, with intricate attention to detail and colour. His work is therefore lovely to look at, but also informative and interesting. Carly hasn't lifted so much as a pencil for weeks now. There's been no writing, drawing or painting done as she just doesn't have the energy. Even reading has tailed off recently. She's happy for me to read to her and I do most days, but as far as taking a book for herself, that doesn't happen anymore.

As I head for home I realise just how much she's missing. A lovely summer evening like this would give Carly a great deal of pleasure. I take my time, trying to savour every detail. It seems a travesty to take it for granted when Carly would give anything to feel the breeze on her face, to watch the last of the sun's colour dip silently behind the hills. The outline of a bird's wings fly in a shimmering silhouette through the day's parting glow and I consciously try to capture the image, sealing it in my memory. All the everyday things take on great importance now because of Carly. She's taught me to notice the least remarkable event and attribute a wondrous meaning to it. Worth is measured in a different way now; existence itself having the highest value of all.

# SEBASTIAN

"You're not getting the hang of this at all are you?" I can't help laughing. Here's the girl who's good at everything. Not just good, she shines at almost anything she deigns to put her hand to; painting, writing, every kind of craft you can think of. Languages, though, are not something which come naturally to Carly. She looks slightly embarrassed and I wonder for a moment if she thinks I'm making fun of her. Gently I lift her hand. She looks really tired; her eyes, dark-shadowed, hang heavy in her pale face. Her cheeks are really thin and she seems very frail tonight.

"Hey, don't worry. It makes me feel good to know I'm better than you at something, that's all."

She smiles at this remark and I'm pleased to be able to reach her. Instinct works well for me now as far as Carly's concerned. Could it be a father-daughter thing?

"You're right I don't get it. I don't find it logical at all. I can't really see me mastering this language, if the truth be told. You might just have to accompany me everywhere and translate for me."

This is good. It sounds like she's coming round to the idea of visiting France with me once she's well. The first time I suggested it she seemed pretty reluctant. I guess Luc's return has probably helped. They look pretty serious so maybe she's thinking she should make a bit of effort for him.

"I suppose that could be arranged," I tell her.

I've absolutely no doubt that she'll soon pick up French once she's actually speaking it and hearing it on a regular basis. This is a

465

difficult situation in which to be trying to introduce new ideas to her. At the same time, though, I don't want her worrying unnecessarily about anything and if she thinks I can be on hand to translate for her then that's fine. I want her to relax, to settle down and to concentrate on getting well. The last thing I want is for her to be getting in a state about speaking French. She's quiet tonight, unusually quiet and it makes me feel a bit anxious.

"Is anything the matter, baby? You seem preoccupied with something."

Shaking her head she tells me she's just tired, but no, she doesn't want me to leave. She can't explain it but she feels a bit scared tonight and doesn't want to be on her own. Placing my arm around her shoulders, I draw her close to me and reassure her I'll stay as long as she wants me to. She snuggles in to the cleft of my arm and I'm filled with emotions new and unrivalled.

Having a daughter is such a powerful gift. I'm completely unable to describe the feelings welling up within me as she nestles comfortably within my hold. Total trust and acceptance of me as I am emanate from her fragile frame. I am her dad and I love her and that's enough for her. She doesn't expect or want any more from me than that. In reality she has it all. Everything I am, everything I have; it's all for Carly. She gives meaning to my life, representing the only good in me. A child born out of a love so deep, so complete, how could she be anything less?

We sit for a few minutes, comfortable in each other's embrace, saying nothing. After a while I wonder if she's actually fallen asleep, because she seems so far away. Turning to sneak a look at her face, her head drops off my shoulder. She doesn't react. There's no startle reflex jerking her head upright, it simply hangs in mid-air like a broken doll. Something's not right.

"*Carlee...Carlee!*" I try to rouse her, but she's oblivious to my voice. Suddenly her body begins the frightening uncontrollable movements I witnessed several months before at Claudine's funeral. She's fitting! Tense curves appear around her spine, her arms and legs flail in a mad, desperate sequence. Panicking I reach for the emergency call button and summon help. This should not be happening. Whatever's wrong it should not be happening! Distantly I hear the alarm sounding, the distinctive repetitive buzz, a siren commanding attention. The response comes immediately; one nurse, followed by another, three and four. Everyone rushes to the scene of the call.

"What's wrong?" the first beginning to scrub up.

"I don't know…she's having a seizure…look at her…"
Abandoning the scrub, she rushes straight through the glass doors. Now I'm scared. This is the first time in six weeks that anyone's entered this room without first thoroughly washing themselves and donning the required gown and mask. The nurse shouts for a doctor to be called and one of the others disappears.

Laying her gently on the bed, we watch helplessly as Carly's slight body is wrenched into fierce contortions. And then, as suddenly as it started, the shaking stops. This stillness is almost worse. She lies limp like a replica of herself, a model without purpose or will. The nurse feels her neck for a pulse. Nimbly moving her fingers to her arm she again places her fingers in position. I cannot take my eyes off her. Is she okay? She's got to be okay.

"She isn't breathing! Get me a doctor in here!"

I feel as if I've imagined the nurse shouting these words. None of this is real. We were just talking. Only minutes ago we were talking, now someone's saying she isn't breathing! I watch as she places her mouth over Carly's and breathes, filling Carly's empty lungs with her own oxygen. Repeating the process, she then places her hands on her chest pressing down rhythmically before sealing her mouth again and continuing to breathe for her. The process is repeated over and over. I can't believe what I'm seeing. This isn't a movie, this is real. Carly's not breathing. What does that mean? Is she going to die? No, don't let her die. Don't let her die!

"Crash team are here," a voice from outside the cubicle calls. Suddenly the corridor is filled with the sound of running footsteps. No-one ever runs in here. Nurses hurry about their duties but no-one runs. Various people rush into the isolation room, none of them bothering to scrub up first. What about the infection risk? Then it occurs to me - it doesn't matter about infection if you're dead does it? Dr Armstrong arrives and he too runs straight in, taking control as his rank warrants.

"Where's the emergency trolley?" The distinctive red trolley appears in the doorway. I've seen it many times, parked like part of the furniture beside the nurses' station. Tonight its drawers are being flung open and the contents thrown across the bed. A tube is ripped from its packaging and a torch-like instrument produced. Expertly Dr Armstrong guides it into her throat. A mask is placed over her mouth and attached to it a kind of pump. He fixes some tubing to the end and a nurse fastens it to an oxygen cylinder. Squeezing the bag, again, again, I realise they're giving her oxygen. Her chest swells and dips in time with the rhythm. More, I think, more. I'm aware of another doctor injecting various ampoules of liquids into her veins.

"More adrenaline!" he shouts and is handed another filled syringe.

"Dear God, let her live." I find myself thinking, "Whatever it takes, just let her live."

I don't know if I've spoken aloud or not, but I realise Dr Armstrong is suddenly aware of my presence in the room. His well-mannered persona has disappeared.

"What the hell's he doing in here? Can somebody get him out ...now?"

I feel a hand under my elbow and know I'm being ushered away from this scene of horror. I can't leave her though. That's my baby. I need to stay with her. I should be looking after her, making sure she's okay. My body resists the gentle pressure guiding me from the room. Two hands on my shoulders turn me to face the nurse. It's Mary.

"Please, Sebastian...let them work on her...this is the best help you can be right now...I need you to do this, come with me."

She looks intently into my eyes and I relent. I allow myself to be led away from Carly as she lies there hanging on to her life. In that instant I feel I've abandoned her. Distantly I hear calls for blood and platelets, for fluids and antibiotics. It seems they're frantically pumping everything they can think of into her precious body in an attempt to force some life back into her.

"Come on, Carly!" Dr Armstrong's voice reaches me even though by now I'm at the other end of the corridor. Willing her to live, I think. The professional, the expert is willing my daughter to live. All the medical knowledge and equipment is at his disposal, but he's drawing on other, higher resources to help her. What does that mean? Are they losing? Shaking my head, I can't accept that. Drawing on every ounce of faith I can muster, I add my own resolve to the determination of the medics. "Come on, Carly!" I mentally urge her. Digging deep into my own spirit I desperately try to reach her, to lift her with my own strength.

I find myself sitting in a small room, one I've never been in before. Mary sits beside me, her hand on top of mine.

"What are they doing?" I ask her. My voice sounds much calmer than I feel. Inside my heart is cracking, but my words sound remarkably calm.

"They're giving her drugs to stimulate her heart, oxygen to help her breathe. They know what they're doing, Sebastian."

I nod. Is it enough, though? Is knowing what you're doing and actually being able to do it the same thing?

"It happened so quickly," I say. This time I sound more croaky. I'm not in control of my voice any more than I'm in control of my emotions. I'm all over the place. She nods simply and doesn't attempt to try to make it better with platitudes. I respect her strength and honesty, but can't help wondering if she's preparing me for the worst. There are no promises, no reassurances that it's all going to be okay. The sound of running feet continues, doors opening and closing, voices shouting. It's all developing a dream-like quality though. None of this is real. I'm watching as an uninvolved bystander. I am not me. This is not about Carly. Closing my eyes, I fervently attempt to block out the urgent sounds of an evolving emergency. When I open them I'm blinded by tears.

## LEN

It's such a strange thing. All the times I've visited Carly and then left her in Sebastian's care, it's been at the back of my mind what might happen if she took ill and I wasn't there. I've gone over the possibilities so often in my head and yet when the call came I was completely unprepared. The phone ringing at ten o'clock at night is a fairly unusual occurrence for me, but not totally unheard of. Often I'm in my study at this time anyway, so it doesn't feel particularly late. Even when the voice on the other end informed she was phoning from the ward, my first thought was that Carly wanted something taken up to her in the morning. I must have seemed really slow on the uptake, my inability to grasp the situation forcing the nurse to spell out to me what had happened. She was very nice, but I felt my blood run cold when she told me Carly had become unwell. I wasn't to panic, but she suggested I make my way directly to the hospital. Sebastian had asked for me, it seems. At least he was with her, I thought. Thank God he was with her.

# SEBASTIAN

The door opens abruptly and Dr Armstrong's huge presence enters, filling the room. He's lost his calm, composed demeanour. He looks shaken and dishevelled, although his voice is controlled, continuing to command authority. There are splashes of blood spattered across his sleeve and I'm unable to avert my eyes from them.

"Sebastian."

I'm scared, more scared than I've ever felt in my life. I do not want to hear what he has to say. I'd rather stay in this limbo state of not knowing than have a horrific truth revealed to me.

"Sebastian…we got her back."

I look up immediately: "She's alright?" Desperately I scan his face, try to read his eyes to glean some evidence for what I think I just heard him say. He moves toward me, stares directly at me.

"No Sebastian, I'm afraid she's not alright, but she is still with us."

Shaking my head in disbelief, I feel frustration building up within me. This stress is making it difficult for me to think; finding words in English is really hard. I wish Len would hurry up. They said they would call someone for me, suggested I might want my wife with me. The only person I could bear to have near me is Len and they promised they would contact him.

"I don't understand," I manage to utter, falteringly.

"I'll be completely honest with you, Sebastian… Haven't I always been honest with you? Carly's very sick. She has an infection…we knew that, but her lungs…well the difference in the x-

471

ray from yesterday and the film I've just examined…well it's staggering. There's no surprise she's having difficulty breathing, her lungs are full of infection. Her body is septic, hence the seizure and the arrest. The question is what now?"

What does he mean? Surely he has a plan. Surely he must have dealt with this before. It sounds so serious, so terrible. My head is spinning. I'm having trouble absorbing all this information and I don't even want to. I want to tell him he's wrong, to shout at him to stop this and just make her better. That's what he's meant to be doing isn't it?

He must realise I'm incapable of speech, because after a few moments pause he continues. "I need to know what you want me to do, Sebastian."

He says it so plainly it's hard to imagine I've misheard him, but he can't possibly have just said what I think he did. What do I want him to do? How the hell would I know what he should do? Is he telling me that *he* doesn't know what to do? I open my mouth and somehow words stumble out of it.

"What *I* want you to do?"

He's sitting now beside me. A brief glance over at the nurse, who remains in the room with us and he resumes. "Sebastian, I understand this is very difficult for you. Carly's really ill, desperately ill. You're her father, her next of kin… yes I need to know what you want me to do. We have two options as things stand tonight. One, we can transfer her to intensive care and ventilate her, give her lungs some assistance with breathing and try to get on top of the infection. The trouble with this though is…like I said she's very ill. It's possible…likely even… that Carly will not recover from this. Her lungs are in bad shape. Her heart, too, has been damaged by the intensive chemo given her before the transplant…it's not a good picture. I'm being blunt, Sebastian and I know this is difficult to listen to, but I need you to know what's happening. You need to make an informed choice about the treatment I'm offering…If we go down this line, there's a possibility, probability perhaps that Carly never comes off the ventilator. She may never wake up."

I'm stunned. I feel detached from this whole situation, as if I've inadvertently got caught up in a film-set of someone else's story. This is not about Carly. Carly came in here to get better, this was not part of the deal.

"And the other option?" My voice is no more than a whisper. Maybe I don't really want to ask the question and part of me hopes he won't hear me, won't answer.

"Well…the other option is that we don't take her to ITU…we keep her here…let you spend some time with her…let her go…"

"No!"

I don't even realise it's me who's spoken, shouted the word. It came without any intention to formulate a reply, an instinctive cry from the depths of my soul. No, I will not let her go. "If she's ventilated she has a chance, yes?"

He levels with me. "It's a technicality…a chance, yes…no more than that."

That's enough for me. "Take the chance…make it happen."

He nods. "That's what I hoped you'd say. I had to give you the option because…well because this might be… goodbye…you may not get her back once she's on life support…you have to know that."

I understand, but I can't go there. I am not saying goodbye to Carly tonight. He stands, shakes my hand.

"I'll set things in motion for transfer. It might take a little time to arrange the bed…perhaps you will want to go and be with her."

I nod again. Yes, of course. She didn't want to be alone. She was afraid, she told me. He's on the verge of leaving when I remember Luc.

"Someone has to tell Luc…he'll need to see her."

Outside the closed door the sound of footsteps running alerts me to the fact that someone has already thought of this. His frantic pace rushing to reach her doesn't falter but passes the room in desperation. This can't be happening, I repeat the words over and over in my mind till they blur into incomprehension. My turmoil is interrupted by the door once again opening and this time Len's face appearing before me.

"Sebastian."

That's all he says. Putting his arms around me, pulling me to him he holds me, sharing this torture as only he can. His body is shaking or is it mine? Emotions spiral up and out of me, now that an understanding spirit is here to help me bear this heart-breaking burden. Together we stand and allow our sorrow to well up within us, spilling out of our private hurt and bridging the chasm between us; united in our love for Carly, in our desperation, our pain.

# LEN

Luc's sneakers lie abandoned by the door. He lies on the bed with her, cradling his darling in his arms. His mouth moves as he speaks to her incessantly; reassuring her, comforting her. His fingers gently stroke her face, his love so exposed. It breaks my heart to watch him. His whole life is here in this room and that whole life tonight hangs precariously by a thread of hope. Sebastian, by my side is a broken man. He called because he needed me. I've never known Sebastian need anyone, anything, but here he is crumbling in front of me, unsure, unhinged.

How I hate this place. Hospitals aren't good reminders for me. The stark, clinical environment is in total contrast to everything that I find familiar. It's also the opposite of everything Carly loves, I think. What a horrible way to die! She wouldn't want to die in here. She would want to be surrounded by the wonderful colours and sounds of nature, a landscape which she adored. Not here. Not like this. I watch as Luc's lips press gently against her cheek and it dawns on me in that instant how wrong I am. Yes here, yes exactly like this. She is surrounded by love, deep and absolute; the warmth of his body around her, soothing her frightened spirit; gentle words of love easing her terrified mind.

Glancing over at Sebastian, I wonder how we'll ever get through this. How will we survive the next few hours of torment? And after? What lies ahead for Carly, for us? Seeing the pain etched within Sebastian's face I know that if love were enough to make her well, Carly would be brimming with energy, laughing in carefree health. I want her to get over this. With all my heart I want Carly to get out of here and back to a life of freedom and possibility. I want her to feel this love pouring out for her, a love which I have never understood, never been able to explain to myself.

When Claudine died, I thought I'd experienced love for the last time. I didn't think I had anything left to give. What Carly showed me was love on a different level. I don't doubt that Claudine loved me in her own way and I certainly loved her as best I was able at that time. What I didn't understand was the depths, the heights which love could be capable of transporting the soul. It hurts to contemplate it. I think it always will, but I believe that's what Sebastian and she shared and went on sharing, despite the self-created distance between them. Luc knows. He knows love in its purest, most fragile form. Strength and dependence, fear and hope; perfectly combined, entwined in each other. Beautiful.

I take a final look. Still he lies beside her, stroking her skin, murmuring softly to her, words I cannot hear. He knows as I do, how delicate this state is, how easily broken a heart can be. Carly lies in his arms, clinging on to her tenuous link with life. This pain, this fear, it's surrounding us, threatening to consume us, but it's born out of love. I know that now. Only because we've loved her so much does the danger of impending separation now hold so much power over us. She asked me once, if I'd known how it would end, would I have changed anything, would I have done it all anyway? The answer was yes, because I knew as Carly did that the pain of lost love is a reflection of the beauty once known. Love tonight feels angry. It aches within my heart, crushing my spirit. Love is brittle and scared and helpless. Love is agony.